The Vampire Project

1

Erika's Birth

by

Kate Bean

Libro Publishing

Libro
Publishing

14 King's Road, Colwyn Bay, Conwy, LL29 7YG, UK.
hello@LibroPublishing.com

First published by Libro Publishing 2023.

First Edition   2023
All rights reserved.

ISBN   978-1-913315-11-5

Created in UK

Contents

Chapter 1

Erika stops just outside the conference room door, takes a deep breath, closes her eyes and exhales. 'Here goes,' she says to herself. Pushing open the large beech wooden door, she smiles. Inside the conference room, she sees a room full of people. At the front a man, slightly above average height, waves her over. Like all the men, he's wearing a dark suit with a light button-down shirt. His tie a deep red. Erika walks over with a smile, her attire, like all the women is similar, dark suits, light tops, tights, and heels. The remaining lawyers and assistants are all mingling around the food on the central table, the beer and wine spritzers are at the end of the long beech wood conference table. On this bright sunny summer's day, the air conditioning is humming in the background, keeping everyone comfortable.

"Erika, I'm so glad you've arrived," Jack says warmly.

"I wouldn't miss it for the world, Jack," Erika replies.

"Before we get started, I wanted to congratulate you personally on the promotion."

"Thank you," Erika replies.

"Shall we get the formal part over and done with?" Jack asks.

"I'm ready."

Jack smiles warmly, "Okay, then." He then calls for attention. This part does not work as well as intended, as only a few people near him hear the call. Someone gets a glass and spoon, tapping them together, causing the hubbub to die down. Presently, the room quietens down and the final vibrations from the glass fade.

"Thank you all for coming this lunchtime, you all know Erika and the last thing I want to do is keep you from the festivities with a long speech. So, with that in mind, please can you bear with me! What am I saying, of course, is that as you know, I love a long speech!" Jack says grinning as he unrolls an exceptionally long scroll.

A few grins and groans ripple around the room.

Jack begins to read, "It is with immense pleasure, that today, the fifteenth of July in this the year of our lord twenty something or other, that I dutifully promote Erika Elliot to the highest order of Supreme Judicial Inquisitor. This new role bestows on her no additional responsibility, no more pay, and no more authority," with those words, Jack hands Erika a framed certificate.

The room erupts in applause. This lasts until Jack quietens everyone down, by making a push down motion with his hands.

"On another related note. Erika's promotion has come through, just in time for her birthday. Coincidence, I'm sure. Starting from when she returns from holiday, she'll be much more elusive as she's agreed to work the Far East desk and will be working nights. I'm sure you'll all join with me in welcoming her to the new role and more importantly will keep her in your thoughts in the long dark nights in the winter," Jack says, gesturing to Erika.

Before she can say anything or respond, the room erupts in applause again.

Erika lets the applause die down naturally before speaking, "Thank you Jack for the induction into the Inquisitorial Order. Recognition as one of the team is always gratifying," she smiles warmly, "and I'm going to miss all of you when I'm working nights and you're working days. It's like leaving, without going anywhere. But rest assured, I'll still be here and will pop in from time to time, distributing my own brand of fun." She shoots a glance at Jack before continuing, "I just want to say, thanks and enjoy the double party, birthday, and promotion. I think as a newly initiated Supreme Judicial Inquisitor, I think it's appropriate for me to say, if you've touched the funny water, no more work for you this afternoon."

Jack magics two glasses of champagne from who knows where, hands one to Erika and says, "To Erika."

The room responds with, "To Erika." The toast made and glasses clink.

"Congratulations, go and enjoy the party. I'll take that and see that it arrives on the wall in your office," Jack says to Erika, as he takes the framed certificate, makes a gesture with his head towards the people mingling around the room.

"Thank you," Erika says, kissing him on both cheeks, before moving into the room. She then circulates around the room, making small talk with various groups as she pensively sips her drink. The conversation revolving around the same few topics, her birthday; promotion; upcoming holiday and working on the Asia desk.

Erika spots her friend across the room and moves quickly towards her. "Elle, you've not got a drink?"

Elle turns and smiles, "No, I put it down and popped out to the loo. How's the party going?"

"You saw, Jack got me good!" Erika remarked, with a quirk to her lips.

"Yes, he did, a classic that one. Supreme Judicial Inquisitor, I don't think we've had one of those before," Elle grins yet again.

"No, me neither. Come on, let's get you another drink," Erika says as she moves towards the drinks station.

"Have you eaten anything yet?" Elle asks.

"No, I'd just arrived, then we had the ceremony, I probably should have something. Drinking on an empty stomach isn't such a clever thing to do," Erika admits.

"No, it's not, you need some healthy food, like crisps and sandwiches! There's some tomatoes and celery, but that just takes up the space we need for cake!"

Erika chuckles, "Yes it does and that would be a waste, when there's strawberry cheesecake waiting it's turn before the Supreme Judicial Inquisitor!"

"Now you're getting into the spirit of the thing," Elle says, getting herself a glass of champagne and refilling Erika's glass. Sipping their champagne, they move down the table to the food station, where to Erika's surprise, there's cheese sandwiches in wholemeal bread, as well as cheese and onion crisps.

"If I didn't know better, I'd think that you had something to do with the organisation of this party," Erika says inquisitorially.

"I may have been consulted," Elle says grinning.

"Excellent," Erika says, giving Elle a clink of her glass.

"I'm sure everyone's already asked this a million times, but what are your holiday plans? I know you said you weren't going away, but have you changed your mind?" Elle enquiries.

Erika shakes her head, "No, no change to plans. I'm going to stay here at home for the whole two weeks. I'm going to relax, go out do some touristy things in London. Maybe visit the Tower of London and I don't know, some of the other things you always say you'll go and see, but never seem to have the time. When was the last time you went to the theatre?"

"Yikes, I can't remember, it's been years, two or three years, I suppose. You?" Erika can see Elle cogitating. "A little longer I think more like three or four years. There always seems to be so much time, and it's right there, so there's no rush. I should try and go in the holidays. Do you want to come one night?"

"Sure, why not. Can I bring Andy?" Elle enquires.

"I don't see why not. I don't have a plan, but I'm sure that there must be something at the National or the Vic."

"If the goal is to go to the theatre, then it doesn't matter what we see, it's the act of going that matters," Elle says sipping at her champagne. Erika nibbles at her sandwich, eating crisps alongside.

"It's funny, this morning, it never occurred to me to go to the theatre. So, thanks," Erika smiles.

"What else are you doing?" Elle wonders.

"I'm going to spend some time with Dominique, she's going to be off too, so I think we'll do some romantic things. I'm not sure what, she's the one who thinks of the romantic things."

"She seems like a keeper, unless your lack of romance drives her away."

"I just don't think like that," Erika said defensively.

"It's quite easy. When was the last time you bought her flowers?" Elle asked.

Erika shrugs a little, eating more crisps, "I don't know, a while. She never asks for flowers."

"Of course, she doesn't. A lady never asks for flowers, it's just something that shows you're thinking of them. That's just one part of being romantic."

"That means there's more?" Erika queries.

"Of course, there's more, otherwise they'd call it giving flowers. It's spending time with her and just her, giving your time. It's walks in the park, or at sunset, or both. Perhaps by the river. It's going on a picnic at the beach or in the park. It's doing cute things together. Do you need an action plan and a to-do list?" Elle says knowingly.

"Clearly yes," Erika retorts.

Elle laughs, "Then you're on your own for that one."

"Typical, all the problems but none of the solutions. Where have I seen that before!"

"You're the new Supreme Judicial Inquisitor, not me. You have the high status and the to-do list with the blank action plan. Besides, at this point, I'm sure she's used to it," Elle says.

"You make me sound so bad," Erika says, feeling a bit guilty.

"I know because you are. What else are you doing?" Elle enquires.

"I think we'll go around friends' house for dinner or dinner party. I'm not sure if the plans are finalised yet, but it will be one or the other, depending on peoples' availability."

"Dinner parties can be fun," Elle agrees.

"I like it when they're themed, like a murder mystery dinner that kind of thing," Erika confesses.

Elle shakes her head in despair, "Of course you do. Always the detective and the lawyer. Do you understand the concept of a break? You know, where you do different things from work. Where people let their hair down, metaphorically, and have non-work fun?"

Erika finishes her sandwich, "Yes, I know what that is. I read a book on it once and there's videos on the internet."

"Exactly my point. Anything else?" Elle takes another sip of her drink.

"Some shopping, I think," Erika says, not very enthusiastically.

"That could be fun, but not for you, so I imagine it's for work suits," Elle says with a knowing nod.

"Amongst other things," Erika says sounding very defensive.

"What about this new job, I still don't understand why you chose to work the night shift. Anyone else could have done it?" Elle had to admit she was surprised when hearing about Erika opting for the night shift.

Erika sips her champagne, "Partly it pays a lot more, I could do with the money, also, because I think it might be fun to visit Hong Kong, Singapore, South Korea, or Japan from time to time. Travelling on the company's expense account must be good!"

"But to do that, you must give up all your evenings and sleep all day. When there'll be lots of noise with traffic and people milling about. Won't you miss all that?"

"Of course," Erika agrees, "but it's only for a while. If I don't like it, I can always talk to Jack and get a different role. It's not like a banishment to Siberia!"

Finishing her champagne and looking at the rapidly depleting drinks station, Elle asks, "What about Dominique? How will this fit in with her, no non-romantic evenings, trips to the theatre, etc.?"

"Go get a refill, I'll wait," Erika says, and Elle vanishes returning in record time with a full glass. "I'm not working weekends and restaurants, theatres, ballet, or opera are all open at the weekend. Don't think I didn't notice the little quip about non-romantic evenings!"

"Someone must keep you on your toes. Well, I'm going to miss you around the office." Elle sounds sad already, as she contemplates missing Erika every day and the fun they have together.

"I know, I'm going to miss you at lunch and all those other little chats. Truthfully, I'm going to miss everyone. As I said in my speech, it's like leaving, but without leaving."

"Don't worry honey," Elle consoled her, "Andy and I'll still go out with you, even at the weekend. Though, I'd like to point out that you don't go to restaurants, the theatre, opera, or the ballet. We already established that."

"That's fair," Erika says, "but we also established, that neither do you. So, you coming to get me out the house is also me getting you out of the house. Let's be honest, that what a Supreme Judicial Inquisitor does."

"I've never heard that before about a Supreme Judicial Inquisitor. They sound very social, but Inquisitors, well, they don't sound social!" Elle says tongue in cheek.

"We're social, like social media," Erika retorts.

"Ah, toxic and evil. Right, got ya," Elle says with a gesture.

"So young, so cynical," Erika says half-jokingly.

"Welcome to the club. If it wasn't for Dominique, would you ever go out?" Elle enquires.

"Probably, sometimes," Erika admits.

"Ooo, will you still be going to the gym, or I suppose on a different schedule?" Elle wondered.

Erika hesitates, "I assume so, I haven't thought about it. Does working nights stop me going to the gym?"

"Maybe, it depends on what time you get up and when they close, or you could go before bed in the morning. Maybe you can find a gym that's open 24/7?" Elle feels rather pleased with her off-the-cuff suggestion.

"We'll have to see, it's one of those things I never thought about. Which means there's going to be others. Like shopping," Erika realized there was a lot she hadn't considered before.

"Deliveries will work fine, they work in the evenings as well," Elle said, trying to be positive.

"Good catch. I'm going to try and use the holiday to move my sleep cycle to days and be up at night. I don't know how long that's going to take to be normal with a shifted day," Erika said thoughtfully, contemplating options and scenarios.

Elle pauses a moment thinking, "If I remember correctly, it takes one day to recover from one hour of jet lag, so I am going to guess about twelve days, to do a full flip. What's the time difference between here and Hong Kong?"

"It's eight hours, so noon here is eight p.m. there," Erika replied.

"Then it should only take eight days to get on to their time zone. You can probably do it in a week," Elle said cheerfully.

"Well, I have a full fourteen days, so it should be fine."

"This means you'll start work at about midnight here, work all night and then what go to bed straight from work and have your spare time in the evening before work. Except your spare time is in the morning rather than the evening. That's too weird," Elle says, slightly bewildered at the whole situation.

Erika nods, "Yes, basically. It does mean though, that I'll have the work I need doing all prepared when the day people arrive, so from that point of view, I will look amazingly fast. I get the instructions as to what you all require in the middle of the night and the first draft of the documents could be ready the following night."

"And that's why this works, and you get paid the big bucks," Elle remarks.

"That and the fact no sane person wants to work nights," Erika retorts.

"There's that too," Elle agrees, "I wouldn't."

Erika grins, "I suspect it's only that. But we do make good money and the firm has good connections, so it's a win all round."

"Except for you."

Erika sips at her drink before replying, "No, I have a good relationship, the money will be handy and it's a good career boost. I'm doing well from this. The only real downside is not chatting and mucking about with you."

"You're going to make me cry and we haven't even had cheesecake!" Elle said trying to make light of the situation.

"I don't believe for a minute that you're going to cry, but the cheesecake plan, now that sounds good," Erika remarks.

Elle leads the way to the cheesecake, grabbing a portion for each of them, together with stainless steel cake forks.

As they move back to their free space, Erika asks, "Have you and Andy chosen your holiday destination yet?"

Caught with a mouthful of cheesecake, Elle pauses and covers her mouth to answer, "We're still back and forth between the Maldives and Goa."

"I've never been to either, so I can't help," Erika admits.

"We'll probably go to the Maldives and have one of those beachfront cabins or huts. It's hard to know what to call them, when they have air conditioning, electricity, and all that," Elle says.

"It sounds nice," Erika says taking another bit of her dessert.

"Oh, you'd love it, gorgeous turquoise blue water, horizon to horizon sunshine, all your meals in a luxury five-star restaurant or delivered to the beach chalet. Yes, chalet, that the right word. Sunbathing, swimming in the sea, snorkelling and, of course, boat trips. I think I'm talking myself into it," Elle says waxing lyrically.

Erika laughs, "I'm glad to have been of assistance."

"What time are you staying until?" Elle idly enquires.

"I'll be the last to leave, it's a party in my honour after all. It seems only polite. You?"

"Until about half of the people have left, then I'll head home early. Although, with an apartment upstairs, you'll probably be home before me," Elle chuckles.

"Probably, particularly if your train has a hiccup."

"You can count on a delay if I leave early, it's the universe's way of punishing me. Do you have any plans for tonight, Erika, as it's your Birthday night?"

"You know that Dominique has plans, exactly what they are, I'm not sure. My instructions are to come over about seven o'clock and wear something suitable. I'm thinking cocktail dress, heels and the usual," Erika says going back to the cheesecake.

"That's all she said. With no hint of if you're going out or staying in?" Elle acts surprised.

Erika shakes her head, "No, but I think it's going to be dinner in, she's planning on cooking something and then maybe a romantic walk by the river, you know, with the sunset."

"If that's the case, then it was her plan!"

"Yes, fine, it will be her plan. But it sounds like a nice evening. Party all afternoon with you all," Erika says making a feeble gesture to the room, "then an evening at home, well, evening in anyway."

"It sounds nice. Better than going to a restaurant and Dominique's an excellent cook. It'll be better than my last birthday, the restaurant was nice, but it was too loud with all the other people and the music," Elle said reminiscing.

"Yes, I remember it well. They treated you well though."

"They did. I know I'm monopolising the guest of honour; you should finish that up, take your champagne and mingle. I'll see you about going to the theatre during your holiday." Elle gives Erika a quick kiss on the cheek.

"Yes mum," Erika says with a grin, but she still finishes her dessert.

"Besides, I have people to schmooze."

"I'll see you over my holiday. Enjoy your schmoozing," Erika smiles.

Elle says, "I will." Before giving Erika a wink, she heads off towards a small group of people.

Erika places her empty plate on the table and with glass in hand, begins another tour of her work colleagues. The afternoon passes in pleasant conversation and as the alcohol drains from the drinks station, the conversations become more honest and slightly louder.

Chapter 2

Erika smiles into the mirror as she finishes the last touches to another immaculate application of lipstick. "Perfection!" she murmurs to herself then does a quick once-over in the mirror to check that her makeup is exactly right. Standing, she walks happily towards the black silk cocktail dress draped carefully over the bed, her matching high-heeled strappy sandals aligned precisely on the floor, creating the impression of an outfit, just without out a body inside!

She sits on the thin peach duvet, wrinkling its neat smoothness, next to her dress, then looks at the clock radio beside the bed, before slowly looking around her bedroom with a deep sense of satisfaction. The ceiling is white, the walls a warm cream colour, which, when illuminated by the sun, look fantastic as they shimmer and glow. Erika contemplates the entire room with a deep sense of satisfaction. The whole room, in Erika's opinion, tastefully appointed, with an oak bed and matching bedside tables and two sets of drawers. The walk-in closet slightly ajar. The remaining furniture is elegant, but not expensive, the prints on the wall are all nondescript abstracts or antique maps. The honey oak parquet floor with its built-in heating system, covered strategically with rugs, creates a warm and friendly feel. She sighs gently. 'Relax, it'll be fun,' she thinks as the butterflies begin to settle. She then sits on the edge of the bed for a full ten minutes, breathing, calming her body and mind.

Erika stands and slips the dress on and effortlessly zips the dress up the left side. The excitement coming back into her eyes as she considers the evening ahead. After slipping on her matching heels, admiring the overall effect in the mirror, she collects a small shoulder bag from the dressing table and walks out of the bedroom, down the hall and into the lounge. Walking over to the picture window, with the balcony beyond, she looks out over the city, as she's on the on the second to top floor of the building in the heart of London. The view's acceptable, despite being on the wrong side of the building for stunning views. She turns and walks towards the front door. As she reaches for the handle, she whispers to herself, "Remember, this is the last day before the rest of your life."

Chapter 3

BING

The lift doors begin to open. 'The sound is always so jarring and loud,' Erika thinks, as the adrenalin dies down from the suddenness, 'why can't they be quieter and less harsh.' As she steps out into the corridor, her heels sink into the deep navy-blue carpet. The whole floor decorated the same, with dark navy carpets, very pale, almost white walls, and a bright white ceiling. The thousands of tiny, but very bright lights provide a constant and uniform light down the whole corridor. But they don't negate the harshness and intensity of the light from the ceiling. Just another innovative idea that didn't quite work in practice! The lights should have provided a nice, pleasant environment, but instead it is too harsh. She walks purposefully, but slowly over the soft and spongy floor, each step, deliberate and controlled. The doors, in contrast to the blue feel of the floor are all black, a deep matte black. They seem blacker, because or perhaps due to the intensity of the overhead light. Care and attention clearly went into the creation of this effect. Presently, she arrives at her destination apartment E. The penthouse floor is the only one to designate accommodation by letters and not numbers. She knocks twice on the door.

Erika waits and is just about to knock again when the door opens. The darkness of the door, giving way to an evening light that seems to engulf the room. "You're early," Dominique says simply, a warm welcoming smile spread over her face.

At 5'6" or 1.68 metres, Dominique is of average height and slender build. Her shoulder length blonde hair just kisses the tops of her shoulders contrasting with her black velvet cocktail dress, black tights, but no shoes. Diamond earrings dangle subtly below each ear, matching the silver pendant necklace. She wears no rings. Her makeup, applied to highlight her hazel eyes, which seem to shift colour as she moves. Everything about her says, successful, but in an understated way.

"The traffic wasn't as bad as I anticipated," Erika replies, a playful glint in her eyes.

Dominique looks sceptical, "The traffic?" she enquires. "From one floor below this one?"

"OK, fine," Erika concedes, "I didn't have to wait for the lift."

"Right," Dominique confirms still slightly sceptically then takes a step backwards so that Erika can move into the apartment. Then they embrace, a warm friendly and intimate gesture. Dominique makes a kiss sound and releases her friend. "You do look beautiful tonight," she says, releasing the embrace and then moves back into the apartment and into the short corridor. Erika follows, closing the door and securing the security chain. She quickly removes her black suede sandals, with the polished silver spiked heels, carefully placing them on the shoe rack behind the door.

As Erika walks down the short corridor, she muses that they must have used the same paint throughout the whole building, as it looks as if the colour scheme is the same as the colours in her apartment. The main difference is the deep luxuriously piled carpet that runs like grass covering the whole floor. No pictures adorn the walls of Dominique's short corridor, only the pair of floor-to-ceiling mirrors near the door, which creates an impossible infinite reflection effect, it's particularly impressive when the lights are on.

At the end of the corridor, the space opens out into an open-plan living room and dining area, with a kitchen off to the left. As Erika glances round the main living area, she takes in the light brown fabric sofa and chairs, the medium oak furniture, which tone perfectly with the sofa and chairs. The printed photographs show only Dominique and Erika, there's nobody else in the images. One, a single large electronic photo frame, where the images slowly change to show Erika in all manner of situations, mostly tourist situations around London and some from what are clearly visits to the countryside. The furniture arranged around a huge, but seldom used, flat screen TV. As she turns, Erika sees Dominique fussing at the table, preparing candles in their holders. "Do you need a hand?"

"Thank you, yes," Dominique replies.

"I fully expected you to have done all this hours ago," Erika comments as she walks over, the carpet pile sinking between her toes.

"I did everything I could last night," Dominique says, moving the candlesticks into the exact perfect spot for symmetry on the table, "but not everything is happy being setup early and you too were early."

"I'm sorry if it's ruining your plans," Erika replies before adding, "what should I do?"

"Pop into the bedroom and bring all the obvious bits out," Dominique glances at Erika with a knowing smile. She then goes back to arranging items on the table.

Erika opens the heavy door to the bedroom, noticing once again, that the penthouse apartments are not just bigger and nicer, but they also have better appointments, the kitchen is nicer, the doors heavier and thicker. Upon entering the room with the same deep lush green carpet, she heads to the bed, where there are four carefully wrapped gift packages and three helium filled Mylar balloons with the number '34' printed in big bold numerals. She gathers everything in one go and returns to the dining area. "Are these what you wanted?"

"Thank you, yes. Just what I was looking for," Dominique says, finishing with the table. As Erika looks on, she has transformed the clutter to a perfect arrangement. The white, red, and black roses arranged in order, with three full sets in a circle in the centre. The two candlesticks on either side with three small tealights arranged around each. The two long red candles giving light high up and the tealights giving light low down, which will make the lead crystal sparkle as the flames dance. The place settings: wine glasses, and napkins all precisely arranged. The napkins folded into a rosebud design, deep red, the same colour as the candles and the roses.

"It looks very nice," Erika comments.

"Thank you, "Dominique says with an excited grin, "Happy Birthday." With that, she presents a wrapped gift, one that Erika has just bought from the bedroom.

While Erika carefully removes the ribbon and tape, Dominique moves into the lounge and places the Mylar balloons strategically around to maximise their effect. "How does it feel to be thirty-four?" she enquires.

Erika sighs softly, "It feels the same and you know it." She removes the jewellery box from its paper prison and opens it with a pop. "Ooo, that looks beautiful."

"Don't get your hopes up, it's only silver and cubic zirconia."

"It still looks beautiful," Erika says happily.

"Here, allow me," Dominique says taking the wrapping paper, box, and bracelet, "Try this one," she says, slipping another box into Erika's hand.

Slowly, methodically and with purpose, Erika de-ribbons, unwraps and then opens the second box and reveals a matching pendant necklace. "Once again, thank you. It looks beautiful."

Dominique again takes the wrapping paper, ribbon, box, and necklace and asks, "Would you like to wear them?"

"I would," Erika replies formally. With that, Dominique places the present debris onto the coffee table along with the boxes and moves back to Erika who offers her right wrist. Dominique takes a couple of attempts to get the clasp shut around the proffered wrist. The necklace is a good deal easier; the lobster claw clasp opens and easily closes behind her neck. The artificial diamond within its circular mount laying flat just below Erika's throat.

"There, that looks good," Dominique offers, surveying her handy work.

Erika's right arm stretches out and she twists it, looking at the new bracelet, watching the light catch and sparkle off the artificial diamonds, then she touches her neck to feel the new necklace. "Thank you."

"May I," Dominique says lightly, but with a theatrical flourish as she gestures towards the balcony, "interest you in a cocktail, birthday girl?"

"You may," Erika says, partially stifling a chuckle.

"Then I will join you outside shortly," Dominique says, as she moves gracefully towards the kitchen. Erika walks over to the sliding door, working the lock and catch, slides it open, revealing the sounds, smells, and liveliness of London on a July evening. The view from the balcony is everything that is missing from the view in Erika's. The Thames stretches out left and right, with Tower bridge off to the right. It always looks spectacular when the lights come on, which they will in an hour or two.

Erika takes her place on her customary reclining chair and simply takes in the view. The balcony covered in artificial grass, that's just a slight shade of green different from the carpet. The recliners, footrests and the table are all nice quality patio furniture, which would look at home in any five-star hotel. The wood nicely maintained and worn just slightly from frequent use. It looks loved, in all senses of the word.

Dominique appears with two crystal champagne flutes, each a work of art. "If you don't like it, just say," Dominique begins, "I know strawberry is your favourite, but the cherry just works so much better." With that, she tentatively hands Erika her glass.

Erika's drink initially looks like champagne, with a twist of orange wedged halfway down the glass. A red syrup like blob on the orange is slowly sending tendrils of red through the drink on convection and bubble currents. Three maraschino cherries sit generating streams of bubbles from the bottom. Around the rim, there is a light brown freeze. "They're not quite ready to drink yet," Dominique comments, placing hers down on the table, "they'll take five to ten minutes. Feel free to watch them while we wait."

"Alright."

Dominique gracefully slides onto her reclining chair and looks out over the Thames a moment before speaking, "There's a couple of things I want to talk about before dinner, if that's alright with you?"

Fascinated by the movement of the red tendrils in the cocktail and the bubbles, Erika answers without looking up, "Yes, that's fine. You're not getting cold feet, are you?"

"No, nothing like that. I just need to be sure that, you're sure."

"So, I worry about you, while you worry about me," Erika says, looking up now from the drink to Dominique.

"Something like that," Dominique confirms, "I just need to make sure a few things are all sorted out first. That and, you're sure."

"You know I'm sure but ask away."

Erika looks at Dominique a moment, then back to the cocktail as Dominique speaks, "Children? Are you sure about not having any?"

Erika looks back at Dominique, "Oh, I see what you mean by questions. We've talked about this before and I am fine with things as they are."

"I know, but it's one thing to say it when you have options in front of you, and an entirely different situation when you don't. Right now, this is a possibility, later, not so much. I'm just trying to give you the option to have an opt-out."

"I appreciate the concern and the opt-out offer, but it's not necessary," Erika steals a glance at her ever-evolving drink as she speaks. Then after a pause asks, "What about you? Ever wanted children?"

Dominique looks at Erika, then her drink and then out into London, Erika begins to wonder if she said something she shouldn't before Dominique replies simply, "I did."

"You did?" Erika says, turning her full attention from the streams of bubbles and the growing red tint. "You never mentioned it before."

"It wasn't the right time before and now might not be either, but you did ask," Dominique said rather sadly.

"Yes, I did, so tell away."

"I had four children, well actually seven, but three died when they were young." Dominique looks to her drink a moment then adds, "But, they're all gone now."

"That's all?"

"For now. I'm sure this will crop up later, so that's all I want to say for now, I had children and it's in some ways comforting to know that your family continues, even though, knowing they will die is distressing. More so now I think." Dominique looks at her drink a moment and then smiles to Erika, "They look ready to drink when you're ready." No sooner had Dominique's words left her lips than an arm adorned with a new diamond bracelet reaches out for her glass. "Happy birthday, my love," Dominique says, then with a clink of two crystal champagne flutes she adds, "May this be your best birthday ever."

Almost as one, Dominique and Erika sip their champagne cocktails, "Oh my goodness, that's lovely," Erika exclaims, "how have we never had these before?"

"Special party drink."

"What's in it? How do you make them?" Erika couldn't believe how good they tasted.

"Do you really want to know, or are you being nice?"

"I really want to know."

"Champagne, I think this works best with a slightly sweeter champagne, fresh eating cherries, about thirty per serving, maraschino cherries, lemon, orange, pure maple syrup, some nutmeg, cinnamon, salt, icing sugar and a couple of spices I'm keeping secret. It takes quite a while to do, but first remove all the stones from the fresh cherries. Then extract all the juice, put it in a pan with some fresh lemon juice and a little of the orange. Hand squeezing gives a better result, the machines sometimes put some of the bitterness of the pith into the juice. Then warm over a medium heat, add some maple syrup and the nutmeg powdered, not grated. Allow to warm until the first bubbles start to appear in the mixture. You should stir it continually. For the glass, get some triple sec to wet the rim and then using equal parts of cinnamon, icing sugar and salt. Make sure they are all a super fine powder, you want it to feel silky smooth on the lips and tongue, not rough and ready. Grind with a mortar and pestle until they are all extremely fine, the sugar will be like this anyway, the cinnamon too, if you buy the right one. Then mix all three together so they are perfectly blended. Then with the damp triple sec rimmed glass put a coating of that mixture onto the rim. Put the maraschino cherries in the bottom, in the arrangement you want, then cover them with vodka, carefully half-fill the glass with the champagne, then place the orange segment or twist into the glass at the champagne level. The thicker you make the cherry sauce, the longer it takes to dissolve into the drink, but the more spectacular it looks. Next add a portion of the syrup onto the orange, being careful to make sure it doesn't or won't slide off, making it cold by keeping it in the fridge works well here, then fill the glass with champagne. Carry carefully to the recipient and allow them to wait and watch for the full effect."

"That's it?" Erika asks incredulously.

"No, it's more complex than that, but I assumed you wanted the quick version," Dominique says, with a knowing grin.

"Indeed!"

"Just to ruin the surprise, there's steak for dinner, with crème brûlée followed by individual strawberry pavlova." Dominique watches as Erika's expression brightens, "I thought you'd like your favourite birthday treats."

"That sounds lovely. Thank you," Erika says, taking another sip of her drink, in another spot to get the fresh frosting from around the rim.

"I just assumed you'd like a taste sensation meal."

"I do and I would. You make the nicest food." Erika sips at her drink again, in a new spot.

"I have planned for three cocktails each, so there's no need to nurse it."

Erika grins, "Good to know."

"Tonight's dinner is going to be as good as food gets, you know that right?"

"Intellectually, yes. But I don't know what that really means for me," said Erika, with an underlying query in her voice.

"It means enjoy it for the hedonistic pleasure that it affords and don't regret any of it," Dominique says encouragingly. "And because your life is too short and because I love you, I'll skip what went into preparing the steak."

"Involved?"

Dominique plays with her drink a moment and takes a large sip, "It makes the cocktail look like an instant drink."

"Then I probably don't want to know. At least not tonight, when I am enjoying it." Erika wanted just to enjoy the moment.

"Probably a wise choice and, let me know about half an hour before you want to eat."

"It's half an hour before I want to eat," Erika says with an impish grin.

"Are you hungry? I should have asked when you first arrived. I'm currently a bit slow, it'll get better as the evening progresses."

Erika nods, "Yes, I'm hungry, so I would be happy to eat sooner rather than later."

"Then feel free to stay here and enjoy the view and cocktail or come into the kitchen, while I put the finishing touches to dinner."

Erika watches as Dominique vanishes into the apartment, turns back to her cocktail, savouring the view over the river. The light is starting to dim, just a little but not enough for the building lights to come on. 'Tower bridge always looks spectacular from here,' she muses.

Erika continues to enjoy the view until the smell of cooking steak wafts through the open balcony door and interrupts her city gazing. She slides out of her chair and walks effortlessly through the lounge and dining area into the kitchen. "I came for a refill."

"Drawn by the smell of very nice grilling steak too, I imagine," Dominique says, taking the now empty cocktail glass.

"That might have spurred me into action," Erika concedes, "that and I thought I should be here, just in case."

Dominique assembles another cocktail as per her original instructions, it only takes a minute while the rest of the meal cooks, "If you're wanting to do something constructive, how about lighting the candles?"

"That I can do, while enjoying a cocktail," Erika says, before extracting the candle lighter from the drawer. Then heads off to light the candles, something at which she is clearly very practiced. "Did you have more things to discuss?"

"Just one and it's a simple question, so no discussion required."

"Alright, what is it?"

"Would you like to postpone tonight's festivities?"

Erika finishes lighting the candles before heading silently back to the kitchen. When she sees Dominique replies simply, "No."

"Fair enough, and you're comfortable with it?"

"I'm excited and looking forward to it," Erika says looking intently at Dominique.

"Alright, then we are a go," Dominique says, walking round to her friend, "I have this for you too." She hands Erika another small gift wrapped present.

"Three of four," Erika comments quietly, as she places her glass on the counter and takes the proffered package. Unwrapping it a little less precisely than the previous two, she removes the ribbon, the paper and extracts the little box from its paper tomb. As the box snaps open, a pair of diamond stud earrings mounted on silver posts stares out of the black box. "Thank you, they're beautiful."

"Part of a birthday set and I'm glad you like them."

"Why so many bits of jewellery?" Erika queries totally overwhelmed.

"I saw them and thought they would like good on you as a set."

"You've gone to a lot of trouble with all this, the food; drink; presents and not to mention balloons." Erika couldn't remember when she'd last had such fantastic presents.

Dominique continues cooking, or at least watching the cooking, "It's no trouble."

"What am I missing?"

"Nothing, you're not missing anything," Dominique replies. "As you correctly mentioned there is one more present which I will give you at dinner and everything else you know. More or less."

"So, no surprises, no sudden change of heart, nothing like that?" Erika says, a playful suspicious tone in her voice.

Dominique starts to turn off the grill and the rings under the frying pans. "No nothing. We have dinner, dessert, some chat. Then some fooling about and finally a walk later tonight or more likely technically tomorrow morning. You don't have plans for tomorrow, do you?"

"None that you're unaware of. I thought the plan was for me to stay over tonight," Erika asks.

"Yes, that's the plan." Dominique starts to dish up the steaks, chips, salad, grilled mushrooms and tomatoes and a small bowl with some sauce. "Feel like carrying something?" she asks, offering the two plates to Erika, who simply transports them into the dining area and sets them at the table.

Following Erika, Dominique brings the remaining items and places them in their correct place on the table. "There's no crackers, no party poppers, nothing but what you see here."

Erika slips into her chair, the same one she always has when eating here. As Dominique takes her place, Erika takes in her friend's outfit. Dominique's dress fits perfectly, like a hand in a glove, yet somehow being more. Hazel eyes that seem to change colour with her mood and the light, and lips that when done up like they are tonight invite a kiss. This is not how they usually look however, so the change is most welcome.

"Please start," Dominique says, collecting her cutlery, "I'd hate for it to get cold. There's nothing worse that cold steak."

She cuts at her steak and adds, "Actually, I can think of several things worse." Erika chuckles and takes her first bite of meat.

"Oh, my goodness, this is amazing," Erika exclaims, her mouth still half-full.

"I said you'd like it, didn't I?"

"I don't know how long it took or what went into it, but it was worth it," Erika says having finished her first mouthful and cuts out the second, "Where did you learn to cook like this?"

"It's just takes a little practice, you pick things up over the years."

"Like how to be a gourmet chef?"

"For example, and I hope you see the irony of it all," Dominique said with an underlying message in her voice.

"Perhaps."

"You will tomorrow," Dominique confirms, "and before I forget, do you want wine, or have you had enough with the cocktails?"

"I know where this is going, so, can we have a glass of wine and I'll stop with the cocktails."

Dominique stands and effortlessly glides to the kitchen and returns shortly afterwards with a single bottle of wine. "Red with steak." Skilfully, the top is unwrapped with a sommeliers knife and the cork extracted. All done with fluid grace and poise of someone who's done this a thousand times before. She pours them both half a glass of wine and places the bottle in what is its predesignated spot on the table. Leaving it to breathe. She raises her glass and offers a toast, "Enjoy your birthday, you're only thirty-four once."

Erika raises her glass and clinks them together, "To birthdays." She sips at the wine and mms, "This is the best wine I've ever tasted."

"Probably," Dominique agrees.

"Expensive?"

"Very," Dominique concurs.

"Thank you," Erika says sipping more of the burgundy liquid velvet.

"Enjoy the tastes and flavours," Dominique says, continuing with her meal.

"I am."

"Just remember, tonight is for the hedonistic pleasures, the sensations and please don't drink too much alcohol," Dominique requests.

"Why? Oh, I get it, that's why you're not drinking too much now."

"Thank you and yes, that's why." Dominique nods her head in agreement.

The two thirty-something women enjoy conversation and dinner until after the second dessert.

"As you were counting, this will be the fourth gift," Dominique says, offering the final gift-wrapped box to Erika.

With slightly less skill than when she first started, Erika carefully and precisely removes the ribbon, the tape and finally releases another black jewellery box. When it pops open, she looks to Dominique and then back to the ring. "How do I interpret this?" she asks, slightly confused.

"Any way you see fit," Dominique says with a knowing playful smile. "It's only a ring. Wear it on whichever finger or fingers you see fit. Although, it will only fit two comfortably." Erika slips the ring out from its velvet base and begins trial fitting it to her fingers. As the process continues, it quickly becomes clear that it only fits comfortably onto her ring fingers, both left and right.

"So," Erika says slowly, "it fits either of my ring fingers only. Which means this is either an engagement ring, when on the left or nothing special, if worn on the right."

"I think we're beyond that," Dominique says, stating the hidden obviousness to their situation.

"We might be, but I have to think of work and the rest of the world," Erika says, considering her options.

"Then you'll have plenty of time to think about it, because tonight is Friday and you have two whole weeks of holiday before going back to work, which, if my calculations are correct, is about sixteen or seventeen days, depending on how you calculate them."

"And tonight?"

"Tonight, you wear it however makes you feel best, hedonistic day remember."

"Right," Erika says and slips it onto her left hand.

"See how easy that was?" Dominique said playfully.

"A little too easy, you're very slick," Erika retorted.

Dominique beams a theatrical grin, "I know." She glances towards the lounge, "Shall we? And feel free to take your wine."

Erika slips off from her chair and heads towards the lounge, and as she catches sight of the balloons asks, "Why three balloons?"

"Simple, one for each decade of your life. I did most things in threes, three sets of three roses, three pairs of tealights. But one set of four, the presents, one for each year. Giving thirty for the balloons and four with the gifts. Your age."

"That's too subtle and clever."

"I know," Dominique says smugly.

"But it's impressive."

"I know."

"Oh, now you know all," Erika teases.

"Not all, but some. But all the things that I planned to be just so," Dominique says, with a smile.

"What next?"

"How about we watch the end of the sunset?"

Erika slips her left hand into Dominique's right and walks with her to the balcony, "Excellent plan."

They slip their hands apart and slide onto their chairs, looking out over the river Thames, the lights are now on Tower Bridge and the whole edifice brightly lit. "You know, I'd forgotten about this," Dominique says taking up her cocktail.

"I assumed that you didn't like it," Erika says, sipping her wine.

Dominique shakes her head, "No, as far as champagne cocktails go, it's probably the best in the world. I was simply busy with other things. You know how it is."

"I do, it's so easy to get wrapped up in doing something and well, forget the other things," Erika says contemplating her life.

"Exactly," Dominique agrees, "and I've had a lot of things to try and get exactly right for tonight. I must be honest; I'm quite nervous about the whole thing. Trying to make it perfect, trying to have you relax and be at ease."

"It has been perfect, better than I could have imagined. I've never tasted food like that before. I am not going to ask how long it took to prepare that dinner and I feel a little bad for my quip when I arrived about having done it all already, when it's now obvious that you spent a huge amount of time and effort on tonight," Erika sips her wine slowly.

"You know you're special, in general and to me, Erika. Otherwise, we wouldn't be doing this whole thing tonight."

"I know, but still."

"Besides, I have plans for all, and I do mean all, of your holiday," Dominique says, the twinkle in her eyes and voice show future intent.

"Are you going to show me off with this fancy new ring?"

Timed to perfection, Erika forces Dominique to blurt champagne cocktail through her nose, the clean-up quite comical, without any tissues or cloths on the balcony. Once she's finished dabbing the last remaining drops of champagne off her nose and onto her hand, Dominique walks briskly into the kitchen and comes back several minutes later. To find Erika still highly amused by the whole incident.

"Very nice timing," Dominique offers.

"Oh, come on, it was amazing timing and pretty funny too," Erika chortles.

"You're going to get my makeup all messed up."

"I'm sure that it'll get messed up between now and going out anyway."

"Maybe, but you don't need to mess it up on purpose."

"I'm saying sorry, but I didn't think you'd react quite that forcefully," Erika says, sipping more of her wine.

"If you drink too much more of that wine, I might have to kill you."

"If I drink much more you might not be able to!"

Holding up her champagne flute, Dominique concedes, "Fair point. So, détente it is then. And no, I am not planning to show you and the ring off to anyone. I'm serious, it's all silver and cubic zirconia, so it has truly little value, to a thief or resale, but it looks extremely nice. I suppose, that's lesson

31

one. Never have things, like jewellery that's so expensive, you can't afford to let it go. That goes for gifts to others as well as for yourself. But you can look drop dead gorgeous without spending a huge amount of money. Remember, elegant, not flashy. The only one you must impress is yourself. I'm already impressed."

"As always you're too kind," Erika says kindly.

"Not really, but now that you're all fat and happy, so to speak. Second to last chance to change your mind?"

"Fat, check; happy, check; hedonistic, check. Changing mind, blank."

"Lawyers and their checklists. You're as bad as pilots," Dominique quips.

"Ooo, what do you know about pilots?" Erika asks, looking over from the muted blues, purples, oranges, and greys.

"Nothing I want to get into tonight. Other than that fact that they generally have aeroplanes."

Erika finishes sipping her wine, "I was hoping for some salacious story."

Dominique goes for the theatrical and places the back of her hand to her forehead, "What kind of woman do you take me for."

Erika laughs aloud, "The kind who knows her way around a pilot?" Dominique joins in the laughter.

"I've met a pilot or two, but nothing more."

"That's what they all say," Erika mocks.

"With good chaste reason I imagine."

"I assume the imagine comes from lack of experience – in being chaste that is," Erika says trying to keep a straight face. The alcohol buoying her levity.

Dominique considers her response carefully while sipping her cocktail, "I prefer to discuss, then negotiate; perhaps consider the risk in the current course of action; then we move on to warnings, threats, and only then direct action. Usually final direct action. That would be lesson two."

"I hope you have these written down, I'm in no position to remember all these lessons. Birthday Girl, remember."

"No, they're not written down, they are for you to remember."

"It's Friday night for Christ's sake," Erika says, finishing her wine.

"Ah, The Terminator reference, got it," Dominique says happily, having got the reference.

"Exactly, well spotted. Now I've finished the wine, how expensive was it?" Erika's curiosity was getting the better of her!

"Very."

"So, you said, but exactly how very expensive, in numbers?" Erika persists.

"If I said, a few thousand pounds, what would you say?" Dominique asks cautiously.

"Then, I'd say, no wine that expensive should be drunk, only stored and traded."

"Then it wasn't a few thousand pounds, it was quite a bit more," Dominique hedges.

"Fine, then keep your wine cost secret, but it seems like a waste."

Dominique offers her cocktail glass to Erika, "Did you enjoy it?"

Taking the glass Erika replies, "Yes, it was delightfully nice. The whole evening has been the best night of my life."

"Then it was money well spent," Dominique says kindly.

"How can you be so casual with money like that?" Erika says, stunned by Dominique's casual attitude to the cost of the wine.

"When you have none, money is the most important thing there is. Think back to when you were a student, you lived as cheaply as you could, saved every penny for the things you thought were important, going out with friends, etc. Then when you earnt a little, your priorities changed. When you had enough for a nice apartment, like the one downstairs, your priorities were different again. Each time as you gained more money, your idea of what a lot of money is, changed, and you never entered the - I have enough money - bracket. But I have. I have enough, so that I can have this apartment, buy you jewellery, make nice meals and have exquisite wine." As Dominique speaks, Erika looks unconvinced. "If you have fifty pounds, spending twenty-five on dinner is an extravagance. But if you have a thousand, that seems acceptable. Now if you have a million, does a thousand sound a lot. What about ten million, or twenty? Just to be clear, I would have been perfectly happy for you to have half a glass of wine and we pour the rest down the sink, if that's what you wanted and would make you happy. That was all that mattered. And yes, we can afford it, otherwise, I'd never have offered it. It's not extravagance, it's living within your means and having a treat."

"I never understood or appreciated that until now. There are somethings that simply don't matter to you," Erika says, considering her friend in a new light.

"Correct, seeing you happy, and knowing that this would be a day you'll remember for the rest of time, that's worth every penny to me," Dominique smiles lovingly at Erika.

"I don't know how to respond."

"I know exactly how, when you finish your drink, or actually, my drink, we'll head in and do the fooling about part of the evening, I was thinking in the bedroom," Dominique looks at Erika a long moment, "If you're up to it?"

"Sounds like a plan and, yes, I'm up to it."

Dominique flashes her most charming grin, "So defiant."

"So, I'm staying over?" Erika enquires.

"You'll wake up here and, if I have my way, spend most of the next week or two here."

"But I don't have any spare clothes, you never said anything about saying a week," Erika protests.

"In case of emergency, I'm sure we could sneak into your apartment downstairs and find an outfit of two," Dominique suggests conspiratorially.

"Oh, a cunning plan!"

"Which is why I'm in charge of all plans. I believe I have a badge somewhere to that effect."

"That wouldn't surprise me," Erika says, finishing the cocktail.

"Had enough? Fancy coming to bed?"

"Yes, I do, yes I have."

Chapter 4

The master bedroom, like the rest of the apartment is spacious and tastefully appointed, but nothing showy. The thin purple duvet, with matching pillow, on the bed still showing the slight indents from the gift packages. "Please sit," Dominique says gesturing to the bed.

"What now?" Erika asks, as she sits properly on the bed, knees together, hands in her lap.

Dominique kneels in front of her and looking her in the eye says, "This is your last chance to change your mind and say no."

Erika nods and a smile sweeps across her face, "We've discussed it before, and I am still going to go ahead."

"Fair enough, that was your last opt-out. From now on, you're committed," Dominique says seriously.

"I know and I'm fine," Erika says, nervous excitement creeping into her voice.

Dominique effortlessly rises to her feet and sits down sideways facing her friend. Erika turns, adjusting her position on the edge of the bed to face Dominique.

"What now?" Erika asks. "Sex?"

Dominique shakes her head, "No, not tonight, but and you'll like this, there's going to be plenty of opportunity for you to indulge your desire for sex later." She pauses a moment and then with a hint of seduction in her voice adds, "There's going to be plenty of sex in your future. It's one of the things that makes being one of us fun."

"How?" Erika asks sounding intrigued.

"That's for another night, tonight, I have other plans," Dominique says, her grin widening.

"What then?"

"Something old and something new. You understand, this is a process, and you have, sorry, we both must follow it through correctly, otherwise, disaster."

"I understand, so what do I have to do?" Erika ponders, waiting for some guidance.

Dominique pauses a moment and looks at her friend, "First, you must drink. Then we both do. You'll probably have a lot of fun, then all will slip away from you. Then finally, you'll feel a tingling all over your body, like the activation of every nerve ending, all at once. Then we'll take it from there."

'Am I doing the right thing,' Erika wonders as she listens, 'it's a big step. Yes, we've been through it many times, it what we want and planned. I can do this.'

Dominique asks, "Ready?"

"Ready," Erika confirms, but the slight inkling of a doubt still hovers at the edge of her mind.

Dominique extends her right arm to Erika, wriggling her bracelet back up towards her elbow. With a single effortless gesture with her other hand, uses a matte purple fingernail to slice open her own wrist, the blood begins to pool out of it immediately. She offers it to Erika's lips, which quickly cover the small cut and she begins to drink.

As the initial sensation of intense burning quickly fades, Erika mms into the familiar, but enjoyable sensation. She's done this many times before and knows what to expect. The anticipation of the sensation is almost as nice as the actual effect. It feels like liquid velvet bliss, time seems to fade, as she focuses on and thinks only about the warm sensation flooding through her body. It feels like the build-up to an orgasm, but before the release.

After some time and Erika has no idea how long it's been, Dominique removes her wrist from Erika's mouth and the blood immediately stops flowing from the cut, then moments later, the cut is gone, as if it had never been. "Step one complete," Dominique comments, but Erika in her bubble of bliss hardly notices, "Now for us both." With that, Dominique stands and moves behind Erika and once again, makes a cut into her wrist, this time, the left with a perfectly painted fingernail on her right hand. Once more, she puts the bloody wrist to Erika's lips, there's no hesitation this time, lips cover the wound and Erika drinks. The sensation of bliss quickly building again.

Dominique pulls the hair back from around Erika's neck and lowers her mouth to the soft and tanned skin. She places a single loving kiss gently on the surface and then, with skill and poise, her fangs, extend and effortlessly puncture the skin. Erika doesn't seem to notice the fangs, caught up in her intensifying bubble of bliss. The initial surge of blood clearly having a positive effect on Dominique.

Dominique begins to drink, begins to feed, taking blood from her friend's neck.

Erika, simply sits still, drinking and being drunk from, her thoughts drifting from total bliss to a faint warning that something is wrong and back again. As time progresses, she cares less about the warning and enjoys the sensations more with every passing second, until the thoughts slowly slide from her mind, and she can no longer retrieve them.

Ultimately the world goes black, and she passes from consciousness, but she continues drinking, until the last possible moment.

Chapter 5

The burning sensation sears through every nerve in Erika's body. The intense pain ripping through her body feels like liquid fire, covering every part of her skin; insides, and all the parts that she didn't even know could feel anything. Her screams echo within her head, it seems to go on forever, but she knows it lasts probably only a few seconds or at most minutes.

As the sensation fades, she rolls onto her back and opens her eyes. The first things she sees after the ceiling, is Dominique sitting next to her on the bed. "Welcome back," Dominique says softly, a warm smile covering her face.

Erika looks at Dominique's face, which looks even more beautiful and perfect now than it did before. She reaches her hand out to touch Dominique and gently caresses her cheek, "I can feel the pores."

Dominique's grin grows wider, she seems happier, "I know. How do you feel?"

"You said it would tingle; it burnt like fire," Erika says, the feelings still raw in her mind.

"Really?" Dominique exclaims.

"Liquid fire," Erika reiterates.

Dominique hesitates a moment, "Now that's interesting. It shouldn't have done that!"

"Is that bad?" Erika enquires.

"No, nothing bad, nothing like that. It just means that you're going to be more sensitive, that's all."

"What like allergic to things?" Erika starting to feel a bit apprehensive.

Dominique looks surprised, confused, then chuckles, "No, nothing like that. It means that you'll feel things more acutely, have more sensitive senses, that's all. It's really a good thing." Erika looks less convinced as Dominique speaks.

Dominique offers Erika her hand, "We're done in here, come on." When Erika's hand arrives in Dominique's, she's helped up and into a standing position. "Are you stable?" she enquires.

Erika lets go of the helping hand and stands on her own a moment, "It looks like it."

"Excellent, then let's go into the lounge."

As they walk out of the bedroom and into the lounge, Erika asks, "How long was I out?"

"A bit over an hour. So, technically, it's still your birthday and it will be for the next oh, almost an hour."

"What can we do for the rest of my birthday then?" Erika asks, thinking of possibilities.

"If your thought is to go out and slaughter all the villagers, then no," Dominique says with a grin.

They both laugh. "I wasn't thinking that," Erika says, but the look in her eye says that the thought absolutely had already crossed her mind.

"Before there's any going out, there are a whole raft of things we need to do and discuss," Dominique says seriously. "For you, the night has only just begun. The first thing we need to cover, is proper technique."

"Technique for what?" Erika enquires, unsure as to what Dominique is talking about.

"Feeding," Dominique says simply.

"Isn't it easy, instinctive?"

"Yes, if you want to take out the whole village. But that's not what we want to do. As I said, it's going to be a long night," Dominique says patiently.

Erika nods her understanding, 'Can't we just get on with the fun parts,' she wonders to herself, "What do I need to do?"

"You're a solicitor, a barrister, a lawyer, so words are your thing, and you'll enjoy this. Basic nomenclature, all those people, the humans, they are known as people. We are all known as family and together, people and family are everyone. Clear?"

"Yes, but why?" Erika asks, clearly unsure what Dominique has in mind.

"Because there are only rare occasions and very private places where we use the real names for things. You never know who's listening when they might hear or record your words. The only time we talk about vampires, is when regarding fiction, such as books, movies, games, that sort of thing. Never about each other and never others. They are family, close family, like you and I, distant family, all manner of in-between. Some family you have a good relationship with, others you don't. But all are family, and we protect family over people," Dominique says, letting her words linger, so Erika understands their importance.

Erika listens and nods as she takes in the updates to her new world, "Understood. People, family, and everyone. What about friends?"

"Do you mean friends or associates?"

"Oh, I think I'm getting it," Erika says, racking her brain for the exact wording, while distractedly thinking, 'it's so hard when the world is so bright, so loud.'

"Until an hour or so ago, you were a friend, a lover, and an associate. Friend, because a friend is a friend. Lover, obviously. That was for your benefit, and we'll come to that later. Finally, an associate, because all those who know and form part of our extended sphere, those who sort of know, at least part of it, they're your associates and you'll have a few. Some to help you navigate the world, some to sustain you, others just because."

Erika considers this all a moment, 'How am I going to navigate all this at once,' she wonders, "It seems like a lot?"

"It is, but it's straightforward and you'll get the hang of it in no time," Dominique says reassuringly.

"I'm sorry, I'm having trouble thinking, it's so loud and bright in here," Erika mumbles, having difficulty concentrating.

Dominique moves quickly to the balcony door and slides it closed, "I'm sorry, I forgot about that," she says on her way back. "Sit down and close your eyes." Once Erika sits on the sofa, Dominique continues, "Imagine a slider, like you see on your phone, there's a label under it marked brightness. At one end is zero, at the other one hundred percent. In your mind, move the slider to twenty percent and then open your eyes."

Erika imagines the slider as instructed, 'This is silly,' she thinks to herself, as she complies, upon opening her eyes says, "What was that supposed to do?"

"Do it again and concentrate," Dominique says reassuringly.

Erika repeats the process, only this time, she concentrates on what she's doing, "Oh wow, that's definitely made the room darker."

Dominique looks like she has just won a major award, "Now do the same thing with sound and the world should get quieter."

Erika directly concentrates this time, no inner dialogue, no comments, just focuses and the constant din of the world diminishes under her control. "That's so cool. What else can I do like that?"

Dominique runs her fingers over Erika's forearm, "I'd would expect skin sensation. Label it correctly and adjust the slider."

Erika closes her eyes and imagines the slider, bringing it all the way down to twenty percent. She touches her own skin, checking the setting. "This is so strange, being able to control my body like this."

Dominique chuckles, "This is a poor way to do it, but I thought it might work with you. It's easier than the fully autonomous way, but that takes a lot of practice, and this seems to be quick and easy, if a somewhat cumbersome way of getting it done. I would adjust the sense of smell too."

Erika does as instructed, and with each adjustment, she is able to make them just a little bit easier and quicker. "This is amazing," she says quietly, "having total control over my body."

"Normally, they would be at about thirty percent, but you're sensitive, so I guessed lower. You should now adjust them so they are about the same as you would have felt them yesterday. Play around for a moment, I have time," Dominique says patiently.

'Talk about irony, the first thing you do as a vampire, is adjust a whole lot of settings, which you can access by sliders, to make yourself just like a human,' Erika thinks when juggling her settings. It takes her a couple of minutes before she's happy, or happy enough. "Can I change them later?" she asks.

"That would be family and yes, you can change them when you need to. Boost the brightness if it's too dark or improve your hearing if you need to. Just be aware, that people struggle to see in the dark, they can't hear all that well, so don't make yourself stick out. This is going to be our most basic rule, you can't ever let any of the people know you or any family member exists. You have a secret you must above all others always keep, no matter what."

Erika nods as she listens, considering the implications of what she's hearing. "What about associates?"

"Every rule has its loophole. And don't push the boundaries of this, there are few things you'll be hunted and killed for, but this is one of them. Understood?"

"Understood, fully understood," Erika says nodding.

"Next topic, food."

"Alright," Erika says cautiously.

"It's always called food, never anything else. One simply never mentions the source. Where to start?" Dominique says considering her options, "I know, you need to eat regularly. First, ignore everything you know from books, films, fiction, etc., it's almost all wrong. Now that is out of the way, eating. You must eat, your body can hold a certain amount of food, you need some to just live, but the spare, that's slowly used as you go about your day, doing things. The more active you are, the more you use. Seems obvious, but nothing you've seen, read, or been told will have covered this. So, you must eat every day. The hungrier you get, the more the cravings to eat will become. At some point, they'll become so intense that you cannot resist them. That's when you've lost control and who knows what havoc you'll unleash. You cannot let that happen, ever."

"That sounds grim," Erika said, frowning.

"It gets worse. We've worked for months to get to tonight. You've done everything you needed to, but there are things that remained hidden from you. There's a huge downside to being family. One, and it's important, there is a monster that lives within you, it's kept at bay, by the way you behave and by keeping well fed. When it gets out, you get the aforementioned havoc. However, the more it comes out, the more likely it is to come out. Sort of a self-fulfilling event. The monster begets the monster. If it ever gets to a point where the monster is omni present, then they will kill you. Because you can't control yourself and you'll threaten exposure of the rest of your family. Do you understand?" Dominique says in all seriousness.

Erika nods, "Oh my goodness, just by not eating I can make a fatal mistake. However, am I to survive! If I don't have anyone to fed from and make a scene, then I'm the one killed." The inner panic begins to show on Erika's face.

"You're not in this alone, that's why we are chatting. I'm going to help you through this transition to make it as easy as possible. There's going to be some theory and some practice." Dominique sits down beside her friend and offers her wrist.

Erika looks blankly at it, "What?"

"Feed."

"How?" Erika exclaims.

"Think about your teeth, extend them, put them into my wrist, then drink. Then you must close the wound."

"How do I do that?" Erika looks blankly at Dominique.

"Lick it."

"That's it?"

"Yes, now practice," Dominique says.

'This is nothing like the movies, where you just find someone lounging about and bite them in the neck and a few seconds later it's done,' Erika thinks. She concentrates, but nothing happens, no fangs, nothing.

"Did you make a slider?"

Erika looks dumbfounded, "For that too?"

"Whatever works."

Erika closes her eyes and concentrates, "Ah fiddlesticks that hurts," she groans, but the fangs slide into position.

"You're such a little robot," Dominique quips.

Erika ignores her as she bites into Dominique's wrist. "Alright, that's enough," Dominique says. Erika tries to pull back but stays locked to the food source. "Fight the urge, stop feeding."

'This is impossible, it's so hard to start and impossible to finish. The taste, and sensation, it's like before, but a thousand times more intense,' Erika thinks as she fights to do as instructed.

"Look at me and stop," Dominique says.

Reluctantly Erika looks at Dominique and seeing the look on her face, redoubles her efforts to stop drinking. Finally, she pulls back, but forgets to close the wound. Dominique does it automatically before blood can spill onto the carpet.

"I'm so sorry," Erika says panicked, "I couldn't stop."

"I know, let's try again," Dominique says, offering her wrist again.

Erika's reluctance is palpable, as she ponders, 'What if I start and can't stop. What if I kill her or make the monster?'

"It's perfectly safe, this is part of the practical and you're doing so well."

"It's going horribly wrong," Erika says worried she's doing it all wrong.

"Oh, you with all the experience," Dominique jibes.

Erika sighs and takes the proffered wrist, this time closing her eyes, and her fangs slide out effortlessly. 'I can do this, just drink a little and then stop. It's simple,' she tells herself as she breaks the skin, the artery and then blood begins to flow. But this time, she has a plan and takes a single mouthful and stops, closing the holes.

"Don't leave a mess, please clean it up," Dominique requests, forcing Erika to lick the blood on her wrist, the desire for more blood evident on her face.

'Oh no, I'm never going to make this work,' Erika thinks, as she licks up the surplus blood.

When she has finished and resisted the desire to drink more, Dominique says, "Well done. I know how hard that was. Ready for a little more theory?"

"Is it going to be like this all night?" Erika asks.

"No, it's going to get easier and you're doing very well, I'm impressed," Dominique says with a warm smile.

"Have you done this before?"

"Yes, but not for a while," Dominique confesses.

"How long?"

"A while, we'll talk about that later. One thing at a time."

"Will it always be this hard to stop drinking?"

Dominique shakes her head, "No, it'll normally be much easier. This week's going to be particularly hard because you're drinking from me. Polite society frown on drinking from family."

"Why? It feels so good."

"That's one of the reasons. You're new, so there's things we do, to make life easier for both of us. You can't really hurt me, even if you were to lose control, I would still be fine, so practicing on me is the safest. The downside is that, to you, I taste fantastic. In practice, nobody will ever taste as good to you as me. There are rules about drinking from family, you just don't do it. It is an intimacy that most cannot cope with and don't want the implications of."

Erika shakes her head, "I don't understand?"

"We have a bond, we've had it for years, and I mean years before you were an associate, if you catch my meaning. But, since you became an associate, and, therefore, became tied to me, that bond has become much stronger. Now that you've become family, every time you feed from me it renews the bond, it becomes strengthened. I'm not bothered, because the bond is genuine, it's pre-existing and frankly nice. But with others, I can't say the same."

"That makes some kind of sense, but I don't really get it," Erika confesses.

"That's because currently you don't really appreciate the power of blood. There are seventy-five places to start, and I don't know which one to start with," Dominique pauses and collects her thoughts. "Blood is now everything, it's the only thing that really matters to you. Sex is a means to an end now, you will want it for a while, because of what you associate it with, but it doesn't matter to you any more only feeding does. I've been around a while and that makes me relatively strong. Because I made you, you'll be strong too. Think of it as strong blood. Each, what shall we call it, generation, the blood gets diluted. So, my blood is stronger than yours, you're stronger than anyone you make, and they're stronger than anyone they make. So, at each point, it gets weaker, because of this, you'll be stronger than most. The upshot is, you don't want to be drinking from family, unless you are desperate, as there are consequences. Only feed from people."

Erika looks uneasy, "So, villagers are easier?"

"Yes, much. But they won't taste the same or feel the same."

"I knew that was too good to be true!"

"I am impressed, by the way. Ready to try again?"

"What already?" Erika says alarmed. 'What if I can't stop and she stops being impressed,' she thinks.

"Yes. Already," Dominique confirms as she offers her wrist again. "This time, drink longer, at least ten seconds."

"What if I can't stop?"

"You can."

Erika slides out her fangs once more and a little clumsily bites into Dominique's wrist, the blood welling up from the two round holes. 'I think I'm addicted, that's the problem,' she thinks.

Dominique starts counting down, "Ten, nine, eight, seven, six, five, four, three, two, one, done."

Much to Erika's surprise, she simply stops right on queue. "How on earth did I just do that?"

"See easy. Now for the fun bit."

"There's a fun bit, the whole things been horrific," Erika protests.

"Stand up with me, sweep my hair away and use your lips to feel the heartbeat in my neck."

Erika does as she's instructed, her normal soft easy touch, becomes clumsy and awkward.

"Did you feel it, as your lips brushed over my neck?" Dominique asks.

"No."

"Try making your lips more sensitive, you have to feel the pulse, or you won't know where it is," Dominique says, gently guiding Erika's actions.

Erika tries again, her lips gently caressing Dominique's neck. "Found them," she confirms.

"Good girl, move your fangs about two millimetres behind the back one and feed. Time yourself, closeup and cleanup."

Moments later Erika sighs as she takes her first taste. The sensation completely different from her previous experiences. Wrists and necks are not the same thing she learns quickly. Reluctantly, she pulls away, closes the holes, and has nothing to cleanup. "How was that?" she asks.

"Almost a professional," Dominique says with a grin. "Now the other side." Dominique tilts her head, offering the other side.

Erika takes a moment to compose herself, gaining confidence, not just in the technique, but more importantly in stopping feeding, finds the right spot, sinks her fangs into the soft warm flesh and begins to feed. As she begins to lose herself in the sensations, feels a tap on her shoulder and suddenly realises what's happening and regains her composure and stops, closes the holes, and cleans up the small amount of blood that escaped.

"Did you get taken in by the ecstasy, you seemed to lose focus?" Dominique enquires.

Erika nods, "Yes, I let it start to sweep me away."

"You must concentrate and focus. It'll get easier with time and practice. Which side do you prefer? Everyone has a favourite?"

"Um, my right, your left," Erika says, after thinking about it.

"Nice, keep that in mind, it'll help in the future. There's one more thing we need to discuss for now."

"What?"

"You're dead! That means there's somethings that are going to be a problem for you."

"Like what?" Erika says puzzled.

"Like tomorrow, you'll be the temperature of that table and as warm and inviting as one too. It'll be much worse in the winter."

"Oh no, I didn't think about that." Erika thinks, 'How am I going to blend in if I feel like a table? A winter table.' "I feel warm. You feel warm," Erika says slowly, contemplating.

"True, but you're cooling down every moment that goes by. I'm not, and we'll come to that later too. In the first instance, let's talk about what this means and what you can do about it. Obviously, you're stuffed!

"That's it?"

Dominique grins, "No, of course not. It's easier in the summer, but consider this, you have mass, your body, so you can warm it up right through, then it will stay warm for hours."

"How?" Erika enquires.

Dominique pauses a moment, then with a smile says, "The easiest way is with a hot tub, or sauna or a bath. The bath is the easiest. You'll have to spend some time, like an hour or more and it must be hot, hotter than normal body temperature. Say forty degrees or a little less, then you stay in until you're warmed all the way through, the warmer on the inside, the slower you cool down. It's a hassle, but it works."

"Is that what you do?" Erika asks.

Dominique shakes her head, "No, I maintain a warm body all the time, it uses up a little food, but I stay like this all the time. The trick is to allow it to change as conditions dictate, cold hands, in winter, too hot in summer, etc. With practice, one can control all aspects. It's how you were able to find my arteries and veins. Most of the rest of our family can't do that." She flicks her eyebrow a moment.

"Can I use the sliders trick?"

"No, this is something different and much harder. In time, I'm sure you'll get it, but not just on day one. There's so much to learn, so much to do, you're going to love it," Dominique enthuses.

"You sound excited by this?"

"Oh, I am excited. This is going to be so much fun," Dominique chuckles.

"Sometimes I worry about you," Erika says shooting Dominique a look.

"You shouldn't. Do you fancy going out for a walk?"

Erika's enthusiasm for going out from earlier seems to have waned a little. Her inner hesitation reflected outwards, "Are you sure?"

"I wouldn't ask if I wasn't sure, and I'll keep you honest and safe," Dominique says reassuringly.

"If you promise."

"I promise," Dominique says, greeted by Erika's smile, "I'll grab my shoes and meet you by the front door."

"Could you get me a jacket please?"

"Of course," Dominique says heading towards the bedroom.

Chapter 6

Walking quietly with Erika, Dominique takes in her surroundings and guides the pair to the railings keeping people from falling into the river Thames. She asks, "How are you feeling?"

"Fine, why?" Erika replies, looking out over the river at a party boat, moving slowly down the river, revellers on the upper deck, drinking and making merry.

"We're outside, new sights, sounds, smells, etc. You know, more stimulus," Dominique says conversationally.

"Ah, right. No, all is fine."

"Then have you adjusted your brightness to the changed light levels?"

"Should I?"

Dominique turns from the river to look at Erika, "I do, I keep everything at a constant brightness all the time, so it's comfortable, but so I can see everything that's going on. Nobody likes surprises."

Erika stares out over the river for a few moments, "Now, that's strange."

"But better, no?"

"Yes, much better," Erika agrees.

"And you can see into the shadows?"

Erika nods, "Yes, why are we out for a walk?"

Dominique slips her arm through Erika's and gently moves to walk down the Embankment next to the river. Each step takes them onto a new paving slab, each almost aligned correctly with those around it. She whispers, "We have many things to cover on your vacation and very little time."

"Sorry, pardon, what did you say?" Erika queries.

"Perhaps more sensitivity on the hearing?"

"Yes of course," Erika says, without stopping walking.

"Technically, I'm pacing you, this is about the speed you should walk when out and about. It feels like slow casual strolling, but it's normal walking pace. Strolling would be more like this." With that Dominique cuts her pace and they walk much slower.

'Now I need to have walking training too,' Erika thinks, while trying to memorise the pace and the changes, "Right."

"Cheer up, your favourite burger van is over there, shall we?"

"I don't think I'm hungry after all that dinner," Erika says.

Dominique doesn't say anything but continues her even pace towards the queue of people at the burger van. At this time of night there's few options for something to eat.

'Why are we getting burgers?' Erika wonders, 'It's late and we already ate.'

Rather than joining the queue, Dominique moves back to the railings by the river and asks, "What do you smell?"

"Burgers, onions, frying, the usual smells," Erika says without much enthusiasm.

"And how does that make you feel? Hungry?"

There's surprise in Erika's voice as she speaks, "No, it makes me feel nothing, it smells like it always does, but there's no hunger, the desire to have one is missing."

"But you love the smell of this place, it's your favourite late night snack spot."

"Yes, it is, but tonight, it's not doing anything for me."

"And it never will, your old food, will have no appeal to you anymore. What was once your favourite will no longer matter. That's why we had steak tonight," Dominique says.

"Is this what it's been like for you all the times we walked by?"

Dominique nods, "Yes, but I've never experienced a burger like you did. To me it was just something, a nothing."

"But you ate them."

"It's what people do. How can I describe it, when someone changes their diet, say they go from being a meat eater to vegetarian, their sense of what tastes nice changes, what smells good will also change. As I understand it, after a while, the vegetarian will smell the meat and either ignore it or find it repulsive. You seem to be able to ignore it. The trick is to smell and taste things for what they are. It's important to be able to distinguish tastes and smells, as people will expect that of you in your interactions. It's not hard, it just takes a little practice."

"So, the steak we had, it will be the same as this?" Erika asks.

"Basically, yes, it will taste different than the burger, but the overall effect is the same. You can eat it, but it will do nothing for you. Those pleasure drugs that were released when you ate the nice food, that's all changed. The new foods will produce that effect, not the old foods. As you've already noticed."

"So, if I eat and drink, then what..."

"Then you go to the toilet, like everyone else. Like before," Dominique grins widely. "But it's not quite the same."

"What does that mean?"

Conspiratorially Dominique replies, "A surprise for later."

"I don't think I'm looking forward to that surprise."

Dominique shakes her head, "It's simply different. Nothing to worry about. Shall we continue?"

"Yes, let's," Erika says, starting to walk, this time by Dominique's side, her pace a little slower than strolling, but Dominique keeps pace and says nothing.

"Are you comfortable with the sights, sounds, smells?" Dominique asks.

"Yes, I think so."

"Good," Dominique replies, then dropping the volume of her voice says, "Remember when we were upstairs, and I mentioned about eating, etc.?" Erika nods her recollection. "Then you need to consider that you're a predator now. All these people are possibilities for you. Always remember that, because you need to control yourself all the time when out and about."

Erika replies quietly, confidentially, "I don't know how to reply to that."

"You just must remember it. Perhaps more importantly be careful of it. Villagers might seem harmless, but they all have pitchforks."

Erika laughs despite herself, "I honestly don't know what all this means and the implications of it."

"I know and it's hard to teach someone all this in such a short amount of time. I said you were special earlier, and I meant that. You're special in the truest sense of the word, not in the more common sense that everyone is special, like daddy's special little angel. And before you ask, I am not getting into religion tonight. You're special and to me that means you'll be around for a longtime." Dominique pauses a moment and takes in her companion's face, her features and the curious expression. "We've been planning tonight for over a year. But I have been planning it a while longer than that. A little-known fact, family, like you, don't tend to last long on average."

Erika's face show more concern that curiosity, 'Why do they die,' she wonders. "Why?" she asks aloud, both concerned and curious.

"It's an attribute thing, maybe they were made for the wrong reason. Perhaps their expectations of life are misaligned with reality, who knows. But many burn out, I mean they have destructive behaviours. Such as excessive partying, going out and being the big-man or big-woman. They get into situations they cannot control or understand. They have an idea that they are invincible, when they're only a little better than average. Some, they can't cope with the idea of forever, it seems fun at first, but time has a way of changing how the world looks."

Erika nods as she listens, taking in all the excessive amounts of information, "So, how old are you?"

"You ask the most complex questions, while seeming to ask such simple ones."

"It seems quite straightforward."

"I know, that's one of the things I love about you," Dominique sighs. "Suppose you're six years old, then someone who's twelve looks old. A forty-year-old looks very old and a sixty-year-old looks ancient. It's not so much the numbers, but the ratio. Do you understand where I'm coming from?"

"Yes, you're saying that age is relative. So old or young is dependent upon the age of the observer. In this case that's me."

"Broadly, to me, I'm just living my life, and this is a single lifetime. To you, it will look totally different, as your frame of reference is different, and it will seem ancient. I don't think we should discuss this any more outside. I'll answer this a bit better later. Maybe tomorrow. I don't really want to fill your head with things that don't matter or worse are a distraction."

Erika sounds a little disappointed, "Understood, but we're talking ten times for ancient. I can do the multiplication from there."

Dominique shakes her head, "That wasn't what I intended."

Erika smiles triumphantly, "But it's what you said." 'Holy smoke, she's over three hundred years old,' Erika blinks in amazement.

"Let's just accept that you're with an older woman!"

"On this topic, the topic of time, it's probably important to understand that you now live outside of time."

"What?" Erika exclaims.

"As hard as it is to hear and maybe understand, time no longer matters to you. You won't age, you don't have to worry about a pension. I think you see what I'm saying?" Dominique's words are met with a nod and murmur. "That doesn't mean you can ignore time. You'll have to work hard as time moves on all day, every day."

Erika looks blank but offers a tentative, "Alright."

"In your bag, you have a smartphone. Years ago, you had a dumb phone, before that, no phone. Before that, people had phones with a wireless handset that only worked at home. Before that, phones were all wires. Before that, etc., all the way back to no phone at all. So, people communicated with telegrams, etc. Now look at it from the other side. Start with the telegram, then you get the all-wire phone, then the partial wire phone, then the dumb phone then then smartphone. That happened over many years, but you must keep up with changes to technology; society; trends and norms."

"I think I understand what you're saying now. Time is unimportant to me personally, but is vital to blending in," Erika clarifies.

"Yes, exactly, and that's another reason why family often don't make it past the first few years. The right mental attitude is necessary."

"And I have that?"

"You do," Dominique confirms with a wink, "otherwise we wouldn't be here tonight."

"So, you've done this before?"

"Yes, but not for a while. I'm particularly happy with the slider trick, that's made life so much quicker for you and easier for me. You're going to have to work out how to make it automatic, or at least changeable on mental command, but this is a good shortcut. Like an upgraded robot," Dominique says mischievously.

"Ooo, like Erika 2.0!"

"See, now we're having fun. I'm impressed though, we've walked past all those people and you've been very restrained," Dominique says, mentally patting Erika on the back.

"Villagers have pitchforks, remember."

"Indeed, they do."

"Can I ask an unrelated question?" Erika asks tentatively.

"Of course, ask away."

"It's about sunrise."

"What about it?"

"What happens?"

"The sun comes up and things get lighter," Dominique says stating the obvious.

Erika sighs an exaggerated theatrical sigh, "You know what I mean. And why are you making this so hard."

"Because it's fun and I do know what you mean. We're back to ignore everything from fiction, art, books, films, etc. From now on, midday is like the old midnight. You go to bed in the morning and get up in the evening. It's why you're working the Far East desk. They are active in their day, which is your night. You're going to have to get used to working nights and sleeping in the day. It's why you're being paid the big bucks."

"So, night is day and day is night? That's it?"

"That's it. The longer you go past dawn, the slower you get and the more tired, just like people do in the night. Come evening, you perk right up after a good day's sleep." Dominique points to the edge of Erika's eyes, "You wouldn't want to get lines, would you?"

"That's it?"

"I'd stay out of direct sunlight too if I were you, sunburn ages you, not to mention the potential for burns."

"Cloudy days?" Erika wonders.

"Fine, no effect. Just direct sunlight. It'll burn and it's hard to heal. Summer is much more restrictive than winter, more sunshine and longer days. But the underground is your friend, and you can travel to almost anywhere all the time underground, on your tube pass."

"Adapt and make the technology work for you?"

"Exactly," Dominique confirms with a grin at Erika's progress.

"How do you heal?"

"That's a lesson for another day. I trust you're enjoying the night air and the walk."

"Yes, thank you," Erika replies.

"Good, because you'll be getting a lot more of them going forward."

"Ah, yes."

"I was thinking perhaps we could go clubbing and this is where it gets awkward," Dominique says.

"How?"

"It's now what, one-thirty, two o'clock, and if you sleep all day, is it clubbing tonight or tomorrow night? Technically, today is today and it's just in twenty hours, but is that thought of as today or tomorrow?" Dominique asks in all seriousness, despite the complexity of the question.

Erika pauses and thinks, 'Is she trying to trick me?' "Um, it's today surely. As it's in twenty hours, and the date stays the same."

"Just checking. But I still think we should go clubbing tonight, after a nice long relaxing sleep. We are on holiday after all."

"Can I stay over tonight?"

"Of course. It's expected," Dominique confirms.

Chapter 7

Erika's eyes flicker open slowly, groggily, the bedroom is dark, but after a few moments she can see clearly, like daytime.

"Morning or perhaps evening sleepyhead," Dominique says with a smile, she's clearly been awake a while. She places a delicate kiss on Erika's lips, welcoming her into the world of the awake.

"Evening already?"

Dominique nods, "Yes, it's a little after six-thirty."

"It feels like..."

"Like first thing in the morning?"

"Yes."

"That's because it now is first thing in the day, your day, not the sun's day."

Erika sounds tired, still sleepy, "I technically know, but it still feels strange." As she sits up, she smiles to herself as she looks at Dominique's pyjamas, some unknown cartoon character, which would seem more at home on a teenager than an adult. 'Even though, she's quite a bit older than just any adult,' she muses.

Dominique slips out of bed and quickly puts on a cream cotton dressing gown, covering her cartoon creatures, "Feel like some breakfast?"

"Yes, that sounds nice. What is there?"

Dominique laughs to herself, but the sound is far too loud for that to hold long, "The same as always!" With that she heads out to the kitchen.

Erika follows moments later, her pink pyjamas, with grey shorts, quickly covered in a silk dressing gown, this one white with red flowers. "What's so funny?"

"There's only ever one thing for breakfast."

Erika performs an exaggerated and clearly fake face-palm motion and sighs, "Of course."

Dominique grins and begins to make a pot of filter coffee, the same as she's done every morning that Erika has stayed over. Only this time, she's making it in the evening.

"Coffee?" Erika enquires.

"Everyone has either tea or coffee for breakfast, so do we. We have cereal, cooked breakfast and all the packets go into the recycling or the bin. Anything you don't eat, goes into the waste disposal unit and is ground up. Cups, bowl, plates and cutlery all go into the dishwasher. The apartment must look like any other lived-in apartment. No exceptions, no corners cut. Though, you don't have to make the portions so big if nobody's here to see."

"That's a lot of pointless work."

"It's only pointless until someone notices that you're not eating food and never have any rubbish. Then they begin to ask all sorts of questions you don't want asked and will not like the answers. Personally, I like the home delivery, as you well know. It's very convenient and they deliver in the evening."

"It's a bit of a waste of money though," Erika protests.

"Money is of little importance, as you'll soon see. Having enough is easy when you have enough time." As the coffee percolates, Dominique heads to the fridge and behind the orange juice, she produces a cardboard carton of strawberry juice. It's clearly labelled as such. She retrieves two large glasses from the cupboard and fills them. "When you finish, we need to wash them up by hand, fill them with orange juice and then put them into the dishwasher." When done, she hands one to Erika.

Erika takes the glass and questions, "Strawberry juice?"

"Try it."

Erika takes a tentative sip, lets it touch her tongue and declares, "New food!"

"It's cold, but there's plenty more, and it's important to feel full. Not over full, just full." Dominique's words are lost on Erika, judging by the look on her face. "Oh dear," she comments now to herself.

'This is the best thing I've ever tasted,' Erika thinks, as she swishes the blood around, letting it coat every part of her mouth. Quickly she lets the taste, feeling and pleasure wash over and through her as she slips into her bliss bubble.

Dominique sips at her breakfast as she watches and waits and waits.

As Erika comes back into the world with a jolt, Dominique says, "I see you like it. More?"

"Yes please," Erika says nodding, clearly looking forward to more. Both glasses are refilled and Erika slips back into her breakfast pleasure bubble of bliss. Dominique simply waits patiently again.

This repeats three more times as Erika gets her fill of breakfast.

"Are you back with us?" Dominique asks tentatively.

"I didn't go anywhere."

"What time is?"

"I don't know about ten to seven."

Dominique shakes her head and gestures to the clock on the microwave, "More like quarter past eight."

"How can it be so late?"

"It appears that you really enjoy your breakfast. Oh, you really enjoyed that. It would seem your sensitivity extends beyond just physical sensations," Dominique says, as if commenting on the weather.

"I'm embarrassed."

"Why?"

"Because I'm doing it wrong."

"You're not, you're doing it your way," Dominique says kindly. "There's nothing wrong with what you're doing. We're going to have to keep an eye on it though. Which means being careful and besides, it might well change over the next few days as you get used to it."

"You think so?"

"I don't know, but it might," Dominique says reassuringly.

"But it might not."

"It might not," Dominique agrees.

"I think I should go and get a shower and think a little."

Chapter 8

As Erika enters the lounge area from the bedroom, she sees Dominique sitting on the sofa, still in her pyjamas and dressing gown. "Are you going to get ready?" she asks.

"All in good time."

Walking over to the sofa Erika asks, "Are you disappointed?"

"No of course not. Why should I be?"

"Because I'm too sensitive."

Dominique laughs for just a moment, "You're worrying about a rare gift as if it is poor trait. Would you ask a fast runner if it was a problem, they were faster than most people?" Erika shakes her head. "Or someone more intellectual than others?" Again, Erika shakes her head. "Then why worry about this gift?"

"Because I'm worried, you're disappointed in me," Erika says reluctantly.

"There's only one way that I'd be disappointed in you, and this isn't it."

'Really, there's a way, but this isn't it,' Erika considers. "What's the way?" she asks.

"There's only one thing that really matters and that's loyalty."

"Loyalty?"

"Yes, loyalty," Dominique confirms.

"Loyalty to what?"

"Not to what but to whom," Dominique clarifies. "Specifically, to each other. My loyalty to you and your loyalty to me."

"That's it?" Erika asks the confusion evident in her voice. 'There's got to be more to it than that,' she wonders.

"That's it. But it's not as straightforward and simple as you imagine, just like your time question earlier. The question is simple, but the answer is very much more complex, because you don't really understand the question, because there's so much more you don't yet know and therefore understand."

Erika comes and sits down next to Dominique on the sofa and they both arrange themselves to face each other, "Alright, why?"

"You know how I said there were people and family, and we are the family part?" Dominique asks, and watches as Erika nods her recollection. "Good, taking that family analogy a little further, any that I have made in the past, they are like your siblings, older obviously, but like siblings none the less."

'I'm not sure I like where this is going,' Erika says to herself. "Understood, at least in principle."

"So, in time, any that you make, well, they too will be bound by loyalty. First to you and by extension to me and further extension to those made by me, to your siblings. So, to speak. I apologise, the analogy is poor, but I don't currently have a better one."

"Once again, I think I understand."

"Good."

"But how do I know who my siblings are?" Erika asks, making air-quotes around the word siblings.

"By identifying yourself as being with me? Or perhaps by identifying me as having made you," Dominique says.

"So, I just tell them that Dominique made me. That's sounds simple enough," Erika says happily having resolved a problem.

"It would be, if we didn't change our names all the time, change our countries all the time and move about and be different people. Which we do. In a few years, maybe ten, maybe fifteen, but no more than twenty, I'll have a different name and a fresh look. But you and I will still be loyal."

"Then what name should I use?" Erika questions.

Dominique pauses just a moment before answering, "Not a name, but a phrase. Ready?" She waits for Erika to acknowledge with a nod before continuing, "The phrase is: She who is without time. She who is love. She who is compassion. She who is vengeance. Please repeat."

"She who is without time. She who is love. She who is compassion. She who is vengeance. Was that it?"

"Yes, that was it. You have a good ear."

"Lots of time spent in court," Erika says with a knowing grin.

"Don't doubt it. Anyone who understands that phrase, they are to be trusted and respected. Anyone who doesn't, well, let's just say, they're less important."

"I'm assuming, once again, there's lots you're not telling me," Erika queries.

Dominique nods, after a short pause says, "There's so much to tell you, but I have to prioritise otherwise you'll be overwhelmed."

"Understood, but can you at least explain the four phrases and why they are there."

"Of course, it's all quite straightforward, as family, we are both outside of time, as I suggested earlier. So, she who is without time, think of it as she who is outside of time, separated if you will. Language changes over time, quite a lot.

So, it might not sound quite right to your ears, but that's what we have. The second, is obvious, she who is love. Someone who can love like a person and perhaps more importantly can love people. She who is compassion is basically the same, only compassion rather than love. Finally, she who is vengeance, is, I think, clear. I might love and be compassionate, but I am not stupid and will not be crossed. You should understand the last one in conjunction with loyalty. I expect loyalty, and I will not be crossed and if necessary, vengeance after the fact. Or as you call it justice."

"I don't understand why love and compassion is such a big deal. Everyone has love and compassion in them," Erika says.

Dominique shakes her head slightly, "People do, family generally don't. Not to people anyway and remember, you need to keep your love and compassion, otherwise there is always the monster within. Which we don't want out."

"I don't feel like that," Erika says.

"No, I don't imagine you do, but you will. It's not even been twenty-four hours yet. Many things have still to happen before you're adjusted to your new way of life."

"It gets better or worse?"

"Don't think of it like that, it's just different, it will be both, if you want it to be. Otherwise, it'll just be different. You're not people, you're now family," Dominique says, then she stands. "I should get a shower, so we can go out."

Erika nods and smiles, as she watches Dominique head towards the bedroom, "I'll see you in a little bit."

Chapter 9

Erika sits on the sofa reading a novel when Dominique returns to the lounge, all dressed up and ready for an evening on the town. Her top has only one strap, the metallic golden flecks in the weave contrasting against the black fabric, a flashy gold skirt comes midway down her thighs, black spider's web patterned stockings cover her legs. Her makeup applied to perfection, dark smoky eyes, lips a very kissable red and cheeks with just enough colour to look fabulous. Her silver heart shaped earrings, match the pendant and chain around her neck.

As Dominique gets closer, Erika puts her book down on the table next to the sofa. "You look devastating."

"I did put in a little effort and, just as a point of order, it's best to have the light on when reading. Everyone expects light when reading."

"Oh flip, I completely forgot. I could just see, with a little adjustment and sorry."

Dominique shakes her head, "Don't apologise, that wasn't why I mentioned it, just being helpful."

"What's that smell, it smells delicious."

Dominique sniffs the air a moment, "I don't smell anything. Or anything specific, or out of the ordinary."

Erika stands and moves towards where Dominique stands, she sniffs the air too and exclaims, "It's you?"

"Me?"

"Yes, you. What have you done?"

"Ah, that." Dominique says, flashing Erika a grin, "I stopped suppressing my scent, now we're going out, I let it come back through."

"You can control your smell?" Erika says incredulously.

"Of course, in time you'll learn how to do it too. In the meantime, I suggest you wear some perfume. I like the tropical one in the blue and pink bottle."

Erika looks at Dominique quizzically. "Why bother wearing perfume, surely, it'll just make it harder to smell the world."

"Everyone smells of something and you don't want anyone to notice you don't smell at all and besides, it'll help with the smells of the evening," Dominique says simply.

"What smells?" Erika queries.

"I'm going to say when you're in a room with five-hundred smells that remind you of the nicest burger you've ever smelt. That smell," Dominique says, a knowing expression written all over her face.

"Ahh!"

Dominique uses the back of her hand to waft air from around her neck towards Erika, "That smell. Like it?"

Erika flashes her fake evil look, Dominique chuckles, "See, that's what I want, and the goal is all villagers pass the night intact. Can you do that?"

"I don't know, I'll try."

"Good robot two point zero."

"Two point one, I've been upgraded," Erika says grinning.

"Already?"

"We robots evolve quickly."

"Apparently."

"When are we going out?"

"Not just yet, I want you to get used to the smell," Dominique says, moving to the sofa and siting down.

"Is that really necessary?"

"Does it make you feel hungry?" Dominique asks, as she adjusts her position on the sofa.

"It's a bit strange, it's definitely pleasant, but I'm full, so, it's like smelling something extremely nice, something that I would normally really want, but the sensation is a bit dulled, by being full. Does that make sense?" Erika says after thinking about it a moment.

"It does, which is why you need to sit down."

Erika sits down elegantly and with poise and grace, "Done."

"Excellent."

"Then if we're here for a while, how do you earn money, I mean really, not what you've told me in the past?" Erika enquires.

"Everything I've told you in the past is true, there's just a little more to it than that."

"Obviously."

"Do you remember that time no longer matters?" Erika nods and Dominique continues, "In that case, consider that you have time to make an investment, let it grow, nurture it and finally use that for additional investments."

"Fine, but how does that work in practice."

"You're a barrister, which means you have clients, you work for a firm, your talents make you money and the firm or company money."

"Yes," Erika says, as the smell from Dominique wafts gently about the room.

"The more the firm charges for the work you do, the more money I make. Which implies, that high fees for your work is in my interests. Now, you might be inclined to move away, as you see the high fees and more money going to me. To stop that, I offer you higher pay. This encourages you to stay and make more money for me."

"I understand this, it's business theory," Erika says, unsure where this is going.

"But I do this with all the barristers, lawyers, fee earners in the company. Some leave and some stay. Over time, I make money from all of them. They make money too and we're all happy."

"And the secret is?"

"There's no secret, I can do that for years, year in, year out. As the business grows, I make more money. I take some out and invest in other things. The secret, if you want to call it that, is that I don't need to worry about having enough for retirement. I'm not going to retire, there is no need for me to grow old and taken care of in a care home. I don't need money for cruises, or all the things people need money for in retirement. I just keep making a little money, every day, and that grows over time, until it's enough to do something else with."

"That's it, you just make a little everyday and it accumulates over the years," Erika says cautiously.

Dominique nods, "Exactly, and don't think that the amounts of money will be trivial because it can quickly add up, if you invest well, get the right people, and manage everything with an eye to the future. What do you think to your apartment?"

"It's nice, not as nice as this one, but nice. It's convenient for work and is located nicely in the middle of London."

"See, someone who's happy with their home. That means you'll stay in the building making a little money each month for the owners. Who in turn will invest that money in something else."

"What's your point?"

"Ultimately, I own the building, the law firm and many other properties, businesses, parts of businesses and other things throughout the world. Build bit by bit over time," Dominique says simply.

"How am I going to do that?"

"The same way, bit by bit, some shares, make a little money. Get some savings from your work as a barrister, invest that into a likely enterprise, etc."

"I don't know how to do any of those things, I've never been an investor or entrepreneur or even a businesswoman," Erika says sounding a little overwhelmed.

"Of course, you have, you do it all the time with your clients. You solve their problems, and they pay you, that's the basis of business."

"Will you help me?"

"Of course, I will, that's what I'm doing now and will continue to do until you're able to do it all on your own."

Erika looks relieved, "Thank you, that makes me feel a bit better."

"I know, I can see it."

"How much are your investments worth?" Erika tentatively enquires, wondering whether she'd get a straight answer.

"This is another of your easy to ask questions, but which are difficult to answer, because you don't really understand the full scope of the question," Dominique replies.

Erika sighs and Dominique grins. 'Is she's ever going to give me a straight answer,' Erika wonders.

"To answer accurately, I would say, I have enough to last until the end of civilisation, even though I don't know exactly when that'll be."

"See, you never answer the question!" Erika says getting exacerbated.

"I do, but you don't understand your questions. You're thinking as the old you thought, but you must start to think as the new you."

"I don't know what that means."

Dominique is quiet a moment, "It means, that before, you were concerned with the way people conducted business, on short timelines, with a view of always having more, with getting something that the others don't have. The new you, needs to move away from that and consider that the only thing you need is food. Everything else is a bonus. We have enough to get by until the end of civilisation. You don't need a job; you don't need heating; you don't need a car or an apartment. All you need is food and there's plenty of that around if needs must."

"And if it smells this nice, I'm good to go. Why do you keep mentioning the end of civilisation?" Erika muses.

"Because that's the end of our resources. Until then, we're as you say, we're good to go. When this civilisation inevitably collapses, and they all do in the end, we'll need to start again. If we're extremely lucky, some of the assets and perhaps goods will be still useful in the new civilisation, but maybe not. Hence, the worst case is you only have food and maybe the clothes on your back. From there, we can start again. Civilisations, inevitably rise, thrive, wither, and die. Usually in that order, but not always."

"That seems a little bleak."

"Why? It's inevitable, you just haven't seen it yet," Dominique says, and holds her hand just below Erika's nose.

"Did you have to do that?" Erika says wearily, "you know how it smells."

"That's the point, to see how you'd react."

"So, I didn't bite it!"

Dominique chuckles lightly, "That's true."

"See, I'm getting better."

"Maybe, but there's going to have to be rules for tonight's activities."

Erika eyes Dominique suspiciously, "What kind of rules?"

"Simple, there's going to be the smell of blood at the club and..."

Erika interrupts, "What?"

"We're going to a place with lots of people, men, and women. Inevitably, some of them will have cuts or nicks, perhaps from shaving, faces or legs. Maybe some of the women are having their period, tampons good, towels bad. Blood is blood. A small amount shouldn't be a problem. It might make you notice, but you're to resist."

"That doesn't sound so bad," Erika says cautiously.

"It shouldn't be. The real problem is going to be if there is a fight or an accident, which does happen from time to time. In that case, I want you to pinch your nose and put your hand over your mouth and head to the women's toilet as quickly and as calmly as possible. I now sound like a safety announcement. That should remove the smell and stop you getting any blood on your lips, etc. It will look to any observer, like you are squeamish to blood and need to be sick. If I'm not there, I'll find you as quickly as I can in the toilets. Clear?"

Erika nods slowly, "Clear."

"And no feeding outside of this apartment, under any circumstances, clear?"

"Clear."

"Good, ready to head out?"

Erika stands from the sofa as she speaks, "Ready."

"Let me grab my bag and shoes and I'll meet you by the door."

"Please could you get me a jacket?"

"Of course."

By the time, Dominique returns from the bedroom wearing black suede shoes, with gold heels and a matching shoulder bag, Erika has put her shoes on and is ready and waiting.

"Thanks," Erika says as Dominique hands her a cream jacket.

With a flourish Dominique asks, "Shall we?" She opens the door, and they head out.

Chapter 10

Erika follows Dominique out of the black cab and closes the door a little too firmly, she offers the cab driver a sheepish grin and mouths an apology. He nods and gently pulls out into the traffic. "I didn't mean to slam the door that hard," Erika says defensively.

"Just be wary of your newfound strength, it's easy to be heavy-handed, as you just did."

"I'll try."

"You'll have to succeed," Dominique says as they head towards the bright lights of Dystopia, the bright red letters covering the whole front of the building. As they approach the line to gain entry, Dominique moves to the right and joins a much smaller line, they are second in the queue.

"It's going to be very loud," Erika comments.

"It is more chance for practice then," Dominique says over the sounds emanating from the club.

At the front of the line, the security bouncer, smiles when he sees them, "Evening ladies."

"And a good evening to you too, Jim," Dominique replies before Erika has chance.

"Occupation?" Jim asks.

"Evil blood sucking fiend," Dominique says lightly, the joke not lost on everyone.

"I'll put you down as a lawyer," Jim quickly taps them in.

"And my friend is a boring evil blood sucking evil fiend."

"Barrister it is," Jim says chuckling.

"On a more serious note, how is the little one?" Dominique asks.

"The little tykes all better. Once he started to recover, he bounced back quick. You know how they are."

"Good, I'm glad to hear that he's back to his little happy self."

"He is," Jim says and gestures for them to go in, "you'd best go in, others are waiting."

Erika glances backwards and smiles, "Of course. Thanks Jim." With that they both vanish through the laser beams and into the thump of the nightclub.

Without any communication, they both head to the left and up the stairs to the upper floor. At the top of the stairs, they're greeted by an usher who without checking passes or identification guides them to an open booth away from the main hubbub of the VIP section.

"After you," Dominique says with a flourish, gesturing into the seating area.

"Why, thank you," Erika replies formally.

"You're quite welcome," Dominique replies.

As they sit down, Erika asks, "How or why do you know Jim so well?"

As Dominique puts her handbag down into its spot, she replies, "Everyone makes assumptions and therefore makes a mistake in who is important and who is not in an organisation. It doesn't matter if this is a company, business, charity, or government for that matter."

Erika looks perplexed, as the sounds of the music from below wash over them.

"Common wisdom is that the managing director, or chief executive are the most important people, perhaps with other senior managers, etc. all playing their part. While I'm not going to argue that they are important, particularly if you want something done. But they're not the ones who have their finger on the pulse. Take here, the manager knows all about staffing, the turnover and stock level, etc. However, who sees and talks to every-single-person who comes in through the VIP entrance?"

"Jim?" Erika offers.

"Exactly, he sees them all, talks to them all and knows what is going on. Partly because he takes the time to be social. He understands that his job is not just security but is hospitality. He looks like security, but makes everyone feel welcome, like he did when we arrived. That little joke he likes, is mostly because he likes you."

"He likes me?"

"Yes, can't you tell? I don't mean romantically, but he's always liked something about you, an attitude, or the way you carry yourself."

"I had no idea."

"I know," Dominique says wryly.

"You never said anything."

"It's not my place, your social interactions are your own. Anyway, back on topic. You'll find the reception staff know what's going on in the business. They see all the people coming and going. They sign in the consultants and the specialists. They know before most of the senior managers and certainly before the middle managers."

"I never thought about it that way," Erika admits.

"Cleaning staff get full run of the building, all area access. In how many organisations are they the most trusted employees? The same goes for security, they usually have full physical access. Something to consider," Dominique says glancing around.

"Normally, those people are some of the cheapest and considered least important people in the company, but from what you just said, they need to be the most trusted," Erika says thinking the implications through.

"Indeed, they do. Drink?"

"Yes please."

"It'll need to be your usual, low profile and all that."

Erika nods, "I was expecting that."

"I'll be right back and remember the rules."

"I'll be good," Erika says, as Dominique stands and heads to the bar.

While she's gone, Erika ponders what she's heard and how it can be useful both from a positive and a defensive perspective. She also considers how this might apply to her own business dealings in the future.

As Dominique walks back from the bar area, a stocky man and her partially collide and the drinks spill. Erika watches the exchange, as the man seems to apologise, and they talk for a few moments. Heads nod and Dominique gestures to the booth they are using. She then brings the partially spilt drinks over and sits down.

"What was that all about?" Erika asks.

"He and his friend were walking to the bar, and we collided. He offered to replace our spilt drinks."

"Is that wise, having a stranger in a nightclub control your drink?"

"As you'll soon learn, it makes no difference to you anymore. You're not susceptible, like you were before, notwithstanding your sensitivity," Dominique remarks.

"That I did not know. So, who is he?"

"He said his name was Bill and his friend is Colin."

"Are we going to spend all night with them?" Erika enquires.

"No," Dominique says reassuringly. "On that note, how are you getting on?"

"Fine, but them coming over is a test, isn't it?" Erika asks her eyes on Bill and Colin as they approach from the bar.

"Yes and no, perhaps a little one. The real test will be when we go downstairs and dance."

"I'm looking forward to and dreading that part."

"You'll be fine," Dominique says, as the two men arrive, four drinks in hand.

Bill places a cocktail on the small table next to Dominique and Colin hands Erika her drink directly. Dominique with a simple gesture says, "Please sit."

As they sit, Bill says, "Sorry about that, I didn't intend to upset your evening like that." Then he raises his glass and says, "To a fun night out."

Dominique retrieves her glass and toasts with the others, "A fun night out." She takes a small sip, then another. Then she glances at Erika. Who smiles back. She then asks, "What are your plans for tonight?" Her hazel eyes seem to sparkle in the light as she moves her gaze from Bill to Colin and back again.

"What do you mean?" Bill asks casually.

Dominique places her drink back on the table, then looking at Erika asks, "Can I have a sip of yours?" With that Erika reaches over and hands Dominique her glass. Sipping it, she looks to Colin, then places the glass on the table.

Looking at Bill, Dominique replies, "I mean, what did you place in our drinks?"

"I have no idea what you mean?"

Dominique's gaze hardens, but her tone is friendly and casual, "Unlike most, I can taste things in my cocktail that aren't supposed to be there, so, I'll ask you once more, what is in the drinks?"

"Nothing," Bill says.

"Then drink them," she says her voice commanding.

Obediently, both men take up one of the glasses and drink down the cocktail in one go. Once they finish, she says, "And your own drinks." To which instruction they consume their own drinks, which look like whiskey and ginger. Dominique waits silently.

"Now you've had a couple of drinks, it's time for you to tell us a little about yourselves. Let's begin with where you work," Dominique commands them.

"We're with the Met," Colin says casually.

"The Metropolitan police?" Erika queries.

"Excellent," Dominique replies, "Doing what?"

"We're sergeants, doing mostly office work," Bill elaborates.

"And back to my original question, what are your plans for tonight?" Dominique continues with her questions.

"We are going to buy you a couple of drinks, with a little extra. Then we'd have sex with you, and you'd not protest or care."

"So, broadly date rape?" Dominique confirms.

Both men nod together, even though Colin speaks, "Yes, that's the plan."

Erika sits silently, amazed, wondering how she did that. Dominique asks, "And as we're getting to know each other, what are your most deeply guarded secrets? Colin first."

Colin replies conversationally, "I'm paid by the mob to help them make evidence disappear. They let me know when they've got a problem and I help clean it up and make it go away."

"And Bill?"

Bill's reply is also conversational, "I really want to have a relationship with another man, but I fear how they'll take it at work. Homophobia is common at the Met. No matter what they say on television. We persecute gay people, both inside and outside the force."

"Well gentlemen, that's been nice. Here's what I want you to do. Anytime you adulterate a drink, you will consume it yourselves, so that you both have half of each drink. Then Colin, I want you to make mistakes when covering up crimes for the mob and Bill, it might be helpful, if you were to be yourself and worry less about other people's opinion of you. I don't ever want to see you in this club or any others around here. Now, I think you should get up and walk out of the club, never thinking of us again. Go now," Dominique says, her voice even, calm, but commanding.

Dominique watches in silence as the two men stand and simply walk out of the club.

"What on earth was that?" Erika asks.

"First of all, did you taste the foreign substance in your drink?" Dominique asks.

"Maybe," Erika says slowly.

"Maybe yes, or maybe, no?" Dominique pushes.

"I did taste something that was a bit off, but I didn't think anything of it."

"That funny taste, was them trying to drug you, as they clearly indicated afterwards. And yes, you're right, never leave a drink unattended when at a club. There are predators everywhere of the vilest sort."

"And them telling you everything?" Erika asks.

"Ah, that takes more than a little skill and practice. Essentially, I can have people tell me things and do what I want. It comes in handy from time to time. Like tonight."

"Can you teach me to do that?" Erika asks, keen to have such power.

"Like so many things, yes, but it'll take time."

"As technically, you've had one and a half drinks, do you fancy a dance?"

"Before we do, I have a question," Erika says.

"Ask away?"

"How does alcohol affect me now?" Erika says her voice a mix of curiosity and concern.

"I don't know for sure, as you're unusually sensitive, but normally, that which you drink as a cocktail for example is at about ten to one, so about a tenth of what it did before. But for you, I would say maybe eight to one, due to the sensitivity. Now alcohol in food now that a different matter. In that case, it's going to be more direct, so you are going to be more susceptible," Dominique says watching Erika's reaction.

"Alright, I understand, I think."

"You're going to dislike this, but as with everything, it's going to…"

Erika cuts Dominique off and says, "It's going to take time. Yes, I am getting that idea."

"Good, because it will."

Erika stands and takes a deep breath, "Let's head downstairs and dance." Dominique stands and they both leave their handbags and jackets and head downstairs to the dance floor.

As they descend the stairs, the sounds of the music and the patrons grows ever louder. Dominique makes a pinching motion to Erika who nods.

"Can we talk about what happened a few moments ago?" Erika asks.

"When we get home, there's some things I'd rather not talk about here," Dominique says as the lasers catch the gold of her shoes and reflect over the stairs. "When we're dancing, I want you to focus your hearing to what I am saying. With practice, you should be able to tune out most of the noise and hear close or reasonably close by conversations."

"Can I dance too?"

"It'd be too easy otherwise," Dominique says as she enters the dance floor. Two thin lines down Dominique's cheekbones and one between her eyes light up creating a stylised arrow forward down her face.

"You never said you were using the UV-active makeup," Erika says almost accusingly.

"I never said I wasn't either. You know where it's kept," Dominique counters.

Erika nods and begins to move with the music and suddenly stops and a broad grin meets her questioning expression.

"Enjoy it." Dominique offers as she starts to move with a poise and grace rarely seen, Erika joins in and they dance together.

Over the next half an hour, Erika and Dominique, dance together, with other people in the general mix and have a fun time. Flowing with the music, feeling the sound wash over them.

Presently, Erika takes Dominique's hand and pulls her back towards the stairs. As they ascend, Dominique comments, "You know, I can hear everything you say.".

"Whereas I didn't hear you singing at all."

"That's probably for the best, my singing isn't all that impressive," Dominique replies.

Back at their booth, Erika says, "I think it's time for us to go home."

"Really?" Dominique replies surprised.

"I think because of my sensitivity, the drugs in my drink had an effect on me."

"That seems improbable," Dominique says, curious as to what's got into Erika.

"Well, somethings wrong."

"What is it?"

"I'm seeing things," Erika says quietly.

"What kind of things?"

"Strange colours."

"Colours?"

"Yes, around people, well some people and some of the time."

"Around me?"

Erika nods, "Not at the moment, but downstairs yes."

"Then we probably should go home. But before we do, you see that woman over there, the one with the blue top?" Erika nods. Dominique continues, "and the man next to her, tell me what they're talking about." Erika moves to stand up. "Not by walking over but listening from here. It's quieter, maybe that'll help."

Erika looks at Dominique wirily, "Fine." She begins to concentrate. 'Now what sliders can I make and change to hear them,' she wonders.

Minutes pass in silence and finally Erika says, "They're arranging a date for a walk in Regents Park. They're going to meet at eleven o'clock and have a walk. Then a coffee and a cake."

Dominique nods slowly, "Well done."

"Can we go home now?"

"Yes, let's go."

Erika gathers her handbag and jacket and watches Dominique do the same. They walk towards the stairs and Dominique smiles at and acknowledges the young man at the top of the stairs.

He smiles back and says, "Are you leaving so soon?"

"Yes, a busy day tomorrow."

"So, we can use your booth?"

"Yes, it's free for the rest of the night."

"Then have a goodnight and I hope to see you both again soon," he says and watches the women descend the stairs.

Erika and Dominique exit Dystopia and hail a cab home.

Chapter 11

Erika swipes her access card over the reader and the out of hours automatic doors swing open, she heads through, followed by Dominique. As they traverse the lobby, a young man, dressed in work casual attire, green polo shirt, with a company logo half hidden behind a fold, new looking blue jeans, and brown moccasin slippers, greets Erika, "Hi neighbour."

"Hi Gavin," Erika replies as she stops.

"Been out having fun?"

"Indeed, we have. What about you?" she says with a grin, all the while Dominique remains quiet watching the interaction.

"I'm expecting my pizza to arrive any minute," Gavin says, the anticipation evident in his voice.

"Isn't it a little late for pizza?"

"Yes, but no, not when you've working late and the company's paying. Only the biggest and best for us," Gavin says with a grin.

"I'll see you later, enjoy your late dinner."

"And the rest of your night," Gavin's tone hints at something more.

Erika shakes her head and with a sigh, starts back towards the lifts, Dominique in tow. At the lift, she presses the up button, and they wait in silence for the lift car to arrive. When the doors finally slide open, they step in and ride to the top floor. Travelling down the same lush carpet as last night, a lifetime ago it seems, they presently arrive at Dominique's apartment.

As the door closes and they carefully remove their shoes, placing them into the shoe rack, Erika asks, "Can I ask questions now?"

"Of course," Dominique says, walking into the lounge and taking her place on the sofa. Erika promptly joins her.

"Where should I start?" Erika says, but wonders, 'What don't I know that I should be asking about.'

"What's bothering you the most?"

"How did such a little amount of that drug affect me so much?" Erika asks. "Is it because I'm sensitive?"

Dominique adjusts her position on the sofa to look directly at Erika before she replies. "I think you're worrying about the sensitivity when you shouldn't. I don't have a good analogy but think about it as if you were a family car before, now you're changed into an industrial sized quarry bulldozer, but one whose paint is slightly more susceptible to scratches. That's your current situation."

"I don't think I really understand," Erika looks confused.

Dominique nods slowly as she hears the words, "No, that's becoming clear. Let's deal with the colours problem first. Tell me what you saw, how and when. All the details you can remember."

"I'm not sure if it started before or after we had the tainted drinks. I think it was after, but I can't really be one-hundred percent sure," Erika says, sounding hesitant.

"Then let's for now assume that it was after, that would be your worst-case scenario, correct?"

Erika nods, "Correct. Then sometimes. No, specific you said. When we went downstairs to the dance floor, it was hard to tell in the lights, the lasers and the general moving of people, but I think I first saw it then."

"Saw what?" Dominique queries.

"It looked like a glow around one of the dancers. She looked like she was glowing a violet or purple colour. It was faint, but I am sure it was real, like a glow."

"And did you see this again?"

"Yes, but not for a little while, I caught it again on a couple talking, but the glow was a more pinkish colour," Erika says.

"You saw it twice, first with one person, then two and in each case the colours were different?"

Erika nods, "Exactly. I saw it once more and this time the man had a grey or maybe a silver glow."

"What were you thinking or doing or perhaps feeling when this happened?" Dominique enquires, looking for additional information.

"I don't know, nothing in particular, I was just walking or dancing. I don't think I was thinking of anything specific or even the same thing each time. Do you think this is because of the drug?"

Dominique shakes her head emphatically, "No, the drug had no effect on you. The amount you ingested would have had no effect on any person, let alone you. No, this is something different."

Erika looks concerned. 'Why me?' she asks herself.

"I've said it before, and I'll continue saying it until you begin to believe it, there is nothing wrong or broken about you. You're doing fabulously well."

"Then why?"

"There are many things that you've not heard of, not learnt, and functionally have no way of knowing even exist. This is one of them," Dominique says, trying to reassure Erika.

"What?" Erika says even more concerned.

"This is a gift, a truly remarkable gift and just to be clear, I've never seen it develop so quickly in someone before and I've seen my fair share. This might be due to the sensitivity you're so worried about."

Erika shakes her head, partly in frustration, but mostly in confusion, 'What's she talking about,' she says to herself. "What?"

"You can see people's moods, their emotions. It's an enormously powerful and extremely useful gift," Dominique says sincerely.

"You've lost me," Erika confesses.

"I know and maybe I'm doing this wrong, it's been a while and things change all the time. Let's try again?"

"I'm prepared to try again," Erika confirms.

"You're a vampire. Agreed?"

"Agreed."

Dominique waits a moment before saying, "Good, that means more than just drinking blood and all the Dracula things you've seen in movies. Sorry, I shouldn't make light of it. You have some new strengths, the most basic of those is well strength. You're much stronger now than you were before, as you demonstrated with the taxi door. You should be able to move faster, much faster than before. You can see in darkness, hear over distance, your senses are all heightened, for better and worse. In short, you're now a predator. Your natural prey is humans. Are we clear so far?"

"Yes, I think so. But..."

Dominique cuts her off before the question forms, "Those things are all run of the mill, most vampires have those enhanced abilities. But, and this is the relevant part, you also get other perks. This ability to read emotions is one of them and in fairness, the perks don't normally start for weeks or even months. So, getting one on your first full day is quite impressive, not unprecedented, but impressive."

"So, it's not something that's wrong with me?" Erika says, the question dripping in surprise.

"Quite the opposite. It something very much right with you. Think for a moment about the possibilities of knowing how someone feels, supposing if you knew if they were happy or sad and they couldn't fake it. Would that be useful?" Dominique asks, letting the implications sink in.

"Yes, that would be incredibly useful."

"Suppose you could tell five different emotions; would that be useful?"

"Yes, even more so. Imagine what that would be like in court, knowing if a witness was lying to you or telling the truth," Erika replies enthusiastically.

"Exactly, although you can't actually tell that, since truth and deceit aren't emotions, but the point still stands."

"Is it real?" Erika asks sceptically.

"It's very real."

"With a little and it seems very little practice, you'll get to recognise and understand well over twenty different emotions and be able to tell people and family apart. Some people can see the aura colours, they can see five, often seven and in rare occasions as many as nine colours."

"How do I do that?"

"Step one first. This skill involves seeing something called an aura. You've probably heard of them already, as a new age phenomenon," Erika nods before Dominique continues. "A colour represents each emotion. Some of the colours are subtly different from each other and this is the bit you'll like. Your ability to see the colours puts you several notches above the skills of those who can see auras. The people I mean. Family will be as good or better. That'll change with time."

"So, I can see more colours?"

"Yes and no, it's not about seeing more colours. It's a bit about that, but it's also about interpreting what you see and being able to see it when you need to. Now the bit that's impressive is that you've already seen some, and that's without trying. As I said before, most impressive. Can you see mine now?" Dominique asks, training in full flight.

Erika shakes her head, "No, it's too bright."

"The brightness of the room makes no difference. Try to get back into that mind set you had in the club. That might help."

"But I don't know what that was," Erika protests. "Why is it always so hard to do something when you're placed on the spot?"

"Would dancing help?" Dominique says with a mischievous grin.

"Very funny."

"Then try this, focus your attention and will on my aura and at the same time, push a little more blood into your brain, eyes and skull."

Erika closes her eyes, 'This feels silly, how do I push blood into my skull!' Concentrating, she does as instructed, and opens her eyes. To her surprise and to Dominique's grin, she says, "You have a violet glow."

"I know. What about now?"

As Erika watches, it shifts colour, "It's now black."

"Very good, and now?"

"It changed to a light blue or maybe a baby blue."

"Close your eyes, turn away. Then open your eyes and look at me. Can you still see my aura?"

Erika does as instructed, "No, wait, yes, it's come back. This is amazing."

"It is impressive," Dominique says emphasising the last word.

"Oh wow."

"If you can still see it, tell me what changes?" Dominique asks.

"Your aura went from normal to a pale faded version."

"Very good. That's the difference between people first and family second. Family has a pale or faded aura. They still have the colours, but more pastel versions. Yes, that's a better way to describe them. Family has pastel versions; people have bright versions."

"So, I can do this on anyone?"

Dominique nods, "Yes you can, and the best bit is that nobody knows that you're looking at their aura. Be aware though, others can see yours and know what you're feeling just the same as you can theirs."

"Oh, yes that's a good point," Erika says, understanding the downside.

"Just keep in mind, that this a serious advantage in your dealings with people and you should never tell anyone you can see auras. They might deduce it, but you confirming it makes them certain. You're better off without them being sure. Clear?" Dominique says.

"Crystal clear. I'm getting the hang of everything being kept secret from everyone."

Dominique smiles, "Excellent."

"Ooo, and your aura just turned violet."

"Violet is for happy, and it just went back to bright from pastel."

"Which makes me people. A happy person."

"Wait, how do you do that, if it represents your emotions?"

Dominique grins a knowing grin, "Not quite for everyone. Some of us can control their aura, present a different emotional face to what they're really feeling. I'm someone who can. It's very handy for training and from time-to-time other things. It makes appearing as people much easier. Heartbeat, that changes normally with activity; body warmth, which changes with activity; aura that changes with mood. If I choose nobody can tell that I'm family. It's my choice. There are other colours that you need to be familiar with, we'll practice those later, but here are a few to get you started. Bright red for angry, red is anger. Orange when someone is afraid. Black if they're being hateful. Excited would be silver."

"How do you remember them all?"

"It's just a little practice. You're soon get the hang of it. The key is to practice seeing them. When you can reliably see the auras, then we can work on what the transitions from one colour to another imply and the subtleties of different colours, such as light and darks. Let's take an example, if my aura is violet and it slowly shifts to a rose pink when someone arrives, what does that mean?"

"It means you're happy that's the violet, then you become something else, I don't know what pink means."

"The rose would imply love and if they kiss and the colour changes to say a deep red, which might well imply passion for the person who just arrived."

"Which means I can see someone's emotions change over time and see how they react to events and their surroundings?" Erika says, her face lighting up with the possibilities.

"Exactly."

"Are there other secret powers?" Erika asks, thinking back to her questions that she doesn't know to ask.

"There are."

"Like what?"

Dominique considers her response a moment, before saying, "Once again, the question is much more complex that you imagine. Let's take the seeing of an aura. You can see and interpret one person at a time, by concentrating and focusing the blood into your head. That works nicely. But it requires conscious thought, which implies you can't really be doing anything else at the same time. What about seeing and interpreting two or three auras at a time. Or a whole group of people. A whole room at a time. Or how about seeing the auras all the time without thinking about it. Or seeing them all the time for everyone in the room."

Erika's eyes widen, "That's possible."

"That and more, like being able to control the colour others see of your aura. Being able to control it so that others see what they want, and what you want them to see, and it changes as they would expect. Did any of those items cover what you were wondering about?"

Erika nods, "Absolutely."

"Well, there's that and much more. Hence, the question is more complex than you think. But, as I have said many times, all these things take time, effort, and practice. We're still on day two, with many more to come," Dominique says reassuringly.

"Alright, I think I am beginning to understand."

"I hope so, because my first goal is to have you in a position to survive. The world is a fierce and dangerous place. Especially for someone like you," Dominique says a serious tone to her voice.

"You mean family?"

Dominique shakes her head, "It's a little more complex than that. I said before that you are special and I mean that, but you won't fully understand what I'm talking about until later. My primary goal is to give you the understanding and tools to keep you alive, well, sort of, so that you can develop your potential. Right now, you have a lot of potential but no real survivability, and you are a target."

"How so?"

"Once again, that will only worry you without giving you any ability to do anything about it. You need to concentrate on what I'm teaching you on how to blend in and stay alive. That's your priority. If you can do that, the other things will follow in due course. There's only so much I can do in a short amount of time."

"Alright, but you're going to tell me what happened at Dystopia?"

Dominique nods, "I said I would explain when we go home and we are home, would you like the explanation, or would you rather wait?"

"You know me better than that."

"Explanation it is then," Dominique says with a smile. "First, you have abilities that normal people don't have, and we should try some of them later tonight, but in this regard, and in time and with practice, you can affect the minds of people."

"What like mind control," Erika says with an edge of excitement in her voice.

Dominique chuckles, "No, not like mind control. What I did was to force them to tell me what I wanted to know. They had no choice, and you can always tell if it worked, by asking them to tell you something they would never normally tell anyone. Like the deepest secrets I made them tell us."

"That sounds like mind control," Erika insists.

"I'm not controlling their mind and making them into a puppet. That's something different. All I am doing is forcing them to bend to my will. They are doing what I want, how I want and when I want. It's not quite the same thing, but I can see how it might at first glance look that way. I'm very good at doing it, so they really had no chance at resisting what I wanted them to do. But, when you're starting out and less practiced, it can be more hit and miss. They might be able to resist what you're doing and not obey you. So, it's important to understand if you have successfully gained control over them or not. There are limits as to what you can do and what you cannot and the better you get at it, the more those limits cease to restrict your activities. I've been doing this a while and am really very good at it. Keep that in mind."

"Alright, I accept that it's something different to mind control, but how do I do it?" Erika asks.

"This is going to be more difficult because you cannot practice this on me. You'll never be able to do it to me."

Erika interrupts, "Why not?"

"Because I made you, or more specifically because I am a generation ahead of you. This will apply to anyone who's a lower generation than you. You can only influence those at your level or below. I am above, this means we cannot practice together. It'll never work on me, no matter how good you get."

"I'm not sure I fully understand the why, but I do understand the result. I cannot force you to do anything. But theoretically I can force people and some family?" Erika enquires, probing the boundaries.

"In principle you can force all people and in practice, most of family. Even if you could force me, because of our bond, you would never want to do it anyway and even if you wanted to, you couldn't. For both the stated reasons."

"But you could do it to me?" Erika asks cautiously.

"Yes, I could, but I would not."

"Have you done it before?"

"No," Dominique says simply.

"Would you tell me if you had?"

"Yes, but as I said, you're special and to me that means something important. To that end, I have no intention of doing anything to you."

"You say I'm special, but I don't really know what that means."

Dominique considers her reply for a moment, "I know and I'm not sure how much to say and when, so that your mind is eased and you're not overwhelmed by the information and, and perhaps or the implications."

"I don't know how to help with that?"

"I know," Dominique says kindly.

"How do you know?"

Dominique grins on of her knowing grins, "Because I can see your aura."

"Of course, you can," Erika says, while thinking, 'Why didn't I think of that before. Of course, she can.'

"Just to be clear, I have been reading your aura every second of every minute of all our interactions. I can read you aura continuously."

"That must be nice."

"It can be helpful. Right now, you're calm, but you keep getting uncomfortable," Dominique says.

"Well, there's so much I don't understand and what you say is disquieting," Erika says defensively.

"No need to be defensive. It was a demonstration, to show what I mean and what we've been discussing. Nothing more." Dominique stands and offers Erika her hand.

Standing Erika asks, "What now?"

"Not dancing, if that's what you're worried about."

"No, I like dancing and I like dancing with you."

"Now you've gone violet."

"You can really do that all the time, regardless of what we're doing?"

Dominique nods, "Yes, all the time. Now, I think it's time to take a break and for you to have something to eat." With that, Dominique points at her neck.

"What here? Now?"

"Yes, from your preferred side."

Hesitatingly, Erika moves towards Dominique and then without much thinking or effort, her fangs slide out and she feels for the artery, as she's trained to do, and her fangs sink into Dominique's neck. Erika doesn't really remember anything after that.

Chapter 12

"I see you're back with us," Dominique says, "I'm guessing you forgot to focus on stopping and only on the pleasure?"

Erika nods slowly, the look in her eyes shows she's coming back to the real world slowly, "Sorry."

"Don't worry, that's why we're taking things slowly and doing everything that needs doing, in a sensible order. I know it's all new and it takes time to adjust."

"You're disappointed?"

"No, not at all. So far, you've done fabulously well. I'm going to let you into a secret, what you're doing now, took me years. So, you have accomplished what took me years in a matter of days," Dominique says with a friendly smile.

"You're just saying that to make me feel better."

"No, I'm saying it because it's true. I didn't have all the help you're getting. I was to all intents and purposes, left to figure all this out on my own. The one who made me, he disappeared after a couple of weeks, and he didn't teach me half of what you already know."

"Then, I'm sorry and I'll try harder."

Dominique nods, "Alright, but now, I want you to see some of the gifts that you've recently acquired. It's going to help with your feelings of sensitivity, I know you're worried about it." Erika looks sceptically at Dominique, "No, I know it, because I can see it in your aura."

Erika sighs, "It's impossible to keep anything hidden from you, as you see everything."

Dominique flashes Erika an all-knowing grin before continuing, "Exactly, now I'm going to punch you in the face. If you don't get out of the way, it's going to hurt, and I mean hurt a lot."

"Wait, what?"

Dominique makes a fist and makes a gesture with it, "My fist, your face. Make sure you dodge it."

"How?"

"It doesn't matter, dodge left, dodge right, it doesn't matter, just make sure it doesn't hit your face."

"Why?"

Dominique says, "Training." As she pulls her arm back and, in a blur, her arm pushes the fist forward and into empty air.

Erika grins up from the sofa, "I dodged it."

Laughing Dominique says, "Yes you did, but I had assumed, but not specified, that you should be standing afterwards."

"I lost my balance as I tripped over the sofa," Erika replies defensively.

"I think you can get yourself up."

"Meanie."

"Predator," Dominique says emphasising the word, "but, did you see how fast I moved and how quickly you responded?"

Standing and arranging her skirt, Erika says, "It seemed normal, natural."

With a sigh Dominique says, "Your turn, you punch me in the face."

Erika looks horrified, "I could hurt you?"

"Humour me, and just so you know, there's no possibility of you hurting me. Your aura gives you away, you're nervous doing this. I could use that against you in a fight," Dominique says.

"I'm a barrister, why would I have to fight?"

"Being able to defend yourself is an important part of your survival. Now punch me."

Erika makes a fist and immediately, Dominique stops her, "Not like that, like this." She then adjusts Erika's fingers so that her thumb is on the outside of her fingers rather than inside. "With your fingers over the thumb, you can break your thumb, it's not serious, but it hurts, and you'll be less able to defend yourself. Survival is the name of the game."

Erika adjusts her fingers and thumb a little and moves for the punch, her hand is a blur as it moves towards Dominique's face, but just as it looks like a solid impact, there's suddenly nothing there.

"Did you see how fast you moved then?" Dominique asks.

Erika nods, "Yes, but you were so much faster."

"Because you weren't trying, you can be much faster than that. Try pushing blood into your shoulder, arm, and fist, like you did earlier with the aura and punch me again."

Erika repeats the gesture and this time, her fist is barely visible, but once again it punches empty space.

"Did you see that? Much better, much faster."

Erika nods, "I did, wow, which was fast, but once again, you're faster."

"True, do it again."

Erika repeats the exercise, and her fist zooms through the air, no sight nor sound, and it cleanly impacts Dominique hand which appears in place of her head. The impact sound is loud, solid, and impressive. A high-speed object impacting a solid object. "I hit you. But it's like hitting concrete."

Dominique grins, "No, concrete would have been softer. Had I been people, your fist would have gone through my head." She pauses a moment, "And I mean right through, brain matter all over your hand and up your arm. It would have been a mess. I see the idea horrifies you because your aura changed colour. But, on the bright side, the target wouldn't have seen it coming."

Erika touches Dominique's hand, the skin soft and warm. 'I'm missing something,' she wonders. "How did you do that?"

"How I do it's not half as important as how you do it. I'm going to suggest a slider marked, soft on one end and hard on the other. Give it a try and we'll see if you can make yourself tougher."

Erika does as Dominique suggests, 'Maybe I should force blood into my skin,' she thinks. Patches over her body flush red, her cheeks glow, her arms redden, her chest flushes and the pores on her skin open a little. "How about this?"

Dominique prods her arm with a finger and shakes her head, "No change, but I see what you did, pushing the blood to your skin. It was a clever idea, but you need to push it to the muscles, not the skin. But I trust you see the effect, it makes you look warm, but your temperature doesn't change. It can be useful in a more limited way to look embarrassed if that's useful. Try again."

It takes Erika a little over an hour to get her body to become harder, attempt after attempt fails, then it begins to partially work, intermittently, then more frequently and finally, she gets it working reliably.

"See, that wasn't too difficult, was it?" Dominique congratulates her.

"How many attempts? A hundred?"

Dominique shakes her head, "I have no idea, I wasn't counting. But it didn't take all that long. What's an hour or so. No time at all."

"You and your outside of time!" Erika jibes.

"Exactly, now, I'm going to hit your hand and I will not miss, no matter what you do. So, make it hard and ready?"

Erika nods and before the nodding is complete, Dominique's hand has impacted into Erika's now hard hand. "Ow, that hurts," Erika protests.

"But your hand's still here and not broken," Dominique counters.

"Is it supposed to be?"

"It would have been if you hadn't toughened up. We can try without if you want to compare, and contrast," Dominique offers.

"I think, I'll skip having my hand broken or torn off."

"If it gets ripped off, you can always get another."

"Can I do that?" Erika asks enthusiastically.

"No."

Erika gives Dominique a withering look, "That's mean."

"I know, but it was fun."

"Can I use fast at the same time as hard?" Erika asks.

"Yes, if it came to a fight, then it would be sensible to have a toughened body, but using the speed, is something you'll have to calibrate. If you're hitting a person, you probably only want to hurt them, perhaps knock them over. That's not something we can practice, but it's definitely not the speed and power we've been doing tonight. Do you remember when I likened you to a bulldozer earlier?"

Erika nods, "Yes, mostly."

"Well, I hope you see now why I chose that metaphor. You have the ability to do some severe damage to everyone. To some more than others. When using your skills, it's best if you err on the side of caution, until you have more experience and finesse."

"Do you think that'll be necessary," Erika enquires.

Dominique nods, "Unfortunately, at some point, it will become necessary. All you can do is be ready. Don't forget, action is the last of our five stages. It would be better if you can resolve any confrontation before you get to action. From a practical perspective, what with you being inexperienced and frankly vulnerable, I imagine the most likely result is someone's death, and I don't imagine it will be yours."

"You keep saying that, but I don't understand why. I'm just a new family member, I'm not as strong or capable as you. So, I'm guessing that most other family members will be stronger, faster, and more capable than me."

Dominique sits back down on the sofa and looks at the place where she knows Erika will sit momentarily. She waits for Erika to sit.

"I've said before and I'll say again, there's so much you don't know. Yes, there are many family members who are both faster and stronger. There are many who are more skilled and you're right, many of them will be able to best you in a fight. That's one of the reasons, why we don't want to be fighting. Resolving disagreements and missteps through other means is your and my best option. But, and this is important, you are already stronger and faster than most. You can do things that many others cannot. Not everyone can move as fast as you can. Not everyone is as strong as you are. Each family member, gets his or her own set of specific skills."

"You mean we don't all have the same skills?" Erika enquires.

"Correct, the skills you have, the speed, the toughness, they're available to you, because I have given them to you.

There are others, which we'll get to once you have mastered the basics of what I've taught you tonight."

"That's interesting, what else?" Erika says intrigued.

"I think three skills in one night is rather good for anyone, seeing auras, speed, and toughness. Please remember that the speed, we've done it only with punching, but you can move your whole body like that and at that speed. But some, like me, can move faster, so you're not the fastest and you should afford anyone who's faster a great deal of respect."

"How can I know who's faster than me?"

"Unfortunately, babe, there's no way of knowing until you see them move. Or worse, don't see them move. I can move so fast, that I can be there and back, and you'd never see me move. So, keep that in mind, even with your super speed and ability to see it, some of us can move faster than you can see."

"That's not possible."

Dominique hands Erika one of the flowers from off the dining room table, "It's possible."

"You never moved. The air didn't move, there was no feeling," Erika says looking confused.

"Just because you can't feel or sense it, doesn't mean that it doesn't happen. Can you see my aura?"

"Yes."

"This is smug because I told you so and you made me prove it. I'll never tell you anything that's not true," Dominique says, her voice reflecting her words.

"Alright, then where were you born."

"But that doesn't mean I will answer your question."

"You can't fault a girl for trying," Erika says with a grin.

"Yes, and you'll have to get up much earlier in the evening to get that past me. I don't know about you, but do you want to go to bed?"

"Already, it's not even dawn!"

"That's a fair point, but you don't have to go to bed and sleep. There're other things we can do before then."

"Like…"

Dominique cuts her off before she can express the thought, "Like things you've never even thought of."

"More training?"

"Of sorts," Dominique pauses a moment, "Yes, training. Let's call it that."

"Alright, I'm prepared for a little training, but first, I want to ask you a question."

"Ask away?"

"Why did you choose me to be family?"

Dominique stands and silently walks slowly, contemplatively towards the balcony window, she looks out at the lights for a moment, before turning back to Erika in the room. "Will you accept because you are and always have been special?"

Erika shakes her head, "I need a bit more."

"I believe that everyone has a purpose in life, if you will, that we each contribute something to humanity, in its entirety," Dominique says. "I see you as someone who'll be here for the long haul. Yes, I know this is going to be a lot put on your shoulders tonight, but I see you being a beacon, in a hundred years, in five hundred, in a thousand. I see you still being here."

Erika looks surprised, "I don't think anyone can live that long."

"You're right, of course, nobody can live that long, but you're already dead, so living in that sense, well, that's not particularly important is it. I use the word live, in the broadest possible sense. Then let me rephrase, I see you being around in a thousand years, and I see you coming into your own, as a leader."

"I'm not sure I should have asked."

"I've been trying to tell you that not all your questions are, shall we say, well advised. But I did say that I would answer them and it's your tenacity for asking questions and the constant interest in what's going on, the why, the how. That's the thing that will keep you going for the years to come. That's a big part of why you're special. Now, is that enough for you to come to bed for some training?" Dominique says, with a hint of something else in her voice, perhaps intrigue.

"I don't know if I'm in the mood now for training, what you've just told me is very daunting. I've been thirty-four for a couple of days and you're talking about how I'll be in five-hundred years from now."

Dominique grins, "I know. But at some point, I must make you pay for the constant questions and the never taking a no for the answer. This is that time."

"So that was a punishment?"

Dominique laughs at the comment, "Far from it. You keep asking and I have at some point to respond truthfully. I can only postpone answers for so long and perhaps, now you'll trust me when I say, that's best discussed later. But I know you and I know you won't. It's part of your nature, it's why you're here."

Erika stands from the sofa, "Then let's go train."

Dominique follows Erika towards the bedroom.

Chapter 13

Waking up, cuddling with Dominique, Erika says, "Mm, you so warm. It's always been nice, but now, it feels different somehow."

"Ah, you mean sucking all my heat out?" Dominique says quibbling.

"Mm, yes, that."

"Vampires!" Dominique states.

"I thought you weren't allowed to say that?"

"I think it's understood in all of society, that women who steal the heat from their partner are vampires. I'm quite sure that most and I mean ninety plus percent of men will agree and a good portion of the lesbians too."

"That's fairly mean," Erika protests.

"Predator, remember," Dominique says, placing a kiss on Erika's cheek. "We're inherently mean to the weaker members of the herd. The young and or the weak. Don't you watch documentaries on television. The lions and the hyenas, they always look for the slow, the lame or the sleepy." With that, Dominique pulls up Erika's left arm and sinks her fangs into the wrist. She drinks for about three seconds, then closing the wound says, "Prey."

"You can't do that," Erika says indignantly.

"And yet, here we are, and I've already started with breakfast," Dominique says happily.

"Did you have to ruin the mood, with talk of breakfast. I'm dreading it after yesterday," Erika laments.

"I know, that's why I'm playing, to make you feel more relaxed."

"You think that was relaxing?"

Dominique raises her arm so Erika can see her fingers and she makes a gesture with the fingers about a centimetre apart, "A little bit."

"You need to work on that."

"Perhaps, but I have been working on your anxiety and I have a solution, literally." Dominique looks mysterious.

"What are you talking about?"

"Come one, if you can wake-up and then jump out of bed, we can get some breakfast."

"Do we have time?" Erika asks.

"We always have time for breakfast. Remember what I said about running down and getting hungry. The monster that resides within and all that?"

Erika groans her recollection and untwines her arm, "See, I'm getting up. It's killing me, but I'm getting up. Why are we getting up so early? Can't we lie-in, we're on holiday?"

Dominique turns over and looks at Erika, she plants a single kiss on her lips, "Holiday is for people. You're in training. Survival training."

"Even now?"

"Even now, what's my aura?"

Erika clearly focuses and concentrates before replying, "It's black. What does that mean?"

"It means that I'm feeling hate."

"You hate me?" Erika is horrified.

"No silly, it's training, what about now?"

"Silver."

"Which is?"

"Enthusiastic or perhaps excited."

"Exactly, well done," Dominique says and, after stroking Erika's cheek briefly, slides out of bed, after slipping on her dressing gown, heads out of the bedroom.

Erika, lingers in bed, relishing the warm spot Dominique has just vacated. Eventually she too must rise, slipping on her dressing gown, she follows Dominique. In the kitchen she asks, "Why do you stay warm all the time?"

Dominique puts two glasses onto the counter, both filled with a deep red liquid, "Partly habit, but it takes ages to warm-up when you get cold, even in the summer. It's much worse in the winter." She slides the smaller one to Erika.

"Am I going to space out again, if I drink this?" Erika says apprehensively.

Dominique shrugs, "I hope not, but I don't know. It's nice that you enjoy it. I wish I could get what you get out of it. That would be a real joy." She sips at her drink, as she does each morning.

Erika on the other hand, takes a tentative trial sip of her drink, then another. "This has a different taste and feel." Dominique nods. Erika continues, "Is this what two-day old food tastes like?"

"No, this is something a little special for you. How does it taste different?" Dominique enquires.

"Um, it's hard to say," Erika says, taking another sip, "it tastes a little thinner, perhaps a little saltier and this will sound strange, but earthy."

Dominique watches as Erika sips more, "How are you feeling?"

"I'm feeling good, exceptionally good, but not spacing out like yesterday. Why?"

Dominique grins, the red clearly present on the inside of her mouth and teeth, "That's my experimental blend number one."

"Experimental?" Erika says, flashing Dominique a suspicious look.

"Finish it up and let's see if it has the same effect as yesterday."

Erika drinks the remainder of her drink, one sip at a time, watching Dominique more than the drink.

"Well, how do you feel?" Dominique enquires.

"The same, I feel very good, it tastes fantastic, it definitely has that earthy taste I mentioned earlier, but it's nice."

"Then it's a secret blend of twenty percent human, eighty percent bovine." Dominique falls silent and waits.

Erika's expression remains neutral, 'It's cow's blood,' she thinks.

"Your aura gives you away. Not keen on the idea I see."

Erika sighs, "I don't know, I never thought about it before."

"If it makes you feel better, and it won't, blood is blood, it makes no difference the source and keeping you lucid is important. I think that the sensitivity will fade over time. But now that we have something that will feed you, we can finesse the formulae and build-up the percentage."

"If you say so," Erika says sceptically.

"I do and don't let your modern sensitivities get the better of you, people have drunk bovine blood for thousands of years. Did you know the people of the Masai Mara mix it in with milk and drink it to this day?"

"No, I didn't know that?" Erika sounds surprised.

"I assume you've heard of black pudding?"

Erika nods, "Of course."

"Well, that's ovine, porcine, or bovine blood, some fat and often a little cereal, like oats. It's fried and eaten as breakfast. Why do you suppose that tradition came about?"

"Don't know, but I assume you're about to tell me."

"Indeed, I am," Dominique says happily. "In times gone by, after the killing of an animal, people didn't want or couldn't afford to waste any part of the animal. That included the meat, the internal organs and, of course, the blood. They created all kinds of preservation methods for all these items. In many parts of the world, it's called blood sausage. In the UK, they make black pudding. The idea is the same, get the blood, mix in some herbs and fat. Put it all into a bit of intestine and you have a black pudding sausage. To eat, they cut sections off and eat it. It contains lots of nutrients and calories. In effect a beneficial source of nutrition. See, nothing to do with family, just sensible use of scarce resources."

"If I'm understanding this correctly, you're telling me that it's perfectly acceptable to drink animals' blood? Is that correct?" Erika enquires.

"Yes, I am, and I didn't think I was being quite that transparent."

Erika flashes Dominique a grin, "You're not the only one who knows the other."

"Then pass me your glass and I'll mix you up a new batch."

Erika slides the glass over to Dominique who begins filling it with a new mixture, "Is this going to be a problem?" Erika asks.

"I don't think so. In truth, I don't know, but I don't think so," Dominique says sliding the glass back to Erika.

"Thank you for being honest," Erika says before taking a sip and then more.

"How about this one?"

"Feeling very nice, fantastic in fact, but not getting spaced out."

"Good, finish that up and we'll try another mixture. This one was thirty percent. I want it to taste nice and feel good, but not too good. Once we understand our parameters, we can slowly increase the amount as you become accustomed to it."

Erika nods between mouthfuls, drinking down her full glass of dark red breakfast blood as quickly as feelings permit. When she's finished, she slides the glass back to Dominique who makes up another batch of breakfast. As the glass slides back Erika asks, "Forty percent?"

"Yes, I'm hoping we'll get to fifty percent, which would be a good result."

Erika drinks the blood and enjoys the sensations, when done she hands the glass back to Dominique who fills it again with a new mixture and hands the glass back.

"Fingers crossed," Dominique says as Erika sips at the drink, repeating her now standard tasting process.

"Mm," Erika murmurs, "this is fantastic." She drinks more, but it's clear that it's a step too far. She begins to enjoy the sensation too much and starts to space out.

Dominique waits patiently drinking her breakfast as Erika enjoys her sensations. As Erika returns to the world, Dominique comments, "That seems to be a step too far. You lost it for a while. Not long, but long enough."

Erika sighs, "Sorry."

Dominique shakes her head, "No, don't be sorry. I envy you."

"What? Why?"

"Because I can't remember when I enjoyed it as much as you are. I might never have enjoyed it as much as you are, and that's my disappointment."

"But I'm the disappointment."

Dominique shakes her head and sips at her food, "No, no, you're not. But this little sensitivity is going to complicate things."

"How so?"

"Tonight's plan was to visit Adam and Anita for a dinner party. As a celebration if you will."

"What are we going to eat?"

Dominique laughs, the amusement written all over her face, "Adam and Anita!"

"We can't."

"We can and I do. They're associates. I thought you knew and understood that?" Dominique says, clearly enjoying herself.

"I wondered, but no, I didn't know."

"This is one of the roles of associates. We'll need to get you your own in the fullness of time, but now, we have other complexities to deal with."

"Like what?" Erika asks.

Dominique simply points at Erika, "How about you?"

"Oh, you mean the drinking?"

Dominique nods, "Yes, that. Now you know what I had planned, do you want to go, or should I postpone our visit a few days?"

"Postpone, I don't want to look silly when we go over."

Chuckling Dominique says, "You worry about all the wrong things. Trust me when I say, they won't be thinking about you. They'll be enjoying the sensation of me."

"There's a lot to remember and so much to get wrong. I just don't know if I..." Erika says, the uncertainty visible to all.

"I don't want to hear it and it's too late now anyway. You're in the do or die part of the operation and dying is not an option. Give me a couple of minutes to go and call then we can have a chat about the subject I dislike the most."

"What's that?"

Dominique says, "Continue drinking, I'll be back soon." With that, she heads back into the bedroom.

Erika drinks slowly trying to sip at her dark red drink, savouring the taste, but drinking slowly enough to not loose herself. She rides the edge of pleasure and oblivion until Dominique returns.

"All done, we have a few days reprieve."

"Thank you. What was the percentage of this?" Erika asks, looking at the remainder of the drink in the glass.

"Sixty percent. I think we'll be going with fifty tomorrow and maybe try porcine instead of the bovine. I doubt it'll make any difference, but we are experimenting."

"Alright."

"It won't make any difference to your body, or your aura focus, etc. It will just help you keep clarity." Dominique says reassuringly.

Erika nods and takes smaller sips from her drink. Dominique reaches out for the glass and when Erika passes it over, she quickly tops it up.

"That should help, I topped it up with bovine," Dominique says passing it back.

"What's this topic we need to talk about that you dislike?"

"Politics," Dominique confirms.

"But you're so good at it."

"I have techniques that help," Dominique says cryptically.

"What do I need to know?"

"Everything."

"That's a bit cryptic and awfully brief."

"This lot," Dominique says waving her hand around her head, "they just love their politics. You'd think any of it mattered."

"You mean people?"

"No, I mean family," Dominique says. "The whole place runs on politics, who's in favour, who's out of favour. Who does what for whom, when, why, where. It's so tedious."

Erika offers her glass, "Maybe you need some of this."

Dominique smiles kindly at the gesture, "Thank you, but this is a bit nicer. That was thoughtful though."

"How about you start from the top and make it clear when it's commentary and when it's fact," Erika suggests.

Dominique looks at the contents of her glass a moment then says, "Yes, sorry. Structure, family like to run things in what they consider to be a modern structure, so we are at kings, queens, lords, barons, etc. A monarchy to all intents and purposes. But, with the distinction that positions, and promotions are via merit rather than through birth or bloodlines, but through favours and deeds done. Support powerful family members and in turn they support you and so on. At least that's what they do."

"They do?" Erika says, looking intently at Dominique.

"I try to keep as far as possible out of it all. The entire system is sordid and not a little squalid for my taste."

"But you still participate."

Dominique sighs, then nods a little, "But only to the minimum extent necessary. If I could avoid it totally, then I would."

"That was commentary. Is there more on the structure?"

Dominique nods, "Long ago, we, that is family, divided up the world into non-overlapping territories. Each one controlled by a king or queen or possibly both and their court. Depending upon the size of the territory, you will see varying levels of titled positions. More levels normally relate to a larger territory. Large can be either geographical or number of people. Larger populations can support larger groups of family. Part of it is practical, there cannot be too many family members in any single space, otherwise, it becomes too hard to blend in. As I mentioned before, some will always do the wrong thing and get themselves noticed, etc. Plus, there's a limit to the food available."

"Understood. And?" Erika says cautiously.

"And, if you want to live in a territory, you must play by the local rules with the approval of the local hierarchy. I'm hoping you can sense how much I dislike all this."

"I do, but I sense that this is going to be as important or more important than some of the other things we've talked about." Erika could feel that things were getting complicated.

Dominique sighs, "Yes, it probably is. Everything that happens within a territory must have the ultimate approval of the king, or a king's representative that acts as if the king was there. This includes significant business dealings, to an extent, it also includes making new family members, and it also includes moving to a new area and setting up residence. There are rules, which I don't want to get into now, as it will be too tedious and burdensome, but we'll cover them in the coming months."

"You seem reluctant to discuss this, which isn't like you."

"Truthfully, if I had my way, I'd have them all slaughtered," Dominique says, a clear bright spot in her discourse, "and we'd start all over again. But I don't get my way and that's not going to happen, so I must deal with what exists and put up with all the silly rules and machinations. When, in fact, I have better things to do."

"Let's go and sit down then you can carry on."

Dominique follows Erika into the lounge and sits in her normal place on the sofa, "To have permission," she says, making air quotes around the word permission, "to make you, I had to jump through all sorts of hoops, get an audience with x, convince y that it was in everyone's interest and finally get an audience with the King and Queen. Then start all over again convincing them that it was a good move for them. That in the fullness of time, it would be to their advantage. Which reminds me, at some point in the not-too-distant future, we're going to have to visit them to introduce you."

"What!" Erika says perplexed.

"Don't worry, they're not a threat to you, it's only a formality, a show of politeness, forced politeness," Dominique sighs. "You see how I hate it? The wasted effort and since they have nothing else to do, it seems like an effective use of time to them."

"You're drifting."

"I know, sorry. What else would you like to know?"

"Is everyone under the rule of the king and queen?"

Dominique nods, "Officially, yes. In practice, we could say no. There's what we will call a criminal element. Not necessarily in the sense of breaking the law and falling foul of the police but operating outside of what the king and queen might do or want. They can present a problem for everyone if they get themselves noticed or do something silly."

"How can I tell them all apart?"

"In practice, you cannot, they look and act broadly the same. It's only when you come across their dodgy dealings that you can recognise them," Dominique says, then pauses to consider her next words. "Which brings us to the law. There are those who investigate and those who enforce. In practice you shouldn't have any problem with either, as you're not going to be doing anything dodgy let alone illegal and so, there's little to worry about here."

"How can you be so blasé?"

"It's not that I don't care, or that this is unimportant, it's that it doesn't matter. Not to me and ultimately not to you."

"I don't understand what you're talking about," Erika says sounding confused.

"I know, but you will. I keep telling you that you're special and you keep ignoring that fact. It's important and you should keep it in mind. When I tell you that something is not to be worried about nor of concern to you, please take that to heart. I mean it," Dominique says, holding Erika's hand in a reassuring manner.

"It's hard, because I don't understand."

"How to explain this again," Dominique says, while contemplating her next words. "In this world, power is different than in the world of people. There, power is normally a function of age, older people have more power and a function of who you know, powerful people tend to know other powerful people. But here, power is getting something done. Fair?"

"It's a bit generic and weak, but I'll go along with it for now," Erika says uncertainly.

"In our world, age does matter, but only because of what it implies. The most powerful are normally the oldest. Being the first made means more time to hone skills, develop abilities and better understand your nature. Where your limits lay. This might be physical, and it might be mental. In most cases both. Being old has disadvantages too."

"Like?"

Dominique pauses a moment before continuing, "Like seeing the world around you change all the time and having to keep up. It sounds like nothing to you now but imagine that you need to move to a new place and that requires learning a new language, new customs, adapting and understanding current technology and so on and so on."

"It doesn't seem that bad."

"No, the first time, it's not, nor the second, but on the twentieth, or the thirtieth, it can become a burden," Dominique says.

"That makes sense."

"So, old family, often lock themselves away from the world and just let it pass them by for a while."

"A while?"

"Hundreds of years in some cases, decades in others," Dominique says, "The idea is to just have a rest from the changes. Of course, it only makes it worse, as you have a lot to learn and catchup on. It's one of the reasons that you don't tend to see many extremely old family members and when you do, people are fearful of them. Partly because they often have fearful reputations. Please bear in mind, that much of this is rumour, speculation and in many cases legend."

"So, how do you get to be old?"

"Simple, by not dying," Dominique says reasonably.

"You know that's not what I meant."

"I know, but you need to be more specific. That's one of the traits that you excel at and will allow you to live a long-time."

"Fair enough, what do I need to do in order to live a long-time?"

"Better. You need to learn the lessons that I'm trying to teach you. We have a lot of ground to cover," Dominique says flashing another of her grins.

"You're avoiding the question."

Dominique sighs, "This is one of the reasons you can become old. It's mostly mental. You have the right mindset to last. Your inquisitive nature, your desire to learn, from people, from books, it all helps make you the type who can thrive over time. Those that cannot, they tend to wither, and when they wither, they tend to either die or fade away. Which almost always leads to unrecoverable death."

"Unrecoverable death?" Erika says sounding intrigued.

"You're already dead, so there are some kinds of dying that are recoverable. I said that some will withdraw from the world, and they effectively sleep for decades or centuries. In practice, you cannot go that long without running out of blood. In that case, you mummify. It's not pretty, but it's not fatal either. Get some food, or lots of food and you'll be as right as rain in no time. Well, in a little time, a few days to a week. You can lose a limb, and have it reattached. The repair of even a severe injury is possible. Various kinds of injury will require more or less time and in the worst cases, might require you to be out of circulation for a time. Think of it as convalescence after a trauma."

"You said that I couldn't regrow a hand, when we were practicing yesterday."

Dominique takes a deep breath and sighs, "Yes, I said that. It's sort of true and sort of not true. Healing is complex and growing bits back can be problematic, always keep the original bits if you can. This is another one of those conversations, which are more complex than you can appreciate."

"Why? You can either do it or you cannot, how complex can it be?"

"Very, because you're new. Do you remember we talked about your ability to see auras?" Erika nods, so Dominique continues, "Well, you have a basic understanding of the skill, as expected, since it is new to you. As you progress, with your understanding of your body, the skill, how to move your blood around and a whole lot of practice and training, you'll be able to do all those other things I talked about. This is true across the board, so something you can't do today, you might be able tomorrow, or the next day or in a year or two. Or longer for that matter. Each skill builds on the one before. More skills mean a bigger base to leverage for more and other skills. You have immense potential, but we must build to get there. So, in the fullness of time, you might well be able to regrow a hand, but that doesn't mean you can do it today. Does that help?"

"It sounds daunting?"

"Do you remember when you were in your first year or two of school?" Dominique asks.

"Vaguely, in parts."

"Near enough. Every year at school, the work you did was the most difficult you'd ever done. It was always hard, and it always pushed you. Yes?"

Erika nods, "Yes."

"But when you look back, even from one year to the previous, the work you did last year didn't seem so hard did it?"

"No and I think I see where you're going with this," Erika says.

"You do?"

"Yes, you're saying that the unknown is always difficult, but as soon as we have learnt how to deal with it, it suddenly becomes easy or at least easier."

Dominique nods, "Broadly, yes. It applies to learning anything, skills, languages, including your so-called secret powers, you name it. So, don't be too frustrated that things are taking time. They will always take time, that's why you have so much of it."

"I'm assuming there's lots that you're not telling me."

Dominique nods again, "Yes, there's still lots more for you to know. But we should continue the politics, perhaps with a walk and we can see the key political sights. Unlike with the people, family politics is a participatory event, so knowing where things happen, does help and for want of a better phrase, will help."

"Alright."

"Then we should get ready and go out," Dominique says as she stands and heads towards the bedroom and the shower, with Erika following closely behind.

Chapter 14

BING

The lift doors slowly slide open, Erika and Dominique step out into the lobby walking casually across the marble floor, their shoes echoing in the silence of night. At the night entrance, they press the button, the door opens with a faint hum, allowing access into the night beyond.

Stepping out, Erika asks, "Which way?"

"This way," Dominique says, turning to her left and walking upriver.

"Are you sure these clothes are acceptable?"

"They're fine, it's early and it's warm. You'll see that other young women are wearing shorts and skirts, crop tops and light blouses. It's summer, just because you're ambient," Dominique quips.

"That's a bit low. Although, it's not such a problem tonight, I'm not looking forward to winter. For that very reason."

"You'll figure it out," Dominique quips lightly.

"Where are we going first?" Erika queries.

"I thought we'd first go to the castle and see where their majesties live, or at least hold court. Just so you know, they are only there when they're on official business. They live elsewhere, as I'm sure you can imagine. Only crazy people live where they work."

"You mean like me?"

"You said it, not me," Dominique quips and they both have a good laugh. "Good, I think that's the first time you've laughed properly since your birthday."

"There's been a lot to do, and it's not been all that much fun," Erika comments.

"Trust me when I say, it could have been very much harder."

"Really, how?" Erika wonders.

Dominique stops walking and regards Erika a moment before continuing, "Really? You must ask how?"

"Well, yes."

Dominique considers her words a moment, before answering, "Then consider, you could have woken up alone, with no idea what had happened, why or what to do. With no help in developing your understanding, your secret powers or any of the rest of it. Imagine what would have happened the first time you had something to eat and how vulnerable you would have been then?"

Erika considers the words for a moment, "Alright, you've made your point. I could have had it much worse. No matter how bad it looks, it can always be much worse."

"Always. Are you enjoying the sights, the lights, and the people. The hassle and bustle?"

Erika muses, 'She's good, I never noticed all the people and the smells, maybe I'm getting better.' "That was slick," Erika retorts.

"If it makes you feel any better, you're handling it like a pro. Although, I suspect it's because you're distracted, rather than because you've mastered that skill."

"You're probably right and we have just eaten," Erika confirms.

"Now your mood has changed, the lighter and brighter version of you was better," Dominique says, clearly enjoying the improvement.

Erika concentrates and says nothing, after a few seconds says, "You on the other hand look a light blue colour."

"Relaxed."

"So, you're relaxed, or you want me to think you're relaxed?"

"I'm relaxed, a walk like this in the summer, is nice. Just remember to keep in the shade, even this late, the direct sun can burn."

"Ah, that's why we're walking close to the buildings, to get shade."

Dominique nods, "Exactly, use your surroundings to maximum effect. It's either do this or wait until later. This seemed nicer. Besides, it's best for people to see you out and about, even if it's late in the day or early in the morning. It arouses less suspicion. Which leads quite nicely to your beautiful tan. You look nice and summery. Making you look more like one of the people and with time, your skin will lighten, a natural part of the transformation. With luck, if we got it right, you'll fade to a normal British white. Rather than the more deathly white, which is problematic."

"Is that what you did?" Erika enquires.

"No, my skin was a little darker than yours is now, so I fit in nicely in the northern environment, as you will too. Not much help in Africa of course, but there's only so much you can do."

"Wow, you think of everything."

"I hope so. That would make everything easier for both of us," Dominique replies.

"How much further?"

"Is this that game children play in the car?"

Erika laughs, "No, I'm just curious, as you never said where it was."

"I didn't say, because it's an anonymous looking door in the side of a building on a minor road. It looks nothing, but is really the seat of power in London, for everyone. There's probably a lesson there, that power doesn't have to be conspicuous if it's real. When it must be shown off, that's when something is amiss."

"That's not what I've seen. Most institutions when they gain power, build buildings, monuments and other displays of wealth and power," Erika counters.

"It all depends upon which path you choose. Do you want to slip under the radar and do your own thing or do you want to be a conspicuous target?"

"Is that the only choice?" Erika asks.

"I'm open to suggestions. I'm always open to suggestions, about this, anything, and everything else."

"What if you're showing off but are not a target," Erika proposes.

"In the world of politics, anyone of prominence is always a target. I'm not sure there's any way round that. Other than not to be in politics," Dominique admits. "The Japanese, I think it is, have an expression, the nail that sticks out is hammered down."

"That's a bit bleak."

"Didn't say it wasn't, but look at the Houses of Parliament, all the members spend all their time vying for the position of Prime Minister. Even the opposition are striving for that. All the MP's all the time. We're here," Dominique says, stopping near a dark blue door, it looks unremarkable.

"That's it?" Erika sounds incredulous.

Dominique nods, "That's it. But look very carefully at the lintel above the door and remember that sigil. That's the one for the current King and Queen. If you see it anywhere else, you'll know that this property or item is theirs. Consider that a warning."

"Warning about what?"

"That you don't mess with the King or Queens' property. They look unfavourably upon that and that just causes more difficulties for no benefit," Dominique says.

"Alright, that makes sense, I was worried that there was something else," Erika says. "I don't plan on causing any trouble."

Dominique laughs, "You are trouble. It's your nature and your very existence. You are a poster child for trouble."

"I don't understand that. I'm not being trouble to anyone," Erika says sounding confused.

"I know and I'm sorry, but I couldn't, not react to that. It was just too funny."

"Once again, I am not in on the joke."

"There's no joke. Honestly," Dominique says with a smile.

"I'm not sure I believe that, but where to next?"

"Well, not far from here there's a restaurant that caters to family, I can point it out, but for obvious reasons, we can't go there yet," Dominique says.

"Alright, lets walk past and yes, I agree, I cannot go in there yet."

Dominique offers her arm to Erika, who slips her hand through, "See, it's not so horrible is it?" As they walk back down the street they just came down and turn right towards the more heavily trafficked part of London.

"Are you going to tease me all the time or are you going to tell me what's going on?"

"Is there a choice?"

"No, no choice."

Dominique makes a play defeated gesture with her head, then says, "There are things I can tell you, but they won't make sense or perhaps you cannot understand the implications of the information, because you don't have the background and framework to utilise that information correctly or perhaps at all. It will be just facts without context. Very much like when you're in court. You must have not only the information, but the context to which that information applies. On top of that, the information must be available in a way that it can be easily incorporated into the framework. I am, currently, trying to give you the framework in which you can create the context to understand the information. Plus, you must be able to understand the implications, both in the short and the longer term. Please keep in mind, that short and long-term, might not be in the units you're accustomed too."

As they walk Erika says, "So, you're saying that I cannot understand?"

"Correct, in that you cannot understand yet. The key here is yet. The understanding at that point, when you can, will be easy and yet profound. It will define you, at least in the short-term."

Erika makes a fist in frustration by her side, "How can I understand something when I don't know what that thing is," she mutters.

"I know you're getting frustrated, but I don't know how to impart so much information to you in such a short amount of time, that you can understand, process and ultimately use it to survive," Dominique says reasonably.

"You could just tell me and let me sort it out. I'm quite clever you know."

"If you weren't, you wouldn't be here with me like this."

"You keep saying that," Erika says.

"Because I don't make new family very often and when I do, they must be special to start with and after, they'll be special forever. Special by the standards of... Oh we're here. That restaurant over there, if you want to eat something different, go in, mention to the person seating patrons that you are family and if all goes well, they'll take you to a different part of the restaurant and you can, for a price, have something different and perhaps to your taste, or exotic or whatever you fancy. Within reasons that is."

"Just like that?"

Dominique nods, "Yes, just like that. Of course, they'll check your aura, no point in the wrong type claiming to be family and getting the wrong end of dinner."

Erika chuckles, "I can see how that would look if it went wrong. It gives a whole new meaning to dinner guest."

Dominique chuckles too, "Yes it does, I never thought of that before. Very witty."

"If we go back home, will you tell me more? More of the things you don't want to tell me and the things I want to know about?" Erika asks.

Dominique nods, "Yes, I will, shall we?" They continue down the road, making turns as appropriate until they're back on the walkway next to the Thames.

"You know, I don't think I have appreciated walking by the river as much as I have in the last few days. I don't know what it is that's made this change. I mean, I know the obvious change, but there must be something else."

"Maybe it's just you are relaxing a little and taking the time to see what's around you. A predator's instinct." Dominique offers.

"You keep talking about predators a lot, but I'm not seeing it in what you do or what you've shown me. Or what we've talked about. Everything we do, is about blending in, going unnoticed and most of all keeping a low profile. None of that says predator," Erika says contemplating.

"Just because we're not going out and eating all the villagers, does not mean that you're not a predator and it doesn't mean that we couldn't. It means that we are choosing not too."

"You didn't answer my question," Erika says. as they amble along the embankment, watching the people interact, the boats and the diminishing traffic.

"Question? Statement more like. But you're correct, I didn't address your points directly. Predators have prey. We covered that already," Dominique says to a nod from Erika. "So, you have the predator's instinct, the innate ability and deep down, the desire. So far, we've kept that desire switched off. It's my hope and goal, that you'll never have to kill to eat. That's why we have breakfast everyday, you have snacks and meals throughout the night. There are lines that once crossed can no longer be uncrossed, and it's only afterwards, that you know you've crossed the line. Functionally, when it's too late," Dominique voice conveys the caution that reflect her words.

"Carry on."

"Predators are generally looking for prey and it won't be too long, maybe a matter of a few months, before you begin to see the world that way. It happens to all of us, it's only a matter of time. I'm trying to get you used to the idea, so when it happens, you will not be surprised or afraid of it."

"But if you're trying to avoid me having the desire and you're trying to do all those other things, doesn't this work against those goals?" Erika counters.

"Yes, yes it does, but while those are my goals, I also must be realistic. I know certain things will happen, just as the sun rises in the morning and sets in the evening. It makes it difficult. But cultivating the correct mental adjustments are critical."

"So, I'm not to feed on the villagers, but at some point, I'm going to want to. Once I have moved past the whole sensitivity thing. Is that what you're telling me?" Erika asks reasonably.

"I'm not sure I would have phrased it that way, but yes, that's probably what we're talking about, or thereabouts."

"Good, I think we're making progress."

As they pass under Waterloo bridge, one then two young men step out in front of them, followed by a third and then a fourth. As Dominique glances backwards, two more appear behind them. As they glide to a halt, she says to Erika, "Stay calm and let me handle this. No matter how it looks. Let me deal with it. And afterwards, I want to know what you saw."

'I hate this kind of thing,' Erika thinks to herself, 'why did they have to ruin our talk!'

Dominique slips her arm through Erika's and with a smile says, "Good evening gentlemen."

The one who stepped out last, dressed in a black leather jacket, jeans, and a pair of brown leather shoes answers, "You made a mistake missy." His chestnut brown hair, neatly coiffed and his accent local, obviously a Londoner.

"I don't see how." Dominique queries.

"Come over here and we'll talk," the young man says, gesturing to the edge of the pavement and to a more secluded spot.

Dominique moves gracefully towards the area suggested, guiding Erika with her, "Are you looking for money?"

The young man looks towards one of the others and says, "Shiner?"

Shiner looks at Erika and nods twice, then nods twice as he looks at Dominique.

"OK," the young man says, "looks like we've got our mark."

Dominique remains completely calm, her voice even and easy, "What's this about?"

"It's about you in our part of town, doing things you shouldn't be doing. Upsetting people."

"Your town?" Dominique queries.

"Our town, when you're in our town, you do things our way," the young man says to the general approval of his companions.

"And what is it, that you want doing your way?" Dominique asks reasonably.

"First of all, payment."

"Ah, so it is a robbery, as I originally suggested."

"We're not stealing from ya. We want you to make reparations for you crossing us and to make good on your obligations," the young man says.

"Reparations and obligations. They seem like awfully long words."

"Are you mocking me?"

Dominique considers his words, "A little bit. They seem a bit beyond you." At this point, she pulls Erika a little closer.

"Don't make me mad, or I'll show you who's boss."

"I'm sure you will, I assume we are now negotiating, so what do you want and what are you offering?" Dominique says simply, her voice calm and steady.

"First, you didn't get permission to make that one," the young man says pointing at Erika.

Dominique smiles amicably as she replies, "I spoke to the King about it personally. All permissions obtained and legitimate."

"Yeah, well you didn't talk to us about it did ya," the young man says his voice quiet, but tone unyielding.

"I've never seen you before, why would I ask you for permission to do anything?"

"Cause we're in charge here and we call the shots."

Dominique considers this as she looks at each in turn, the young man with the leather jacket, then another, in jeans and a heavy metal T-shirt, the third, Shiner dressed in jeans and a different branded t-shirt. The two who had originally stood behind her, were now off to the side and looked more menacing. Both dressed in ripped jeans, boots, and jackets, with various badges sewn onto the sleeves. They all look quite formidable. Turning to Erika, Dominique whispers, "See why I dislike politics." Then to the young man who's in charge, she says, "In charge of what?"

"This whole area, it's our turf."

"And what about the King, Queen, Lords, Barons and the Ladies?"

"Not important, our turf, our rules," the young man states.

"I see and about that negotiation, what is it you want and what are you giving in exchange?"

"Firstly, you insulted us, by not asking for permission. We ain't bin paid for that permission and nobody crosses us," the young man says.

"So, you keep saying. What do you want and what will you give to get it?" Dominique requests again.

"We know what you are, we know you're like us. So, you know what we can do and there's six of us and two of you. Not fair odds I recon."

"What do you want to resolve this misunderstanding?" Dominique prompts again.

"We want you to promise that you'll never do it again, or we'll kill you. This time we's gonna let you live."

"Is that everything?" Dominique asks calmly.

"No. We want her dead, now tonight."

"You want me to kill her?" Dominique says, holding on tightly to Erika.

'These people are crazy, I've only just been reborn, now they want her to kill me,' Erika thinks in a bit of a panic.

"You know that this situation is fraught with risk, you could get hurt, I could get hurt, she could get hurt. If things go badly, one or more of us could die. Is that what you want? Is it all worth that?" Dominique says, still perfectly calm.

"We ain't interested in your trying to weasel your way out of it. Those are our terms and that's final. You crossed us, now you pay," the young man demands.

"And if I don't want to pay?" Dominique asks.

The young man looks to his companions and grins, his fangs slipping into sight, "Then you pay a different way."

Dominique loosens her grip on Erika's arm and moves in front of her friend, looking her in the eye says, "I'm sorry."

'Oh, my goodness, she's going to kill me,' Erika thinks in a panic.

"I'm sorry, sorry that you've got to witness this. I didn't want you to see anything like this and I know you're scared." Dominique makes a tiny cut in the inside of her lip and allows a few drops of blood to bead out. She then kisses Erika, allowing the blood to flow over Erika's lip. As Erika instinctively licks it off, she relaxes a little, taking the edge from her panic.

"We can hear what you're saying you know."

"It's not supposed to be secret," Dominique says to the young man, then to Erika asks, "Please tell them who made you, just to be sure."

Calming down Erika says, "She who is without time. She who is love. She who is compassion and she who is vengeance, made me."

"I don't care who made ya, and the meaningless gibberish you just spouted," the young man says.

"Wait a mo," the man with the heavy metal T-shirt says, "I've heard that before and this might not be a good idea."

"Who are you?" Dominique says, her voice now much more authoritative.

"Um, I'm Matthew, but everyone calls me Matt."

"Well, Matt, that's interesting. Where did you hear that?" Dominique looks at him curiously.

"The one who made me, he made me remember it and gave me instructions in case I ever heard anyone say it."

"Did he now, and what were those instructions?" Dominique says intrigued.

"He said I should be careful and show respect."

"And are you?" Dominique asks.

"I'm trying and maybe I'll save your life."

"Maybe, when this is over, I want to talk with you alone."

Matt looks confused but nods his acceptance and agreement.

"What are you doing Matt?" the young man asks. "You're telling her everything."

"I think we should let them go and forget about it," Matt says.

"Why would we do that, they're gonna pay and that's that."

"I don't think I can hurt them," Matt says, uncertainty clear in his voice.

"Fine then sit out, but you'll pay for it later."

Turning back to the young man, Dominique says, "Just to be clear, I don't think I can kill her, not for you and not when the King gave me permission, that's a step too far."

"In that case, you know what we're gonna do to you," the young man says, menace in his voice. "Expect you both to die."

Dominique closes her eyes and sighs. She makes no attempt at initiating an attack or run away, she simple stands there with her eyes closed. After a couple of seconds, she looks from one to the other of her young male assailants. Her eyes linger on each, skipping over Matt quickly.

"Alright, I'm ready," Dominique says. "Whatever you're planning now would be the best time ever to walk away and go home. I have warned you and there will be no additional consideration given."

"Screw you," the young man says.

Moments later the young man and the four other assailants fall to the floor their hands tearing at their faces, blood begins to pour down from the wounds in their flesh.

Dominique turns to Erika, "Pinch your nose, cover your mouth and don't move."

Erika nods and mumbles something though her hand. 'What on earth has she just done,' she wonders in horror.

The young men continue to tear at their own flesh, ripping bits off and generally disfiguring themselves.

"When I leave, you will forget about me and my friend. You'll never think of us again. If you survive, you'll never attempt to do me or Erika harm again. If you think about it, or try, you will rip your own flesh off your body until the damage is so intense that you can no longer heal the wounds. Then you'll die. If you tell anyone, then you'll rip their heart out and drag them out into a place to meet the sunrise. You'll all meet it together in one last blaze of glory."

Matt looks horrified as he stands rigid on the grass next to the pavement. Erika looks more distressed than Matt as she holds her hand over her mouth. Dominique looks calm and collected.

"Now leave this place and don't let anyone see you, you wouldn't want to upset the people would you." Dominique lets the last threat hang in the air as she turns back to Erika looking at her kindly, "I did say I was sorry."

'How can she be so calm after that, there's nothing in her face, just a friendly smile to me,' Erika wonders as she looks at Dominique.

Turning to Matt, Dominique says, "Now, where did you hear that phrase?"

Matt nods several times quickly, "Yes, of course. I heard it from the one who made me. I told you this already."

"But who, what's his name? More importantly, what does he look like?"

"His name is Jonathan, but that's quite new, he's a bit taller than me, mousy brown hair and..."

"I know who he is. Is he still into his politics?"

Matt nods again cautiously, "How can you know who it is. I only gave you a height and hair colour."

"More importantly, if Jonathan made you, why are you associating with these individuals?" Dominique asks, gesturing in the direction the assailants scampered away.

"He wanted me to know who they were and what they were doing, I was learning more about them for him."

"Interesting, please tell him, I want to meet him tomorrow evening, and to be clear, I'm not asking, I'm instructing. Tomorrow, I want a meeting. We can meet by the river, I don't like it here all that much, so we can meet by Cleopatra's Needle, just down there. Nine o'clock should be fine."

Matt nods hesitantly, "Um, who should I say want to meet him."

Dominique smiles a warm friendly smile to Matt, "His maker."

Mat's eyes seem to bulge out of his head, but he nods his agreement.

"Thank you, Matt, why don't you go and make the arrangements," Dominique says, her voice kind and friendly.

"OK, thanks," Matt says and walks away, at a brisk human pace.

"We should get out of here and somewhere that smells a little better," Dominique says, as she takes Erika's free hand and walks at a casual pace away from the edge of the bridge.

After walking a few hundred metres, Dominique stops and says, "You can remove your hand now from your face, it should be alright."

Erika nods and tentatively removes her hand, sniffing cautiously at the air before finally dropping her hand.

"Questions?" Dominique says before Erika has the chance to say anything.

'Questions, where on earth to begin,' Erika thinks.

"How are you feeling? Do you need another little kiss?" Dominique asks.

"You know how I'm feeling and no thank you, that was a neat trick by the way," Erika says.

"I thought it might help."

"It was a bit mean though," Erika says.

"No, I thought it was kindness. There's no point in you becoming distressed over something that you have no control over. I think I handled it appropriately."

"They ripped their own faces off!" Erika couldn't believe what she'd just seen.

"Yes, they did and believe me when I say, it's going to hurt and take a good deal of time to heal. I doubt we'll ever see them again," Dominique says, sounding satisfied.

"I don't even know where to begin."

"I know, shall we head home and chat about it there?" Dominique offers.

"Yes, please."

Dominique nods and says, "Good." As they start to walk, she fishes her mobile phone out of her bag and sends a message, she slips the phone back into her handbag.

"What was that?"

"Just messaging a friend."

"What about?"

"This," Dominique says, gesturing around with her finger, "this should never have happened. Frankly, I'm a little upset that it did and more than a little annoyed."

"Is that why you did what you did?"

"Action is action. If you're going to deal with thugs, you must make sure they'll think twice about doing it again. Let alone to me again."

"And that bit about sunshine?"

Dominique sighs, "We'll talk about it at home." With that, she and Erika walk back home, seeing the sights, but blocking them out, each in her own thoughts.

Chapter 15

Dominique closes the front door of the apartment then removes her shoes. While waiting for Erika to place her shoes in the shoe rack, she intently watches her friend, looking for changes in her mood. When Erika has finished and begins walking to the lounge, Dominique places her shoes carefully on the rack and, as she turns to head to the lounge, there's a knock on the door.

Dominique turns and opens the door; Erika moves back to see who's there and looks surprised to see Gavin. Dominique makes an exaggerated sweeping gesture inviting Gavin into the apartment. "Thank you for coming."

"You messaged, I'm here," Gavin says casually.

Erika walks towards the front door as it closes, "You know each other?" Erika says confused.

Gavin looks questioningly at Dominique.

"Yes, we do," Dominique offers simply by way of reply.

"But you never said anything?" Erika questions.

"There was never anything to say. Shall we move this into the lounge and perhaps to the sofa and chairs. And if you need anything help yourself," Dominique replies.

"Gavin has free run of the apartment?" Erika asks.

"The public parts," Dominique confirms as they move into the lounge.

"I'm guessing Erika doesn't know who I am or why I'm here?" Gavin murmurs.

"Correct," Dominique replies.

"No, no I don't. I thought you were just my next-door neighbour," Erika exclaims unhappily.

"I am your next-door neighbour," Gavin says with a smile.

"And?"

"And I'm making sure you're safe," Gavin says keeping his smile.

"And the pizza?"

"All part of being a normal person. Can you see my aura?" Turning to Dominique, he asks, "Can Erika see auras?"

Dominique nods, "Surprisingly, yes."

Erika concentrates and shortly afterwards nods, "Yes. I can see it. It's pink, silver, and violet, with the colours blending it to one another, like mist drifting from place to place. I know silver is enthusiastic or maybe excited, violet is happy, but I don't know what pink is, I saw a darker pink earlier, but not this colour pink."

"I told you she could see them already," Dominique comments.

"That's impressive. Just so you know, the pink, the lighter pink is most likely sympathy, empathy, concern, sensitivity, or compassion. It can be any of those things. To me now, it means compassion," Gavin says casually.

"Does that mean you can see mine?" Erika asks.

"Yes, I can see yours, you don't look all that happy," Gavin remarks.

"Tonight's been very stressful and you being here is a surprise."

"I imagine it is," Gavin says. "Can I take you up on the offer of a drink?"

"In the fridge, use the strawberry juice, not the raspberry or grape," Dominique replies, "I'm fine for now, would you like anything babe?"

Erika shakes her head, "No, I'm fine too."

Gavin nods and heads towards the kitchen.

"Where would you like to start?" Dominique asks Erika from her position on the sofa.

"I have no idea. Too much has happened in such a short amount of time, that I have no idea how to process it or where to start. Firstly, Gavin's family. How did I not see that before? What the flippity-flop, happened tonight by the bridge. What did you do and how did you do it? Who is Jonathan and how does that fit in with what happened tonight?" Erika says, blurting it all out at once.

Gavin chuckles as he sits down in the chair opposite the sofa, "So I sense you have questions."

"All your questions are good and valid. The one that nobody's said that interests me is how did those ne'er-do-wells know that you were new and that I'd recently made you? That's very timely information, as it was only a matter of a few tens of hours ago. Not only did they know, but they also knew where we were. I don't like any of that," Dominique says looking at first Erika then Gavin.

"Before I talk about anything, I want to know who Gavin is, he's clearly not a random person who just happens to live next door to me," Erika says, looking at Gavin, then settling on Dominique for the answer.

Dominique glances at Gavin, then replies, "He's your guardian angel, so to speak."

"Guardian from what?" Erika asks.

"From anything you might have needed protection from. Well, at least when I wasn't there. He's put a lot of effort into being your protector during the day, when I've been sleeping," Dominique clarifies.

"Why didn't you have an associate do that, while you were sleeping?" Erika asks reasonably.

"Because I trust Gavin more. I also know that he could faithfully protect you from anything that could have happened during the day," Dominique replies.

"I thought everything was so much harder during the day, slow, tired and all that?" Erika queries.

"It is, which is why he's made a huge effort these last few years to look after you."

Erika turns to Gavin and gives him a half smile, "Thank you."

Gavin smiles fully and warmly back, "There's no need for thanks. I was happy to have helped."

"But that only half answers my question," Erika says.

"Interesting that she noticed that," Gavin comments.

"She always notices that," Dominique says, looking at Erika. "Do you know how we are using the analogy of people, family, etc.?" Erika nods, "Then from a practical purpose, Gavin is your brother. Older brother, but brother nonetheless."

"So, you made Gavin?" Erika said thoughtfully.

Dominique nods, "Yes, a while ago. Which is how he knows that you might be able to see his aura. Everyone I make, that he makes, and you make, will or at least should, be able to see auras. So, he knew that you should, but he also knows how new you are and it's frankly surprising that you can see them already. It took Gavin a couple of months. But, as we speculated already, that might be your sensitivity that's helping here."

"How much can she do?" Gavin asks to nobody in particular, but sort of to Dominique.

Dominique makes a flourish with her hand to indicate that Erika should reply.

"Um, I can see auras, but I don't know what all the distinct colours and changes mean. I know a few colours and the difference between bright and pastel. I can move quickly, and I can make my skin or muscles hard," Erika says hesitantly, looking for support from Dominique who says and does nothing. "I also have some sort of sensitivity, so eating is problematic. No, it's especially nice, fantastically nice, but I think it's probably a problem for that reason."

Gavin looks to Dominique, "And?"

"And she's progressed far beyond where you were at this stage. Being able to make her skin and muscles hard, as she puts it, is easily enough to stop a bullet or..."

Gavin spits his mouthful back into the glass, "Already?" he asks regaining his composure.

"You asked."

"So that will apply to any physical attack? Fists, claws, teeth, etc.?"

Dominique nods, "Yes, all of those things."

"How long does it take to prepare?"

"We've only done it once, last night and it took a while, an hour or so. But she tried to push blood into her skin, so the technique while wrong was smart. I think the next time, it will happen much quicker, as she now knows how to do it."

"Holy smoke, it took me a week to get that working," Gavin exclaims.

"As I said, she's doing very well. But," Dominique says, looking back at Erika, "but she doesn't believe me."

"Maybe Gavin wasn't very quick at learning," Erika offers.

Gavin bursts out laughing, "Could be."

Dominique watches Gavin for a few moments, while he stops laughing, "Don't be cruel Gavin." Turning back to Erika, she says, "Gavin, until you, Erika, was the fastest learner I've ever seen."

"Why didn't you tell me this before?" Erika enquires.

"I did, but you don't believe me."

"Do you remember how Rebekah responded when I got the hard body, and she couldn't?" Gavin asks.

Dominique nods as Erika speaks, "Who's Rebekah?"

"She's my sister," Gavin says, turning to look at Erika.

"Like I'm your sister?" Erika asks, the tone in her voice suggests there might be something she doesn't understand yet.

"No, she's his twin sister," Dominique says. "She's his older sister. Talking of Rebekah, where is she? I thought she was supposed to be in London with you?"

Gavin shakes his head, "She's in London, we're a team! So, obviously I have no idea where she is or what she's doing. Oh, and she's going by Laura now."

"What's the point of the two of you being here if you don't know where she is?" Dominique enquires, clearly dissatisfied at the situation.

"You know what Rebekah's like, she's all team, until she has an idea and then it's team Rebekah. I don't know where she is. But I imagine that there's lots of people that are unhappy about it."

"Yes, it's probably true," Dominique nods ruefully.

"If you want her, you can always request her presence."

"It would be nice for her to be about, with what happened this evening, but for now, she is probably best off doing whatever it is she's doing. Interrupting her isn't always the best plan," Dominique says.

"Fine, I'll do nothing to try and find her," Gavin says, looking at Erika asks. "Has she told you, that you're special?"

"Please don't get me started on that," Dominique chips in.

"She's mentioned it on more than one occasion," Erika confirms.

"And she doesn't believe it," Dominique comments.

Gavin sips at his drink before responding. "I'm impressed that the smell of my drink isn't having any or much effect on you," he says to Erika, adding: "It would have had a huge effect on me when I was like you."

"I think it's my sensitivity, as strange as it sounds, but it seems, that when I'm otherwise engaged or distracted, I don't notice the smell. Or maybe I do notice, but it's not important to me. Being full probably helps. We had breakfast a few hours ago," Erika replies.

"And you don't believe her?" Gavin asks.

"I do, but it doesn't mean anything to me. She says I'm special, but I don't know what that means. She's talked about a framework to understand things in and that I need to build that first, otherwise, it all just becomes meaningless information. Which frankly is just frustrating. I think she was going to tell me things, just before the thugs waylaid us at the bridge."

"How well do you two know each other?" Dominique asks them both simultaneously.

"Less well than I thought," Erika replies first. "We are neighbours, casual chat friends. We've never spent any real time together, just the hello in the corridor and the occasional casual talk."

Gavin nods, "Essentially that. But I know what she was and what she is now and what that means, in more detail than she does. Since I've been through what she's going through now and going to go through over the next few years."

"Then, I'm going to assume that you don't have much of a personal relationship. Like I do with both of you," Dominique says after a short pause to allow the others to jump in and add more detail.

'Where is she going with this, it seems like we're just going round in circles. Or at least not getting anywhere,' Erika thinks to herself. 'Does that mean that they're lovers too?'

"Firstly, my relationship with Gavin, is non-sexual," Dominique says, looking from Gavin to Erika. "As you'll remember and hopefully appreciate, that to us, that's all of us, there are things that matter more than sex. Let's address some of the problems of the night, rather than making more. Fair enough?"

Both Erika and Gavin give their assent, with both general sounds of agreement and nods of their heads.

"Alright then, lets deal with what happened at the bridge. I think you, Erika, misunderstood my apology at the bridge. I was apologising for the inevitable smell and distribution of blood, although, I think you thought it was something different."

Erika nods, "Sorry, I thought you were going to kill me."

"I know, I saw that in your aura, which is why I tried to reassure you and keep you calm," Dominique agrees.

"Are you serious?" Gavin says.

"Yes," Erika replies indignantly.

"You know that Dominique will do everything to keep you safe. That's why I'm here." Gavin adds.

"How do you know?" Erika asks.

Gavin chuckles, "Because right now, you're the most important thing in her world. You have been for the last few years."

"What?" Erika says surprised.

"You're the most important thing in her life. Rebekah and I being here is proof of that. I dare say, she'd have all of London killed before she'd let anything happen to you," Gavin says looking puzzled at Dominique. "Haven't you told her any of this?"

Dominique nods, "Yes, not in those exact words, but yes, I've told her this. I keep trying to tell her she's special, but it doesn't seem to make any difference."

"You've never said that to me," Erika says protesting.

"I've never used those exact words, but I have tried," Dominique replies.

"Then allow me," Gavin says. "You, Erika, are the most important thing or person or whatnot in London. You have been for the last couple of years. Since just before I moved in next door to you. Dominique made the previous occupant a fantastic offer to move out. He, or they, moved to a nicer and larger apartment on this floor, all for no cost. That freed up my apartment, so I could be next door. This enables me to keep an eye and or perhaps two, on you. See, you're safe. Proving I did a superb job."

"Was there any threat?" Erika asks seriously.

"No," Gavin replies, "but if there was, I was ready."

"So?" Erika queries.

"So, the point is, you've had someone looking out for your wellbeing long before the other night," Gavin looks at Dominique, "Not that I'm implying you're not looking out for her all the other times."

Turning to Dominique Erika says, "You set this all up a couple of years ago?"

"A little longer than that, but it depended on how the bits before went. It's impossible to see how events will unfold until they unfold. But I do like to be prepared and I had time," Dominique says.

"I don't know what to say?" Erika says, but thinks, 'how can I create a framework in this mix of information and revelation?'

"You can say, how fast are you?" Gavin asks.

"I don't know how to answer that question, because I have no framework to answer it in," Erika says to Dominique's smile.

"Dominique?" Gavin asks.

"Faster than you'd expect and much faster than average," Dominique offers.

"And technique?" Gavin prompts.

"Poor to average. What you'd expect. Some pointers and assistance would be of help."

"That I can do, if you're up for it?" Gavin says to Erika.

Erika shrugs, "I have no idea. If you say so."

"Excellent," Gavin says, "then you've got yourself a training session. I'm sure you've got time to fit a couple in."

"I suppose so," Erika says uncertainly.

"Good. Now what happened at the bridge?" Gavin asks.

"Glossing over the fact Erika thought I was going to kill her; we had an encounter with six thugs. They seemed particularly well informed, which I didn't care for. I want to come back to that because that's probably critically important. I don't know why, yet, but I think it is," Dominique says.

"OK," Gavin says, sipping at his drink.

"We met Matt, who was made by Charles. He recognised the key phrase Erika said," Dominique says.

"OK, so we have a close family member, and I haven't seen Charles since I've been in London. But then I have been keeping an extremely low profile."

"Charles is currently Jonathan, just for clarity's sake," Dominique says.

"I'd assumed as much."

"Matt seems like a nice young man; he was polite and friendly up to a point. It seems that Jonathan is looking into these thugs and Matt was his inside-man. Which, we unfortunately ruined. Erika was brave, there was a bit of a mess, when they ripped their own faces off, but we endured it. Though I imagine the smell was overpowering, but they left and then we did too. I messaged you and we all met up here."

"You missed out the death threats," Erika says chipping in.

"Yes, I did. They wanted me to kill Erika, or they would kill us both. Hence the ripping their own faces off," Dominique confirms.

"And your final threats," Erika prompts.

"I did as you can imagine, suggest that they should forget about us and if they tried to do anything to harm us, or get anyone else to do the same, they should go out in a blaze of glory," Dominique adds.

Gavin shakes his head, "Your poetic license is as lame as ever. Blaze of glory?"

"I don't understand," Erika says.

"Blaze of glory is her little joke for burning up in the sunshine. In case you didn't get it, she told them to destroy themselves in the sun. They will catch fire and burn to dust. It's not a pleasant way to die," Gavin clarifies.

"I see," Erika says looking intently at Gavin.

"On that note, how tough is she?" Gavin asks.

"She should be fine in the shade, any shade. Deep shade would be best, but I think any shade will do," Dominique says.

"Even in summer?" Gavin prompts.

Dominique nods, "The closer to midday, the more shade I would suggest, but I think she should be alright with some. Obviously in the depths of winter she'd be fine all day. But it's best to start out cautiously."

"Wait, did you just say I can walk in the sun in winter?" Erika asks.

"Yes, but it's not that simple. You can only do it if you have made your body hard. Technically we are calling it hard, but it's like everything else, more complex than that. You're really becoming resistive. Resistive to impacts, to sunlight, to puncture, etc. It's easiest to think of it as toughness at the beginning, as it's easier to conceptualise," Dominique says as a response.

"So, some way to go on that then," Gavin says.

Dominique nods, "Yes and she must do it by an effort of will. Her skill requires concentration, so she doesn't see auras all the time."

"That makes sense, but it's impressive she can do it at all at this point," Gavin says.

"I'm here you know," Erika says.

"I know babe," Dominique says kindly. "Gavin's trying to see how far you've developed and what he can do to help. Over and above keeping you safe."

"So how did you make them rip their faces off?" Erika asks.

"Basically, the same way I got those men in the club to tell us their secrets and give them suggestions. It's the same basic skill, but it's a little harder to do on family than people. Groups is harder than individuals, etc. I think you get the idea. This isn't something we can practice together. While you might be able to influence Gavin, he's far too strong for you to make it work. He can resist you too easily and it will be too dispiriting," Dominique says.

"Could he resist you?" Erika asks.

"If she chose too, no, I couldn't," Gavin says to Dominique's shake of the head. "Just the same as you couldn't. Just as you wouldn't be able to resist me if I tried."

"So, it's something I will be able to do?" Erika enquires.

"In the fullness of time, yes," Gavin says. "Now, because you probably don't know much about fighting, the act of tearing someone's face off, makes it much harder to heal. Partly because you can't just go out in public with a face partially missing, but partly because it's a sensitive part of the body, lots of nerves, lots of blood vessels and it's just harder to heal than the same damage to your arm for example. It's a devastating attack. Depending on how good they were at it, it could take anywhere from seven to ten days to heal properly, assuming they have good access to suitable food. How old were they?"

Erika shakes her head, "No idea. How can you tell?"

"I don't know either," Dominique says, "I would guess relatively young and somewhat weak. They didn't put up much resistance."

"What about the other part, that bit that's making you uncomfortable," Erika says looking at Dominique.

"Do you have anything Gavin?" Dominique asks.

Gavin shakes his head, "No, nothing of use. My thought is Jonathan is your best source here. He should have many contacts in the city, especially if he'd been here a lot of the time."

"That's fair," Dominique says.

"Rebekah, I mean Laura, would probably know something, knowing her, she's probably got some contacts. Contacts who should know something useful," Gavin adds.

"That's likely too. Can you try and get in contact. I would rather you do it than I?" Dominique says.

"OK," Gavin agrees.

"Then how about you two spend some time practicing fighting," Dominique says, "I'll watch and think."

Gavin stands and places his glass on the coffee table, "Come my young friend, shall we?" He offers Erika his hand.

Erika glances at Dominique who nods, and she takes the offered hand and walks over towards the balcony doors with Gavin. Dominique stays in the sofa, watching and thinking.

The rest of the night passes quickly with everyone engrossed in their individual activities.

Chapter 16

Erika heads into the bedroom to get her and Dominique's handbags. Leaving Dominique and Gavin in the lounge.

"It was good of you to come round; I know you need to get to bed," Dominique says to Gavin.

"Yes, I thought it was best, even though nothing's happened all day. I've put out the request to find Laura. But I don't know how long it will take to hear anything back, assuming, that's what she wants," Gavin replies.

"I understand. Tonight, should be straightforward. We're meeting friends."

"Are you going to introduce Erika as a fang-mate?" Gavin asks.

"Probably. It makes sense. There's not point in keeping it a secret from him."

"Are you sure he can be trusted?" Gavin enquires.

"I don't see any reason he wouldn't be. Do you?"

Gavin shakes his head, "No, but I'm trying to be careful. There's no need to take unnecessary chances. Well, if anything goes wrong, I trust you'll take care of it."

"I do."

"I know. Anything else?" Gavin asks smiling.

Dominique shakes her head, "I don't think so, enjoy your sleep and I imagine we'll see you tomorrow or the day after. If you hear from Laura, please arrange for us to meet up."

"I will. Enjoy your night," Gavin says.

"Enjoy might be a bit of a stretch but thank you."

"Night," Gavin calls towards the bedroom.

Erika appears with the handbags, "Night Gavin," she says with a smile.

With that all three of them head to the front door and put on their shoes. Gavin leaves first with a smile. Dominique and Erika, walk slowly down the hallway, in the opposite direction to Gavin. At the lift, they travel down in silence. It's only after exiting the building that conversation resumes.

"And my aura is?" Dominique asks.

After a short pause Erika replies, "Baby or light blue, the pastel version."

"Good."

"Am I going to have to keep doing that, what was the word, melee fighting again?"

Dominique nods and makes a mmm sound, "Until Gavin is happy, and you don't need to anymore."

"But why?"

"Because what he's helping you with, could one day save your life," Dominique says, heading to the railings by the river, where she stops and looks out over the water.

"What are you looking at?" Erika says, joining her.

Dominique turns and looks Erika directly in the eye, "I know you have a problem with confrontation."

"I don't," Erika protests weakly, but indignantly.

"You do. You've had that block ever since I've known you, which means, it predates your legal profession, so it has nothing to do with court."

"I did have a problem with confrontation, but it's one of the reasons that I went into litigation and did the whole adversarial court appearance events," Erika reluctantly confirms.

Dominique remains quiet a moment then says, "I think that you've found a way to make you think you've dealt with it, without actually dealing with it."

"Why do you say that?" Erika queries.

"Think about it. The court room is a well-controlled environment, with the proceedings choreographed, who does what. When they do it. Who's in control at any one point. All looked after by the judge."

'Oh, I hope this isn't true,' Erika thinks to herself, 'but it might be!'

"Even if I'm wrong, you still have the problem. It was extremely clear last night at the bridge. Come on, lets walk," Dominique says, turning to walk off.

Erika turns and they start walking towards Cleopatra's Needle and their meeting.

"If you're right, what do we do about it?" Erika enquires.

"Baptism by fire is the best option," Dominique replies.

"What?"

"In at the deep end. The next time we have a situation, like last night. Unless I say otherwise. You're to deal with it," Dominique says simply.

"I've no idea how to do that," Erika protests.

"I trust you're listening to Gavin and taking on board all his suggestions? Learning techniques?"

Erika nods, "Yes, I'm doing both."

"Then you'll be fine, and I'll be there. You know he was right; I'm not going to let anything happen to you. Regardless."

"I'm not ready for that," Erika protests.

"Of course, you are. Now, on to tonight's meeting. Jonathan, originally Charles, should be friendly. I've not seen him for a while, but he's your sibling too."

"Did Gavin really say fang-mate earlier?"

Dominique chuckles, "You heard that. It's part of his sense of humour. He thinks its funny."

"It's quite witty," Erika confirms.

"I suppose. Anyway, Jonathan might be able to help us with our unknown problem. The who and the how so quickly."

"Do you think Matt will be there?"

"Probably, but, just so you understand, Matt is younger than Jonathan, but you are Jonathan's peer, not Matts'." Dominique says, glancing sideways at Erika.

"I think I need to discuss this with you and Gavin. Everything you say, is right, but he seems to explain it better."

Dominique mimes a stabbing motion to the heart, "You wound me with your harsh words."

"As if."

"He might be of assistance, granted," Dominique says loftily.

"What else with Jonathan and Matt?"

"No idea, we'll have to see how it goes."

"Will they be on time?" Erika asks, clearly curious.

"Yes."

"And he will show up," Erika asks.

"Yes."

"How can you be so sure?"

"If I asked you to come and meet me if you hadn't seen me in years, would you?"

Erika nods, "I would."

"Besides, I didn't make it a request."

"I remember that," Erika says.

"Because of that, he'll know it is important. If it was, otherwise, it would have been a request."

"We're here, but no sign of them?"

"There's still ten minutes before they're late, we should sit on the bench over there," Dominique says, pointing to a bench nearby facing the water.

They walk over and sit down when Erika asks, "Is Jonathan like Gavin?"

Dominique replies, "What do you mean?"

"Well, you asked Gavin to look after me, not Jonathan, there must have been a reason for that."

"Ah, yes. Gavin is exceptionally good at what he does, and this is part of that. Jonathan has a different inclination. He's very much into his politics. Always has been, I imagine he always will be. Gavin and I have that in common, we don't like the politics. But I understand and respect that someone must be. I'm glad it's not me," Dominique explains.

"Are you expecting me to be like Gavin?"

Dominique shakes her head, "No, I expect you to be like you. Follow your passions and interests. That's why I respect Jonathan. I would respect him a good deal less if did something that wasn't himself."

"What is it you think my passion is?"

"That's something for you to know and to tell me, not the other way round. And our visitors have arrived," Dominique says standing up from the bench.

Erika quickly stands up as she watches the two men approach.

Matt, dressed now in a white polo shirt, dark blue cargo shorts and a pair of sports shoes, speaks first, "I hope we haven't kept you long?"

Both Erika and Dominique smile at Matt, Dominique responds, "Not at all, we were just enjoying the evening, the pre-sunset dusk. Don't you find it pretty? The colours, the way they reflect on the river and the buildings."

Clearly caught slightly off balance by the question Matt murmurs, "Yes, sort of."

"I find it endlessly fascinating. It's different every evening. I don't know how long you've been around, but it's worth spending a little time from time to time, to enjoy the beauty of nature and of civilisation," Dominique says. "That really applies to you too babe."

Erika takes the time to look around at the impending sunset. Jonathan's attention divided between the sunset, Dominique, his general environment, and surroundings.

Dominique moves closer to Jonathan, taking in his appearance, khaki knee length shorts, loafer shoes and a white button-down collar shirt. It looks nice, but not exactly casual. She takes in his form, his movements and with a wide smile, embraces him in a warm friendly hug. Jonathan reciprocates and the two hug like old friends.

Jonathan whispers, "May I?"

"Of course," Dominique responds in a whisper, with that, Jonathan sinks his fangs into Dominique's neck and draws blood from her body. He drinks for five seconds, then abruptly stops, closing the wound and giving her a gentle kiss on the lips. "Oh, that was nice," he comments.

"It's nice to see you too Jonathan, anyone else?" Dominique says with a smile.

Erika shakes her head, clearly embarrassed. 'Can you do that in public, just like that,' she wonders.

Matt hesitates, obviously tempted, but decides better of it and shakes his head, "Maybe another time."

"As you wish," Dominique says kindly, "Shall we sit or walk?"

Matt shrugs and seems to have no preference, Erika makes no effort to respond, simply watching the other three. Jonathan simply says, "I'd rather walk, if you don't mind. I don't feel completely comfortable here."

"So, I gathered," Dominique says. "Lead on. Oh Erika," she says turning to Erika, "did you see their auras?"

Erika nods, "Yes, when they first arrived."

"Can you still see them?"

"Yes," Erika confirms.

"What do they tell you?"

Jonathan and Matt look bemused at the exchange.

"Matt when he arrived was, I think uncomfortable, but as the talk started it became more relaxed. Not exactly calm, but less orange and more blues. Jonathan, his has been strange. When he arrived, it was like Matt's, then it went a dark red, then it too went blue. The red was when you were hugging."

Jonathan smiles, not quite a chuckle, but close, "Oh, I see what you're doing. You're learning. What do you think the dark red means? The one you've clearly not seen before or often before?"

Erika shakes her head, "I don't know, and I'm not prepared to guess in front of all of you."

The response elicits a laugh form Dominique, "Matt, would you please help her out."

Matt looks helplessly at Jonathan, who ignores his non-verbal plea, with a sigh, he says, "Lust or intense sexual desire. Something of that nature."

"Thank you, Matt," Dominique says kindly, "that was helpful."

Jonathan doesn't seem bothered at all, "Let's go upriver."

With that comment, they all turn and walk slowly up the embankment, towards the Houses of Parliament.

"Do you feel more comfortable upstream?" Dominique asks Jonathan.

"Yes, this isn't really my territory, so being here is potentially problematic," Jonathan replies, while Erika and Matt listen.

"This would be the politics you so enjoy?"

"It would, my territory is upstream from here, and it takes time and effort to travel outside it. As you well know, but don't care about," Jonathan comments wryly.

"That's true. Are you enjoying yourself?"

"You mean with the politics and the life in London?"

Dominique nods, "Yes, that."

"Yes, I think so. It has its good points and the bad."

"And this is currently a down. I can see it, clear as day. I see you're not controlling your aura," Dominique comments.

"No, I've found that in many places, it's easier not to and I didn't want you to misinterpret anything that happens tonight with either Matt or I."

"Matt has already proven himself to me and you don't need to. You should know that by now," Dominique says matter-of-factly.

"Well, I haven't seen you in a while and, well, I just didn't want any misunderstandings. I didn't know why you wanted to meet."

"Because, I haven't seen you in decades. Well, that and what happened last night with the thugs that Matt was a part of." Dominique pauses and looks at Matt, "Doesn't that mean you were out of your territory too?"

"Technically, yes," Matt confirms, "but..."

"But," Jonathan says, "but, currently, things are not that easy. Can I tell you something and you all promise to keep it secret?"

Erika and Matt both simultaneously say, "Yes."

"Maybe, as far as is practicable," Dominique offers.

"Oh, come on Vicky, how hard is it, just this once, to be helpful," Jonathan says, traces of exacerbation in his voice.

"If I need to tell someone, and I really mean need, then I will tell them," Dominique says, "and it's Dominique now."

"Yes, sorry," Jonathan says, "Matt did tell me, and I forgot."

"Which is not like you at all," Dominique says.

Jonathan sighs, "No, sorry."

"What's on your mind?"

Jonathan moves closer to Dominique and whispers, "The King and Queen are losing their grip on the city."

Dominique stops a moment, then starts walking again, "Are you sure?" Her pace change upsets everyone else's pace and momentum.

"I think so."

"Run it past me, how do you know," Dominique turns to Erika, "and I'll want your analysis on this. You too Matt," she says glancing to Matt.

"Matt's thoughts will be biased with my own," Jonathan says, "but, that incident last night with you two, that wasn't a one off. It and others like it have been happening all over London for the past few months."

"Then you might be in luck, the twins are in town," Dominique comments nonchalantly.

"They're here? Why?" Jonathan asks, an edge of concern in his voice.

Dominique slides her finger towards Erika, taking Jonathan's gaze with it, "Though, in fairness, we don't know the whereabouts of Rebekah. So, if you see her, please let her know I would like a chat."

"I haven't seen her, but I'll keep an eye out. But this is now one more thing to worry about," Jonathan says.

"Don't worry about things, it'll give you wrinkles. Don't you read any of the magazines or watch the adverts?"

Unable to help himself, Jonathan laughs, "Don't tell me you've been caught up in the consumerism of the age?"

"Of course not, but it made you laugh. I consider that a triumph."

"She does this to me all the time. You have no idea," Erika says looking at Dominique.

"Of course, she does," Jonathan says, his voice clear and friendly.

"Matt, please accept my apologies for rudeness, but how old are you?" Dominique asks.

Matt looks to Jonathan for guidance, this time he nods, and Matt says, "One hundred and ninety-two."

Erika looks surprised, Dominique nods slowly, "Thank you. That helps." Turning back to Jonathan, asks, "What other evidence do you have that they're losing control of the city?"

"The gang that Matt was with, they're one of many. I suspect that they are all coordinated to either bring down the current reign or are at best capitalising on the weakness of the King and Queen. There seems to be gangs like last nights in all the different territories, wreaking all kinds of havoc, clearly, it's bad for keeping order, but most importantly, as you saw, they're not too worried about exposure."

"How did they know that Erika was new and that I had made her? This is bothering me and to a lesser extent Gavin," Dominique asks.

"Gavin?" Jonathan asks.

"Jacob, the twin. Rebekah is going by Laura. Just so you know."

"Oh, right, so Gavin is on this too? Matt never mentioned him."

"Matt was correct, he wasn't there. He mostly keeps an eye on Erika during the day," Dominique clarifies.

"He's on babysitting duty, now that's funny!"

Dominique shakes her head in admonishment, "Now be nice."

"Alright and it's best not to forget who he is," Jonathan tentatively agrees.

"Precisely, now back to our problem. How did they know about Erika and me. At that point, it had only been a few tens of hours and I didn't think anyone, but Gavin knew."

"We don't know," Matt says, "but we have some theories."

"Don't keep us all waiting," Dominique says.

Matt clears his throat, "We suspect, that someone in court is either controlling the gangs, or at least supplying them with information. The problem is, they seem to have quick, actionable information. Which fits with someone high up in the court knowing and passing it along. However, if you didn't tell anyone about you and Erika, then I don't see how that fits with our known information. If nobody in court knew that you'd made Erika, how could they pass it along. If they didn't, how did my gang know. I don't know, Joey, the leader, never told me how he got the information, just that he knew things."

"Could it be a coincidence?" Erika asks.

Jonathan shrugs, "I don't know, but I feel it's critical that we find out."

"Could all this be a shade?" Dominique asks.

"It could, that possibility has crossed my mind. A way of seeing who's loyal and who's not," Jonathan suggests.

"What's a shade?" Erika asks, cutting Matt off for the same question.

"A feint or a ruse. A deception with, as Jonathan says, the intent to determine who's loyal and who's not. With the information available, we have no way of knowing if this is a shade or not. I don't feel like I know enough about the goings-on in town to know one way or another and I don't think I want to expend that kind of effort either. Sorry Jonathan," Dominique says.

"I wasn't expecting you to, it's a surprise to see you and any assistance, let alone help is always appreciated and I do know how you feel about politics," Jonathan says.

"As we seem to be the anomaly," Erika says, "does it make sense to focus on how they knew about us or me and what that might say or lead to?"

"OK," Matt says, "when have you been out and about?"

"I've only been out for walks twice; I mean there's not been much chance. Today is my third outing. Which means, yesterday was my second. I'm sorry, I don't really know how to count days, when they run evening to morning, rather than morning to night. It's confusing with the day change in the middle of the day. I'm sure I'll get the hang of it, but just now, it's complicated," Erika says.

"And where did you go?" Jonathan prompts.

"Up and down the river. We also walked to the door of the King and Queen's court, the castle; they waylaid us on the way back home," Erika adds.

"It's possible that the gang knew that Dominique was going to make someone new. That's public information and they've been following her, then when they saw her with someone, and that new person had a pale aura. Well, then they would know," Matt says.

"It would explain you as an anomaly, but if that's true, then it doesn't get us any further than when we started," Jonathan says with a sigh.

"No, it doesn't," Dominique says, "you said there were other groups. Where are the members coming from. Making new members it tightly regulated and the one's we met yesterday, they already knew. They were years old, your typical I'm special because I'm family, but other than that, unremarkable. Lots of bravado, but not much else."

"That was one of the things Matt was hoping to find out, but after months, he came to the same conclusion as you," Jonathan adds.

"What do you want to do?" Dominique asks.

"I need to keep digging and find a solution that works for all the facts I have. Maybe, this is real, and London is up for grabs," Jonathan says with a grin.

"You fancy yourself as King?" Dominique asks.

Jonathan smiles, "It has a ring to it don't you think."

"I suppose," Dominique offers, "but you know that's not how I see the world."

"I know, but this is my thing," Jonathan says.

"We'll do what we can to help. Have you changed your mind about a hug Matt?" Dominique asks.

Matt looks uncertain but shakes his head, "No thanks. But thank you for the offer."

"You should," Erika says, "it's really nice."

Dominique shoots a surprised look at Erika who shrugs. Matt smiles and says, "I'm sure."

"Then short hugs all round and we'll see you soon," Dominique says and hugs first Jonathan and then Matt, Erika does the same.

"Goodnight, ladies," Jonathan says with a smile, as they part company and go off in different directions.

"That was interesting, don't you think?" Dominique says as she turns for home.

Chapter 17

Erika and Dominique walk slowly back along the embankment towards home. The lights now illuminating the city, dancing over the water, and rippling as boats move the water slowly towards the bank.

"What did I you make of all that?" Dominique asks.

"There's a lot going on and I think it's going to be complicated," Erika replies.

"That's fair."

"Something's been bothering me for a little while, on a different topic," Erika says tentatively.

"What is it?"

"The other day, you said you, then you said, we, have enough money to last until the end of civilisation. What did you mean by that?"

"Which part?"

"Let's start with the civilisation part."

Dominique says nothing for a few seconds, when she finally speaks, asks, "Where would you like to start?"

"How about the end of civilisation?"

Dominique's grin comes through in her voice, "Once again, your question is much more nuanced and complex than you imagine. This seems to be a speciality, that I perhaps hadn't noticed before."

"There's more than one?"

Dominique nods, "Oh yes, many more. I could probably narrow it down to four, maybe three. Depending upon the detail you want to get into."

"There's four types of the end of civilisation?" Erika asks, the incredulity clear in her voice. "You are saying there are four ways that civilisation can end?"

"More, but we can start with the easy three, does that make it manageable?"

"Yes, please go ahead."

Dominique theatrically clears her throat, "Alright, imagine a recession, something that boosts the unemployment a bit, businesses close and spending drops."

"That's easy, we've had recessions and civilisation didn't end," Erika confirms.

"Fair enough, but just because something doesn't happen every-time, doesn't mean it cannot happen at any time. Let's take the example of an office building. They're normally owned partly by the owner and partly by the bank. It only takes a percentage of tenants to leave. It doesn't matter what their contract says, if they have no money, then they will leave and you, the owner, will be out of pocket. Do you have enough reserves to keep the building payments going when the recession continues?"

"I don't know, that's hard to answer," Erika replies cautiously.

"Exactly but get it wrong and you lose the building to the bank. Now all the money you put into the building is gone and it's now the bank's problem. But you lose all your investment. It's not the end of the world, at least not yet," Dominique continues.

"That doesn't seem so bad for an end of civilisation."

"Bear with me, if that recession gets a bit worse, then it becomes a depression. Now, a depression is a totally different beast than a recession. First, many people will not just be out of work, but they'll struggle making house payments, car payments, their mobile phone, streaming services, everything. At some point, they then struggle to have somewhere to live and ultimately struggle to find enough food to eat."

"What about unemployment benefits and help for those out of work?" Erika suggests.

"That's fair, but where does that money come from?"

"The government."

"And they get it from?" Dominique prompts.

"Taxes."

"Which come from?"

"Workers."

"Thank you," Dominique says, "and in a depression, what are you short of?"

"Workers."

"Exactly, so the government must borrow money. That comes from those who think the government can or will pay it back later. If nobody thinks they'll get their money back later, then no loans."

Erika considers it for a moment, "But that's quite extreme. Nobody buying government bonds. Large numbers of people out of work."

"It's not particularly extreme, it's different than now, but that's what the end of civilisation will look like, something different from now. Different than everything being fine. That's by definition, I would suggest."

"That's true," Erika confirms.

"Then you're going to love the next bit. So, people start getting short of money, which will cause all kinds of problems. Supply chain disruption, which will have knock-on effects, in distribution. What's the rule, that civilisation is only nine meals from anarchy?"

"Yes, I think something like that," Erika concurs.

Dominique nods, "Which means, that after about three days, people start to get unhappy about the lack of food or at least perceived availability. Another interpretation is that after three days without food, people get very hungry and therefore unhappy."

"That makes sense."

Dominique grins, "It would seem that people have their own monster within when they get hungry, doesn't it."

"Oh, I never thought about it like that. So, in this regard, we're the same."

"Yes and no, just remember when they get hungry, their options are different to yours. People don't and will not do, what you will, so similar, but different. Back on topic, what do you think people will do when they're out of food and no real prospect of more food any time soon?"

Erika considers her words carefully, "Riot and looting, most likely. They'll want food for their family, for their children, wife, husband, that sort of thing."

"That's my expectation too. In the event of rioting and looting, what do you do?" Dominique asks.

"I don't know."

"Be somewhere else. There's nothing gained by being around out of control crowds. They'll hurt you just as soon as ignore you. Anything in their path is either a barrier or worse, they'll see you as competition and want to put you out of the contest. Which would be bad for all concerned."

"Then what can I or we do?"

"First of all," Dominique says, "you need to make sure you can eat. In turn, this means you're probably best served by making sure that some of them can eat too. Your kindness will serve you well. Think of it as farming. You keep your herd alive, and then you have food. That might mean providing them shelter and food, or maybe only food. If you think you can get by without the assistance, then feel free to skip it. Your own preservation takes priority."

"That sounds cold?"

Dominique shakes her head, "No, there's nothing more you can do. The worry is that they see you as trying to take their resources and they will be desperate, so you become a target. You see yourself as separate, but they do not have that clarity and understanding of the situation."

"So, I should exploit the situation?" Erika asks tentatively.

"You're a predator, that's what we do. I mean, functionally, you're a barrister. From an honest look at society, what beneficial value does a barrister add?"

"We help people with the law," Erika says, indignation creeping into her voice.

"Law, which originally helped people, now serves the lawyers. Parliament creates new laws every day. Which isn't a surprise as most parliamentarians are solicitors of some stripe. It's all they do in parliament. When do they remove old laws? That's a question to you," Dominique asks.

"They don't, the politicians only create new ones."

"Which benefits the lawyers, solicitors, and barristers. Rarely is the intent to help the taxpayer."

"That's a bit cynical," Erika says.

"Tell me how I'm wrong?"

Erika considers the request, "Nothing is coming to mind."

Dominique waits a moment before continuing, "Anyway, back to your original question. It's necessary to have access to a suitable food source, securing your own when necessary is sensible. That might mean overseeing the organising of a food bank, or setting up the equivalent of a soup kitchen, as they did in years gone by. In general, it's best to use buildings of others, such as a community centre, a church, or maybe a disused office building. In this situation, there will be many empty buildings."

"If I'm understanding correctly, try and help, but keep a low profile and ideally ruin other people's property first."

"Good girl," Dominique confirms with a grin.

"That's it?"

"No, of course not. Remember that building we had before. Suppose you kept it, or you had already repaid the bank loan. You now have a large asset, that nobody wants, because the occupancy rate is dropping as more companies go out of business. At some point, you must decide, do you keep the building, continue with the maintenance, or sell it very cheaply to someone who thinks the world will get better soon, or at least much sooner than you do?"

Erika, getting into the swing of the conversations replies, "Once again, it's impossible to know. It will depend on the situation on the day."

"Excellent. I see an entrepreneurial future for you," Dominique says happily.

"Now you're mocking me."

"Not at all, this is exactly what we're talking about. How to deal with a collapse. Let's assume you keep the building. You're now offering maintenance work and need materials. If they're available, then both should be available at a discount. The merchant will want to sell products and the worker will want to eat. A win for everyone. For as long as you can afford the building and its upkeep."

"And if I sell?"

Dominique nods, "Then the problem goes away, and you lose the difference between the investment and the sale price. Probably a lot."

"This all seems straightforward," Erika says, "so what's the catch?"

"There's no catch. You need to ensure that you stay alive. The important part is that the people around you will be losing their grip on reality. Or perhaps their definition of reality will begin to diverge from how they saw the world before the depression and how they see it now. That change will be very profound. They will do the things that desperate people do when times are hard. Seeing success when they are failing, will not make them happy. You need to factor that in too. If the depression goes on too long or is too deep, then all bets are off."

"What?"

Dominique continues, "We've never seen a full economic collapse in such a connected and integrated situation. Look at your smartphone. It's made of parts manufactured all over the world, all brought together in the same place and turned into a pocket computer. Your trainers, your shorts, top and your handbag. They ship parts from all over the world to make them. I don't mean just the finished parts, but the raw materials too."

"I never thought about it that way. If payments get stuck, for any reason or the flow of materials gets stuck, this could all collapse?" Erika asks, as much as states.

"Exactly and we've never seen a civilisation so interconnected with all the others before. The world is now almost one interconnected whole. If one-part collapses in the wrong way, it could easily bring the rest down."

"That's two, I think. They're both economic and one could lead to the other. I see how that could work. What next?"

Dominique walks to the railings and looks out over the river, when Erika joins her, she says, "This one you'll like. It's called the PAW scenario."

"PAW, what does that mean?"

"Patience, it means post-apocalyptic wasteland," Dominique says.

"That sounds grim."

"And it is. It assumes that there's been a complete collapse of civilisation, such as after a nuclear war. Feeling cheered up yet?" Dominique says with exaggerated chipperness.

"Now they're just fantasy scenarios."

Dominique nods, "Of course it is, right up until it happens, then it's no longer a fantasy."

"So, it is a fantasy," Erika confirms.

Dominique glosses over the confirmation, "On the bright side, radiation shouldn't affect you. Try to avoid the blast and the fire, other than that, you should be fine. The trick is surviving afterwards."

"Wait, what? Run that past me again."

"Avoid the blast because it can tear you, limb from limb and obviously debris in the wind. Fire, fire is bad for you, bad for the skin, bad for the complexion and hurts. If it gets bad enough, you die."

Erika chuckles, "Again."

"Again," Dominique confirms, "but the convenient bit, is that people all over the world have worked out how to survive afterwards. Which is extremely helpful."

"How do you know?"

"The internet. There are websites for everything, including the post-apocalyptic wasteland scenario. Now, from a practical point of view, much of what they need, we don't. We have no need for medical supplies, water purification systems, guns, tents, warm clothes, cool clothes, waterproofs. You get the idea. But, their surviving, well, that's good for you. Once again, we do what we can to keep them alive. Those that can survive, you help, those that cannot, those well, you get the idea," Dominique says, slipping her arm through Erika's arm and continuing their saunter towards home.

"That simple?"

Dominique pauses a moment, "Well, not quite that simple, if there are no people, you can always hunt animals. Which will be easy for you, as you've already gotten past the hard part."

"I have?"

"Yes, you have. Most family will turn their nose up at animals, but they're just as nutritious as any other source. They taste different, but they'll keep you alive just the same and the feeding rules are the same, don't kill them unless you have no other choice. Farming is better than hunting. As we've already crossed that barrier, you should be fine. I've done it before now, it's not as nice tasting and the sensation isn't as satisfying but being alive is better. Many will not make it past that barrier."

"What else?"

"Well, we've considered financial collapse, but there are other possible triggers," Dominique says walking lightly, despite the topic of conversation.

"Such as?" Erika asks.

"Such as, plague, which is a type of biological pathogen that runs rampant and finally causes an economic collapse. Practically, no matter the trigger, the final collapse will be financial, I think, because everything in modern civilisation is based on money. At some point it all comes down to money or finance. So, a disease causes people to stop working, perhaps from fear or maybe death. They then stop working and that causes the problem. Just look at what happened in the fourteenth century with the Black Death. It caused people to be fearful of interacting with other people. Which caused them to isolate themselves from each other, which in turn stopped them trading, which then cut the production of good and services, which in turn caused the economy to collapse due to lack of commerce. Once that happened, how did people get enough money for food and other products. In fairness, that situation is not like today, as they, the people, were mostly self-sufficient. In that they could grow their own food, make their own clothes, etc., in the modern world, people cannot grow their own food or make their own clothes, etc. If you cannot do that, then the collapse will be worse."

"Which means you think it will be worse?" Erika prompts.

"I'm not thinking in that sense, I am only answering your original question. But, yes, it could easily be like that, and I do think when it finally collapses, it will be very inconvenient. Probably the worse ending of civilisation."

"Why?" Erika asks.

"Why? Because everything is now so interconnected, and nobody can do anything, let alone everything for themselves. Let me ask you a question. What items or things, can you or anyone you know, that you need daily, can you or they produce?"

"What me?" Erika asks, the pitch of her voice rising significantly, "I can't make anything. That's the point of having supermarkets to buy food, clothes shops to buy clothes and all manner of speciality sources of goods and services. The specialist produces a better product or service for less input resource. In practice, it's cheaper and easier than doing it myself. It's why I'm a barrister."

"Exactly," Dominique says enthusiastically. "That was my point, nobody is self-sufficient, which means in the event of a collapse, it all vanishes. Let's consider the obvious. What happens without electricity?"

"I suppose the lights go off and you cannot access entertainment, fridges and freezers stop working and people have to go home from work," Erika says cautiously.

Dominique nods, "Yes, all of that, plus, what about water, which needs electricity, so does sewage. The transport network, computers to communicate with each other, the failures cascade. The more systems go out, the more subsequently fail, which causes more to go out. This process continues until there are no systems working. If we lose electricity, then we quickly loose civilisation. I don't see any way around that. Do you?"

"Businesses have generators and battery backup systems. We have some at work. The building has generators to provide power to all the apartments," Erika says.

"It does, but how long will that last and what happens if the systems outside the building don't work. The building's design called for the generators to cope with sporadic intermittent outages, not for a long-term civilisation wide calamity," Dominique counters.

"Then, what you're saying, is that if the power goes out for any length of time, then civilisation ends?"

Dominique nods, "Essentially, yes. In that case, we have resources up until that point and then we're on our own. More or less."

"Once again, that's bleak."

"Anything you've thought about, isn't a surprise. That's one of the things that sets you apart. Imagine that civilisation ends, what do you do?" Dominique asks.

Erika shakes her head, "I don't know."

"Assuming I'm not about and that you're on your own, you must survive. That means blending in with the other survivors. Ultimately, they're your survival. Which might mean, you do need medical supplies, as you need to keep them alive. You might need access to food, as they need to eat. So on and so on," Dominique says, prompting Erika.

"All right, which makes sense. My goal is to survive no matter what."

"Almost," Dominique says, "but you must do it in a way that maintains your loyalty to me and to those of your close family. If possible, you should work together. Them and you, to everyone's mutual benefit. After all, together we are stronger than each one individually. This will make more sense later."

"Just to clarify, my first priority is to my survival, then to helping my immediate family, then to helping those who can help us?"

Dominique nods, "Exactly, that is your priority. It's, of course, easier said than done, but that's the general plan."

"How do you know when there will be a collapse?"

Dominique shrugs, "I don't have any special insight. I read, see what the leaders are doing, what they say and what's happened before. Taking all those things together, I imagine a collapse will happen. Not today and not tomorrow, but sometime. It will take a huge change of attitude in the political leadership of the country and by extension all countries to avert it and I don't see that happening anytime soon."

"Why not, people can change their vote and get better leadership." Erika counters.

"Perhaps," Dominique offers, "but I don't see any better leadership on the horizon. I don't see any entrenched interest wanting to give up their power, privilege, or position. The world, or perhaps, I should say, people don't work like that. They never have done, and I don't see this batch suddenly changing that trend."

"But people can change."

"They can, but they don't. It's as simple as that. You hear people all the time, complaining that evil has overtaken the world and that the evil doers will receive judgement in the afterlife. But that is a way of simply abdicating responsibility for doing anything in the here and now, and hoping that someone, in this case a god, will make them pay later. Otherwise, it implies that the so-called evil people will benefit from their evil and there's no sanction on them later. In essence they get away with it. When, in fact, the people responsible are more than happy with this arrangement, as it means they can get away with it, and they do. Simple really."

"How do you know that's true?" Erika enquires.

"I don't, but I believe it to be true. They get away with it, because everyone wants someone else, in this case a deity, to take care of it for them. Nobody wants to interrupt their nice cosy life," Dominique says simply.

"Then why don't we do something about it?"

Dominique turns and looks horrified, "Why would we want to do that?"

"To make life better for people."

"Can you imagine what would happen if all the peoples of this planet suddenly started agreeing with each other and getting along?" Dominique asks, horror draining from her voice.

Erika shakes her head, taken aback by Dominique's reaction, "No, not really. People would live a better life and there's be less conflict and death."

"There absolutely would be less conflict and death. But considering human nature, what do you think they'd start doing?"

"I don't know?" Erika replies innocently.

"They'd look for something else to wage war and generate conflict with. Any guesses as to who that might be?"

The light of understanding begins to light up Erika's eyes, she offers, "Us?"

"Exactly, us! There's a reason, that we spend so much effort ensuring that they don't get along. A word here, a provocation there, it doesn't take much, but it requires constant attention and constant vigilance. That all takes time and effort, that's better utilised elsewhere. But luckily for you and for all of us really, that's handled by others. We absolutely do not want them collaborating and getting along. For you, for me, that would be worse than a nuclear war. The PAW scenario is a better outcome than what you just proposed. So please, don't mention such dangerous things to others, they might not be so understanding." Dominique warns.

"What?"

"You just proposed the genocide of our race. Not everyone will take such proposals in the spirit in which you intended them."

"I...," Erika stumbles, "I didn't mean that."

"I know, but others might not be so generous. So, please keep that to yourself."

Erika nods, "I will."

"Good, now those other possibilities, war is an obvious one, win or loose, it could be bad either way. Loose will almost guarantee a loss of civilisation. Famine, that's another easy one. The cause of crop failures could be war of course, but the cause isn't as important as the result. There are some others, but it all ends basically the same, the only change is the starting point."

"How do you know all this?"

Dominique grins, "The internet. There's so much you can read and learn. People have thought about just about everything. Every scenario for every outcome and starting position. All of it you must read, absorb, and learn. A little experience to understand and separate out the good from the bad, the plausible from the implausible. That kind of thing. On the forums, they bounce ideas off each other, refining the question, the answer, and the solution to both. It takes time, but it's been going on for years. You can learn almost anything there. Fantastic invention."

"This is how you use technology?" Erika says, slightly disappointedly.

"I use it to make me and mine better, stronger, and more likely to be here in the future. As far as I can see, there's no better use for it. If people are going to help me, why would I stop them."

"That's very mercenary."

"Predator, remember," Dominique says, with an evil grin.

Erika shakes her head woefully, then nods, "Yes, I do remember."

"Then it's time you started to think as a wolf and not the sheep."

"How?"

"It'll take time, but the most important thing you can do, is to be open to the change. You are not one of them, they don't represent you and basically you shouldn't identify too closely with them."

"But a few days ago, I was one of them," Erika insists.

"And now you're not, which is why I said, it will take time for you to make the change, but to do so, you need to accept the shift in your perception. Until you make the shift, you cannot adapt," Dominique falls silent for a few moments. "Perhaps we need to find a way to make this whole thing feel more real to you?"

"How? What does that mean?" Erika says, alert to impending possibilities, not all of them good.

"I don't know just yet, but I'm sure I'll think of something. Oh, and does that answer your question?"

"I'm not sure I really remember what the question was."

"Then I'll take that as a yes. But, if you think of something else, please feel free to ask. I do so enjoy these walks and our chats," Dominique says with a mischievous grin.

"Really, I find them quite daunting and somewhat uncomfortable."

"Then perhaps you should ask more questions and get used to the answers," Dominique says, taking in the small amount of activity along the riverbank. "On the topic of uncomfortable, are you looking at everyone's aura as we walk past?"

"No, not really," Erika replies, looking at the aura of the nearest person.

"You should be, the more you see, the more frequently you do it, the easier it becomes. In future, do it all the time to everyone you see. You can always ask what the colours mean, but make sure you see the aura on everyone."

"That's going to be quite tiring."

"Yes, it is, so you'll sleep well when we go to bed."

"You know it requires concentrating and moving blood and all that?"

Dominique nods, "I do and the only way to get better is to do it more and there's no real danger at the moment to you practicing and doing it correctly."

"Alright, I'm doing it now, but if I stop chatting, you'll know why," Erika says reluctantly.

"Fair enough, do you fancy a long walk or straight home?"

"A short walk and then home."

Dominique grins, "Short walk and then home it is."

Chapter 18

Erika closes the front door as Dominique unzips the sides of her trainers, slipping her feet out and placing them onto the shoe rack. Erika does the same and then walks into the lounge.

"What's my aura?" Dominique suddenly asks, clearly changing the topic of conversation.

Erika pauses momentarily, "You're happy."

"Good, it's getting quicker."

"Maybe, it doesn't feel like that, it feels like a lot of work, that never seems to end."

"Then trust me, it's getting quicker, and I think you're concentrating less on doing it too. Which, honestly, is excellent progress," Dominique says supportively.

"Can I have something to eat?" Erika asks, "I've been doing this for ages and frankly, I'm feeling a bit worn-out."

"Warm or cold?"

"Warm?" Erika says questioningly.

Dominique sits on the sofa, places the cushion behind her back, sits partly towards the front and partly towards the side; and then pats the space between her legs, "Sit here." Without speaking, Erika silently sits between Dominique's legs and leans back, to see a wrist appear in front of her face. Erika takes the offered arm in both hands and puts it to her lips. Her fangs extend, they puncture the skin, and a warm, sticky fantastic tasting liquid runs out. Erika cups her lips around the wrist, the wound and begins to drink slowly. Dominique stays quiet as Erika slowly drinks from her wrist.

As Erika slowly drinks from her wrist, her head resting back on Dominique's shoulder. Dominique with her spare hand caresses Erika's head, gently caressing the hair.

Time passes and Dominique says, "Time to stop."

Erika stops drinking, licks the wound closed and relaxes with a sigh, "That was nice."

"Good," Dominique says, "I hope it makes up for all the aura practice."

"Mm, yes. Why does drinking from you, not make me go all spaced out?"

"Because, when you drink from my wrist, you drink very slowly. When you drink from the glass, you drink much quicker, at least you consume much quicker. The rate is what keeps you with us."

"Then, if I drank from the glass very slowly, it would have the same effect?"

"Yes, that's most likely the case. But, and this is the problem, you're going to have a real struggle with controlling the rate from the glass. It's just too easy to drink quickly or at least too quickly," Dominique says, as she drops her arm into their shared lap.

"Alright, then I'll stick with your mixture, which seems to work quite well, at least for now."

"Yes, it does," Dominique agrees, "one step at a time, I'm sure that over time and I mean weeks and months, the situation will improve."

"I hope so. Can I ask a couple of questions?"

"Of course, ask away."

Erika pauses a moment, "It's about things that we're vulnerable to. Does garlic affect us?"

"Only as far as making your breath suspect. It's not fantastic at the other end, but I wouldn't worry too much about it from a safety perspective," Dominique says lightly.

"Good, that's been a worry. What about all the other things."

Dominique sighs and places her hands over Erika's tummy, "I see where this is going, and I've been dreading this talk. Not because it's all that complex, but because it's so large."

Erika grins, "So, there's a topic you dread!"

"Just remember, where your neck is, and my mouth is. For the sake of confusion."

"Point taken."

"In common circles, you're a creature of evil. I think that's fair, and most sources will back that up. Is this where you are going with this?" Dominique enquires.

Erika nods awkwardly, "Yes, mostly."

"What do you know or think you know or worse, suspect you know? Don't bother distinguishing between the three, they're all the same for the purposes of this conversation. I'll imagine the rest."

"What about barriers or circles made of salt?" Erika asks.

"Ideal for making margaritas, if you have some lime or triple sec on the rim of the glass, otherwise, not of much use. The obvious exception is for icy pavements or paths. It can help with that. As far as mortal danger, it counts as a zero. Waste of time and effort."

"People sleeping with a circle of salt around their beds?"

"Salt is salt, it makes no difference the shape of the pointless barrier."

"Um, are we evil?" Erika asks hesitantly.

"Please protect me from movies," Dominique comments, "no, you're no more evil than you were last week. So average."

"What?"

"It's perspective. If you take the perspective of someone who doesn't have much money, lives in poor conditions, without access to running water, must scrimp and save and perhaps uses dung to cook. Then yes, they will see you as evil. You have too much, so evil you are. Simple."

Erika play bumps Dominique's leg, "You know that's not what I mean."

"I know, but you didn't ask a proper question. So, what I did respond with was perfectly correct. Even if it's not quite what you were looking for."

"Then are we creatures of evil cursed by God?"

Dominique traces her fingers over Erika's stomach, "No, we're not creatures of evil, cursed by God. Does that help, do you feel better?"

"No, because I think you're now answering my exact question, but avoiding the spirit of the question."

Laughing Dominique responds, "There's no pleasing some people."

"You avoided my question again."

"There's nothing about you that's evil. You are inherently a good woman; you always have been. You're not inherently cruel, you don't try to be spiteful or anything like that. These are all reasons why you'll be here for the long haul." Dominique clarifies.

"To clarify, I'm not evil?"

"No, you're not and you shouldn't worry about it. Some people are evil or what you think of as evil. But you're not one of those people." Dominique hesitates, then adds, "Those thugs we saw last night, you might as well include them in what you call evil, they were looking for trouble and to make others' lives less pleasant. That's not you."

"And what about in the biblical sense of evil? You know, in league with Satan?" Erika prompts.

"You want to talk about religion, when we were having such a nice evening?"

"Maybe."

Dominique pauses a moment, "Fair enough. Then let's get some of the religious iconography out of the way. Crosses, they can make nice jewellery, they have no effect on you, unless you choose for them to. Holy water, in a push can be a drink, but in all truth, it's normally too dirty to consider like that. Once again, if you choose a phobia, that's one some choose. What else do we have, wooden stakes. Best to avoid those, they can do some damage. They won't kill you but if pushed through the heart, will make you immobile and from there, vulnerable. What else do you want to know about?"

"What else is there to know about?"

"Mystical sticks and branches, they're just decoration and perhaps an inconvenience. You're not a demon, so bells and seeds have no effect on you either. To all intents and purposes, you're a normal person who's now deader than a door nail. With the added benefit that you can walk about and talk. You're a supernatural entity. That means you exist outside of nature."

"Is that all?"

"No, not quite. There's a belief that a vampire cannot enter someone's home without an invitation," Dominique offers mysteriously.

"Yes, I've heard of that."

"It's a myth, it has no effect on anything. There's nothing special about a house or a place someone lives. You can enter any house you like, apartment or flat. There is one restriction that you should be aware of."

"What's that?"

"Most people lock their doors and breaking them down makes a lot of noise and draws unwanted attention. The same goes for windows, smashing them makes noise, draws attention, and can cut your hand. So, if needed, best to use a hammer. Better still, be friendly and people will invite you in and offer you coffee."

"Now you're playing with me."

"A little bit," Dominique concedes, "but you're worrying about fiction and myth. Where do you think these myths and legends come from?"

"I don't know, where?"

"From us of course. By placing false information into fiction, books, movies and the like, people know how to defeat a vampire," Dominique grins. "All immensely helpful, to us that is."

"Which means it's all fake? All made-up and untrue?" Erika asks sceptically.

"Mostly, yes, as previously mentioned."

"Then where do we come from?"

"No please don't go there," Dominique says, doing her damsel in distress hand pose, with the back of her hand against Erika's forehead.

"Are we descended from Cain?"

"Didn't I just say, don't go there?"

"You did, but are we?"

"No," Dominique says emphatically, with an air of certainty.

"That's it, just, no?" Erika queries.

"Yes, no."

Erika pauses a moment thrown off, as she thinks, 'This is the first time she's ever answered a question yes or no.' "I didn't think you could answer a question so succinctly?"

"Well, that one was easy. You don't normally ask easy questions. They're normally complicated in ways you don't understand," Dominique says defensively.

"But not this one, one that I thought would be complicated. With an easy answer, you got it down to one 2- letter word."

"Correct."

"How can you be so sure?" Erika prompts.

Dominique sighs, "Because all religion is a human construct. This is part of that and so, by definition, it's also made-up. Simple deductive logic."

"All true, assuming your foundational premise is correct."

"Which it is," Dominique says confidently.

"You seem very sure."

"I do, because I am."

'This really isn't going so well,' Erika thinks to herself. "How can you know that your foundational premise is correct."

"It's simple, but you won't believe me, or won't want to believe me," Dominique counters.

"I will."

"I doubt it."

Erika holds the hand over her tummy, "I will."

Dominique sighs, "Alright here goes. Religions are a chain of beliefs. We'll start with Christianity. I'm telling you; you aren't going to like this."

"Get on with it."

Dominique makes a deep sigh before continuing, "Right, Christianity is a product of the Cult of Mithras, Judaism and Zoroastrianism, all three went into the foundation of Christianity. Some will claim that there's aspects of Hinduism, we'll cover that shortly. Judaism, that you already understand, the Cult of Mithras was a cult of mysteries cantered around the worship of the bull. Zoroastrianism, well that's a little more complex."

"You're making this up?" Erika protests.

"No, no I'm not. The First Council of Nicaea in about 325 anno domini codified what you now think of as Christianity. That's over three hundred years since the birth of Christ. Or if you prefer, more like twelve or thirteen generations. Very few people have memories beyond death. But going back a bit. Judaism, that came from a blending of the wisdom of our friend Zoroaster and a little Hinduism. Zoroastrianism and Hinduism shared a common religious ancestor, which had an ancestor, etc. Because of that, I know that they are all human constructs and therefore the answer was no."

"You're having a joke at my expense." Erika insists.

"You asked and so I am delivering. In fairness, if you take Judaism, over time, which evolved. Let's take a step back. You're familiar with the idea of heaven and hell?"

Erika nods, "Yes."

"Well, Zoroaster created that idea, well in truth, he expanded on an idea from the ancestor religion that his system was based upon. But he was the first to codify those exiting beliefs into a religion or practice. The creation of all religions happens this way, or thereabouts. Someone, someone usually clever and charismatic will expand on ideas already present in society. Those ideas become crystallised and if the proponent of the new way of thinking can get traction for his ideas, then the new religion takes off. Often, they use bits from existing belief systems, this makes it easier for people to accept and adopt the new ways. A classic example of this is the date of Christmas. It subsumes the pagan winter solstice festival or festivals, depending on where you are."

"How do you know all this?" Erika asks.

"Then if you go back a little further, then you get the magic beliefs, which happened before the god related beliefs. One led directly to the other. Then if you trace the magical systems back, they get more straightforward as they connect increasingly with the land, fertility and the growing of crops. See, it's all quite simple. Oh, and the curious thing, is that Zoroastrianism and Hinduism seem to have a common ancestor and that they are almost the opposite of each other. Good gods in one are bad in the other, etc. It's all remarkably interesting. The interesting part of Judaism is that they started off with a pantheon of gods, in that they acknowledged the existence of the many, but they celebrated and worshiped the one. Then over time, they dropped the many and focused on just the one."

"How do you know all this is true?"

"The internet of course, you can find out all kinds of information. Didn't I mention it earlier? I'm sure it was only a few hours ago!" Dominique says with an air of narcissism.

"You did, but you also said, that it was important to know the difference between the true sources and false ones. How do you know that the ones that you found were true and not the false ones," Erika asks.

"I have my ways. Now what's fun, is that Islam derives from Christianity and Judaism. Then if we look at Christianity alone, we have the two major or perhaps three major denominations, Orthodox, Catholic and Protestant. Then all the offshoots of those, such as the Seven Day Adventists, Church of Latter-Day Saints and on the Catholic side, Opus Dei, the Jesuits. The list goes on and on. They all claim to have revelation from God, as they are all derived from the same foundation, they use the same god. But go back a little and there are more and other gods and goddesses."

"This is a whirlwind of information," Erika says, struggling to keep it all together and process it into her frame of reference.

"It gets better," Dominique enthuses, getting into her stride, "you're worried about the devil or Satan, well, there's no worry there. Originally Satan as we know it, is from the Jewish tradition and he was an angel of God, a judge, tasked with finding the worthy and the unworthy. Well, technically separating them from each other. That, over time, morphed into something else, until he became in the Christian tradition a figure of evil. It's all easy to find and easy to follow. More importantly, it's all an artificial construct devised by humans to make the world seem a better place. Well, that and to exercise control over the followers, get them to give the leaders money and power."

"If all of that's true, then why do people follow religion?" Erika asks cautiously.

"You smell very nice," Dominique says, brushing Erika's hair to one side, "may I?"

"No and stop avoiding the questions."

"Spoil sport," Dominique says letting the hair drop back into place. "That one, I don't know. Maybe it makes them feel better. Or perhaps, by doing what everyone else around them is doing, they feel more connected to the group. That question is beyond my knowledge and understanding."

"I can understand that I just thought I'd ask."

Dominique makes a theatrical show of inhaling, but getting no rise from Erika, continues, "Now, if we look at the rituals of the different religions, then things do become interesting. Let's take the idea of ritual sacrifice in Judaism, which, of course, flows into Islam. Who do you know who would be interested in draining the blood out of animals when they're slaughtered?"

"You're kidding?"

"No. Who?"

"Family?"

Dominique kisses Erika's neck, "Exactly. It's very clever. Embed yourself in the priest structure, convince people that God needs the animals drained of blood, to make it holy. Then for the sacrifices, render the flesh inedible, which is fine, as you already saved the useful part. Then make a big show of burning the lamb and rendering it waste. What would please God more than making it worthless and so giving it away for free."

"That's very clever."

"I agree, I wish I'd thought of it. Like all things, over time it changes, morphs, and adapts. Until the people do it without thinking, they produce vast amounts of spare blood which when captured, ends up in the fridge. Waste not, want not and all that." Dominique kisses Erika's neck again.

"If you don't stop that, I'm not going to continue to cuddle."

"Fine. So, you see it's possible to make a religion useful for us. I have no issue with them saying prayers over my food. I know what it means and why it's there. It's funny that all the people thinking that it's important have no idea of their history or religion. I suppose that's the power of it, people blindly following what they're told by people who know better. Or at least claim to know better."

"Assuming what you've said is true, I don't see why people follow religions," Erika says.

"Well mostly, they don't know any better. Who in the church is going to explain that people over the centuries made it all up to enrich the church and the priests?"

"None, I suppose."

"None indeed. Which means, the congregation isn't going to know. Go back in time, I have no doubt that it started out as something other than a power grab, but as power accrues, organisations or the people in the organisations in this case, want more power and wealth," Dominique says. "It's one of the reasons that we need to be low key and keep out of sight. When you have power and are visible, others will see that, and it then makes you a target. Being a target is bad. It's one of the reasons that I don't want to have anything to do with politics. See, ultimately, it all comes back around to the same few themes. Power, money which gives power. Prestige, which gives money and power. But, when someone knows you have power or money, they can try to take it away. If they don't know, then well, let's just say it's better if they look elsewhere."

"I can understand that. It makes for an easier and safer life."

"Yes, it does. It's one of the reasons, that I don't appear to have much money. Enough, but not much. I have an apartment, but no car, no flashy jewellery, no flashy clothes. Everyone who knows me in both business and my personal life, can see that I live within my means. Which implies that they don't look too closely at me, which then helps to keep a low profile."

"Once again, that makes sense," Erika says, leaning forward out of Dominique's embrace.

"See, simple, as I said at the beginning."

Sitting up and looking at Dominique properly Erika asks, "Is what you said all real?"

"Yes, all of it. Why?" Dominique says nodding.

"It just sounds so extraordinary, so impossible."

"I've been around a little longer than you and seen and learnt a little more. I'm not trying to pull rank or anything like that, but from what I've seen, it's all true."

"I'm still reeling from the possibilities of all of this." Erika admits.

"Why? Isn't it straightforward?"

"The way you say it, yes, but there's more to it than that. The church's teaching, that I've received all my life that there is a God and that going to church will save my soul."

"I don't really know anything about saving your soul, but the church is just a building with people in it. Did you ever hear of the Nag Hammadi scrolls?"

Erika shakes her head, "No, I don't think so."

"Well," Dominique says moving to a more traditional sitting on the sofa, "they paint a different picture of early Christianity than the one present in the Christian bible, the one you're familiar with. The Gnostics, consider Satan to be the inspiration for the bible. See how they built on parts of the earlier tradition but interpreted it all differently. It's really fascinating if you investigate it in any depth."

Erika holds out her arm with her wrist pointing up.

"Is that for me?" Dominique enquires coyly.

"Yes, it is. Enjoy."

Dominique's fangs slide down and in a single effortless motion, they've done their job and she begins drinking from the offered wrist. A minute passes before Dominique stops and closes the wound. "Now that was nice. We should do this more often."

"It's better when I have your wrist," Erika says a tinge of disappointment in her voice.

"Yes, but fair's fair."

"Is what you've told me true? Or have you been telling me a tall tale?" Erika asks.

"To the best of my understanding and knowledge, it's all true."

"Can you prove it?" Erika asks, "Any of it?"

"Prove is an exceedingly high bar, particularly with history. Being a barrister, you should know that the further back in time one looks, the harder it becomes to find proof."

"That's true, to an extent."

"When we next get the opportunity to talk with Gavin, we'll ask him for his opinion. Fair?" Dominique suggests.

"Yes, that's fair. Although I suspect he will tell me exactly what you want him to tell me."

Dominique chuckles, "You've only been one of us a few days and already you're a cynic. And yes, he probably will, because it's the truth, or at least near enough what happened, for the purposes of our conversation."

"What are we going to do for the rest of the night?"

"I was thinking a little aura practice and some melee training. Just because Gavin's not here, doesn't mean you shouldn't continue training. Then we'll go to bed a little early...," Dominique says.

"Some holiday this is turning out to be."

"Shouldn't have fallen in with a bad crowd and gotten yourself dead, should you."

"Fine, your plan is acceptable."

Dominique grins knowingly, "I know."

Chapter 19

Erika slides her feet into her slippers and walks from the bedroom to the kitchen loosely tying the silk belt of her dressing gown. As she arrives, she sees Dominique is not there, but in the dining area, sitting at the table. Dominique has nothing in front of her, just an empty table. "Is everything alright?" Erika asks, a hint of concern in her voice.

"To the best of my knowledge, everything is fine," Dominique replies.

"Then why are you sitting at the table?"

"I'm waiting for breakfast," Dominique says simply.

"What?" Erika asks confusion evident in her voice.

"Breakfast, you know, the meal you have when you first wake up after a long sleep."

"I know what breakfast is."

"Excellent," Dominique says brightly.

"Oh, you want me to make breakfast?"

"Exactly."

"What are you having?"

Dominique grins, "My usual."

"Right! Which is which in the cartons?"

Dominique shakes her head, "That's for you to work out. Don't forget you're on half and half."

"Sometimes you're so cryptic and it's mildly infuriating."

Dominique's grin reappears and widens, "I try."

"I have no doubt," Erika says, moving to the refrigerator and removing the relevant cartons. She sniffs at both and then retrieves glasses from the cupboard. "I think I have this correct. The earthy one is mine, right?"

"If you say so."

"You're going to make this hard on purpose, aren't you?"

"No, I'm giving you the chance to make the choice and an opportunity to learn and be in charge," Dominique says.

"I get all that by making breakfast?"

Dominique grins again, "Yes you do."

"Fine," Erika says pouring out one full glass and another with half from one carton and the rest form a second. "Do I need to mix them?"

"Pouring like that should be good enough, but you can if you want."

"I'll try it without and then stir it if necessary."

Dominique nods approvingly, "The efficient option."

"Good, because nobody likes to think of it as lazy," Erika says, bringing both glasses over to the table, she sets one down in front of Dominique.

"Thank you."

"And you're sure this one is mine?"

"Yes, sure," Erika says, sipping at her drink.

Dominique takes a sip of hers and laughs, "Very funny!"

Erika grins, "Do you like it?"

"And yours?"

"Fifty-fifty as per the recipe."

"And mine?" Dominique says.

"Raspberry."

"Alright," Dominique says, sipping at her drink.

"You're taking this awfully well."

"Food's food," Dominique says simply, before sipping at her drink again, "although, I'd prefer the strawberry next time. As I'm sure you knew."

Grinning Erika says, "I'll see what I can do."

"You do that funny girl."

"I will. On a different subject, what are we going to do tonight?"

"I don't know, I don't have any real plans. I was thinking we need to reschedule with Adam and Anita. We still need to go round there for dinner."

"I thought that was too risky?"

Dominique sips at her drink several times before replying, "I have noticed something about you, and I don't think we have any problem with that in the future."

"What's that? What have you noticed?"

"As I think, I mentioned before, it looks like you only seem to get all spaced out when you drink too fast. If you drink slowly, it's fine. When you drink from the wrist, you seem fine. So, I'm thinking that it has to do with you drinking too much too quickly. The irony is, the hungrier you are, the faster you're likely to want to drink. Which will, of course, make the problem worse."

Erika noticeably takes smaller sips of her drink, "Is that true?"

"It seems to be, you can drink from my wrist without problem, but if you drink from the glass too quickly, you lose yourself. I don't know this with certainty, but it is my working hypothesis."

"Well, that might be good news. As having a solution is a step in the right direction. Correct?" Erika says, sounding happier about the subject.

Dominique finishes her mouthful before attempting a reply, "In theory yes. We'll have to see how it pans out in practice. But step one is to have a theory and then to test that theory."

"Then on the basis of testing theories, what do I need to do?"

"Nothing yet, but we'll see."

"Alright. Then, on the general subject of socialising with Adam and Anita, I need to bring up another social event."

Dominique's eyebrows rise as she listens and then drop as she speaks, "What social event?"

"On Friday, when we were having my birthday and promotion party at work, I was talking with Elle, and we agreed to go to the theatre over my holiday."

"And did you two have a play in mind while hatching this genius level plan?"

Erika finishes her drink before replying, "No, I thought you'd know something good. What do you mean by genius level plan?"

"Well, do you plan on eating Elle and I'm guessing Andy's coming too, so are you planning on eating him?"

"What? No, of course not," Erika retorts.

Dominique nods slowly, "Right, you're not planning to do it, so it'll be a surprise to everyone when it happens."

"What? No, it won't they're my friends, our friends."

"True, but that's not the dynamic here, is it. Things have changed since Friday lunchtime. Do you remember the Friday evening events?"

Erika makes an exacerbated face, "Of course I remember. It was fabulous."

"Good, because it's important to distinguish dancing at Dystopia and sitting next to someone who smells so very nice for several hours. In the first case, you have a lot of generalised smells. In the second, you have a few smells that get more intense and interesting as time goes on. They will become all you focus on. I'm not sure that you're ready for that yet, but you've already made the commitment, so we'll work though it as best we can. Trial by fire, I believe they call it."

"If you think we need to, we can always postpone or cancel the theatre visit. I wasn't really thinking about all the potential problems when we were talking."

Dominique finishes her drink, "I know. We'll muddle though. It's just that you might not enjoy the play as much as you might otherwise. Anything you fancy seeing?"

"I have no idea what's on."

Dominique slides her chair backwards and looks longingly at her glass, "Please miss, is there more?" Not waiting for a reply, she heads into the lounge and retrieves a tablet computer and quickly begins working the controls, she suddenly stops and catches Erika collecting glasses, "Did you mention which theatres you wanted to visit?"

Erika pauses a moment, "I think I mentioned the National Theatre and the Vic."

As Erika prepares more drinks in the kitchen, Dominique walks back to her chair at the table. "There's Othello at the National. Getting tickets for that should be straightforward." She continues typing on the screen and scrolling. Finally pronounces, "There's nothing at either the old or young Vic that I'm interested in seeing."

"Is there anything else on at the National?" Erika asks, sitting a glass down in front of Dominique.

"Romeo and Juliet, something called Jackie's Journey, I'm not sure what that's about. Volcano the mind boggles as to what that will be. I think I'd rather watch Romeo and Juliet than something too avant-garde. Sometimes plays go too far. Although Romeo and Juliet, does have a suitable amount of gruesome death. No blood, but they'd only use fake blood anyway." Dominique sounds a little disappointed at the last thought.

"I'll mention it to Elle and see if they want to have dinner first."

"Now that's brave, eating out and then a show. If possible, skip the dinner, I don't want you under too much pressure. Besides, the play starts at seven-thirty and runs for about three hours. So, I'm not sure what we could do that would give us dinner after work and allow us to get to the theatre," Dominique says, collecting her drink and sniffing the glass.

"Well, there's options."

"I'm not going to have fast food. Eating is enough of a concession, without stooping that low."

"Then what do you suggest?"

Dominique sips at her drink a moment, "You could propose takeaway, eaten at your apartment. That'll seem more natural, as she's been to your place before."

"Alright that works. I'll call her when we've had breakfast."

Dominique shakes her head, "Best to do it now, it's later than you think." She gestures at the clock, "See."

Erika puts her glass down and sighs, "Alright, I'll be back in a few minutes, and don't steal my drink."

Dominique grins innocently, "Would I?"

"I don't know, probably. I've heard that vampires are sneaky," Erika says standing and heading to the bedroom.

"Allegedly," Dominique quips as Erika disappears.

Dominique sips at her breakfast while she waits for Erika's return.

As Erika leaves the bedroom and appears in the main living area she says, "Done. She's going to come to my house straight from work on Friday. Andy will come from work and should be here, or thereabouts, by six. Which means, we have time to eat and then make it to the theatre."

"Good, what did you agree to get for food?"

"Chinese, I'll get a selection. Give them most of the food and say, we're watching what we eat, trying to stay in shape after overindulging already on my holiday."

Dominique takes another sip before replying, "That's a good plan."

Erika grins triumphantly, "I thought so."

"You did well. That's a workable solution to the problem. But we're going to need to have a chat."

Erika narrows her eyes, "Chat about what?"

Dominique shakes her head slowly, "Eating."

"Didn't we talk about that before?"

"Talk no, mention yes," Dominique says.

"What else do I need to know?"

"I've told you that you're special. I've said it several times and I know that you don't believe me." Dominique holds up her hand to stop Erika's protestations. She continues, "It's the nature of us, that you don't understand. We're not entirely natural, but we sort of are. We're not exactly supernatural, but we sort of are. This makes it all very tricky."

"Now I don't understand," Erika says with a sigh.

"A truly supernatural creature wouldn't be created from a natural one. They would be purely supernatural. I suppose the most obvious example would be an angel. They're not made from people, but spring into existence fully formed as angels."

"Didn't you say that all religions were created by people for power and wealth."

Dominique sighs, "I did, please focus on the specifics of the example, not the wider picture. Whether angels exist or not doesn't matter for now, it's the bigger picture that does. Now, where was I? Yes, you're part natural and part supernatural. It makes for some interesting problems. Eating people food, is one of them. At least in passing."

Erika pointing says, "You're being vague."

"And you're pointing and not eating breakfast. It's widely accepted, and it might or might not be true, but widely accepted that we all descend from a first or original vampire." Dominique takes a large mouthful of blood and lets it settle in her mouth before swallowing. "This batch is much better. Then each one made, they're a little less strong than the one who made them."

"So, each generation, becomes a little weaker than the one before. It doesn't really make sense, but I'll go along with it, since you're the expert on this." Erika concedes.

"Basically, yes. As each generation, as you say, becomes weaker, they loose abilities and capabilities over time. While you can eat, there are many in London who cannot. I'm going to say that they're too weak to process people food through their system. You can, but many cannot."

Erika takes the glass from her mouth, before sipping and asks, "Why is that?"

"I don't know, but I've seen it and in some it causes such a reaction that they will literally vomit it back up, along with some of the food they've drunk."

"That sounds ghastly," Erika says. "But, alright, but why does it matter?"

"It matters, because, if they believe that family cannot eat and they see one eating, it means that you're somehow different. Different isn't good in this case. It singles you out and therefore makes you a target."

Erika relaxes a little and sips at her drink, the red clinging on to her teeth, "This goes back to your theory on being noticed."

"Believe me, it's more than a theory. But yes, standing out like that isn't so good. For someone like me or Gavin, it's much less of a problem, as we can take care of ourselves if something goes wrong. You're not currently in such a position."

"This is part of why you're with me all the time and Gavin lives next door, right?" Erika asks.

"Correct. Family like you are exceedingly rare, rare in a way that honestly you won't understand, even if I tell you. And before you ask, I'm not going to tell you."

"Will you tell me soon?"

Dominique nods with her mouth full, once it's empty, she replies, "I will. I promise. I don't want to keep things from you, but I must prioritise what I tell you and that means the things that do matter today, not those that are academically interesting."

"Alright, it's frustrating, but alright."

"Good, now back to food. Not this," Dominique says, gesturing with her glass, "You can eat, you will sort of digest it. It's complicated, but the bacteria that lives in your gut, the healthy bacteria, etc. that you see in the adverts and all the rest, it will continue to sort of process the food, but you cannot absorb the nutrients, as they don't do you any good, so they will just pass through. Which is why I mentioned about the garlic. Ingesting it is perfectly fine, but your digestive system doesn't work the same anymore. So, it will pass through semi-digested. By semi, I mean for you, maybe twenty percent digested, the rest," she shakes her heads, "not digested. I imagine that you've already noticed that."

Erika nods, "It's hard to miss it."

Dominique chuckles and takes another sip, "Yes, it's hard to miss. But you get used to it. On the liquids side, you can ingest any liquid that you like, I mean food wise, but the only thing that will give you nutrition is the red stuff. Drink alcohol if you want, coffee, tea, hot chocolate, it doesn't matter. All the liquid will be absorbed, all the rest, that passes through and out with the faeces."

"So, liquids are acceptable and solids to be avoided?" Erika asks cautiously.

"Yes, sort of. You need to eat a little, so that your digestive tract moves things through. You can't let it stagnate too long, as it contains material, and you don't want it to rot. That would be bad, but eating too much, will put a strain on your body. You'll get a feel for what works and what is going to be a problem. But, like so much here, you need to be careful and work with your body. Which is why you're drinking half and half, and this is much nicer that your first oh so transparent attempt."

"Are there any foods that are better or worse than others?"

"Not really, just like all the experts advise, everything in moderation. Fibre is always helpful, but you'll just need to work it out for yourself. I imagine that some foods will work better than others for you. Just as some work better than others for me."

"I think there's a wrinkle in your plan. You said before, that in the event of a collapse or a PAW event, that I could get by just drinking from animals. But this seems to say I must eat people food too?" Erika asks, trying to clarify the apparent discrepancy.

Dominique holds the blood in her mouth a while and swallows slowly before answering, "Both are true. You can get by, but, if possible, keep the digestive system moving. If push comes to shove and you're not going to eat for a while, you can always clean it out. The exact details of that I'm going to leave to your imagination and an internet search. If you don't already know how. Starting it up again is slow and less than comfortable, but straightforward."

"So, how does that work?"

Dominique wiggles her glass, indicating a refill. Erika sighs, quickly finishes hers and starts to become spaced out. "Too fast, I think. Concentrate and you'll get though."

As instructed, Erika fights through the sensation and keeps her focus. A moment or two later says, "That was close and thank you."

Dominique winks, "You're welcome, babe. If you want more, have some, but I would like some more please."

Erika pours out another glass for Dominique and half for herself. As she returns, Dominique speaks, "Everything you do requires blood. Whether warm or from the fridge doesn't in practice make any difference. It also makes no difference if it is human or animal. So, to use what you call your secret powers, which requires the use and direction of blood. When you make your body hard, that uses blood. When you want to make your body restart digestion, which you must do, if you want to eat people food, then you need to use blood. You use a certain amount of it every day. The more active you are, the more you need. That's why we have breakfast every day. But, as you probably have noticed, if you don't do much, you don't feel the need for anymore. But when you're active, you feel the need for more. Which is why looking at auras all the time makes you hungry. For the record, I think you probably need more than you've had so far today. Your goal should be to always be full. That way, if you ever must exert yourself or be without for a time, you're still in excellent shape and the monster within is, well, kept deep within and under control."

Erika sips at her drink more slowly than before, "So, blood is everything. Is that why Jonathan wanted to taste yours when we met at Cleopatra's Needle?"

"It's a little more that that. You know how you feel when you drink from me and how the drink you have tastes?"

"Yes, you taste so much better, this is a distant second."

"Exactly. Any vampire tastes so much better than a person. So, when given the chance of a friendly drink, most will take it. Jonathan is like you, only a bit older, so he tastes the blood very similarly to how you do. Although he doesn't have the sensitivity, so it doesn't taste quite as good to him as it does you. But, to him, I taste fantastic, and he hasn't had anything like this in a long-time."

Erika sips at her drink, "Then a vampire would always like to drink from another vampire?"

Dominique hesitates, "Yes and no. The blood of another vampire will taste better than a person, but there's significant risk from drinking from another vampire."

"What's the risk?"

"Generally, it's either considered at best as rude, or at worse as an attack. It's common to drink a vampire's blood in combat. It weakens them and strengthens you. So, they can easily perceive the drinking of their blood as a threat to their life and most will react in that way."

Erika stops drinking, "That sounds like a good reason to not to do it."

Dominique grins, her fangs sliding into place, the red blood staining the inside of her mouth, a small amount deliberately on her lip, "Unless you want to kill them."

"Now that's creepy."

"Not suitable at the dinner table?"

"No, we're sophisticated here," Erika confirms.

"Anyway, if you want to talk about fighting and combat, you'd best talk to Gavin. He'll happily teach you all there is to know."

"You don't know how?"

Dominique shakes her head, "I do, but I just don't want to get involved. What are we going to do today or tonight, are you used to the idea that a day is really part of two days yet?"

"I don't know to the first and no to the second."

"Then let me give you a shortcut," Dominique says. "Think of the two parts as Monday and Monday plus. The plus part running into the next day."

"That makes sense," Erika says, "I'll give it a try."

Dominique quickly drinks the remainder of her drink and says, "Then perhaps you'll have an idea over a shower and getting ready?"

"Perhaps, but probably not," Erika says, sipping at her drink, not rushing.

"I'm glad to see that you're not rushing it. We'll get ready as soon as you're finished."

Chapter 20

As the automatic doors close behind them, Dominique slips her arm through Erika's and guides her as they walk down to the river, then onwards towards the Tower of London.

"We're heading towards the city?" Erika says curiously. "What's down there?"

"The usual, buildings, the Bank of England, that sort of thing. Nothing, in particular. I just felt like walking in a different direction tonight. Do you mind?" Dominique says simply.

"No, I was just curious."

"Walking towards the dawn, it doesn't have the same ring as riding off into the sunset, does it?"

Erika chuckles, "But we're not making a movie, are we?"

"No, we're not. Life as you know it isn't a movie," Dominique says, slipping her arm out from Erika's, her walking gait improving as she does so.

"Technically, is this life?" Erika asks. "You know. You know what I mean?"

"It is, it isn't, it's what you make of it, now you have it in abundance."

Erika reflects on Dominique's words before replying, "So, the label doesn't matter. It's what you do with the time that matters."

"Exactly. That's all that matters in this regard. People love their names and labels for things. I assume it makes them feel better," Dominique says.

"Don't the labels and names help?" Erika enquires.

"To an extent, I think, so long as they don't become the focus of everything, which I suspect in the current era they are. Just look around at all the movements, the labels, the safe spaces and the like. Society is becoming polarised by any, and all trivialities. Things that don't matter in the slightest. I don't just mean from my perspective, but from the participants perspective. Which leads me to suspect it's not a natural development but orchestrated by an unknown actor," Dominique says, continuing to walk, not paying any attention to the look of surprise on Erika's face.

"Who would do that?"

Dominique shakes her head, "I don't know, but the list of candidates isn't all that long."

"Seriously?"

Dominique sighs slightly, "How do I start? I know. Who do you know, who might care and could do something about it?"

Without thinking about it, Erika replies, "Us, family."

"Exactly, they're the most likely instigators. That doesn't mean they're doing it, most likely they have associates to do it for them, either willingly or unwillingly. But it's unlikely they are acting by themselves. That's not the smart way of doing things."

"Supposing you're right, what's the end goal?" Erika asks reasonably. "I mean, if you're going to all this trouble, there must be some advantage to it, otherwise, why bother. Cui bono?"

"Yes, who benefits. That would depend on who's doing it and why. Just to be clear, I do not have that information," Dominique says, looking momentarily at Erika.

Erika feigns surprise, "You mean there's something you don't know the answer too!"

"Every once in a while, it seems so," Dominique replies, playing along.

"Then what would cause someone to do this?" Erika asks, dropping the game.

Dominique stays silent a moment thinking, then gestures to all the buildings around them, "Do you see all the buildings and all the cameras?"

Erika nods, "Yes, they're everywhere. I think London has the most cameras per capita of anywhere in Europe, or maybe the world."

"I'll take your word for it, as it doesn't really matter. Not that it makes it any better if there were less. Now, you have about fifteen years left."

Erika interrupts before Dominique can either continue or finish, "What? What happens then?"

Dominique gives Erika a quick admonishing look, "If you don't interrupt, I can finish. You have about fifteen years before we need to move and adopt new names. To that end, you'll always be known to us as Erika, regardless of what names you have later. Curiously, everyone seems to return to their original names as often as they can. I suppose it's just the way people think."

"You're drifting off topic," Erika prompts.

"So, occasionally, we need to move, setup home in a new place, etc. Now, the cameras make that more difficult. Suppose you wanted to move to Manchester. That's not going to work, as your image is everywhere, any move to Manchester will not give you a new lease on life. You'll still be associated with this Erika, as you were today," Dominique says, shaking her head slightly.

"What can we do about it?" Erika asks reasonably.

"In the short term, not much. We could move to Hong Kong for a while, then somewhere else. They don't keep records indefinitely, I hope, and warehouses seem so susceptible to fire."

"So, the warehouses and storage facilities just burn down?" Erika asks, suddenly extremely interested in the conversation.

"Sometimes, it's one option," Dominique says casually.

"Which implies there are other options?" Erika prompts.

Dominique chuckles, "There's always other options, ranging from the small to the large."

"Would you care to elaborate?" Erika asks.

"It would be my pleasure, but as you've just asked a question, in the Erika style, one that seems simple but has a large set of unknown ramifications, the answer will be long and complex," Dominique flashes Erika a knowing grin. "Well done on that!"

"If I knew which questions would be simple and which complex, I probably wouldn't have to ask in the first place," Erika says, knowing how this is progressing.

"That's a very good point, but it changes nothing," Dominique says with a smile. "Shall we start at the beginning?"

"Ooo, a story."

"Certainly. Once upon a time, there was a great civilisation, that ruled all the known world. Every attempt at commerce resulted in bountiful trade. Every military endeavour resulted in glory. The civilisation prospered, it grew, and both the people and the leaders were happy. This went on for generations. Then one day, the civilisation collapsed, and nobody lived happily ever after," Dominique says, with a flourish.

"Is that the story of the Roman Empire?" Erika asks making a sad face that the end of the story.

Dominique shakes her head as she walks, "No, that's the story of just about all empires and civilisations. They do well, grow, flourish and then decline. Nobody knows why."

"Do you have a theory?"

"Theory?" Dominique says, shaking her head, "No, not a theory. It happens because the power behind the throne or whatever you want to call it, simply gets bored and walks away. Sometimes, they're killed, but mostly, they get bored."

Erika stops a moment and forces Dominique to stop too, "How do you know this?"

Dominique takes Erika's hand and starts walking, "We need to keep moving while having this kind of conversation, you never know who's listening." She pauses a moment to let the words sink in then continues, "I know, because it's obvious."

"No, it's not," Erika says, enjoying the warm hand.

"Actually, in this case, it is. You come across a young civilisation, maybe a group of people wanting to do better. They're keen and eager. What they don't have is the skills, the long-term planning, and the ability to see the big picture with enough dedication and time to see it through. People, have a noticeably short horizon for getting things done. Look at businesses, they think in a year or two, maybe six months, depending on the age and structure of the company. Established, but small businesses think five or ten years ahead. Publicly traded businesses think about the next financial statement they must release. Professional managers, they think only about how to make money for themselves from the business they are supposed to be running on behalf of the owners. When, in fact, they're running it for their own benefit. Then you have politicians, they only care about lining their own pockets, see the commonality here, they also want re-electing, so they can line their pockets some more. Repeat until they get too old or do something silly, that gets them deselected for an election. Marital indiscretions are a good option there," Dominique says.

Erika looks deep in thought as she replies, "That's it?"

"Of course not, I'm just getting started. The point is that people will choose the path of least resistance and maximum short-term gain. Family on the other hand, have all those proclivities, but have the advantage, that they can keep the long-term in focus. Therefore, that budding civilisation or the group that wants to make a difference, if they catch the family's eye, well things might work out differently," Dominique says.

"Alright, I see where you're going with this, and it makes a sort of strange sense. Did you ever do this?" Erika asks.

"Me?" Dominique questions surprised. "Good grief no, never. Don't you remember what I said about politics?"

"I was just asking. You seem to know a lot about it," Erika replies.

"Knowing is different from doing. Anyway, what tends to happen is that the associates tend to do very well, civilisations become empires, they flourish and the power behind the throne has fun, building up the empire. But, and this is the crucial part, at some point they tire of it. Perhaps there's no more territory to conquer, maybe they have done all they can. Just because you're immortal, doesn't make you smart or knowledgeable. Case in point our bridge friends. So, they stop for some reason. The reason isn't all that important. What matters, is that they stop."

"So, they stop, but why the decline?" Erika asks.

"The decline is because the people didn't really know what they were doing. The first batch, which was working with the family member, they were probably competent and could keep things going, but then, what about their successor and theirs? They have no idea and people can only stay in power for so long, forty, fifty maybe sixty years. Most don't make it that long. Illness, political machinations, accidents, the list is long and death inevitable," Dominique says conversationally.

"So, the civilisation collapses due to incompetence?" Erika asks.

Dominique continues, "It's a little harsh, but yes, that and corruption. The new people don't have the background, they don't have the experience and the guidance, which was never a natural part of the civilisation, so it vanishes. The institutions that remain tend to look inwards and turf wars start. Remember, the guiding hand would have stopped this in the past. The infighting and power struggles, all of which would never have happened. This goes on and slowly over the space of a few decades, maybe a century, the civilisation degrades and decays. At some point another civilisation takes over as they have strong leadership."

"And this happens to all of them?" Erika enquires, keeping her hand in place.

"I'd say the vast majority," Dominique confirms.

"What about our civilisation?"

"I don't know about you, but it seems that this one started to decline after the Second World War. Therefore, I would assume that the hidden hand ruled the British Empire, they left, etc. and the decline began. It's debatable at this point if the hidden hand guides the United States of America, I think they were, but clearly are not any longer. So, I would expect them both to slowly decay and go down," Dominique says simply.

"That's a disaster," Erika counters.

"Not really, it's by the by. If this fails, we'll simply go somewhere else," Dominique says matter-of-factly.

"It matters that little?"

"It doesn't matter one jot," Dominique says, squeezing Erika's hand reassuringly.

"But we live here."

"Then we'll live somewhere else," Dominique replies. "It's really that simple. Don't let trivial things like that bother you."

"But...," Erika begins before Dominique cuts her off.

"Don't worry, now that you are outside time, all the things that once mattered, you'll see don't matter anywhere as much. Many of them don't matter at all. We don't need the economy; we don't need the civilisation. Don't get me wrong, they're nice and having a dry, warm apartment is nice too. Having entertainment on hand whenever we want it, that's also nice. But it's not necessary or important. In fairness, what are you worried about?" Dominique asks, keeping Erika's hand in her own.

Erika hesitates a moment, "I'm not sure, maybe it's the whole idea of civilisation going away and it not mattering. For my whole life it's mattered. Now you say it doesn't matter. That's a leap from where I am or was to where we now seem to be. That and, if there's no certainty, how do we get by from day to day?"

Dominique smiles reassuringly, but it's not clear if Erika sees it for what it is. "If you live long enough, you get to see all sorts of things that you never thought you'd see. In many cases, things you'd never even thought possible. By that I mean, you never even thought about them, let alone thought they might be possible. Imagine that you live in the seventeenth century, in say sixteen-fifty, would you consider international jet travel possible? Would your imagination have been vivid enough to have imagined that people could move from continent to continent in hours? I doubt it, the concept wouldn't have even entered your mind, so the conception of a jet airliner would never have crossed your mind. It was so far outside your realms of possibility that conceiving it seems impossible. Now, that's how the world really is. The longer you live, the worse that effect will become and at some point, you accept it and move on. It's not that you're without certainty from day to day. That exists and remains. Today will be very much like tomorrow and yesterday. But one day, that won't be true and then we move on."

"You make it all sound so matter-of-fact, like it's something that happens every day," Erika says, slipping her hand out of Dominique's hand, then placing it around her waist.

Dominique reciprocates the action and adjusts her walk to match Erika's, "To me, it is matter-of-fact. It's happened before and it'll happen again. I have a theory, a belief if you prefer, that the final downfall of civilisations comes about because of corruption. That doesn't have to mean envelopes filled with cash, although that's not precluded. What I mean is the corruption of purpose. When an institution stops serving those it's meant to serve and focuses only on its own inner power and priorities. Often to the detriment of other related institutions, that's when the corruption has passed the point of no return."

"Does that mean, that for a certain amount of corruption, there's a possible way back?"

"Yes, I think so. Now, the corruption that we're talking about is institutional corruption. This isn't where a corrupt official wants a bribe to let you off a parking ticket or to speed up the passport application. That low level corruption is easy, with the right will and dedication, to correct and irradicate. It just requires a concerted desire. No, what I'm talking about is even more difficult to irradicate, simply because the participants don't want it eliminated. Let's take the example of politics. You know it's bad when people quip, that they know that corporate interests can buy politicians, but they didn't know they were so cheap. You've heard that?" Dominique asks, glancing around.

Erika nods, "Yes, I've heard that."

Dominique nods, "Then what path does someone have to change the dynamic? Can they vote more? Vote for someone else? Well, for parliament, you have the choice of voting for any candidate that the parties decide to let you vote for. Only the major three parties have any chance, so any vote for an independent is all but guaranteed to go nowhere. So, you get to choose from the people that the establishment decides you can choose from. To be clear, it doesn't matter what establishment means in this context. What matters is that your choices are already predetermined. So, you vote. Someone becomes a new member of parliament. Do you suppose that they allow reformers who want to stop the corruption from winning?"

"Well, I don't know," Erika says weakly.

"I'm going to go out on a limb and say no. I don't think the corrupt will want the non-corrupt joining their club. Once a little corruption begins, at first, it's hidden and probably doesn't benefit the corrupt very much, then it slowly grows as the participants all want more. Until it's in plain sight and nobody knows what to do about it. How does one reform a corrupt institution that is happy being corrupt and has only one goal and that's to become more corrupt?" Dominique asks reasonably.

Erika shakes her head, "With difficulty?"

"If you're lucky and you're probably not. Eventually the institution only serves the institution and not society in general. At that point, collapse is better than continuation for all but the institution," Dominique says.

"Then what do I or what do we do?" Erika asks.

"Nothing. It's not our problem and not our concern. That's for the people of the country to deal with. We have our own concerns, which sometimes align, sometimes don't. When they do, we cooperate or intervene, otherwise we leave well alone," Dominique says.

"Then why are you telling me this?" Erika asks conversationally.

Dominique walks a few steps before responding, "Because there are things that do concern us and therefore, concern you. Those we need to focus on and, perhaps worry is the wrong word, but consider."

"Like what?" Erika asks now intrigued.

"If things get bad, and it looks like they are. We might have to act. You remember that we have a five-stage escalation plan. There's an incredibly good reason for it. Firstly, it stops emotional reactions to situations. Tempers can flare and people say and therefore do things they might later regret. Well, when things get serious, we can discuss and threaten, etc. but at some point, we might need to act. You saw that at the bridge. It was necessary and I did what was necessary," Dominique says carefully.

Erika slips her arm from around Dominique and stakes a step sideways, then asks, "Is your aura correct?"

Taken aback by the change in topic, Dominique hesitates, "Yes, I think so. Why?"

"Then what does blue mean?" Erika asks, moving back to Dominique's side.

"Generous, why, do you doubt me?" Dominique enquires.

"No, I'm practicing, and I didn't know what that colour meant."

"So, sometimes action is needed and it's not always clear who should take that action," Dominique says, putting the conversation back on track.

"What kind of action?"

"Better question," Dominique replies smiling. "That depends on the situation, but you're technically now in an organisation that doesn't exist."

"If it doesn't exist, how can I or anyone else be in it?" Erika asks reasonably.

Dominique looks around slowly, taking in her surroundings, the river, the buildings, the rooftops, all of it. When that process is complete says at little more than a whisper, "Because you are a junior member, but a member and one day, you'll get to know what happens."

"That's extremely vague," Erika whispers back.

"Thank you," Dominique says, again in a whisper.

"That wasn't supposed to be a compliment," Erika whispers. "Do you mean something like the Illuminati or one of those level ninety-nine Freemasons? Something like that."

Despite herself, Dominique laughs, "It wouldn't be much of an organisation that doesn't exist if it had a name, a logo and a headquarters, with a website listing now, would it?"

Erika sighs, "I suppose not."

Whispering again, Dominique says, "I keep telling you that you're special and you keep ignoring it. But you are."

"Not this again," Erika says interrupting.

"This again," Dominique whispers, "There's a few of us, including the twins and Jonathan, along with others that you don't know, who make up a group when everyone agrees we'll take action."

"Wait what," Erika says, interrupting again, "If you're an organisation that doesn't exist, then how do you meet to discuss things?"

Dominique whispers, "When the time comes, you're included and there's more than one way of meeting. It doesn't have to be in person. Did you ever try video chat?"

"That's it, you meet via video chat?" Erika says deflated.

"Of course not, I was playing with you. The important thing is not how we meet, but what the topic is and the resulting action. Do you remember I mentioned earlier about the cameras all over the place?" Dominique asks, speaking at a more normal volume.

Erika nods, "I remember."

"Good, that's becoming a looming problem for us. A hundred years ago, there wasn't much to worry about, a few images in a filing cabinet. It was unimportant to us. But now, all these years later that has become pictures in lots of filing cabinets, which became images on computers. Now, they are all shared by all the companies and governments and that makes life potentially awkward for us, I don't mean you and I, I mean all of us in the larger sense of us," Dominique says ruefully.

"And?"

"And something needs doing about it. I don't see anyway presently, and I accept, that I'm not an expert in the technologies involved, so I might be missing a solution, out of this. Those images all must go away. The associations to all of us regarding those images need to go away. This is a potentially existential threat and I have no intention of dying over something so trivial," Dominique says.

"Can't we just make people delete the images?" Erika asks reasonably.

Dominique hesitates, "Perhaps. But I don't see how that's a long-term solution for everyone. It might work for you and me today, but can you guarantee that you get all the images of you deleted? I mean them all, not one left associated with anything that's traceable back to you?"

"That seems more difficult." Erika concedes.

"Then how do you do it, guaranteeing that we can slip into another identity and continue somewhere else?" Dominique asks.

"I suppose, you need to get rid of the surveillance system in general and stop it being used in the future," Erika says, considering the options.

"And how do you suppose we can do that?" Dominique asks.

"Oh no," Erika says, as the realisation dawns on her.

"Oh yes," Dominique replies, "which is why it needs to be a group decision."

"Who's in this group?" Erika asks quietly.

"The family elders," Dominique says whispering.

"How can I be an elder, I'm only a few days old?" Erika replies quietly.

"Because you're thinking in years, not generations," Dominique whispers back.

"I don't understand."

"Of course, then think of this. Normally, the oldest of us are the lowest generation, the closest to the beginning. But, because of the way things work in practice, what matters is not the age, but who makes you. If the one who makes you is an elder, then by definition, you'll be a little less of an elder. In generations, not in years. So, you can be both an elder, in generation, and young, in years. Which is you. I'm an elder, in generation and older in years. Does that make sense?" Dominique whispers, waiting for a response.

Erika considers what she's heard for a long-time, her steps quiet over the pavement. Presently, she nods, "Yes, it makes sense, logically. I don't really know if it's useful to me though."

"Right now, I don't think it's all that useful. But it fills in another piece of the puzzle as to who you are, what you'll be and what that might mean going forward," Dominique says, stopping and looking around. "You know, there's nobody around tonight. Shall we walk back the other way?"

Erika nods, "Yes, that's fine." She pauses before adding, "Am I understanding correctly, that while you don't control anything, collectively, if we choose, we can change the world?"

Dominique turns round and sighs, "Yes, but no. Our ability to change things is extremely limited, as I think you already understand. If, and it's a big if, collectively we decide that things need changing, then there's several paths, but they mostly mean this all goes away. The technology, which really is the source of the problem. The rest is, of course, collateral damage."

"And if I want to, I can influence this?" Erika asks clarifying.

"I'm not sure I'd go with want, but yes, at this point you're part of the process," Dominique says reassuringly.

"I don't know what to say to that," Erika says, walking in step with Dominique.

"There's not much to say, you've just had your world changed again and it feels strange. I have been warning you about this for the last few days. That there were things you would need to know, but they would be hard for you to integrate into your world view," Dominique says carefully.

"I'm going to need some time to understand this and see how it applies to me," Erika says, regaining a little composure.

"Years I imagine," Dominique says warmly, "but, I don't see anything happening for several years yet, maybe a decade."

"That's reassuring," Erika says sarcastically.

"Good, I knew you'd see it from the practical side," Dominique says, ignoring the sarcasm.

"I was being sarcastic."

"I know, but I'm not letting your newfound power interfere with my walk," Dominique says, as they walk back upriver, discussing the nature of corruption and its implications to a stable civilisation.

Chapter 21

Several days pass, during which Erika spends time honing her skills, learning more about feeding and getting her sensitivity under control. She also spends hours practicing her melee skills with Dominique; gaining the ability to anticipate actions, providing correct countermeasures, and generally honing all her skills. The topics covered aren't those previously discussed. Basically, Erika spends her time concentrating on everything practical and studiously avoiding asking easy looking but awkward questions.

As the days of her holiday tick by, it gets to Friday night and the big day of the theatre visit. Getting up early, at around four-thirty in the afternoon, Erika struggles to wake-up and get going for the evening.

Taking advantage of Erika's tired state, Dominique rolls over and kisses Erika, who's first instinct is to protest the kiss in her sleepy state.

"Mm, is that fair," Erika asks through the kiss.

"No," Dominique replies, "but it feels nice."

Erika coming to her senses, returns the kiss and they smooch a little.

"I didn't appreciate it when you said getting up early would be hard. I thought what we were doing before was early. This is punishing," Erika says, struggling to keep her eyes open.

"We have a plan and time is short," Dominique says. "So run and get the bath going, and don't forget to use only hot water. We need to warm you up and only have an hour to do it."

"I know, I know and I'm going," Erika replies, struggling to put one foot in front of the other. Seeing this, Dominique, having much less trouble, passes her and begins filling the bath with hot water.

"The sooner you get in, the sooner you'll warm up," Dominique says, commenting, "There's no need to be too awake in the bath, just submerged."

Erika shuffles sleepily to the bathroom and stripping off her pyjamas, climbs into the now slowly filling bath. She sits down and lets the hot water slowly climb up her skin.

Minutes later Dominique returns holding a glass of deep red velvety breakfast blood. "This should help a little," she says hopefully.

Taking the glass, Erika sips at the contents, "Thank you. This tastes nice."

"Good," Dominique says, watching the scene unfold. "You're going to have to lie down and submerge yourself, the more of your body that's in the water, the better. Hotter is better too."

"But I can't drink lying down," Erika protests.

Watching the predicament Dominique sighs, "You're right, that's awkward. Let me go and see if I can find a straw or two." With that, she disappears out of the bathroom. Erika does her best to submerge into the deepening water while sipping her breakfast.

Presently, Dominique returns with two straws, each with a yellow spiral stripe, "Here, these should help," she says, as she bends the tops over and hands them to Erika.

"Much appreciated," Erika says, putting the straws into the glass and using them to lay back into the bath, allowing the deeper water to cover her whole torso. "How long am I doing to have to be in the bath?"

"Until five-thirty, I think, we can't leave it any later than that, as you still need to get made-up and dressed. Look on the bright side, you'll feel all warm all evening. That should be nice," Dominique says kindly, as she turns the tap off, stemming the flow of hot water.

"There's something you're not telling me about this isn't there?" Erika asks suspiciously.

"No, not really. You must drink breakfast and get as warm as possible. There are things you can do to make the process work better. Send blood to the skin, then bring it back to your core. Keep repeating this process for the next hour, or fifty minutes. It should heat you up quicker. Then when you've finished breakfast, you can duck your head under the water. From time to time, every five minutes or so, I'll bring a kettle of boiling water to keep the temperature up." Dominique grins at something not said.

"Go on, what else? Finish the thought," Erika prompts.

"Oh, I was just thinking, if we do this right, we could boil your head," Dominique says, doing her best to keep a straight face.

"I'm assuming you've done this before and know what your doing?" Erika asks, a hint of concern in her voice.

"Done it before, yes, boiled my own head, no," Dominique quips.

Erika sighs and hands over her empty glass, "A refill please."

Taking the glass Dominique heads back out to the kitchen. While she's gone, Erika slips her head under the water, allowing the hot water to envelope her face, scalp, and hair, allowing the heat to slowly seep into her body.

After a minute or two, Dominique returns, with Erika's breakfast glass refilled and the straws in place. She doesn't bother to prompt the submerged Erika, but simply begins to pour the boiling water into the bath. This causes Erika to re-emerge from the depths of the water. "You're refill madam," Dominique says with a flourish and grin, hiding the now empty kettle behind her back.

"Thank you," Erika says taking the glass. "You know, I can see the kettle!"

Dominique grins, "I know, but this makes the game more fun. Feeling any warmer?"

"Technically, probably yes, but it doesn't feel like getting warm, it feels very strange," Erika says, after sipping her drink.

"That's because it's a new sensation. You didn't really feel the getting colder, so the getting warmer will feel strange. But, with luck, the warmth is seeping into your core. That will enable you to keep warm all evening. We'll make sure you wear some insulating undergarments, as a base layer if you will. That should make sure that you feel normal for the festivities. Having said that, you must put the effort in now, to get as much heat into your body as you can. The hotter you can be now, the longer and more convincing it will be for Elle and Andy," Dominique says, placing the kettle on the floor.

"I know, but it seems like a lot of work," Erika says.

"It is a lot of work, but in fairness, it's mostly laying down work. One which gets you breakfast delivered with straws. What more could a young woman ask for?" Dominique says, raising an eyebrow questioningly.

Erika chuckles around her straws, "Off the top of my head, I can think of several things."

"I'm sure you could. But until you can do this yourself, this is all you have," Dominique says, before collecting the kettle and heading back out for more boiling water.

This cycle repeats itself, while Erika slowly warms-up in increasingly hot water. Dominique brings her breakfast and oversees the kettles of boiling water. At the end of the process, Dominique gives Erika the washing items from the shower and encourages her to wash quickly.

"You should get dried and dressed as quickly as possible. Our goal is to seal in the heat. I've laid out everything on the bed and then, I'll get showered and clean up the bathroom. It should only take a few minutes," Dominique says, taking the washing materials into the shower.

Erika heads into the bedroom and looks over the clothes on the bed, they don't look like a casual summer outfit. Thick tights to go under jeans. A thermal vest to go under her long-sleeved top and over the bra. A lined cream jacket and brown boots. The outfit looks stylish but is more than the skimpy clothes people normally wear in the middle of summer. She has only just got the clothes on when Dominique appears fresh from her shower.

"This looks nice, but a little warm," Erika comments.

"It should be fine," Dominique comments. "The theatre will be air conditioned. Elle and Andy will dress up a bit, even if Elle doesn't change after finishing work. They're going out for the evening, you'll see everyone else dressed like this, perhaps without the warm underlayer, but we need to keep you warm. I can't afford tonight for Elle to notice there's been any change in or with you. The night's going to be hard enough as it is. When do you think they'll arrive?"

"Elle will be punctual; they'll arrive at exactly six o'clock," Erika says. "Probably within a few seconds of the hour. We should be downstairs before they arrive."

"We need to be there before them anyway, as that's where the food will arrive, I imagine it will arrive about five minutes early. That's what I requested when I placed the order," Dominique says, finishing dressing, a blue silk cocktail dress draped over her contours, simultaneously hiding, and emphasising her shape. A matching blue silk jacket rests on the bed, next to their shoulder bags.

"I'm ready when you are," Erika says, looking round for anything that she's forgotten.

Dominique shakes her head, "Make-up!"

"See, the boiled brain isn't a good look," Erika says, zipping over to the dressing table and applying make-up very quickly, but precisely.

"When you're ready, go downstairs, I'll tidy up here and meet you at your place," Dominique says patiently. "And don't forget your jewellery."

"I'd have forgotten that too," Erika says, "Why am I forgetting everything?"

"Because you're panicking or at least rushing and not thinking. Relax, we have plenty of time. Oh, and pull as much blood into your body as you can, until our guests arrive, then when you interact with them, push the warm blood into the bits of your body that touch them, hands, cheeks, that kind of thing, lips, etc. then pull it back, to keep it as warm as possible. You're mostly covered, so it will keep the heat in, but your fingers will need extra attention," Dominique says gently.

Erika finishes her make-up, pops birthday earrings into her ears, Dominique carefully fits the necklace with a kiss around Erika's neck, then claps the bracelet around her wrist. "Now you look ready," Dominique comments with a smile. Erika then pops her new ring onto her left ring finger.

"Thanks," Erika says, heading out of the bedroom to collect her boots which are by the front door. She leaves the apartment and takes the lift down to her floor and walking down the corridor smiles to herself, at what a wonderful life she has.

At her apartment door, she unlocks it and walk in, slipping her boots off and putting warm slippers on. Entering the lounge area, she quickly tidies a few items that look unsightly; she deliberately leaves the balcony door closed to keep the draught out. Then into the kitchen, putting plates and bowls into the oven and sets the dining room table. Erika carefully opens a bottle of rosé wine and pours four glasses, setting them at each place setting. Surveying her handiwork, satisfied that all is in place and looking good, she heads into the bedroom and tidies that up too. With that task complete she heads back into the lounge to read. No sooner had she sat down, than a knock on the door prompts her to abandon that plan.

At the door she's greeted with a beaming smile from Elle and a grin from Andy, which indicates that they'd been joking around being silly. "Am I missing a joke?" Erika asks, gesturing them into the apartment.

"Oh no," Andy says. "We were just being silly, imagining the carpet being much deeper, so you waded through it."

"It was funny at the time, now it seems silly," Elle says, as she and Erika kiss cheeks, followed quickly by Erika and Andy doing the same.

There's another knock on the door, this time, the food delivery courier offers an insulated bag. "Chinese for Erika Elliot?" the young man asks.

"That's me," Erika says, "please come in." With that the young man follows her into the kitchen. They unpack the bag, placing the dishes onto the counter and Erika gives him a five-pound note and her thanks. They walk to the door, and he departs just as Dominique arrives.

"Evening all," Dominique says gently, with a smile.

"The foods just arrived, so I need to sort it out," Erika says, closing the door.

Dominique removes her shoes, quickly followed by Elle and Andy. They all proceed into the lounge.

"Do you need a hand?" Dominique says, looking at the table.

"It would help," Erika replies.

"Alright," Dominique says, before kissing Elle's cheek then Andy's, "Nice to see you both again."

"Oh, why don't you two get started on the wine, I just poured it out a couple of minutes ago," Erika says, gesturing to the table and the wine glasses.

"Now that's a sound plan," Elle says, heading towards the table. "Where should we sit?"

"It doesn't matter, choose your glasses and therefore seats," Erika says, "We're not set on ceremony here."

Elle and Andy choose wine glasses and head out to the balcony, they slide the door open and look at the view over London, it's nothing like as spectacular as the one from Dominique's apartment.

In the kitchen Erika gathers the cardboard boxes and puts them into the microwave on full power for three minutes giving everything a quick heat through.

Dominique removes the plates and dishes from the oven and places them on the counter, she doesn't bother with a cloth, simply picks them up, despite them being too hot for a human to handle.

Erika makes a mental note to draw it to Dominique's attention later that she hopes that Elle and Andy didn't notice the plates from the oven trick while they enjoy the view.

Erika removes the items from the microwave and places the boxes on the side, opening each one in turn, emptying the contents into hot bowls. First the rice, then chips. Followed by the beef and mushrooms in a black bean sauce, sweet and sour chicken Hong Kong style, then chicken and ginger with spring onions. The prawn crackers go into a large serving bowl. The dipping sauce gets its own warm bowl.

Just as Erika's about to get a cloth to carry the first of the items into the dining area, Dominique takes her arm and, over the beef, with her fingernail slices open Erika's wrist, allowing a couple of tablespoons of blood to dribble into the dish, she then moves the wrist quickly over the sweet and sour sauce and allows a little less blood to flow into the dish. She then moves her mouth to the bleeding wrist and after a quick suck, closes the wound. Then she checks Erika's cuff for evidence and satisfied gets a spoon and begins to stir the blood into the beef dish. Seeing what's going on, Erika does the same with the sweet and sour sauce. She doesn't comment on what's going on. It's always best to leave some questions for later!

With that complete, Dominique uses a tea towel to take the plates and prawn crackers into the dining area. Erika follows doing the same with two dishes. She repeats this process to retrieve all the dishes, placing them on the table. Once she's laid out the warm plates, Dominique gathers Elle and Andy from the balcony and after closing the door, follows them to the table. Back at the table Dominique asks, "Who's sitting where?"

"I'm here," Elle says, "and Andy's there."

"Then I'll sit here, as it's the closest to the kitchen," Dominique says, making the arrangement with Elle next to Andy, who's next to Dominique, then to Elle as they go around the table.

"Cheers," Andy offers lifting his glass to all. Collectively, they clink glasses with a group cheer in response.

"Help yourselves," Erika says. "There should be plenty to go around, and I did order things I know you like." She directs that comment towards Andy.

"Oh, I see that," Andy says, "I like all of this."

It takes only a few minutes for Andy to have a selection of everything on his plate, with plenty of sauce on the beef. As he sprinkles salt on his chips, Elle watches and her hand poised to intercept the salt, only a light sprinkling covers the chips, but Dominique notices the exchange. Elle does the same, but has less of the egg fried rice, but more chips. Dominique takes rice, a little of the beef but a lot of sauce, a couple of chicken balls and a generous helping of sauce, while skipping the chips. Erika opts for the chicken with ginger, a little of the beef. a little rice and chips. They all dip into the prawn crackers as they eat.

"Have you decided on a holiday destination yet?" Erika asks.

"Yes," Andy replies being first to finish his mouthful, "Mauritius."

"Elle was selling it to me last week at the work's party," Erika comments, "When are you off?"

"Ah, it's not booked yet," Elle says, "but we're hoping for the end of September, so about nine or ten weeks from now. It should be hot, but not too hot."

"That's so British," Dominique comments to Elle.

"Isn't it just." Andy chuckles.

Elle exclaims, "You should come with us. Remember, horizon to horizon sunshine, golden beaches, and crystal-clear water."

Erika glances to Dominique who replies to the unasked question, "Feel free to go, but I can't. I have other commitments."

Elle looks expectantly at Erika, "Then, I don't think I can," Erika replies, "I don't want to be a spare wheel. Maybe next time when she's got more time to plan. It amazes me that's she's always so busy."

"Some of us have to earn a living," Dominique quips.

"Don't I know it," Andy chips in.

"Fine," Elle says a little deflated. "But next time!"

"How long is the flight?" Dominique asks.

"About fifteen and a half hours," Andy says. "You leave one day and arrive the next. Normally in the afternoon and arrive the following morning, so you sleep on the plane and spend the night flying, eating, drinking, relaxing, and sleeping."

"That sounds like a long time," Erika says.

"I love flying, it's the most amazing thing imaginable. You get on the plane in London and the next morning you're on the other side of the world," Dominique says. "How amazing is that!"

"Have you been to Mauritius?" Andy asks.

"No, but I've flown all over the world," Dominique says, watching Erika slowly picking at her food and sipping at her wine. Elle on the other hand, is eating her dinner with enthusiasm.

"Anywhere fun?" Andy asks.

"No, mostly business related," Dominique concedes.

"Where did you get this Chinese?" Elle asks. "It tastes absolutely amazing."

"It's just the usual one, that we use for work, they're close and offer good food at a good price," Erika says. "Maybe they have a new chef?"

"I don't know, but I agree, it does taste much better than I remember," Andy says.

"The beef's nice," Dominique comments casually, joining in the compliments.

"I'm not surprised you ordered from there. We should have this more often," Elle says, continuing with her dinner. After a couple of prawn crackers, she asks, "Have you thought of going vegan?"

Dominique ejects a few grains of rice from her mouth as she splutters and laughs, before being able to cover it with her hand.

"What's so funny?" Erika asks.

Composing herself and regaining her control, Dominique asks, "Can you imagine Erika as a vegan? That's just too funny."

Erika gives Dominique a look and says, "Why?" The other two look baffled as they look at Dominique.

"Imagine a world, not any world, but Erika's world without, strawberry cheesecake, which is for dessert, cherry cheesecake, pavlova, Eaton mess, chocolate eclairs, cream cakes in general, chocolate cake, Victoria sponge cake with strawberries, anything with cream or cheese. For good measure, lets add in bacon, beef, chicken, fish, and crispy duck," Dominique says, ticking items off on her finger as she speaks. "I doubt that's a comprehensive list."

"There's vegan versions of all those things," Erika protests, entirely missing the point.

"There are things that purport to be substitutes for those things, but have you ever tried any?" Dominique counters.

"She does have a point," Elle says interjecting, "we had some vegan cheesecake over lunch last week, or earlier this week, on Tuesday. It didn't taste or feel like cheesecake. I wouldn't want it again."

"Did it feel like a cross between rubber and plastic, but somehow sticks to the inside of your mouth?" Dominique asks.

"You've had it," Elle confirms.

"When they serve it at a meeting it's a good excuse to be on a diet," Dominique adds.

"You people are so cynical," Andy notes.

"Speaking of cynical and now you have some food and wine in you, what's wrong with you?" Dominique says, a little too directly.

"What do you mean?" Andy asks cautiously.

"I saw you wince earlier, and you seem extra chipper. So, I am assuming that something is wrong. And the holiday of a lifetime is also curious," Dominique says, going back to eating slowly, but effectively.

Andy looks at his wife and after a moment replies, "My kidneys are failing. They don't know how, it's probably the viral infection I had back in February. But I have about a year before I need to go on dialysis and then I need a donor for a new one."

"I'm sorry to hear that, Andy," Erika says compassionately.

"And when were you doing to tell us this?" Dominique asks, ignoring the compassion angle.

"Maybe after the play. You would probably notice it then anyway as the pains get worse as the day progresses," Andy replies, slightly defensively.

"I think we can put a positive outlook on this, I'm sure a good diet, some exercise and some drugs will sort this out," Dominique says to surprised looks. "What? Isn't that how it works. I've read the studies, watched the documentaries, etc."

"It's not quite that simple," Elle says. "Once his kidneys shut down, they'll just be useless lumps in his body. Then he needs dialysis and with luck, we might be able to do it at home. I'm assuming that you've never been extremely ill?"

Dominique shakes her head, "No, not really. I was quite ill at one point as a child, but not since. It's been quite a while."

"This isn't how I want to spend my evening at dinner and the theatre, discussing my demise. I want to have happy thoughts, like Erika being a vegan or jetting all over the world," Andy says, going back to his dinner.

"I'm sorry," Dominique says, resuming the appearance of eating her dinner.

"When we're finished at the theatre, would you like to go out for a drink?" Erika asks to Dominique's surprise.

Elle shakes her head, "No, we must catch a train and it'll probably be the last one or close to it. It finishes at about ten, right?"

"Yes," Dominique replies, "But it might be a little earlier or later, depending how the performance goes. But it should be about then. Plus, we will need some time to filter out, etc."

"You could always stay here for the night," Erika offers, ignoring the look from Dominique.

Elle looks at Andy and says, "We could?" Andy nods in agreement and Elle replies, "That would be nice, but where would we sleep?"

"You can sleep in my room, and I'll stay with Dominique," Erika says with a smile. "But you'll need to show yourselves out in the morning, as I will be sleeping. Trying to switch to nights, remember."

"Oh yes, of course. I remember," Elle says. "How's it going?"

"I've got the switch done, which was good until today, I had to get up especially early this morning, I mean afternoon, to get ready for tonight. You see how it gets confusing?" Erika replies, nibbling on a prawn cracker. Andy digs into the remains of his dinner.

"I do and it's funny to watch," Elle says, with a friendly smile, "But we can see ourselves out. We can go first thing and get an early train home."

Erika shakes her head, "No need for that, just have some breakfast and leave when you're ready. But I won't be around to say good morning."

"Thanks," Elle says, with a warm smile. "Much appreciated."

With that complete, they finish their main course and have a dessert consisting of Dominique's homemade strawberry cheesecake, made just the way Erika used to have it and a splash of cream. The conversation drifts only over easy and fun topics, no more mention of Andy's illness or looming difficulties. At the appointed time, they head out to the theatre.

Chapter 22

Andy, Elle, Erika, and Dominique walk upriver to the theatre. Erika sports a casual brimmed hat, keeping any errant sunshine off her head. At the entrance, Dominique collects the tickets for Romeo and Juliet and the four head towards the Olivier Theatre.

"Anyone need the toilet before we go in?" Dominique asks. "It's going to be at least an hour and a half before the interval."

"How long until it starts?" Elle asks.

"I don't know," Dominique replies, "but it's due to start in about ten minutes. I don't imagine it'll start on time."

"Then let's find our seats and then see how we go," Elle offers.

With general agreement to this plan, they all head into the Olivier Theatre and find their seats. Not the best, but not the worst either. Their seats are next to the aisle close to the middle of the stalls in row H.

"Who wants the aisle?" Andy asks. "Any preferences?"

"I don't mind, I'm happy to sit anywhere," Dominique says.

"I'm easy," Erika says.

"So, I've heard," Elle quips.

"Very funny," Erika replies.

"Then how about I sit in, then Elle, Erika, and Dominique sits in the aisle seat?" Andy suggests.

To a general shrug and agreement, they settle into their seats. Then just as they sit down, Elle stands up and says, "Now for the loo. Any takers girls?"

Andy sighs as the three women stand and proceed to leave the theatre to head to the toilets.

"I'm glad that Andy told you about his medical problem," Elle says. "He's being a man about it. He doesn't want to tell anyone; in case it makes him look bad or weak; or something, which is clearly silly isn't it?"

Dominique and Erika nod agreement, "If we don't know, how can we help or be sympathetic."

"Exactly," Elle replies. "I sometimes wish he would be more expressive with things that bother him."

"If there's anything we can do, you just have to let me know," Erika says, with a smile and a touch of Elle's arm.

"I know," Elle replies and then sighs. "Is that the queue for the loos?"

"It looks like it," Dominique confirms. "We have time, I think."

They wait in line, as they shuffle their way towards the door. The queue moves quite quickly, as women shuffle in and yet seem to stream out. At the door, Dominique says, "I don't need to go, so, I'll wait out here. There's no sense in filling the toilets with more people than necessary."

"I don't either," Erika says grinning, "so it looks like you're going in on your own."

"Thanks friends," Elle says grinning, as she heads through the door.

Erika and Dominique move away from the door and find a quiet spot. "There's a lot of people?" Erika says cautiously.

"Yes, there are," Dominique replies with a malicious grin, "so you're going to have to be on your best behaviour and try to ignore all the people. There's nothing much I can do here and under no circumstances can you mess with the villagers."

"I know, but how?" Erika asks.

"Dial down your sense of smell, try to ignore it. Then concentrate on the play. It's going to be extremely difficult for you," Dominique replies. "If it all gets to be too much, we can always step out or leave. But it would be best if you show your determination and willpower. I don't really want to have to explain to Elle and Andy why we must leave early."

"And if it gets too much?" Erika asks.

"When it gets too much, you can always hold or squeeze my hand. Just be careful that you don't make me bleed. That would introduce a whole new set of problems," Dominique says by way of reassurance. "I would like to point out, I did say this wasn't such a good idea."

"You know, I can smell blood, when we were in the theatre," Erika whispers.

"I know, I counted over ten different sources," Dominique says with a grin, "but I'm sure there are many more than that. There's a lot of people, easily a thousand I would guess."

"So, what do I do?" Erika asks, as several theatre goers flit past.

"It's no different than Dystopia, pinch your nose, hand over your mouth and head to the toilets. That's the only plan we have," Dominique confirms.

"Alright. I understand," Erika whispers back.

"I'm here with you and we'll get through this, try to enjoy the play and not worry about the what-ifs," Dominique says. Not long after that Elle emerges as part of the stream leaving the toilets.

"Feeling better?" Erika asks as Elle joins them and they head back into the theatre to take their seats. The usher opens the doors for them as they approach and head quickly but quietly to their seats. The introduction to the play has begun and they listen as they head to their seat. They filter in and take their places. Sitting comfortably in the plush seats, they settle into the beginning of the play.

As the first act progresses, Erika comes under increasing stress. She takes Dominique's hand and holds it tightly. After a few minutes, Dominique whispers into Erika's ear, "Try not breathing. It will not remove the smells in your nose, but it will stop more coming in."

Erika does as she's instructed and simply stops breathing. This helps and she relaxes a little the grip on Dominique's hand. The play progresses and they all seem to be enjoying a first-class performance.

This arrangement continues, with brief moments of more difficulty as evidenced by the grip on Dominique's hand. Then the darkness recedes, and the lights come up, indicating the interval.

"Wow, that, was fab," Andy offers before anyone else can comment. "What happens next?"

Now the lights have come up, Erika tries to compose herself, fighting back her instincts with all the delicious smelling food, wandering around. The smells too intense for her to easily cope with.

Dominique smiles warmly in Andy's direction, "I'm guessing this is your first play here?"

Andy nods, "Yes, I've not seen a play since I was at school and that was nothing like this."

"Do we get ice cream?" Elle asks.

Dominique looks at the young woman and nods, "If you feel the need, yes. I'm going to skip it, I had enough at dinner."

"Having Chinese and cheesecake for breakfast is my limit. It's too early for ice cream," Erika says, looking a little off colour.

"If you're getting them E, I'll have chocolate preferably, but I'll have vanilla if that's all they have," Andy suggests.

"I'll get them," Dominique says, "What would you like Elle?"

"The same please," Elle says surprised at the offer.

"We'll be back shortly," Dominique says, offering her hand to Erika.

"Sometimes, you two are too cute as a couple," Elle comments to a wink from Dominique.

With that Erika and Dominique head out of the theatre to the concessions and quickly join the queue for ice cream.

"How are you doing babe?" Dominique asks quietly.

"The play's good, but it's hard to concentrate on it," Erika confesses.

"I know, not enough to distract you," Dominique offers.

Erika nods, "Right."

"Don't worry, we're halfway through. Would you like to sit on the aisle for the second part, rather than next to Elle?" Dominique asks.

Erika nods enthusiastically, "Oh yes, that would be nice. It's hard sitting there, with the smell all the time. Even doing as you suggest, it's still staggeringly hard to resist."

"I know babe and you're doing really well," Dominique says. "I'm doing all I can."

"I know," Erika says softly.

With the new plan in place, they discuss the play until they have procured two ice cream tubs and little wooden spoons. Heading back to their seats, Dominique says, "Don't forget to hold my hand, it can help."

"I know and I have been," Erika replies. "It does help."

At their seats, Dominique slips in first, allowing Erika to sit at the aisle. She leans over Elle and hands Andy an ice cream, "Chocolate, as requested, sir."

"Thanks," Andy says with a smile.

Dominique says, before handing a tub to Elle, "And yours as requested my lady."

"Thank you," Elle says adding, "What's got into you, you're in a very good mood."

"Nothing, I just felt like playing. It must be the medieval atmosphere," Dominique says sitting more comfortably.

"Well, it's nice to see you kids having fun," Elle replies, prying the lid off her ice cream tub. "Is Erika, okay?" Elle asks. "She seems a bit distracted."

Dominique glances at Erika and back to Elle, "I think she's up too early and the idea of breakfast in the evening as an evening meal, coupled with going out and doing evening things when she's only just woken up is upsetting her rhythm."

"Hm," Elle says unconvinced.

"That and I think her tummy is a bit queasy, which I think is the real reason for her passing up ice cream, which let's be honest isn't Erika is it? Missing a dessert?"

Elle taking the first scoop of her ice cream nods in agreement, "No, she doesn't pass up dessert, even for breakfast. Is she okay?"

"I hope so," Dominique says. "The play is good, and I hope she's enjoying it. Though, I have my concerns, which is why she's sitting on the aisle."

Elle sighs, as the lights dim and the theatre goes dark, "I understand."

Erika fighting harder to contain her desires as the minutes pass, periodically squeezing Dominique's hand harder from time to time, until at one point, there's a distinctly cracking sound, which causes a few people nearby to look around. Dominique does the same looking for the source of the sound, despite it coming from the bones breaking in her right-hand. A look of horror washes over Erika's face, but Dominique shows no outward sign of recognition. It just passes her by, as if nothing had happened. Erika relaxes her grip and begins to let go before Dominique's left-hand pushes Erika's hand back on to her own and holds it in place. Telling Erika that everything is all right.

With the bones already broken, there's nothing much more for Erika to break, so the repeated crushing of Dominique's hand has negligible effect on Dominique but does help Erika as the play progresses.

Ultimately, the play ends exactly as expected with the lovers showing their undying love for each other. After the curtain call and the civilised clapping which always accompanies these performances. Erika looks over at Dominique's crushed hand with most of the bones broken, only to see she's clapping sophisticatedly just like all the other patrons.

As the clapping from the encore dies down, Elle says, "That was fantastic. I'm so glad we came to see this."

Andy nods in agreement, "I'd love to come back and see other plays in the future. This was great."

"We really should do this again," Erika says, refocusing on her companions.

"Yes, we should," Dominique agrees. "Shall we head out?"

"Can we wait until the crush has gone?" Erika suggests.

"Fine by me," Andy replies to general agreement from the others. The four-sit chatting amongst themselves as hundreds of people file out of the theatre. As the throng subsides, they gather their things and head towards the door. At the first available opportunity, Dominique slips her hand through Erika's arm as they head out. Seeing this, Elle does the same with Andy and together they proceed out of the theatre and into the now dark river walkway.

At the river they turn right and head back down the Thames, back towards Erika's apartment. During the short walk, they chat about the play and the different funny and tragic parts.

The focus as with every viewing is what would you do for love. Would you kill yourself if your love dies. Dominique keeps Erika snuggled tight as they walk. Erika on the other hand, uses the fresh air as an opportunity to clear out the smells of all the people from the theatre, her mood brightens a little and she seems to relax a little bit.

At the apartment building, they see Gavin returning from a run, his T-shirt drenched, his trainers looking worn. "Evening," he offers to Erika, as they meet at the automatic door.

"Evening Gavin," Erika replies with a pinched smile.

He looks over Dominique and their guests a moment, then asks Erika, "Been out anywhere nice?"

"To the National Theatre," Erika replies, as they cross the foyer to the lifts.

"I need to go and be more cultural," Gavin says nodding slowly. "But there never seems time, what with work, etc."

"Oh, I'm sorry," Erika says, gesturing to her companions, "This is Elle and Andy." Then turns to Gavin, "And this is Gavin, he lives next door to me."

"Nice to meet you both," Gavin offers, "I'd shake hands, but I've been out running, and they might be a bit sweaty."

"Nice to meet you, Gavin," Elle and Andy say together, but out of synchronisation.

As the lift arrives and the doors open at the bong, Erika says, "Elle and Andy are staying over tonight."

"That sounds nice," Gavin says casually.

The lift doors close and the lift whisks the occupants to Erika's floor. The doors effortlessly slide open and deposit the occupants onto the lush carpet.

"I'll only be up about half an hour," Gavin says with a grin, "so please keep the noise down." He then winks at Erika.

"You're impossible sometimes," Erika says to Gavin, as they walk down the corridor towards Erika's door.

Suddenly Erika lunges forward towards Elle, her fangs descended. Instead of sliding them into the soft skin of Elle's neck, she's met with the solid wall that is Gavin and a hand over her mouth from behind that belongs to Dominique. The moves are complete no sooner than they began. Elle and Andy continuing to walk down the corridor blissfully unaware. Neither Gavin nor Dominique say anything. Dominique's hand slips from over Erika's mouth and the three move down the corridor with a horror struck look on Erika's face.

At the door, Erika unlocks and opens the door gesturing everyone inside.

"Night all and it was nice to meet you both," Gavin says with a little wave, as he continues down the corridor to his apartment.

Inside, Dominique holds Erika's hand, as Erika says, "The place is yours. You know where everything is."

"You're going so soon?" Elle protests.

Erika pulls Dominique closer and smiles, "I have some post theatre plans of my own."

"Right," Elle says knowingly. "We might do the same," she says with a wink.

Erika, Elle, Dominique, and Andy, all give each other a hug and a cheek kiss and say their good nights. Then Elle and Andy step inside, closing the door. Erika and Dominique quickly head upstairs to Dominique's apartment.

Chapter 23

No sooner than Dominique and Erika have removed their shoes than Erika turns to Dominique and says, "I'm so sorry for letting you down."

Before she's finished speaking, Dominique has wrapped her arms around Erika, holding her in a close hug, "You've nothing to apologise for."

"But I," Erika says, her voice breaking, "but I let you down,"

"No, you didn't babe," Dominique says softly. "You did really well."

"But I was going to bite Elle," Erika says, her voice faltering.

"Going to, planning to, yes, but you didn't," Dominique says softly, reassuringly,

"Only because you and Gavin stopped me," Erika counters weakly.

"Yet Elle doesn't know anything about it and I'm sure Gavin won't tell her," Dominique replies reassuringly.

"But...," Erika starts before being cut-off by Dominique.

"But nothing. I don't like and don't need to engage in pointless what-if games. You either did or you did not. In this case, you did not. That's the bit that matters, it doesn't matter if you intended to and did not. What matters is the did or in this case the did not," Dominique says caressing Erika's back, reassuring her.

"But I lost control, and I would have...," Erika begins, relaxing slightly.

"You probably would, if things had been different, but they weren't," Dominique says, pulling back slightly. "You've been family for how long?"

"About a week," Erika admits.

"A week," Dominique agrees, "All bar about half an hour. In vampire years, that's a week. Or looked at from another perspective, it's one fifty-second of a year. Which when the normal measure of time is in the decade or century, it doesn't seem like particularly long. I know, you're trying, but you need to put your triumphs and I hesitate to use the word failure to one side, so I'll stick with missteps. You spent the whole night, a good three hours at the theatre plus another two hours of socialising without any problems. Frankly, I'm extremely impressed. I did say at the beginning this was not a terribly good plan and you did so much better than I imagined."

"I did?" Erika asks hesitantly, looking Dominique in the eye.

"You did. I was fully expecting a problem of some kind in the theatre. I didn't think you would have a problem with dinner, and you handled yourself impeccably. I did think that the theatre would be too much. But to my pleasant surprise, you handled that well. It was unfortunate what happened at the end. Any idea why that happened?" Dominique asks, taking her first step towards the lounge area.

"I don't know," Erika offers weakly, following along.

"Yes, you do," Dominique says, her warmth present, but the firmness returning to her voice. "Be honest, to yourself and to me."

Erika stops walking, closes her eyes, and takes a deep breath before exhaling, then speaking, "I'd been concentrating all evening, fighting the smells and the desire to just feed," Erika says, with the words suddenly just pouring out. "Then in the corridor, I started to relax, as we were home, and I thought the risk had passed. I'd been fine during dinner, and I think I let my guard down too quickly or maybe just let it down and then I was overtaken with the desire to, you know, to bite Elle."

"Why Elle, why not Andy?" Dominique says.

"Um, I think she just seemed the one. I didn't really think about it. It was an instinct," Erika says, after a moment's consideration.

"Alright," Dominique says, "and just so you know if I'm disappointed, I will tell you. There will be no misunderstanding. Now sit with me on the sofa and let's talk about the interesting things that happened this evening."

Erika sits down on the sofa, allowing Dominique to sit between her legs and lay her head back onto Erika's shoulder. "What was more interesting than my slip?"

"Well, in the first instance, you seem to be over your sulk or low patch from the other night. I would consider that an interesting development," Dominique says, getting comfortable.

"I wasn't sulking," Erika says protesting, "I was overwhelmed by what you said and what it implied."

"I've been saying the whole time, that you're not ready to have the answers to questions you ask and the first time I give you the full answer, you sulk for a couple of days. I was beginning to wonder if I should watch daytime TV and then use that as an excuse to kill myself," Dominique says seriously.

"You can't you're already dead," Erika quips.

"Then it goes to show, I wouldn't even get that satisfaction. That's what you're not-sulking was doing to me," Dominique replies.

"Sorry, I didn't mean to do that," Erika says.

"And yet you did it for days, so was it deliberate or not? And if it was an accident, does that make you incompetent?" Dominique asks.

"I don't know, maybe," Erika says bemused.

"Exactly," Dominique says triumphantly. "Now to the interesting matters at hand. Were you looking at auras all evening?"

"Most of it," Erika says cautiously, "it got a little overwhelming in the theatre, but mostly. Why?"

"Alright, lets start at the beginning. What did you see and remember from when you first saw Andy and what did you see with his aura later?" Dominique asks.

"Let me think," Erika begins, "When he came in, he looked happy, incredibly happy. Now you mention it, he seemed overly happy."

"And then later?" Dominique prompts.

"Then later, he looked, I don't know, for a few moments, he's aura was brown. I don't know what that means."

"Brown is unhappy or at the extreme bitter," Dominique says.

"And it had some dark grey and dark green," Erika adds.

"That would be depressed or perhaps uncertain, it will depend on what other colours are around at the time," Dominique adds, "The dark green is typically, envious, or jealous, something like that. So, unless you have more colours. Put that together."

"Alright, that all makes sense. If he's extremely sick, he's going to put a brave face on it, but his true feelings are going to show through from time to time. So, being unhappy, envious, or depressed all make sense. I could also see him trying to put a brave face on it, particularly for Elle," Erika says thinking it all through.

"Yes, it does," Dominique confirms, "but what should you do about it? If anything?"

"You mean more than you already did?" Erika queries.

"Yes, more than that," Dominique confirms.

"Why did you put some of me into the dinner?" Erika asks, without prompting.

"Think it through, what effect will that have on them? And on us?" Dominique asks, leaving the questions hanging until Erika replies.

After giving it a little thought, Erika says, "For you and me, it makes it taste a lot better. It makes it taste much nicer."

"Alright, that's fair," Dominique says, "it did certainly make it much nicer from my perspective. But that wasn't the reason I did it. Although, I won't pretend that I didn't like it. What about for the others?"

"Oh, for Elle, it will give her a nice taste and a good feeling," Erika says. "Is there anything else it will do for her? But, for Andy, it will taste nice and improve his mood. It will also heal him?"

"I don't know about heal him, but it will or should, give him a little boost. Did you see how his mood improved after dinner and he seemed better within himself? That's about all that small amount will do. Don't forget there was only about three tablespoons worth in total, spread out between all of us and some wasted. It's why we don't normally put it into food. Taking it direct is more enjoyable for all parties."

"I understand that, but why did you do it?" Erika asks.

"There are a couple of reasons, first, I thought there was something wrong with Andy. It turns out, I was correct. I couldn't know what was wrong, but I did know something was wrong," Dominique says. "But I might well have done it anyway. You're going to need associates and Elle might be a good possibility."

"What?" Erika says an edge of surprise creeping into her voice.

"You will need associates. She's a good friend, she works at the same law firm as you do, but she's around in the daytime, when you're not. It would give you a much-needed advocate into the business, during internal discussions, and during decision making. She could be there to work on your behalf," Dominique says. "And with the new Andy situation, you could fully heal him and transform their lives. He wouldn't need dialysis or a transplant. You could give him his kidneys back, as if they never became damaged in the first place."

"That's very calculating," Erika notes.

"It is, but that's how life now is for you. Predator, remember. You need to put your long-term interests first. In time, people will seem to flit in and out of your life, as they don't last all that long. Short lifespans," Dominique says, as kindly as she can.

"Yes, but...," Erika begins.

Dominique interrupts, "You had this problem a couple of days ago, which caused the non-sulk. I know it's early for you, but this mindset change is going to have to happen, or you won't survive. I'm doing everything I can to keep you safe and enable you to thrive. I know it's confusing and difficult, because it means changing everything about your life and your outlook."

"It's not just that," Erika says. "But it seems so cold. So uncaring."

"It might, to a human, but it's not. It's a necessary part of being who you are and how you can and must live to survive and thrive," Dominique replies. "You're going to need associates. The best kind are ones you like, they can help you and you can help them. The way things look currently, Elle and Andy are viable candidates. Besides, tonight, they demonstrated that they're compatible with you."

"What do you mean compatible with me?" Erika prompts.

"Because this is new to you, you won't have appreciated that not everyone can become an associate. Sometimes, they're just not compatible. They can't take the blood, or perhaps can't take it from a particular donor," Dominique says.

"Just to clarify, you're saying not just anyone can be my associate?" Erika asks.

"That's correct," Dominique says, "you'll find that most people will be compatible, but not all. As far as I know, there's no way of knowing ahead of time. They just must drink from you and see how it goes. It if tastes nice and they enjoy it, so much the better. If they vomit, then it's not going to work for them. The test is easy, hence the upgrade to dinner. Everyone enjoyed it and so everyone enjoyed their evening."

"That's it?" Erika asks.

"Not quite, they'll heal well over the next few days, so Andy might well improve a little. Elle will heal anything that might need healing. The effect will be gone by this time next week. Probably a little quicker than that. It depends on how much they use up and how much healing, etc. they need. Andy will go through his supply much quicker as he is already sick," Dominique says, wiggling slightly, to get more comfortable. "It's nice to have you warm again."

"What if I don't want to make them associates?" Erika asks.

"Then everything will progress as it does today. Elle will get old, and Andy will lose his kidneys in a year or so from now. You have the power to change that course, or not, as you see fit," Dominique says simply.

"That's a lot of pressure, just like with the fate of the world," Erika says.

Dominique considers Erika's words a moment, "I don't see it that way. She's your best friend, you went to university together and became lawyers together. I would have thought that the decision was easy and obvious. I agree, that if Andy hadn't become ill, it would have been more difficult. But she is, and he's ill, so it's quite simple. You can help them, and they can help you. Why would you hesitate?"

"Because it doesn't seem that simple to me, she's an old and dear friend. How could I do that to her, without her permission?" Erika asks.

"Who said anything about without her permission?" Dominique says. "I don't remember mentioning that."

"I just thought," Erika says slightly confused. "I don't know what I thought. I think I assumed that I just do it to her or to them."

"Don't be silly. You are mixing up the: is it a sensible idea, with the how to do it," Dominique says. "So, step one, is it a sensible idea. I think it is. Everyone wins and you get to keep your best friend young and healthy for as long as possible. Your thoughts, on the sensible idea part?"

Erika sighs, raising and then lowering Dominique's head, as her chest expands, "Yes, it's probably a good idea."

"Thoughts, not simple agreement," Dominique prompts.

"I've not really thought about having associates, so the idea of Elle and Andy becoming associates is frankly a strange concept. I understand that I was one of yours but taking one of my own seems strange. I could make a difference in Andy's life, for the better. You're right, Elle being at work during the day looking out for my interests is a fantastic idea. It could make my life easier at work and she could give me advanced warning of things I might need to know. It makes a lot of sense," Erika says.

"Then I think we're in agreement, that it's a good idea," Dominique says recapping. "Which leads us to the practical implementation. This is quite straightforward. You simply tell them that you're a vampire and that you'd like them to be part of your team. The benefit will be Andy's cure and Elle won't grow old."

"What, we just sit down over a coffee, and I explain all that to them?" Erika says to Dominique's laughter.

"Hardly," Dominique says wiping a tear from her eye, "No, you first need to be able to use your and I'm using your phrase here, mind-control techniques to cover your failure scenario. So, if it goes wrong, you can reset their world, as if it never happened. That's the pro version of how to do it. In practice, when the time comes, we'll do it together and it won't go wrong."

"You do this to me on purpose, don't you?" Erika says, poking Dominique in the ribs.

"Yes," Dominique replies simply, "Yes I do."

"Why?" Erika asks.

"For the same reason I give you every time you ask, because it's fun!" Dominique says with a grin.

"You're impossible," Erika chides.

"Perhaps, it's you not me that's impossible. I'm doing my best, you know," Dominique says, as her grin fades. "Anything else you want to ask about this evening? And I'm not going to explain the play or what happened or why the body count is so high."

"There's a couple of things, lets start with me crushing your hand. What happened, what did you do, how did you do it?" Erika asks, as she gently caresses Dominique's arms.

"That feels nice," Dominique comments. "That's fairly straightforward, you squeezed too hard and broke the bones in my hand."

"But you never reacted, you only looked around to see where the sound was coming from. When you knew full well it was from your hand. I thought you could make your body rock hard?" Erika pushes.

"All those things are true, but what was I to do? I was trying to help you. I needed you to get through the play. That was part of my way of doing that. Nothing more, nothing less. You did squeeze extremely hard, but yes, I could have stopped that happening. But here's the curious part, it was less effort to have you break my bones and to heal them than it was to become suitably hard. It was just practical. That and I wanted you to feel what it was like to break someone's bones," Dominique says, as her grin returns.

"You're playing with me again," Erika protests.

"No, I'm trying to give you a wide range of experiences in the shortest amount of time possible. You must be fully autonomous by the first day of back to work, which is in what about nine days," Dominique says. "So, you knowing that you can easily break the bones in my hand, shows you how easy it will be to do that to other people, who might not be able to heal quite as quickly as I can. What was your other thought?"

"Gavin's appearance was most timely and opportune," Erika says coyly.

"I'm sure it was nothing more than a coincidence. I imagine he knew that you'd been out all evening with me and thought it was an appropriate time for a run to keep fit," Dominique says simply.

"Except, if I understand correctly, he's dead and cannot get fit or for that matter unfit. So, why would he be out running when he can move like lightening?" Erika asks pushing again.

"Maybe, just maybe, because that's what men in their late twenties do. They go running, they lift weights," Dominique says. "It's one thing to say you do it, but to be truly believable, you must physically do it. I think I see how this is going and where I can help. What's the best way to fake packing a suitcase?"

"I don't know?" Erika says.

"It's easy, you pack the suitcase as if you're going for a trip. Then pull a couple of items out and repack it. That way, it will look like a packed suitcase," Dominique says.

"That's because you packed the suitcase," Erika says. "There was no fake about it."

"Correct, but to everyone you've packed a suitcase. The same applies here. If his lifestyle includes going for a run, then he must go for a run. The sweating was a nice touch though," Dominique says impressed.

"How so?" Erika asks.

"Generally, we don't sweat, technically, if you can get warm, run the heart, etc. even while sleeping, you can with effort sweat, but generally it's too much effort. So, either he was showing off, unlikely, or he tipped a bottle of water over himself and nobody's going to lick it to see if it's water or sweat. And if they did, he could just say that he poured a bottle of water over his head because he was hot. It's quite simple to be convincing. People tend to accept the solutions that are appropriate to the situation. I don't know why he didn't want to shake Elle and Andy's hands. You're guess is as good as mine on that one," Dominique says.

"But it was very helpful that he was there during my lapse," Erika says not entirely convinced.

"I think I could have handled you on my own. You're only a week old. Not all that much of a challenge," Dominique quips.

"So, you say," Erika says lightly.

"Yes, I do. Now, would you like to go and play vampires and villagers?" Dominique asks.

"How does that work?" Erika enquires.

"Come with me and I'll show you, villager," Dominique says lightly, as she leans forward, but her voice suggests something else entirely.

Chapter 24

Dominique watches the black cab pull-out into traffic, then turning to Erika, says, "At least you didn't slam the door that time, which is a marked improvement."

"I've been practicing, and I am trying," Erika says, looking towards the door and the long queue, which is unusual for the VIP guests.

"I see it too," Dominique comments, "I wonder why the queue is so long?"

As they join the end of the queue, Erika asks, "Is there an event going on tonight? Or something like that?"

Dominique shakes her head, "Not that I know of. It must just be one of those things, where on some random night it's just busy. Hopefully, the queue will go quickly. We shouldn't have to wait long."

"And if we do?" Erika asks.

"Then we pull rank and move to the front," Dominique says simply.

"How do we do that?" Erika asks. "Use our powers of persuasion?"

"That could work, but hardly necessary. We can just walk in, but I prefer to get a feel for what's going on and what people are expecting, so I don't mind waiting a little while," Dominique says by way of explanation. "But patience only lasts so long."

"All interesting, but you didn't really answer my question," Erika prompts.

"Oh, sorry," Dominique says. "It's simple, because this is one of the businesses we own."

"Really?" Erika asks surprised.

"Of course," Dominique says, "it's always better to frequent safe places. Those you own are normally safer than those owned by others."

"How so?" Erika asks.

"Well, firstly, all the staff are known quantities, because they've been employed specifically because you trust them, at least they're mostly trustworthy. Secondly, you know their vested interests, like keeping their jobs and those who are only here for the fun. Those looking for the money and a career, they're the best. It's easy when you can see their emotions. Which I trust you're currently doing to everyone," Dominique says.

"I'm doing my best, it's hard with so many people. I must focus on one at a time, even though I did see more than one that first night," Erika protests.

"Yes, you do, that's how you develop the skill, the more you practice the easier it will become. The quicker you can master this; the easier life will be. This is a foundational skill. Start with one person, then two, then groups and finally everyone at once all the time," Dominique says. "It'll take a few years to get everyone all the time, but that's one commodity you have in abundance."

"Alright, I'm trying and practicing," Erika says with a resigned edge to her voice. "It's hard work you know."

"I know and you're doing well," Dominique says, as they shuffle forward.

As they chat back and forwards, they move closer to the front of the line and after about ten minutes are at the front.

"Evening ladies," Jim says with his customary smile and cheer.

"And a pleasant evening to you too Jim," Dominique offers.

"Evening Jim," Erika says with a grin.

"And your occupation tonight ladies is?" Jim asks grinning.

"Blood sucking evil fiend," Dominique says casually.

"I'll put you down as a lawyer then," Jim says, clearly having fun.

"And Erika here, she's a boring blood sucking evil fiend."

"Barrister it is as usual," Jim says chuckling, clearly never tiring of the joke.

"We seem to be busy tonight?" Dominique enquires.

"Yes, I think there's a party of some sort. They're going to fill the VIP section and with luck they'll behave," Jim says, clearly hoping for the best but not expecting it.

"Thanks for the warning," Erika chips in.

"And all's well with the family?" Dominique asks.

"Yes, they're all fine," Jim says, "Now you two, stop holding up the line, I have more guests to welcome. Go on, shoo." With that he makes a shooing action and encourages them into the club.

Like always, the noise washes over them quickly, followed by the signature laser display. They head to their left and up the stairs to the VIP floor. At the top of the stairs, the usher smiles, greets them warmly and shows them to their open booth away from the main activity.

As she sits down Erika asks, "Are we going to continue coming here every weekend?"

"Perhaps not every weekend, but most, yes," Dominique says, slipping into the booth next to Erika. "Why do you ask?"

"Well, I was wondering, if there wasn't better use of our time?" Erika asks.

"You don't like the party scene?" Dominique asks by way of a reply.

"I do, but things have changed," Erika replies.

"They've not changed all that much," Dominique says looking at the people around the lounge. "Look around, there's all kinds of people here, what more could you want to practice on, to see and understand? Plus, in the fullness of time, you'll find plenty of opportunities to practice your seduction techniques."

"I don't think I see the world the same way you do," Erika replies.

"Perhaps not, not yet anyway," Dominique says, "but I think you'll see it more my way over the coming weeks and months."

"You're probably right, but I'm still trying to get a feel for the changes," Erika says. "It's not as easy as you think and I'm going to bet you don't remember quite how hard it is."

"You're almost certainly right on multiple counts there. It's been a while and I don't remember as well as I might have and anyway, this time is different to when I went through these changes. Your challenges and problems are different than the ones I experienced. So, to that extent, you're correct. It is different, both easier in some regards and much harder in others. But this is really a conversation for at home not here," Dominique says.

"Yes, alright, when we get home," Erika says understanding.

"Now, would you like a drink? Your usual?" Dominique says, "Or do you feel like celebrating a work success and having some champagne?"

"Really, I thought we were keeping a low profile," Erika asks.

"Lowish," Dominique says with a grin, "but not too low. A girl's got to have fun."

"Then yes please," Erika says with a grin. "That sounds nice."

Dominique slips out of her seat and walks over to the bar. She waits her turn and the bartender, takes her order explaining that it will be a few moments and he'll bring the drinks and glasses over. Just as she's about to return to her seat, Dominique pauses and looks at the woman sitting alone a few places over. Eying her momentarily, Dominique goes to speak to the woman before returning to Erika.

"Excuse me," Dominique says to the woman and when she looks up, continues with a warm smile on her lips, "I'm sorry, I hope you don't think I'm being rude, but you seem to be sitting alone in a nightclub."

The woman looks at Dominique a moment then with a gentle sigh says, "I'm waiting for some friends."

"Of course," Dominique says with a warm smile, "but you didn't all come together?"

"No, they are supposed to be here by now, but I just got a message to say they're running late," the woman says.

"That's unfortunate," Dominique agrees. "Did they say when they'd be arriving?"

"In about twenty minutes," the woman says unhappily.

"Would you care to join Erika and I, over there at the booth," Dominique says. "No strings attached, just a little chat and maybe a laugh or two. I've been where you are, sitting alone in the club waiting. It's not fun."

"Um, I don't know," the woman replies, looking torn. "I don't know if I should."

"Then have a drink on me and if you change your mind, I'll be over there," Dominique says gesturing to where Erika's sitting. Gesturing to the bartender, who comes over quickly. "Please get this lady whatever she wants and put it on my tab would you please." He nods his agreement and Dominique with a smile to the woman walks back to Erika to await her champagne.

"What was all that about?" Erika asks, as Dominique sits back down.

"I ordered our drinks; they should be over shortly," Dominique says.

"And?" Erika interrupts.

"And, I had a little chat with that woman. She's here alone, and if you've been watching her aura, she's not particularly happy about it," Dominique says.

"I did see that, but I didn't know why, until now," Erika says. "I also saw how it changed just before you started to talk to her and how it changed while you were talking."

"Good. So, I invited her over and bought her a drink. Then came back here," Dominique says knowingly.

"Do you think she'll come over?" Erika asks, looking at the young man bringing their champagne and glasses over.

"Of course, she will," Dominique says with complete confidence. She thanks the young man as he expertly arranges the glasses and champagne in its silver bucket on the table. He pours two measures, letting the fizzy liquid glide down the side of the glasses, keeping the froth to a minimum. Once finished, he quickly disappears after ensuring all is well.

"How can you be so sure?" Erika asks, watching the young man disappear.

"Because I charmed her," Dominique says simply.

"What's that?" Erika asks intrigued.

"It's the reason we're here tonight," Dominique says cryptically.

"You know what I mean," Erika prompts, reaching for her glass.

Dominique makes a show of sighing, "I showed her my, not so inconsiderable, charm. So, she'll want to come over and chat. Just wait and watch."

"Alright," Erika says sipping at her drink.

Dominique reaches for hers and offers a toast, "To life."

Erika echoes, "To life." And clinks glasses. "How long will it take?"

"A couple more minutes," Dominique says confidently. "She's currently fighting with herself to decide if it's sensible or not. Deep down she knows it's not in the generalised case, but she really wants to. So, that will win out and she'll come over."

The two women continue chatting about this and that, Erika knowing better than to push about the ability to charm. Another conversation for at home. A few minutes later, as predicted, the woman comes over with a Strawberry Daiquiri.

"Would you mind, if I joined you?" the woman asks gingerly.

"Of course not," Dominique says a warm smile on her face, "I invited you earlier. So, you're still welcome."

The woman smiles, and as she sits says, "Thank you."

"But, only until your friends arrive. You can't stay longer than that, it wouldn't be right," Dominique says with mock seriousness.

The woman relaxes visibly and sips at her drink.

"I'm sorry, I'm being rude. I'm Dominique and this is my friend Erika," Dominique says gently, the charm always present.

"Hello," Erika says with a smile.

"I'm Sharon," the woman says returning the smile.

"I know this is a little strange, being asked over by two complete strangers," Dominique says. "But we've all been in your position, and I just thought, offering was the nice thing to do."

Erika nods as Dominique speaks, then adds, "It's horrible to be all on your own."

The three women talk about this and that. Time passes, the laughter ebbs and flows with the conversation. In time, Sharon's friends arrive, and they spot her and wave.

"That's my party," Sharon says chuckling from the previous comments, "I should join them."

"It's been nice chatting with you Sharon," Erika says warmly, the enjoyment in her eyes.

"And if you ever find yourself in that position again and we're here, feel free to come over. I've enjoyed the last half an hour," Dominique says.

"Me too," Sharon agrees.

"We tend to be here on Saturdays, just so you know. Fridays, sometimes, but normally Saturday if we're going to be here," Dominique clarifies.

"I'll keep that in mind, and I'll stop and say hi next time I see you," Sharon confirms.

"I look forward to it and I hope you enjoy the rest of your night. Happy dancing," Dominique says with a warm smile as Sharon stands up, flashes Erika a smile as she turns walking towards to her friends.

Once she's out of earshot, Dominique whispers, "Now listen to what they say." She sips quietly at her drink while Erika listens.

Erika to sips at her drink, when Sharon's party move off, she turns to Dominique and says, "That was interesting. She spoke very highly about how nice you were and how it was nice of us to invite her to spend time with us."

"I predict that's she'll be here next Saturday too. So, we can chat with her again next weekend," Dominique says simply.

"How can you be so sure?" Erika asks.

"Charming, remember," Dominique says, "she's going to want to spend some more time with us and particularly me. This is something you're going to have to learn how to do."

"Clearly," Erika confirms.

"There was a good reason for showing you this, it's going to be critical to your interactions with everyone going forward. Particularly in situations where you want people to have a favourable impression of you," Dominique says, refilling their glasses.

"Is this a new secret power?" Erika asks.

Dominique sighs, "You and your cartoon people. Yes, if you want to think of it that way, then yes. It's basically the same scenario as the bridge, but the complete opposite. That was control, this is more persuasion."

"Ah, more mind control," Erika says misunderstanding.

"No, it's nothing like that. It's both more subtle, sophisticated, and much harder to detect," Dominique says, resigning herself to the simplistic explanations.

"I think I understand," Erika says nodding.

"We'll see," Dominique says finishing her drink. "Laura's coming for a visit tonight."

"Gavin's sister Laura?" Erika enquires.

"The one and the same," Dominique replies. "So, we have a little time for dancing and one more drink before we must head home. Fancy a dance? And don't forget, club rules apply."

"I remember, hold breath, etc." Erika confirms.

"Then let's dance a little," Dominique says with a grin.

Chapter 25

Settling back onto the sofa, having swapped outdoor shoes for slippers, Erika arranges herself comfortably. Her voice cautious as she asks, "What happened at the nightclub? You said we'd discuss it back at home."

"Alright, give me a second," Dominique says, as she also settles onto the sofa, looking directly at Erika. "First, were you looking at Sharon's aura, the whole time we were talking?"

Erika nods, "Yes, I think so. Why?"

"What did you notice, what did it tell you?" Dominique asks.

"We talked about this in the club," Erika says.

"We did but indulge me," Dominique counters.

"As we discussed, she was unhappy that her friends left her alone, they didn't arrive when they were supposed to and that left her feeling abandoned and isolated. With, I would like to point out, nothing to do and nobody to speak to," Erika says.

"All true, how much of that did you get from her aura?" Dominique asks.

"Well, I knew she was unhappy, but I didn't know why," Erika replies.

"Good, as far as it goes," Dominique says, "but there was more you could have known. The fact she was alone and unhappy meant one of two things, either her friends had not arrived yet, or they had ditched her. Either one would be ideal for a predator looking for a weakling at the edge of the herd. If you see the analogy."

"Alright, so you saw that she was unhappy, then your experience gave you some possibilities as to what might be going on. All of them made her vulnerable," Erika confirms. "That makes sense, which implies that anyone in such a situation might well be vulnerable too."

Dominique nods, "Exactly. Now, there's the possibility that it's a trap, but very few people can fake an aura and even fewer would do so in a nightclub. But, as you saw, I didn't do anything overt, I just offered her some company and someone in that position might well like some company. The key was that it was subtle, so even if it was a trap, I did nothing that would spring it on me. As she did want some company. It can be very boring being alone in a nightclub. I then upped desirability a little by making coming and chatting very enticing. That was the charm, or you could think of it as the charisma part. You must always be on the lookout for a trap or someone trying to gain one over on you. Don't forget, you're not the only predator out there, remember what happened last week?"

Erika nods, "I do remember and I'm taking your advice."

"First of all, let's think of it as charm or charisma on tap. It's there for you to use at any point on just about everyone. Now, what I did is hard to explain, but should be relatively easy for you to do. It's much easier to do than the fear I used at the club and at the bridge. That's harder, because if it goes wrong, you're in trouble. The charm, well, if that fails, nobody really knows. I suppose one is active, the fear, and the other more passive, the charm. That would be the best way to think about it," Dominique says holding Erika's gaze.

"Understood," Erika says, "but how do I use it?"

Dominique grins, "Now that's easy. Push the blood to your brain, like you've been practicing, but this time, think about being charming. Think about how much they like you and how they don't want to be out of your sight. Think about how they want to be around you all the time. Like all these skills, the more you use it, the easier it becomes. But a word of warning, this will work on family, and they might well notice what's happened. They might not be able to stop it, but they might well not look favourably on you for doing it to them. Just a word of warning. And on that topic, when Laura comes later, she'll almost certainly try it on everyone. It's one of her party tricks."

Erika thinks for a moment, "You told me how to do it, not how to use it."

Dominique sighs just a little, "You're right. The best places are when you want or need someone to feel positively to you. So, in the club, I wanted Sharon to come over, so I made her feel happy, positive thoughts towards me. That's really it."

"Can I try it on you?" Erika asks.

"Of course, but I'm almost certain to notice, and even if you get it right, it will almost certainly have no effect," Dominique says, "but the practice is good."

Erika, like with all these attempts, puts too much effort into preparation, as if that matters. She clearly concentrates as she gathers her thoughts and pushes blood into her head. Minutes tick by and nothing happens. Then more minutes pass.

"That was almost it," Dominique says, "I felt a little something. Not quite what we needed, but you're getting there."

As with previous attempts at mastering a skill, it takes quite a while longer before she gets the effect again. Only this time it's much more pronounced.

"Oh, I felt that," Erika says happily.

"Good, because I did too. That was a good attempt, you'd have gotten Sharon's interest with that. I think it might just have been enough to get her to come over. So well done and that took what, forty minutes?" Dominique says, giving Erika a congratulating smile.

"And this is what it feels like to be on the receiving end," Dominique says, as Erika receives the full force of Dominique's charm offensive.

"Wow, the effect was quick and intense," Erika says impressed. "You just blasted me with charm, and it took you no time at all and I really felt it. I want to be with you, to do things to please you. It's an intense feeling, I just want to make you happy."

"I'm sorry but it's important you can feel what happens. Now that was much more intense than is useful for general activity because you felt it so strongly. But I wanted you to get an easy feel for what it's like. Don't worry, it will pass soon, or at least soonish," Dominique says sheepishly.

"So, I'm going to feel like this all night?" Erika asks.

"Yes, probably," Dominique concedes.

"Great," Erika says with a sigh.

"Don't worry, it will help when Laura comes round later," Dominique says cheerily.

"You know these little pep-talks make it worse right?" Erika states.

"We'll see, what looks worse now, might not be later. I hope the warning is clear," Dominique says.

"It is, but I don't understand the why behind the warning," Erika says getting slightly frustrated.

"I already said, Laura will fill the room with this to see who's susceptible and who's not paying attention. She won't care who knows, that's not the point," Dominique says.

"So, she does it because she can," Erika asks.

"Partly because she can, partly because she finds it fun and there's no repercussion with us. It's just part of her being her," Dominique says simply.

"Alright, I'll do my best," Erika says.

"And you wanted to talk about something else when we got home?" Dominique asks.

"It will make me sound like I'm complaining," Erika says, "but I'm not sure that you fully appreciate how hard it is to do all the things you want me to do all at once."

Dominique nods as she listens, "You're probably right, I don't really remember how hard it is and I know getting accustomed to the new body, the things that you can now do and the things you can't do any longer. It's not easy, I know that."

"Carry on," Erika prompts.

"When I did it, there wasn't all the technology which works both for you, in that it makes things easier, but it also makes it much harder as you need to be more careful. But I think I have managed all those parts well for you. For now, at least," Dominique says. "The bits I know you're talking about are all the other things, which have to do with you adapting to the new way of thinking and the so-called secret powers."

Erika nods, "Yes, that. I don't know if you know how hard it is to completely change your world view and drop everything you know and take on a new way of seeing and interacting with the world."

"I don't," Dominique concedes. "When I was in the position you are now, the world was simpler and there wasn't the pressure you're under to learn everything so quickly. For that I'm sorry, but I don't know of any other way to do it."

"Tell me what you're trying to do and why," Erika says encouraging Dominique to continue.

"I've told you before, I'm trying to get you ready to go out into the world on your own. There are some who would take advantage of you. Of your strength, mental and physical, of your blood and of your potential," Dominique pauses a moment. "Even though, I keep telling you that you're special, you don't and currently cannot understand what your potential means. Partly because you don't have the framework to process it. Look what happened the other day and that wasn't a particularly significant conversation."

"It seemed pretty important," Erika says. "We were talking about deliberately collapsing civilisation."

"Exactly," Dominique says with a smile, "that makes my point directly. It's not significant, but you think it is. Civilisation will collapse whether we do it or not. We are only quibbling about the timing and what damage happens to us in the interim. I know the former is inevitable, it's the latter about which I am more concerned."

"You don't care that millions of people might die?" Erika says incredulously.

Dominique shakes her head, "No, millions, billions, it doesn't matter to us. What matters is that civilisation doesn't continue, otherwise we're all killed. That would be the tragedy. Your perspective is still human, but it's only been a little over a week and that'll change soon. When you begin to see what they are and understand what you are. And what you are to them."

"What do you mean, what I am to them?" Erika asks, her attitude changing quickly.

"We keep hidden and quiet, trying to mind our own business and keep our affairs separate as much as possible," Dominique begins, "but that doesn't mean that our existence is as well-hidden as I would like. Take that incident at the bridge. Do you imagine that we're the first family or people that they accosted? I doubt it, I would expect they had done that to many others. I don't know their goal or motivation, but I don't think it involved keeping our presence secret. That will have repercussions on both all of family and, specifically, the King and Queen. Don't forget that London is one of the top territories in the world. Destabilise here and there will be repercussions elsewhere. Jonathan can explain this all to you better than I can. It is after all, his thing."

"If I am understanding correctly, I am still thinking like a human, because I don't understand enough of what's going on elsewhere?" Erika says thinking it through. "But you haven't told me enough to give me a detailed framework to allow me to understand the bigger picture from a family perspective. Is that correct."

"In a roundabout sort of way, yes," Dominique confirms, "but like with all these things, it's not that simple. You're doing the people thing and wanting a simple explanation, but there isn't one. The world is complex, the problems are complex and the solutions difficult at best. I honestly don't want to see millions of people die. That doesn't make me feel good or happy, but, and this is important, I want to see you dead less. That means, if I need to choose between keeping you alive and millions of them dying, I will always choose you. Since this is all new to you, you don't know how much preparation I've put into making these two weeks work as well as I can and including last night's wobble, we're doing well and on plan."

"I appreciate you wanting me to be alive," Erika says, then realises something. "Wait, you have a plan for all of this?"

"Of course, I do, you didn't think that the trips out and all the other set piece events are random, do you?" Dominique says surprise evident in her voice. "Though the theatre last night and dinner was not part of my plan, but it went as well as could be expected."

"So, you planned out the whole two weeks?" Erika asks pushing.

"The broad-brush bits, there's plenty of things you must learn, practice and there's not much time to make it work. Remember, when I said you've done more in days, that I did in years. That's still true, if all goes well this coming week, you'll be ahead of where I was in my first ten years. Admittedly, you have a teacher, and I didn't. But you also have Gavin to look out for you and to train you in the things he's good at. Who knows, we might yet get something useful out of Laura too. Though, my hopes are not so high there. If she cooperates, she can teach you the charm much quicker and more effectively than me, but so far, she's been off doing whatever it is she's doing and before you ask, I don't know what she's doing, I have a theory, but I don't know."

"I don't know what to ask next," Erika concedes.

"We could always go back to the ending of civilisation that seems to upset you no end," Dominique suggests unhelpfully.

"I don't know if I should ask, but there are things worse than that," Erika asks, then suddenly understanding the perspective, "From a human perspective?"

"I don't know about that," Dominique says, "I don't have that as a perspective. Mine is concerned about you, about Gavin and Laura; Jonathan and Matt. Mine is family related. What affects them, that affects all of us, so it's important to me. From that perspective, yes, there are things more important than the end of civilisation. While you will have input, should the need arise, your opinion will not be the dominant one. Almost everyone will be happy to get rid of civilisation if it means preserving us. Their perspective is much closer to mine than yours and in time yours will be closer to mine too."

"This is the bit I am struggling with," Erika says, "it's the matter-of-factness. The cold detachment in the whole event. I understand that the people don't matter to you, and I suppose that in time, my attitude will align more with yours as they matter less to me. But inherently, it just seems wrong."

"I think I know how to sort this out," Dominique says. "How much concern did you have for the beef animal that went into your steak, the one you had on your birthday? Your final meal if you will. How much did you care about that cow or steer or whatever it was? How much did you worry about that animal or any of the ones that died the same day and, in the months, since?"

Erika hesitates, partially thinking and partially looking for a way out, eventually she says, "Not much." From the look Dominique gives, prompts her to add, "Not at all. I didn't and don't care about them. They're just food, something you eat to get by."

"Bingo," Dominique says a broad grin covering her face. "Do you now know where my perspective is focused and why it doesn't bother me?"

"I do, but that doesn't mean I like it," Erika protests.

"It has nothing to do with liking or not liking it. It simply is. I don't imagine that you've thought much about it, but where do you think breakfast comes from?" Dominique asks.

"The fridge," Erika says, ducking down a little.

"Exactly, the strawberry comes from people, the raspberry from the abattoir. Neither is as satisfactory as drinking direct, but there is a definite convenience for the former over the latter," Dominique says.

"I have been meaning to ask about that," Erika says. "Is it something I should ask now or leave for later?"

"I'd be inclined to leave for later. For now, just assume that it's all sourced mostly ethically. One comes from voluntary donations, the other purchased as part of the waste process. All convenient, but not necessarily the best way to think about it," Dominique says, waiting for the inevitable questions.

"Alright, I'll back off and not ask any more about it," Erika says. "I trust you on this as with everything else."

"Good," Dominique says with a grin. "We wouldn't want you to have an unfortunate accident, would we?"

"No, I wouldn't," Erika confirms. "How long do we have until Laura arrives?"

Dominique glances at her watch, "An hour, maybe an hour and a half. Something like that, I don't know exactly when she's going to arrive. I imagine she'll come with Gavin."

"Understood then maybe we have time for a drink before she arrives?" Erika asks with a smile.

"Fridge?" Dominique asks.

"Only if there's no other options," Erika replies.

Chapter 26

"No, of course not," Dominique says, as she's interrupted by a knock on the door, "Hang on, let me get that," she says standing from the sofa and walks quickly to the front door, her slippers making hardly a sound. Upon opening the door, she's presented with Gavin's smiling face.

"Evening," Gavin says, his smile even more pronounced.

"Please come in," Dominique says formally.

"Why, thank you," Gavin replies equally formally, despite his beaming smile.

They both have a chuckle as Gavin removes his shoes and they head into the lounge, where Erika sits on the sofa.

"Evening Erika," Gavin says, as he enters the lounge area.

"Nice to see you again," Erika replies happily.

"Now that's over and done with, aren't you a bit early?" Dominique says. "I thought Laura was due in about an hour?"

"Possibly," Gavin offers, "I have no idea. I didn't know she was coming round here tonight."

"Then at the risk of being rude, why are you here?" Dominique asks.

"No offence taken," Gavin says warmly, "I came round to see how Erika's getting on." He pauses a moment, then adds, "After last night."

"I'm doing fine Gavin thank you," Erika replies. "Other than the shaky moment in the corridor, I've been coping fine."

Gavin looks to Dominique who nods, before adding, "We went to the nightclub tonight and she was fine. So, I'm not too worried about that."

"Well, that's good news," Gavin says with an infectious smile.

"Then I'll leave you two to it, for an hour anyway," Gavin says, "I want to be here if Laura's here."

"Just before you go," Erika says quickly, "I have a question if that's alright?"

"Anything, just ask," Gavin says kindly.

"Dominique and I were talking the other day about religion, and she said I should ask you about something," Erika says. "Are you able to stay and chat about it a little?"

Gavin doesn't respond, instead the looks at Dominique who simply nods twice. "I'd be happy to answer any questions you have. But, I need to say, her thoughts on religion and mine don't differ much."

Erika gestures to the sofa and the chair giving Gavin free rein to sit where he feels comfortable. "Then I have a few questions," Erika says, as he sits in the chair opposite her.

Gavin glancing to Dominique asks, "Is there any of that strawberry in the fridge?"

"I'll get you a glass," Dominique says and heads to the kitchen.

"We were talking about religion the other day," Erika says, "and Dominique said that basically it was all made-up by people and family and that it had nothing to do with any kind of god."

Gavin nods as he listens, "Alright, what do you want from me?"

"What can you tell me about religions," Erika says, choosing her words carefully, "I had the impression that you had some insight that would help me."

"I'm going to assume that you're religious?" Gavin says cautiously.

"Sort of, I go to church sometimes, but I was raised in a Christian household and in the Christian tradition," Erika says honestly.

"And how's it been?" Gavin asks.

"What do you mean?" Erika asks, as Dominique returns with a glass of deep red blood. She hands it to Gavin and sits down on the sofa.

"Thanks," Gavin says with a smile, "Ooo, and it's warm too. Perfect."

"Just as you like it," Dominique says with a nod of her head.

"I mean, what's it been like going to church lately?" Gavin clarifies.

"I've not been that much lately, they're semi-welcoming," Erika confirms.

"No gay marriage then?" Gavin says.

"No," Erika confirms, "that's exactly what I was thinking about."

"Well, if it makes you feel any better, if you think it's bad telling them you're a lesbian, imagine what it will do when you mention you're a vampire, or better still a lesbian vampire," Gavin says in all seriousness.

Dominique stifles a chuckle, but Erika ignores her and answers, "I don't imagine it will be much better."

"Neither do I," Gavin says, "and I don't imagine that it'll get any better anytime soon. I am assuming that Dominique told you that all religions are basically a human creation. That they have nothing to do with any god or deity?"

"She did and that's what I want to talk to you about," Erika says following Gavin's words with nods.

"I think I have to warn you that this conversation is going to get very uncomfortable very quickly," Gavin says. "There's nothing good that's going to come from this. After the sulking, are you prepared to accept that?"

"We're calling it a non-sulk," Dominique says chipping in.

"Then after the non-sulk," Gavin clarifies.

"Do I have a choice?" Erika asks.

"You always have a choice," Gavin says surprised, "there's always a choice. It doesn't always help, but there's always a choice."

Erika hesitates a moment, "Then I choose to know."

"Then if she told you what I expect her to have said, that every religion is based on previous religions and that they all form a chain from the basic to more complex. The goal at every step is for those in charge to remain in charge and for those that follow the religion to give power and money to those in charge. Does that sum it up?"

Erika nods, "Yes, that covers most of the big picture parts. My question is how does she know. I know the information is on the internet, I checked, but how do we know that information is correct."

"How much has she told you about us?" Gavin asks.

"Not much, mostly that time isn't important to us and that we need to focus on other things," Erika says. Dominique remains steadfastly silent.

"Has she told you anything about Laura or me?" Gavin asks, glancing at Dominique.

Erika shakes her head, "Nothing much, other than you're here to look after me in the daytime and that you're a twin brother and sister."

"Then there's a fair amount you could know about us. I'm guessing that you don't know much about Jonathan either?" Gavin asks.

Erika nods, "You're correct on all items, we've been concentrating on other things, like getting me to see and understand auras, on practicing your melee moves and that sort of thing."

"Understood," Gavin says clearly considering his options. "Then we probably have a little more to discuss than you imagine."

"Like what?" Erika asks.

"Like everything," Gavin replies. "Let's start with your religious questions. You want to know how she knows, or I know that it's a human creation. How old do you think I am?"

"If she's three hundred and forty, you have to be younger, Matt is one hundred and ninety-two, so I am going to say, about two hundred years old," Erika says a question in her voice as she finishes.

Gavin looks perplexed as he listens, then looking over at Dominique who simply shrugs.

"I hope you're looking at auras," Dominique says in general, "because from here, Gavin looks perplexed and he's not the only one."

Gavin regaining his sense of place, replies, "I don't know how that would work. Jonathan is what, five hundred and twenty or thirty years old. So, I don't know how Dominique could be three hundred and forty."

Erika looks to Dominique and says, "But you said ten times my age?"

"It was an example and I'm sure I mentioned at the time, that you'd misunderstood what I was saying," Dominique says bluntly.

"Well, Jonathan is much older than that and he's the second youngest of our group. You're the youngest, obviously," Gavin says. "Laura and I are a fair bit older than that. Which is how we all know that religion is all made-up, we've seen it change and morph into what the current leaders needed and wanted. Look at Christianity, over the last what twenty years, being gay was anathema to the church. Now today, it's tacitly accepted. What's written in the bible is either God's word, and therefore immutable and strictly followed, or it's not. It can only be one or the other. In my view, it's clear that it's purported to be God's word, but it's something else. That something else, is whatever the ruling hierarchy need. They adapt and reinterpret the written words as they see fit. Over time, what once was, will no longer be and so it morphs and changes to reflect and adapt to the prevailing social conventions."

"How can, you be sure?" Erika pushes.

"Because you and I have both lived through that change," Gavin says. "Either it's cast in stone, or it's not. If it's not, then what value other than control does it have?"

"Then let's for the sake of argument, say that you're correct," Erika says. "Then where does that leave me?"

"I am correct," Gavin says, "and it leaves you where it always has, with a choice. You can either follow along or not. I too was raised in a religious household, but once I saw what was happening, I came to understand that it was all man-made."

"You were religious?" Erika asks curiously.

"Of course," Gavin says openly, "we both were. We were raised as Jews back in the day. But over time, I saw how our religion morphed. If you look at what God's chosen people believe, it makes no sense. How can there be different sects if there's one religious' text and one word of God? It makes no sense."

"So, did you choose to be Jewish, rather than Christian or was it just what your family did?" Erika asks, clearly enjoying the conversation.

Gavin looks once more at Dominique who gives nothing back.

"What does his aura tell you?" Dominique asks Erika.

"That he's confused, or at least perplexed," Erika replies automatically.

"Good," Dominique replies.

"When I was young, Christianity wasn't an option," Gavin says simply regaining his composure.

"Why? Because you family was strictly Jewish?" Erika asks.

Cautiously Gavin replies, "No, because Christianity hadn't been invented." He looks to Dominique for support, but none is forthcoming.

Erika looks shocked. "Your aura gives you away Erika," Dominique says simply.

"You're over two thousand years old?" Erika says incredulously.

"Yes, I am, quite a bit older," Gavin says regaining his composure.

"Gavin's what, three thousand years old?" Dominique says adding to the confusion.

"Three thousand three hundred and a bit," Gavin says, "I can give you the exact number, if it matters."

Erika shakes her head, "No, three thousand three hundred is good enough. I had no idea that when she was talking about plenty of time, she really meant thousands of years. I thought it was just talk for the newbie."

"Why would you think that? Didn't she tell you that she'd only tell you the truth?" Gavin asks perplexed once more.

"She did," Erika confirms, "but, it never occurred to me that we were talking in such long-time scales." Turning to Dominique she asks, "So, how old are you?"

Dominique shrugs, "I don't know."

"What about approximately, I mean, it must be older than Gavin," Erika prompts.

"I don't know, but at a guess, I'd say, maybe eighteen or nineteen thousand years, it might be a little less, but I don't know. It was never that important at the beginning," Dominique says with a shrug.

"So, I've been dating an older woman," Erika says with a grin, but her expression and aura shows something else.

"In fact, as far as we can tell, perhaps the oldest woman alive, or well, you know what I mean," Gavin says.

"So, when you say, that religion is a man-made construct, you know it for a fact, because you saw it develop and when you talked about icon magic and the like, that was because you had first-hand experience with it?" Erika asks.

Dominique nods, "It is."

"Then where were you born?" Erika asks Dominique.

"It was before names," Dominique says simply.

"Well, what country then?" Erika asks, still not grasping the significance.

"It was before countries," Dominique says simply.

"What do you mean before countries?" Erika asks.

"I mean the concept of a country didn't exist. It was before countries. When I grew up, places didn't have names, there was no need. You knew where you lived and that was all you needed," Dominique says simply. "In the modern era, everyone likes to name everything, from their cuddly toys to body parts. Everything has a name. I think this is because of writing. As writing becomes everything, so things must have names, otherwise, how can you write about it. You need writing to communicate over large distances, which, in turn, means everything must have a name. We didn't travel over long distances, didn't need to write things down and so, didn't need to name everything. We knew where we lived and everyone else too for that matter."

"I think I understand what you're saying, but it seems so, so other...," Erika says, then pauses to collect her thoughts. "Then the village you were born in, is it now a city?" Erika asks, her trepidation at the subject overridden by her quest for knowledge and understanding.

Dominique shakes her head, "No, it did grow a bit, in the years after I left, but it was swallowed up by the sea when it rose."

"When was that?" Erika asks.

"I don't remember, ten or eleven thousand years ago, it might have been a bit longer," Dominique concedes.

"And what about you Gavin? Where were you born?" Erika asks enthusiastically.

"It's in what's now called Jordan," Gavin says. "We grew up in a small town. There's not much to say, it was just a normal town, doing normal things. But over time, you see the changes and it's strange to see, when you remember what it was like before."

"Do you miss it?" Erika asks.

"I don't think about it," Gavin says with a shrug. "I have other things to think about and one of the things you'll learn is that it doesn't pay to dwell too long on the past."

"What do you mean?" Erika asks.

"I mean, the curse, if you want to think of it like that is that we live forever. Never growing old, never getting ill and all of that. Which means everyone you know, will die, and every place you know will be gone, but you will still be here. The only thing we have is each other. That's what Dominique discovered and it's why we behave the way we do, so that we have some continuity in life, something, or someone that's there for us. That's me, it's Laura, it's Dominique and it's you," Gavin says looking Erika in the eye.

Erika looks surprised, "Me?"

"We are scarcely changing in a world of constant change," Gavin says. "I'm sure Dominique has already told you that you have to change a little bit every day, so that the world doesn't change without you?"

Erika nods, "She has."

"Good, if nothing else, do you see how you can fit into the group?" Gavin asks.

"I'm beginning too," Erika agrees.

"You understand that Dominique has a plan for all of us before we're made. That she chooses us very carefully, with just the right mix of personality, drive, and inquisitiveness?" Gavin asks to receive nods from Erika. "Then you know that we're putting in a lot of effort to keep you safe. The world's not quite as safe as she's probably lead you to believe. The threats come from people and family..." Dominique shakes her head and Gavin stops speaking.

"There's more?" Erika says, not seeing Dominique's gesture.

"There is, but not for today," Gavin says. "Suffice to say, the world isn't a safe place, but I'm sure you know some of that, hence the non-sulk."

"Alright, I get the idea. Can I then ask Dominique about her life, you know, before?" Erika asks.

"Don't ask me, ask her," Gavin says directing the conversation elsewhere.

"Ask away," Dominique says.

"What was lifelike all those years ago?" Erika asks, failing to get a sensible question out.

"Very much like today, lots of work and not enough fun," Dominique says.

"My question was poor," Erika says, critiquing herself, "what I meant, was when did you get married? Because I know you had a husband."

"It was before marriage," Dominique says simply. "But to answer the question you meant to ask, I was with my, I suppose we shall call him partner, we had a commitment ceremony in front of the village. We then, as the custom of the day, built our house. It took most of the summer and part of the autumn. Marriage is a comparatively modern idea, based, of course, from an older principle. Anyway, we built our house and made our bed, then when the autumn came, we harvested our crop and used the straw to finish off the outside of the house and cover the bed in straw and animal skins. When you get together, the village donate animal skins to the newly partnered couple. I don't want to say married couple, as it was something else, which doesn't have a name. That was what we did. From then, we had a family and raised our children."

"How old were you when you did this?" Erika asks enthusiastically.

"I don't know, fourteen or fifteen," Dominique says struggling to remember, "Years weren't as important then as they are now. Everyone now obsesses with how old they are and how old everything else is. Back then, it didn't matter. When you were old enough, you were old enough. Children helped the family, by planting seeds and tending fields. Nowadays, it would illegal, but then, it was a matter of survival, life, or death. If you, as a family, planted enough food, you got to eat through the winter. If not, then you didn't and could starve to-death. So, it was in everyone's interest to work and have enough to eat and the other practicalities of life."

"So, at fifteen you were a housewife?" Erika says stunned, "With all the responsibilities that goes along with that?"

"You make it sound so, I don't know what, somehow sordid. It wasn't like that, as you grow up, you spent time with your grandparents, learning skills, like how to make things, knives, axes, tools of all kinds. They taught you how to weave, make leather, everything. They were like a modern practical school. Then you went with your parents to do work. So, grandparents were for learning, parents for doing. I suppose things changed over the years, but I don't know when."

"So, you could teach all the historians about history. Tell them where they're going wrong and what they need to know?" Erika asks.

Gavin and Dominique chuckle simultaneous, "I could," Dominique says, "but that wouldn't be very sensible would it. People don't live that long and technically, to correct Gavin, I'm not the oldest living person on earth, I've been dead for almost all that time. Spritely, yes, but dead. It would be best to not forget that."

Erika nods, "Understood, but I have so many more questions. I don't know which one to ask first."

"Well, I'm not going anywhere, so you can always ask tomorrow, when you know which one to ask first," Dominique suggests.

"I know, why did you make Gavin?" Erika asks, as there's a knock on the door.

"Hold that thought," Dominique says heading for the door.

Chapter 27

No sooner had Dominique opened the door than a dark-haired woman smiles and quickly enters the apartment.

"I'd invite you in Laura, but there doesn't seem any point," Dominique says, the sarcasm evident in her voice.

"Thank you," Laura says, "but I don't think it's really necessary."

However, even having invited herself in, Laura doesn't proceed into the apartment proper, after placing her bag on the floor, she waits for Dominique to close the door, then wraps her arms around Dominique and says, "I've missed you."

Dominique completes the friendly embrace and hugs Laura back. As she releases the hug, Dominique comments, "But not so much as to come and visit."

"I've been busy," Laura says, as they walk into the lounge proper.

"Of course, you have," Dominique says her voice even.

"I have and just so you all know, Jonathan will be coming over later," Laura comments, even though she hardly acknowledges her brother or Erika, her attention fully focused on Dominique.

"How is tonight's visit going to go?" Dominique asks.

"Fine," Laura replies.

"Evening Laura," Gavin says enthusiastically. However, Erika remains silent.

"Gavin," Laura says hardly glancing his way.

"Erika, this is Laura," Dominique says formally, but unnecessarily.

"Hello, Laura," Erika offers, watching Laura intently.

Laura glances in Erika's direction and says, "I know who she is!"

"You said you were going to be nice," Dominique says. "Are you being jealous?"

"What?" Laura says surprised. "Who? Me? No, of course not."

"Then you can start being more friendly to people," Dominique says. "I'm not in the mood for a difficult night."

"Jonathan mentioned something about that," Laura comments.

"Oh, what did he say?" Dominique asks.

"He warned me not to make my usual style entrance, with the charm burst," Laura says, looking only at Dominique.

"Well, that explains that," Dominique says looking over at Gavin, who simply shrugs. "Will this be true for the whole evening?"

"Yes," Laura states matter-of-factly.

"Alright, this is irritating, and I'm not in the mood for irritating either. What's the problem, what's wrong and why are you being so standoffish?" Dominique asks, in her typical blunt style.

Laura sighs gently, "I was hoping to spend some time with just you and I arrive to find the apartment almost full and Jonathan's coming later."

"How old are you?" Dominique asks.

"Old enough," Laura replies.

"Then suck it up like a big-girl and be friendly. There are drinks in the fridge," Dominique says, gesturing towards the kitchen.

"And cold drinks?" Laura says pouting.

Dominique holds out her wrist, "But you still need to get other drinks from the fridge."

Laura shakes her head, "Thank you, but no thank you."

"Are you going to sulk all evening?" Dominique says. "I've had enough of that this week. Whether it's a sulk or a non-sulk, I've had enough."

"But I've only just arrived," Laura says perplexed.

"You have, but you arrived in a bad mood and tonight, I don't care. Either snap out of it or come back tomorrow when you're feeling better," Dominique says, sitting back down on the sofa next to Erika.

Laura looks to Gavin for something, support, information, a friendly smile. She receives none of them from him. After an additional imploring look, he says, "Erika's still feeling human and doesn't like the idea of the end of civilisation and being part of the decision-making process. She's not taken it well and it's been stressful for the last few days, and it doesn't look like anyone's in the mood for your neediness."

"Decision time Laura," Dominique says, glancing at Erika.

"Fine," Laura says cautiously, "then I'm going to get a drink from the fridge. Can I at least have it warm?"

"There's a Christmas pudding container in the cupboard next to the microwave. Use one of the glasses in the same cupboard. Only use full power for twenty seconds. That will be just about the perfect temperature," Dominique says, looking back at Laura.

"Thank you," Laura says clearly unhappy as she walks into the kitchen area.

"I'm sorry about that," Gavin says to Erika. "She gets funny sometimes and it looks like today is one of those days."

"No need to apologise for her Gavin, she's old enough to know how to behave," Dominique says. "We both know what's going on and why, but it leaves Erika out and that I'm not happy with. And yes, I do know she can hear me."

"Am I right in thinking that this is really about me?" Erika asks, looking from Laura in the kitchen to Dominique.

"Yes and no, it's more about her than you, but you know how people get. She likes the idea of being my favourite, even though such a thing has never happened. She acts like it anyway. But, as you noticed, she doesn't put much effort into being here. Just with the rewards of being here," Dominique says, her attention fully on Erika. "So, no it's not about you, but you're the excuse for today's behaviour."

"So, there's nothing I should do? Or could do?" Erika asks.

Dominique shakes her head, "No, nothing. We must let it run its course and either move on, or she's coming back tomorrow. But as Laura went to the kitchen to get a drink, she's decided to stay. I think."

"Perhaps you'd like to ask my charming sister, about her experience with religion," Gavin suggests.

"I'm not sure I want to interact with her," Erika replies.

"She's not normally this bad, I don't know what's going on with her tonight," Gavin says, "but it might be fun."

"If you want to, feel free, but I'm not going to," Erika reiterates.

"I know," Dominique says, "there's no need if you don't want to."

Laura comes back into the lounge area, glass in hand. "Why is there cows' blood in the fridge? You could have mentioned that the strawberry not raspberry was the way to go."

"Sit down, why don't you, in the chair," Dominique suggests, indicating the empty chair. She waits until Laura is sitting before continuing, "Erika, has a sensitivity to the human, so we're mixing it half and half. It's as simple as that."

Laura now turns to Erika and in a possible attempt at building bridges asks, "What's wrong with you?"

Rather than replying to Laura, Erika speaks to Dominique, "Is she trying to be unpleasant?"

"It's hard to tell," Dominique says, glancing at Laura, "it certainly seems that way."

"No, no, I didn't mean it like that," Laura says quickly. "I meant, why can't you drink human? Does it make you sick?"

"No, it doesn't make her sick," Dominique says, knowing that Erika will not engage now. "She likes it too much. It's too nice, so she loses herself for a while. On the plus side, she's doing well with seeing auras. So, the sensitivity is helping and hindering."

"She can see auras already?" Laura says sceptically.

"She can see auras and is getting to understand the changes," Dominique confirms.

"That's impossible," Laura states assertively.

"Improbable, yes, but not impossible. Or you think she's lying about it?" Dominique asks.

Erika watches Laura carefully, taking in her aura, posture, and facial expressions as she listens. Gavin watches with disinterest.

Realising what she's said and what that implies, Laura begins to back-pedal, "I don't mean that she's lying, I mean that I've never heard of anyone progressing that quickly before. And I'm expressing my shock by stating that it's impossible. When, as you say, it might only be improbable."

"And you doubt me about? About what?" Dominique asks, her tone more neutral than the words suggest.

"I don't doubt you at all," Laura says the uncertainty creeping into her voice.

"Good, then let's have that all cleared up," Dominique suggests. "What do you want to discuss?"

"I'd rather wait until Jonathan arrives, otherwise we must go through it twice. Once now and again when he arrives," Laura says more conciliatory than before.

"Then to pass the time while we wait and to allow you the least opportunity for further disharmony, would you care to continue our discussion on religion?" Dominique asks amiably.

"Is this a trick?" Laura asks cautiously.

Gavin laughs, "Now, you become cautious? No, it's not a trick. Erika's just learnt, as far as I can tell, that you're much older than she had expected and that our experiences give us a certain perspective missing by almost everyone, people, or family."

Gaining a little confidence back, Laura asks, "What was the question?"

"Are religions made-up by humans, by a god or gods?" Gavin offers, simplifying the previous conversation.

"What did I you tell her?" Laura asks.

"I told her that religions are made-up by humans, mostly, and that she shouldn't worry too much about her relationship with her church," Gavin says. "I didn't think they would take too kindly to her being family and she shouldn't take that too personally."

"That's all?" Laura asks.

"No, but that'll do for now," Gavin replies. "What are your thoughts?"

"Well, obviously it's all made-up. You only must look at it for a little bit of time to see that," Laura says, "Even in the last few decades, the Christian denominations, proves it's made-up as they went from women are incapable of serving God in any official capacity, to them becoming priests and bishops. If that doesn't tell you that they make it up as the wind shifts, then what would?"

"An official announcement," Gavin offers.

"I doubt that they even realise that this is what they are doing. They, the church leadership, probably don't realise that this is what they are doing. People who reach for power, rarely see that they are corrupting the very thing they claim to cherish. But that cherishing is really a vessel for their own ambitions and power. This is what you see in the church now. Well, over the last few hundred years," Laura says, her confidence returning slowly.

"Then why?" Gavin says. "How do you, who clearly dislike Erika, show her that what you're saying is the truth, rather than another attempt at hurting her for no apparent reason?"

"Why does everyone think that I dislike Erika?" Laura asks, clearly bemused.

"Perhaps everything you've said, your attitude since you arrived and the fact you've not helped one jot in the last two years to help keep her safe," Gavin says, the accusation clear in his voice, but not his expression.

Dominique's low interest perks up at Gavin's words.

"I," Laura says, but then sips at her drink, ignoring the looks from the rest of the room, "I don't dislike Erika. I don't know her. We've never met, and I've never spoken with her."

"And yet tonight would have been a perfect opportunity for you to have had your first conversation with her, yet you came in guns blazing and at the risk of overstating the case, you've not won any friends. So, her first impression of you is completely negative. Why should she ever warm to you, or have any respect for you?" Gavin asks.

"I didn't mean to," Laura replies weakly.

"I doubt that you thought about anything at all other than Laura and how you could impress Dominique," Gavin counters. "I've expended a lot of effort blending in here, living and working, to keep Erika safe. Other than going off and doing what you want, what have you contributed?" He pauses a moment then answers his own question, "Nothing."

Laura protests, "I've been helping, just in a different way."

"So, you say," Gavin says dismissively, "but, we've not seen any help or support for two years and I have no idea how you ever think you'll make it up to Erika. She's not going to talk to you, because she has a dislike of confrontation, and you came in here in full confrontational mode. It might be fun for you, but it's not for her."

"I had no idea," Laura says weakly.

"No, you didn't, and you never thought to check or ask. You did your bull in a china shop routine and made everything about you," Gavin says, "but you're supposed to be here to help her."

"I...," Laura starts before she's cut off.

"So, I'm going to ask again, how are you going to make this right? She's supposed to be loyal to us, and that includes you, but you've done nothing to show her that you're loyal to her. So?" Gavin says, sitting back in his chair, indicating that he's finished with this bit of conversation and it's now all up to her.

Laura looks at Erika, directly in the eye and says, "I'm sorry Erika. I didn't intend for our first meeting to be like this. I'm not going to ask you..."

"Stop," Dominique says, cutting Laura off, "I'm not going to listen to you justifying to her what you did or try to make it right. You know that I love you like a sister. I have done for all these years, but that doesn't mean I have to listen to you witter on. If this is about you looking good to me, then you've failed totally. If it was to make you like wise and powerful to Erika, once again, you've failed totally."

"Why are you being like this?" Laura asks sounding hurt.

"Why?" Dominique says, "Because you only had to come here tonight and be nice. I know that's in you, so I don't understand why you didn't do that. You know what she is, you know what she means to us, to us all, but still you behaved like this. I don't understand why and at this point, I'm not sure I care to know. Frankly, I'm quite disappointed."

Laura looks like she's been physically struck, "I didn't intend any of this to have happened like this. I was looking forward to meeting Erika and I didn't know she's sensitive and neither did I know she's adverse to confrontation. Isn't that a bit of a problem in our society?"

"As Gavin said, you're going to have to decide how you are going to make it up to her and how you can gain her trust and respect. She's, after all, done nothing to you that would justify your behaviour. And yes, it would be, but we have plenty of time to work on that," Dominique says her voice even and calm.

"Is it because we can live for ever and that you've all lived for thousands of years," Erika says to Dominique, "that none of you believe in God?"

Dominique looks at Erika a moment and smiles, a warm, kind smile, "We've never talked about God."

"We were talking about it earlier, you, Gavin and me," Erika says.

"We were talking about religion," Dominique says, "you didn't mention anything about God or gods."

"What's the difference," Erika asks, "isn't religion about God?"

"Religion is about controlling people, gaining influence and power," Gavin says. "God is an entirely different conversation."

"Then, is there a God or gods?" Erika asks.

"I have no idea," Gavin replies.

Dominique shakes her head, making a neutral gesture, "I have no knowledge one way or another. There could be a god or gods and there might not be. But religion has nothing whatsoever to do with God. It uses the concept of a god to cower people into submission. They use Zoroaster's ideas of good and evil, and created a system where the powerful could get away with anything in this life, because punishment would or perhaps would happen in the next. Of course, if there isn't a next life, they get away with all kinds of malfeasance. Which, if you are part of the ruling power elite, is perfectly fine with you. Do what you like here now and worry about the consequences later. It has the added benefit, that the non-elite can be convinced that justice will come later, so there's no need to worry if the system now is imperfect. Sort of a double protection for the malfeasant."

"That's very cynical," Erika says, "as I have, I think mentioned before."

"You have and that doesn't make it any less correct," Dominique replies, as Laura keeps quiet and sips at her drink.

"Look at it this way, how do you think that the church, and I don't care which one you pick, I don't really care which religion you choose either. How do you think they became rich and powerful? Where did the money come from; how were the huge buildings built; who paid for that; what about their political power? Do you think they will give that up easily?" Dominique asks. "Then consider the kinds of people that rise to the top of organisations like that. What kind of people are they?"

"I suppose," Erika says uncertainly.

"You're a good person. You're honest, more or less, and you have a good moral compass. That's why some of this is hard for you to accept. Because you think that everyone is like you. Some are, many are not and some, they're ruthless powermongers who'll stop at nothing to get their way," Dominique says. "The irony is, now that you're one of us, you would have no difficulty doing that. But, and the irony's irony, is that you don't want to do that. Right now, you want to save all the people from the likes of those people. Whereas, in time, you will realise that it's not worth the effort thinking and worrying about it. There're many things we can do but choose not to. Because it's not in our nature, so to speak."

"Is this what you've been talking about all this time?" Erika asks.

"No, not really. This is one tiny aspect of a larger picture," Dominique says, glancing at Gavin. "We're here for the ages. You're here for the ages. In a thousand years, you'll be still here, but everything you know right now, will be gone. The people; buildings; civilisation; technology, all of it. It will evolve, morph, and become something new. You'll see it, adapt slowly and we'll cope fine. It's part of what we do."

"Can I ask a question?" Laura says cautiously.

"If, and only if, it's friendly and related," Dominique offers.

"It is," Laura says. "It's about the changing language. Lots of people now seem to be saying tu, like in the word tut, but with the last t missing. Should we be doing that? Changing how we speak?"

Dominique looks at Gavin who shrugs, "I don't know," Dominique says. "I've been hearing it more frequently over the last few years and it's now cropping up on TV and the radio, so perhaps we should be prepared for it. What do you think Erika, you're our contemporary expert?"

"Me? I'm not an expert," Erika protests.

"Of course, you are," Dominique says warmly and with a knowing grin, "You're the only one who's younger than three thousand years old. That automatically makes you the expert."

"I don't know," Erika says a little too quickly, "but, I've heard it happening more and more over the last few years too, so in perhaps in five or ten years, it will be said one way and written another, then I suppose people will agree on a new spelling and it will be officially tu and the too will then be old fashioned," she hesitates a moment. "I see the problem and why you'd care, why we'd care. It's a real problem, isn't it?"

"Yes, it is, and I didn't think it important enough to discuss, but it will be important in a few years, I agree with you on that," Dominique says. "See, you're already contributing your unique insight into the wider group."

"Now you're making fun of me," Erika says with a smile.

"Not this time," Dominique says her face warm and friendly. "This time it was genuinely helpful."

No sooner than she's finished speaking than there's another knock on the door.

Chapter 28

Dominique closes the door after Jonathan and Matt step through. They quickly remove their shoes. Jonathan's dressed in a white polo shirt and kaki shorts and Matt has a light green T-shirt and blue shorts. They arrange their trainers neatly with those next to the shoe rack.

"Can you please bring my bag in with you?" Laura calls from the lounge.

Dominique grabs Laura's bag and follows her guests into the lounge. "You'll need to get some dinning chairs, unfortunately, the others are all in use."

"Not a problem," Matt says and quickly brings two chairs into the lounge, one on either side of the sofa.

"Would you like anything to drink?" Dominique asks, as she hands Laura her bag.

"Thank you, but I'm fine," Matt says with a smile, then turning to Erika, grins, "Evening." Jonathan shakes his head by way of a reply.

Erika returns the smile and says, "Evening Matt." Then turning to Jonathan adds, "And you Jonathan."

Jonathan makes a small bow with his head, "Evening."

"I assume you all know each other?" Dominique says more for Matt's benefit than anyone else's. She looks at the nods and then sits down. "Did you have any problems getting to come over?" Dominique says to Jonathan.

"No, it just takes a little time, the politics of it all," Jonathan says, he doesn't seem perturbed about the hassle.

"I don't mean to rush because I don't know what we must discuss. The detail and the scope," Dominique says. "I don't know who's going to start, etc., so please start as you see fit."

Jonathan and Laura look at each other and are clearly deciding on who's going first. After a few seconds, Jonathan says, "Then I'll start. As you all know, Matt and I have been looking into the rise of the gangs in our community. We know some of it, but know much less than Laura, who's been looking into it from a different angle. Firstly, I don't believe that the King and or Queen know anything about it. In itself, this is a grave concern, as there should be very little that they don't know about, and this is not the kind of thing that would be in that category. They should know about this, the scope, the implications and be dealing with it. From what I can tell, they simply don't have any idea that it's happening. Laura?"

"That's my understanding too," Laura says, licking a stray drip of blood off her lips. "It seems that there's one gang and only one gang in each of the thirty-two principalities. There's not that many in each one, the gangs range in size from six to eleven members. It doesn't seem to have any relationship to the size of the principality. I am speculating, but I think it's to do with how long the recruitment drive has been going on. Or perhaps just the availability of recruits. To be clear, they made some for this purpose and others are genuine recruits. It's not clear to me where they resourced recruits and the criteria used to select them. I don't think it probably matters. Matt and I have talked extensively about this and neither he nor I can provide a recruitment motive. For those made for a purpose, then it's simple, they don't know any better. Which is both an advantage and a problem to us. The advantage is that they don't know any better, so rehabilitation isn't an option. The problem is they can and are breaking the laws all the time."

"As you know, I spent some time with one of the gangs in this area," Matt says, "In that time, I did get to find out the name of their leader, he goes by Tai Lin. But, as Laura said, we don't know the motivation or reasoning behind the converts. And as you know, my gang had an accident after trying to extort Dominique and Erika. The interesting bit with them is that their information was incredibly accurate. They knew Dominique had only recently turned Erika. They knew the where and the how. That shows that they had exceptionally good access to information. In some areas, better than Jonathan. Which, if you think about it, is problematic."

Laura digs through her bag as Jonathan speaks, "I'm not saying that I know everything that's going on, but I didn't know that Erika was one of us, until I found out from Dominique the following day. So, their information was exceptionally good and up to date. That wasn't general court chatter. We didn't know it had happened. We knew it was happening, at some point, but you know how this works. You get permission and then sometime later, you make your new family member. So, the timeliness was or is curious."

"For those of you who think I haven't been doing my job, I have been doing what you knew I would be doing, out gathering information. Doing what I always do. With that in mind, I have identified threats and where necessary taken care of them. Just as you apparently did at the bridge," Laura says, slightly defensively, both Matt and Jonathan notice. She puts a folder onto the coffee table before continuing, "But, in my travels, I have identified both the location and habits of the different gangs. All of them! There's more useful information in the folder. Things like the ringleader, the exact locations that sort of thing."

"Thirty-two is a lot of gangs," Erika comments, seemingly happy to talk in this conversation.

"It is," Jonathan says, turning to Erika, "which leads to one obvious question. Why are there gangs in all the areas controlled by different Princes? Which then leads to the obvious follow-on question, why don't the King and Queen know anything about it? At this point, I think we have a discussion."

"I know what you two are like, sorry Matt, I don't know you well enough. So, I'm sure you've speculated on the why, which is what matters in the first instance," Dominique says.

Laura nods, "We have and, as hard as we try, it keeps coming back to someone wanting to take over London. It seems they want the Kingdom."

Jonathan nods his agreement, "I see it the same way. If they can create enough chaos, and keep the King and Queen in the dark, they can mobilise a political coup, by rightly showing that the current leadership is unable or unwilling to rectify the problem. This will create support for the coup plotters and probably give them the votes and power to depose the current King and Queen. It's quite simple and, therefore, quite clever really."

"And if they fail?" Erika asks.

"If the plot fails, then it's only some thugs that the King and Queen can have cleaned up," Jonathan says. "Nothing really to trace back to the plotters, it seems to be all done at arm's length. I mean, there might be a small possibility of one of the plotters discovery but I don't think that's likely."

"Why not?" Erika prompts.

"Because the one that we've identified as the leader, is none other than the Kingdom's Head of Security," Laura says, "but, we're sure there's at least one other and probably two other senior figures, however we don't have names yet. The Head of Security is Tai Lin, we're quietly confident of this, as I've seen him at three of the gangs' strongholds."

"And who's the Head of Security?" Gavin asks, finally joining in.

"His name is Andrew Haig," Jonathan says.

"So, Tai Lin is Andrew Haig," Gavin confirms. "Why the Chinese sounding name? Does he look Chinese?"

Jonathan shakes his head, "No. He looks as Chinese as I do."

"Then why the name?" Gavin asks.

"I don't know, but I'm assuming, because it sounds nothing like Andrew and it has a slight menace to it, invoking the triads and their reputation. I can't think of any other reason," Jonathan says. "But, if what we think is true, then I doubt that the choice is an accident. So, he chose the name carefully. Tai Lin has a reputation, as does Andrew and they're quite different reputations."

"That's good to know," Gavin says.

"Then, we need to decide what we're going to do, if anything," Dominique says. "We, Jonathan, and I, did discuss cleaning this up and making Jonathan King. Do we still want to do that?"

"I'm not sure that we do," Jonathan says. "The situation isn't as we believed when we talked last weekend. It looks more complex, and I don't like the idea of a coup d'état. It was one thing when it looked like they were being incompetent. Having things run correctly is important. But this whole situation as it currently stands doesn't sit right with me."

"Erika, what do you think we should do?" Dominique asks.

"Me? I don't know," Erika says too quickly. "I don't know anything about the politics of family society."

"Suppose it's nothing to do with politics or society. What if it's about doing the right thing. What then?" Dominique asks. "What if this is a morals question?"

"If it's a morals question, then you need to do the right thing. No matter what. Or perhaps I should say, no matter what, so long as it isn't bad for us," Erika says. "I mean, isn't that what we're trying to do, have a moral and good life?"

"Indeed, it is," Dominique says. "So, what are you all thinking?"

"I don't think I'm thinking anything," Jonathan says. "But I can't speak for Laura."

"I don't have any plan either," Laura confirms.

"Then what would you like?" Dominique enquires.

Laura goes back to sipping at her drink, probably to make sure she's not the next one to speak.

"As surprising as this may seem," Jonathan says, "I think we need to support the King and Queen. It's wrong what's happening, and I accept they do appear to be over reliant on dishonest courtiers, but in this situation, what can they do? What could I do in that situation?"

"Then do you have a proposal?" Dominique asks.

"Well, first of all, does anyone disagree that we should be supporting the King and Queen?" Jonathan asks.

To general shaking of heads, Dominique says, "In that case?"

"I'll be honest," Jonathan says, "I have mixed feelings about it. They're in one of the most prestigious territories in the world and they have lost control. I accept that the loss of control is a deliberate plot and not something organic, but I can't help feeling that there's something not quite right with their reign. I mean, shouldn't they know about this and be sorting it out themselves?"

"There's the right and wrong of it," Laura says, "but there's also the do we help them aspect and if we do, at what risk to ourselves?"

"Go on," Dominique says.

"Well, we're working on the assumption that Tai Lin or Andrew is the top of the pyramid. What if he's working for someone else, and is only an operative?" Laura says. "What if there's others involved that we don't know about?"

"That's distinctly probable," Gavin says. "What else do you know about Andrew? What do you know that might be useful in settling this problem?"

"To the best of my understanding and research, he's a ninth generation out of Bristol. He's been around the block and is about the same age as Matt. He's ambitious and so, could easily be working with or for someone else, someone we don't see. Everything I have done is observational with a little research. If I didn't see it, I can't be sure of it. As you know, it's possible to communicate with people and I wouldn't know about it," Laura says. "So, I cannot be sure he's at the top. There's no information to say he is, or he isn't. There's simply no information and I've not been able to develop any. But I have had limited time."

"Erika?" Dominique asks.

"I have no insight," Erika says. "I also have a disadvantage in that I don't know what any of you are capable of."

"Our capability isn't really of concern," Dominique says. "We could have them all gone by morning. What matters is the correct course and as you rightly pointed out, without endangering ourselves."

"Then let's assume that Tai Lin, I mean Andrew, is working for someone else. How does that complicate things. How much more powerful would they need to be? They're capability is obviously limited, otherwise they wouldn't need to resort to Andrew doing their dirty work. Plus, if he is this capable, why share the prize?" Erika says, clearly thinking like a trial lawyer.

"Could there be a sixth or even fifth involved?" Matt asks, "I mean as the one that Andrew is working for?"

"I've not heard anything about such an individual," Laura says, "but we're running around town, and nobody knows about us, so once again, I can't for sure say no, but I don't think so."

"And if there is someone like that pulling the strings?" Erika says. "What can we do about it, and can we mitigate that risk?"

"From what I've heard," Gavin says, "I don't think there is anyone pulling the strings, but if there is, I don't think they're a threat."

"And if they are?" Erika prompts. "What then?"

"Then we deal with it when the situation arises," Gavin says. "This doesn't seem too onerous. We're dealing with between two hundred and fifty and three hundred family members. That's quite a lot, something could always go wrong dealing with that many. However, they're all spread out in various parts of London. It's not like we're dealing with one group of three hundred. We also would need to deal with the King and Queen and the infiltrators in court. This is going to be difficult to coordinate if we choose to do anything."

"Assuming we're going to do something, who does what and when?" Dominique asks.

Gavin looks to Laura who nods a couple of times, "The way I see it, Jonathan and Matt cannot participate. They need to stay clean with the royal court. That leaves the three of us. So, three teams, Laura and I clean up the gangs, you and Erika deal with Andrew and the King and Queen. You might have to deal with the infiltrators too. I don't think we can help much with those unless you want to switch roles with me?"

"You know, that might work nicely. You and Laura dealing with the gangs. That makes a lot of sense. Erika and I can do the other bits as you've outlined. It will be a good opportunity for Erika to have a stab at her confrontational problem in a semi-controlled environment," Dominique says confirming Gavin's plan.

"You're going to drop her into a hostile situation so soon?" Laura queries. "Is that wise?"

"It's not like she'll be alone," Dominique says. "I'll be there supporting her. Besides, she's been under Gavin's tutelage, so she should be able to handle herself against the gang members at least. Jonathan? Matt? Questions or comments?"

"I agree that we need to be distanced from this," Jonathan says. "Because we either need to remain in court or leave London."

"I'm planning on staying for the next ten to fifteen years," Dominique says. "So having you in place makes sense."

"I don't feel qualified to comment," Matt says. "You all seem so much more knowledgeable."

"What including me?" Erika says incredulously.

"Yes, you did well," Matt says. "You fit right in. If I didn't know better, I'd believe that you've done this before."

"Maybe I do this as a hobby?" Erika quips.

"Perhaps," Matt says grinning, "but your aura says something different."

"It's difficult being the only one who cannot control their aura," Erika comments.

"Oh?" Matt says, "You're not the only one. I can't do it either."

Dominique looks to Jonathan, "What?"

"He doesn't want to practice," Jonathan says simply.

"Matt, you're going to have to practice," Dominique says looking at him, "I'd hate for Erika to be able to do it before you. And just so you know, she can already see multiple auras. It takes some effort, but she's making rapid progress. You've been warned."

"I have just thought of something," Matt says. "Coordination will be a key. Erika and Dominique will need to have taken out Andrew and his group before you two can start. Otherwise, he might well be alerted and not show up. I suppose that's going to be our job, to make sure Tai Lin shows up at the right place at the right time. That's going to require the right bait. I don't know what that is, but I'm sure that you'll think of something."

"Coordination should be straightforward, as long as everyone is in position and there will only be thirty-one gangs, as Dominique and Erika will need to deal with their one," Gavin says. "Laura and I can handle the rest, but we're going to need to start as early as possible. Night at this time of year is short and there's quite a lot to do."

"Then we need to start on a plan, pulling together all we need to do and the timing of it. We need to make sure that everyone's smartphone knows about the others for tonight. Then delete the contacts, as necessary," Dominique says.

With that, the group begins to plan their operation in detail. This takes the rest of the night.

Chapter 29

Just before sunset, Erika and Dominique arrive at a black door to the left side of the disused Aldwych Tube station. Dominique dressed nicely in light-blue three-quarter length trousers, a halter top, and trainers, looks around the door, the frame, and nods, asking, "Do you see the code?"

Erika, dressed in designer jeans, a black T-shirt and light denim jacket, sporting her own trainers, looks over the door and frame, but shakes her head, "No, I'm not seeing it."

Dominique points to a faded torn sign in the middle of the door, "Just above the sign. See it now?"

Erika smiles, "Yes, six, two, nine, three, three, four."

"Excellent," Dominique says, typing the numbers into the keypad. Almost instantly as she presses the Accept button, the sound of an electronic lock clicks and clunks as the locking mechanism disengages and, with a gentle push on the door, it swings open. Glancing over at Erika she asks, "Are you ready?"

Erika takes a deep breath and holds it a moment, clearly preparing, "Yes, clear mind, looking for aura, body hard."

"Good," Dominique says, "and if everything starts going horribly wrong, you hold my hand and do not let go, no matter what. If you must fight, do what Gavin taught you. He's exceptionally good at what he does, and this is what he does."

"I will," Erika says confidently.

"And as we discussed, all the talking, you do it," Dominique says. "I know you're not comfortable with confrontation and this is going to be hard, but baptism by fire and all that. I'll be here the whole time, right next to you. We'll do what you think is right."

"I know we discussed it last night, but I'm not sure I'm the best choice for this," Erika says trying one last time to wriggle out.

"We did and made the decision. Tonight, you're in charge. Confronting your fears is the only way to overcome them," Dominique says. Then flashing a grin to Erika adds, "And tonight's that night."

"Just to be clear, if it comes down to it, you aim to kill, no prisoners, no wounded, only bodies," Dominique says, the grins quickly fading.

Erika nods, "Only bodies." She makes a flourish and adds, "After you."

Dominique makes a show of an exasperated look, "So gallant," she quips.

"I try," Erika says, following Dominique into the darkness beyond the door.

Dominique wends her way through the corridor and down the stairs, working her way slowly under London. Presently, they meet a young woman, who asks, "Who are you?"

"I'm Erika and this is Dominique," Erika says, "We're here to see Tai Lin."

"Are you expected?" the young woman asks.

"Probably," Erika says with a smile. "That's why we're here!"

"I don't remember him mentioning he was expecting you," the young woman counters.

"I'm sure that we're the reason he's here tonight," Erika continues, her tone warm and friendly, "If you don't mind me asking, what's your name?"

"I'm Jane," the young woman says.

"Nice to meet you, Jane," Erika says with a smile.

"You'll need to follow me; I can't have you wandering around on your own," Jane says, "You might get lost."

"Then please lead on," Erika suggests.

"I don't think so," Jane says, "you can go first. Though that door."

"Fair enough," Erika says warmly. "Just to be clear, we're no threat to you."

"So, you say," Jane says, "but you don't get to be old by making silly mistakes. So, you go first."

Erika sighs gently as she walks, following the corridor, then down more stairs. Eventually, they get to another door, Jane unlocks this one with another combination keypad. She pushes the door open and beckons them to enter. Dominique entering first, followed by Erika and then Jane.

"Knock on that door there," Jane says, pointing to a door across what is clearly a recreation room. "Wait until he calls you in and be polite."

"I'd expected more people here," Erika says. "Where's everyone?"

"About," Jane says cryptically.

"Thank you for your help and assistance," Erika says with another smile.

"Sure," Jane says but doesn't move. She stands by the door and watches Erika and Dominique cross the recreational space. She glances at the large screen TV, which is currently off, and then back to the women as Erika knocks on the office door.

After a few seconds, a voice says, "Come in." With that invitation, Erika turns the door handle and enters the office, closely followed by Dominique. To her surprise, an elaborately decorated office presents itself, making her own look positively spartan.

As they enter, Tai Lin stands and gestures to the chairs on the other side of his desk, "Please sit."

Erika heads towards the chair, she sits gracefully in the offered seat. Dominique moves slower, taking in the whole room as she does so. Finally, she sits into the chair, as Tai Lin sits into his. The door remains open.

"Thank you," Erika says with a smile. "Tai Lin I assume?"

"Yes, that's correct and you're being very polite, especially after what you did to my friends last week," Tai Lin says conversationally.

"Civility is the cornerstone of cordial relations," Erika says warmly.

"And yet, you don't travel alone," Tai Lin says.

"Can you blame me," Erika replies, "particularly after what happened? Sometimes, it's unsafe for a young woman to travel after dark, and I believe it's now dark."

Tai Lin chuckles coldly, "It's always dark in here."

"Where exactly is here?" Erika says, "I saw the tube station, but hasn't it been closed for decades? You seem to have a nice setup down here. Is it part of the old tube station?"

"I think originally it might have been. I don't honestly know," Tai Lin says, "but we've been using it for some time. I don't know the history, and I've never bothered to check. I've never had the need. If you're wondering about exits, the only way out of here is the way you came in."

Erika smiles a disarming smile, "No, nothing like that. I was simply curious about the underground tunnels. I imagine that there's many that virtually nobody, but family know about."

"Probably, but that's not why we're here is it," Tai Lin suggests more than asks.

"I'm not entirely sure why we're here," Erika says. "It seems to me that there's a great deal of, shall I say, machinations, going on in London. Why don't you tell me a little about what you're planning."

Tai Lin laughs hollowly, "And why would I do that?"

"Because I asked nicely," Erika says warmly.

"It'll take a little more than that," Tai Lin says, as his laughter dies down.

"I was hoping that it wouldn't," Erika says her warm smile still present. "I was hoping that we could have a civilised chat and we'd all leave here happy."

"I'm being rude," Tai Lin says, "can I offer you both a drink? I have warm and fresh, and I have bottled, it's a little cool, but palatable."

"Thank you, but no," Erika says. "I had breakfast before I came out."

"And your friend?" Tai Lin says. "Would she? She doesn't speak much, does she?"

"I think she's fine for now too," Erika says. "I think it's best if only one of us does the talking. It leads to less confusion."

"As you wish," Tai Lin says. "Do you mind if I drink?"

"Feel free," Erika says, "but I would appreciate it if it was only from a glass."

Tai Lin grins, "Clever. I like the way you're thinking." He turns and retrieves a bottle from a cupboard, takes a glass and fills it with a deep red coloured liquid. Erika can instantly tell from the smell that it's human blood.

"I hope you enjoy your breakfast," Erika says warmly.

"Unfortunately, I've been up for some time, so this is more like an early morning snack," Tai Lin says.

"Then you have my sympathies," Erika says. "Perhaps, you could enlighten me as to why your friends threatened me last week?"

"They are trying to cause a little trouble here and there," Tai Lin says sipping his drink. "You and your new family member were convenient. It's not personal, just business or more accurately politics."

'Mm,' Erika thinks, 'he doesn't know that I'm the new vampire. Interesting!'

"So, it was just a case of wrong place and wrong time?" Erika suggests.

"It was a little more than that," Tai Lin says.

"Such as?" Erika prompts.

"Well, for starters, newly made family tend to be very unstable. Their makers tend to be very protective, so it's a good combination for disharmony, between both parties and society at large," Tai Lin says. "So, any discord created helps with destabilising society."

"And yet, that didn't work out as planned?" Erika prompts.

"So, it would seem," Tai Lin says. "It's not entirely clear exactly what happened but you'll be pleased to know that they're all healed by now. Well, all but one, he's still got some lingering scars, but in a day or two, he should be better."

"I'm glad to hear that they're all feeling better," Erika says.

"That was particularly slick, by the way, the disfigurement, meant they couldn't go out for about five days, which, of course, meant that acquiring food could only be done by others and most of my friends aren't so keen on the bottled stuff," Tai Lin says, sipping at his drink.

"Well, it was a very public place, and we don't want people seeing things they shouldn't see," Erika says. "Now do we?"

"Your point's made," Tai Lin says placing the empty glass down on the table.

"Thank you." Erika says warmly.

"Now, if you don't mind," Tai Lin says, "we're going to need to wrap this up and finish the job we started last week."

"That's a shame," Erika says warmly still smiling, "because I still have more to discuss, and I can tell you that my friend has been enjoying the conversation. You're eloquent and she very much appreciates that."

"Thank you," Tai Lin says, glancing at Dominique for a moment. "But I'm a busy man. I have important business to attend to. Matters of state you understand."

"I do understand, but I have to insist," Erika says warmly.

"I'm sure you'd like to, but, as I said, I have matters to attend to and my friends have their orders too," Tai Lin says.

"I should probably have asked this when I first came in, but do you prefer Tai Lin or Andrew?" Erika asks, to a flicker of a smile from Dominique.

"What do you know about that?" Tai Lin says slowly.

"Well, I know who Andrew Haig is, I understand his relationship with Tai Lin," Erika says warmly. "What I don't understand is, why you chose a Chinese sounding name, when Andrew seems perfectly courtly."

"Now, I'm unhappy," Tai Lin says. "That's privileged information."

"As I thought was clear when we arrived. I have done my homework and I'm not too worried about our current situation," Erika says still smiling, her voice kind, even and friendly.

"But you should be," Tai Lin says hesitating slightly.

"Why's that?" Erika asks. "I thought we were having a civilised conversation?"

"Only for as long as it amuses me," Tai Lin says.

"Then as you appear to be running short of time, I have to insist that you tell me who, if anyone you're working for and who else in the court is working with you?" Erika says warmly, her smile natural and dances as she speaks.

Tai Lin looks at Erika a moment, clearly focusing on her intently. 'I bet he's looking at my aura,' Erika thinks. Then he repeats the same intense look at Dominique and all remaining colour in his face drains away.

"You brought a sole hunter with you?" Tai Lin says the panic clear in his voice and demeanour.

Just as Erika's about to speak, the idea of a soul warrior pops into her head. She pauses and then starts to speak, "I thought we had already agreed, that after dark, a young woman needs some sort of protection. You know, from things that go bump in the night. Not like a soul hunter, but more a soul warrior."

At Erika's words, if it was possible for someone panicking to move that panic to a new level, that's exactly what Tai Lin does, "You brought a soul warrior? Here?"

"It's not safe out. Surely you can understand that," Erika says her happy smiling demeanour now contrasting with Tai Lin's panic.

"How?" Tai Lin manages to get out.

"I assume that you can see auras?" Erika asks kindly.

"I've only heard about it; I've never seen aura like that. But everyone knows what it means, the blue with the gold sparkles or flecks. They're the only ones who have aura like that."

"Perhaps, understanding is of secondary importance to the answering of my questions," Erika suggests. "We can discuss the importance of seeing auras early in the conversation rather than later. But first, who else is working with you, Let's start with in the court?"

"I only know of one person in the court, but I know he has contact with like-minded individuals," Tai Lin says, trying to regain some composure.

"And outside of court?" Erika says. "I don't mean your gang friends."

"There's nobody outside of us and those in the court," Tai Lin says quickly.

"For some non-orange reason, I don't think you're being completely truthful with me," Erika says.

"You can see aura too?" Tai Lin asks.

"A little," Erika admits. "But enough to know when people are being dishonest with me. I will not ask again."

"There's nobody. Just me, my contact in court and my friends out in London," Tai Lin says. "That all there is."

"And how many friends out in London to do you have?" Erika prompts.

"I don't know, I don't control that," Tai Lin says. "Each group controls their own membership, but I'd estimate three hundred, maybe a little more."

"Thank you for that information," Erika says warmly. "Now, what else do you need to tell me, that I haven't asked yet?"

"I haven't told you the name of my contact in the court," Tai Lin says, his voice gaining a minuscule amount of composure.

"I already know his name," Erika states.

"Anything else, something useful?" Erika prompts.

"I think that's everything," Tai Lin says, "but I don't see how this information's going to be useful to you. You'll never get out of here and all my friends will continue doing what they do."

"I wouldn't worry about us. I have no doubt that we won't have a problem leaving fine." Erika says. "I'm wondering, will you be resigning as Head of Security?"

Tai Lin looks surprised at the question, "No. Why?"

"I was just curious as to how you were going to deal with your treachery?" Erika asks, "I mean, the King and Queen rely on your integrity to help them run London and you're," she pauses a moment, "you're not all that reliable."

"They'll never believe you that I have anything but their best interests at heart. I'm a loyal and reliable subject," Tai Lin says with a sly grin.

"Yes, that might be true," Erika says. "But it does make a couple of assumptions. Not all of which might be valid."

"Like what?" Tai Lin says uncertainly.

"Like we don't go and let them listen to the recording of this meeting," Erika says her warm smile infuriatingly still in place.

"I can see how you're having fun," Dominique says evenly. "But other than the fun, is there anything to be gained in continuing this conversation?"

Erika turns to Dominique, "I thought I was the one dealing with this?"

"Of course, you are," Dominique says. "I don't think he has anything more to tell us and we do have an appointment with the King and Queen. I don't want to be late."

"Fine, you win," Erika says to Dominique. Then turning to Tai Lin, she says, "It seems we have other business, matters of state. You know how it is. So, we will say our goodbyes and see you another time."

"You'll never made it out of here alive," Tai Lin says.

"Are you referring to your eleven friends outside?" Dominique says.

"Yes," Tai Lin says his confidence fighting the fear.

"There's not a concern," Dominique says. "They're all already dead, unrecoverably dead I mean." She turns to Erika and says, "If I forget, remind me to get the King and Queen to have this place cleaned up."

Erika nods, "I'll try."

"Thank you," Dominique says with a smile. "Now, one last loose end to clean up. Andrew, what shall we do with you?"

"Let me go and I'll leave the city for ever," Tai Lin suggests.

"That's one option," Dominique concedes as she slides her chair back and stands. "Or we could try something else."

"Like what?" Tai Lin says.

"I'm not Erika, so my solution will be a little less convivial," Dominique says, "and she did put so much effort in giving you a chance." No sooner than the last word has left her lips, than those same lips are around the artery on Tai Lin's neck, as she drinks.

Erika looks surprised to see Dominique on the other side of the desk, but not as surprised as Tai Lin, who feels his life ebbing away. Dominique doesn't seem in any hurry to finish her drink.

Erika waits patiently while Dominique enjoys her drink, then they leisurely leave, passing the completely dead bodies of Tai Lin's gang members.

Chapter 30

Erika pays the taxi driver, giving him a little more than requested. Dominique waits momentarily for Erika to exit the black cab. The taxi pulls away, joining the light early night traffic, Erika says, "What do I need to do?"

"Be polite and leave the rest to me. You did well earlier. This should be straightforward, but you never can tell. So be prepared, just like we did before. Remember, the official reason for the visit it to introduce you. Then I have a few revelations for them afterwards," Dominique says, flashing Erika a kind smile.

"No charm?" Erika enquires.

"Correct, no charm or other powers. It's best to keep those to ourselves. I'll explain why if you need to know when we get home," Dominique says, as they approach the dark blue door. "Ready?"

"Ready," Erika replies, she draws in a deep breath and exhales.

Dominique simply twists the door handle and pushes it open, just like any house front door. They step inside and close the door. The light in the lobby is very dim by human standards, just enough to make it clear that a human is in the wrong place. Dominique leads Erika, deeper into the lobby, then up a grand stone staircase. At the top, they turn left down the corridor and stop at a closed door, guarded by a well-dressed attendant. He wears a dark-grey three-piece suit, white shirt, a dark red tie sporting a Windsor knot, black well-polished shoes and has an air of importance.

"Can I help you?" the attendant asks.

"I hope so," Dominique says. "We here to see their Majesties."

"Do you have an appointment?" the attendant asks.

"I believe that we do," Dominique replies conversationally.

"Name please?" the attendant asks.

"Dominique and Erika," Dominique says. "We're a little early, but it's generally better to be early than late."

The attendant consults a paper list and nods as he finds their name on the list. "Yes, you're about forty-five minutes early," he says, "but, I can probably fit you in sooner. We've had a no-show, so things are running ahead of schedule."

"That would be most convenient," Dominique says with a smile to Erika, who smiles back.

"If you could wait over there," the attendant says, gesturing to some chairs. "It should only be a couple of minutes."

"Thank you," Dominique says, and they head over to the seats and wait quietly, talking seems so out of place in the silence of the corridor.

The wait is more than a couple of minutes, but a little less than ten, when the attendant returns and says, "Please follow me."

Dominique and Erika stand and follow the attendant through the double doors, down another corridor and then enter yet another room. At the doors on the other side of what is clearly an anti-chamber, the usher takes responsibility for them. He looks quickly at everyone, seeing that all is in order, nods his agreement and acceptance to the attendant, who departs silently with a confirmatory, yet curt nod.

"Which one of you is Erika?" the usher asks.

"Me," Erika says, "and that's Dominique."

"Thank you. I'm Adrian and I'll be introducing you tonight," Adrian says. "So, before we begin, don't do anything stupid. That will only end badly. Please be polite, and ideally, don't talk across each other or others. It only leads to confusion and makes everything take so much longer."

"Thank you," Dominique and Erika both say in unison.

"I believe this is your first time Erika," Adrian continues, "but you don't have anything to worry about. They're both extremely nice and looking forward to meeting you. If they ask you anything, which other than a few pleasantries, they probably won't, just answer honestly. They can see your aura."

"Thank you, Adrian, that's very kind," Erika says, clearly slightly nervous.

"Shall we?" Adrian asks. "Before your nerve fails?"

"Please," Erika replies.

Adrian steps forward, knocks twice on the door's built-in knocker. He waits twenty seconds, timed on an elegant watch on his wrist, then simply opens the door. As it swings open, much to Erika's surprise, rather than an elaborate throne room, there is a boardroom table, with executive style chairs at each of the sitting positions. The King and Queen sit at the head of the table, assistants to their sides and a couple of people standing behind them. All eyes follow Erika and Dominique as they cross the space between the door and the chairs. As they walk, Adrian says, "Your Majesties, I would like to present Dominique, who is already known to you and Erika Elliot." He then turns to Erika and Dominique, adding, "Please sit down," and he gestures to two seats at the opposite end of the table, a good six metres from the King and Queen.

Dominique puts her bag down on the floor and pulls the chair from the table before sitting down. Erika copies Dominique and sits, pulling her chair into the table. Adrian leaves, closing the doors firmly shut, making hardly a sound as they close.

"It's nice to see you again," The King says, looking at Dominique, his voice deep and rich in tone. He's dressed in a dark-blue three-piece suit, just like the attendant, looking just like any other successful businessman. If it wasn't for the time of day, it could be any business meeting at any corporation in the world.

"And it's nice to be permitted an audience once more," Dominique says warmly.

"How could we turn down a request from Jonathan," the King says. "You know he's one of our favourites."

"I didn't," Dominique says slightly surprised, "but I can understand why."

"Of course, you can," the King replies, "and he's said nice things about you too Erika."

"Oh, come on Richard," the Queen says, her voice full of impatience, yet feels languid, "get on with the introductions." She too is dressed in formal business attire. Her white blouse contrasting with the deep, yet muted purple suit.

"Yes, my love, I'm getting there," Richard replies, "I know that this is stressful Erika. I don't mean it to be, but the unknown often is like that. Then to keep my wife placated, which is always a good plan," he chuckles at his own joke, to which his wife rolls her eyes, he continues, "I'm Richard, King Richard and this is my Queen, Zoe, so you may call us Richard and Zoe when we're alone, but formally, it's King Richard and Queen Zoe."

"See, that wasn't so hard was it," Zoe says looking at Richard.

"No and I was getting to it," Richard says to his wife.

"Thank you," Erika says.

"I'm a little surprised that you're here tonight," Richard says. "I honestly thought you'd drag out bringing Erika here. They usually do and then they show up on the last day of the month's grace period."

"I truth, I was going to leave it until the third week, but something has come to my attention that I thought you might be interested in," Dominique says her voice warm and friendly.

Richard's warm demeanour slips a little and he becomes more business like, "Oh?"

"It's a very delicate matter," Dominique begins, "something that I would rather discuss with you in private."

"I'm sure that anything that you can tell me, you can say in this room, and it will remain in confidence," Richard says, glancing at his wife. "You know this."

"It's not my confidence that I'm concerned about," Dominique says. "It's a delicate matter and I fear that you're going to be unhappy when we finish our conversation." She watches the expression on Richard's face briefly change to confusion and then back to his warm demeanour.

"Now you have me intrigued," Richard says.

"Is this something I should stay for?" Zoe asks.

"Yes, I think you should stay," Dominique says with a nod of her head.

"Then I'll stay," Zoe confirms.

"I'll defer to your judgement on those present in the room," Dominique says, "but the matter is sensitive and potentially time sensitive."

"I think I'm happy with those currently present," Richard says. "Now what does this pertain too?"

"Simply put, kingdom security," Dominique says simply, "and I would like to point out, at this point, that I am simply the messenger."

"I don't think I'm liking this but carry on," Richard says, "and I understand that you are the messenger. Which implies that there will be no consequence to you for delivering the message."

"Thank you," Dominique says.

"Oh, Dominique," Zoe says, a twinge of concern in her voice. "What are you mixed up in?"

With a smile Dominique says, "Me? Nothing, fortunately."

"Good," Zoe replies, sounding happy at the clarification.

"So?" Richard prompts.

"First, I have something for you, not exactly a present, but a token," Dominique says and lifts the bag up from the floor beside her chair and puts it onto the table.

"What is it?" Richard asks, curiously.

"The Head of Security," Dominique says, undoing the bag and removing a transparent plastic bag containing Andrew Haig's severed head. The bag sealed, keeping the blood and more importantly the smell contained. "Remember, I'm the messenger."

Richard makes no move or reaction, other than to say, "That's some token." Others in the room are not so stoic, audibly gasping at the sight of the severed head.

"This is just the beginning; it gets worse from here," Dominique says. "In terms of seriousness, not gruesomeness."

"I think we've had enough gruesomeness for one night. Don't you, my love?" Richard says to Zoe, even though he's still looking at Dominique. Zoe shakes her head slowly, unhappily.

"I'm not sure where to begin from here," Dominique says. "I didn't know how you'd react to the head."

"Where did you get it from?" Richard asks.

"Yes, I appreciate the help," Dominique says. "I think the best thing is to start with the fact there's a soul warrior running around London cleaning up Andrew's mess. Let's get the serious bit out of the way first."

Richard looks to Zoe and then back to Dominique, "Why's there even a soul warrior in London? Let alone what are they doing? And why?"

"Andrew, it seems, has been mixed up in what I will euphemistically call ill-advised activities," Dominique says, "to which the end goal would be a replacement in the current hierarchy."

"Replacement?" Richard queries.

"At the very top," Dominique confirms.

"I see," Richard says, "and how far had this activity progressed?"

"Well into implementation," Dominique says evenly.

"I am guessing then that the soul warrior is cleaning up this, implementation?" Richard asks.

"That would be my expectation," Dominique agrees.

"I am also expecting that there's proof of this?" Richard asks.

"Some," Dominique replies as she digs into her bag again and retrieves an A4 envelope, "There's some pertinent information in here." She makes no attempt to slide it across the table.

"Please continue," Richard says, looking briefly at the nondescript white envelope.

"As far as I understand it, the broad outline is as follows. The conspirators, intended to replace the current rulers of London. Their plan was primarily political. Create disharmony in each of the principalities, to that end, Andrew had gangs of family, doing things noticeable to humans. They were trying to sow discord within our community too. They appear to be very well-organised and extremely well-informed. For example, only hours after I made Erika, they knew. Very few people in London knew I was making a new family member and even fewer knew it had happened. Therefore, I concluded that their resources were widespread, and their knowledge detailed," Dominique says.

"Interesting," Zoe comments.

"It seems the plan was to get the princes on his side and use that as a way of replacing you," Dominique says simply. "It seems that he had it all planned, and the implementation proceeding as intended. I imagine it was the soul warrior that disrupted their plans."

"Do you believe that Andrew acted alone?" Richard asks.

"I don't know if you heard of Tai Lin?" Dominique asks, sidestepping the question.

Richard glances to Zoe, who shakes her head, "No, I've not heard of him or her."

"No, I thought not," Dominique says. "Tai Lin was the name of the gang ringleader who was terrorising the streets. The instrument of change if you will."

"And where is this Tai Lin now?" Richard asks.

"His head is in a bag on the table," Dominique says simply.

Richard shakes his head, "That's so disappointing. We trusted him."

"I know," Dominique says. "Which leads us to discuss his accomplices."

"You know more?" Richard asks, knowing the obvious.

"Firstly, there were the gang members. As I understand it, the soul warrior is dealing with them, probably as we speak. So, there's truly little to worry about in that regard. Secondly, that leaves us with external and internal accomplices," Dominique says. "From the information given to me, I don't believe there are any external accomplices. That's the good news."

"And then that means there's bad news," Richard says unhappily.

"As always, you're correct," Dominique says. "There's unwelcome news. It seems that there's several bad apples in the barrel. Which is why, I was interested in keeping this discussion private. I don't know who the people are."

"That's not so helpful," Zoe comments.

"Let me rephrase," Dominique says, "I know their names, but not who they are. I hope that clarifies."

"Can you tell me?" Richard asks.

Dominique pushes her chair back from the table and picks up the envelope. She slowly and purposefully walks round the table and presents it to Richard, who takes it. But, before he can open it, Dominique says, "Before you open it, I should say, that there's more in there than just a name." She looks at Richard a moment and then turns and returns to her chair, pulling it back towards the table.

Richard waits for her to sit down, "Then what else is in the envelope."

"A list of gang headquarters. I imagine that by the end of the night, there will be thirty-two locations all over London that require a cleanup team. I can't imagine that the soul warrior cleaned up after himself," Dominique says.

"Yes, as I understand it, tidiness isn't one of their strong suites," Richard says.

"I think that covers all I need to say tonight," Dominique says. "There's a letter from the soul warrior in the envelope with everything I've said, or at least from his perspective. If I have made any mistakes, the envelope version is the more accurate."

"I understand," Richard says. "You've done us all an incalculable service. I'm truly proud, thank you."

"You're quite welcome," Dominique says. "Oh, there's one more thing, I almost forgot! James Knightly and Brandon Anderson, those are the co-conspirators known to the soul warrior."

No sooner had the words left Dominique's lips, that the attendants intercept both men as they attempt to leave the room, their speed no match for the better positioning and the fact the attendants were already standing.

"Now that is disappointing," Richard says to the room in general, as he pushes his chair back, walking towards where James lays pinned down to the floor. Brandon struggling to get free, but that window of opportunity now firmly closed. Kneeling next to James, he asks calmly, "Who else betrayed me?"

"I never betrayed you," James shouts struggling. "She's made it all up."

"Perhaps," Richard says, "but I'm not going to cross a soul warrior and it seems that you'd have got away with it if it wasn't for him." He stands back up, walks over to the table, picks up, opens the envelope, extracts the pages, each one on standard photocopier paper – rather anti-climactic for such an important document. He reads each word carefully, then when he's finished each page, hands it to Zoe, who in turn does the same. When they've both finished Zoe places them back into the envelope. "It might be best if all you ladies left the room. We have somethings to discuss."

Dominique and Erika push their chairs back and stand. Zoe does the same. "Thank you both," Richard says. "We'll be in touch shortly to wrap this up and if you see the soul warrior, please thank him on our behalf."

"I doubt I will," Dominique says.

"I doubt it too, but we're grateful nonetheless and I would like him to know that," Richard says, moving back towards the pinned down figures.

With that Zoe joins Dominique and Erika, then all three of them exit through the large doors they originally entered through.

Once outside and the doors closed, Zoe turns to Erika and gives her a hug, she turns to Dominique and does the same. "Thank you both," she says, "I know you took a real risk to do what you did and I'm so happy that you did."

"I'm just doing my part," Dominique says with a smile.

"I don't doubt that at all," Zoe says with a warm smile. "I need to go, I have to get those sites cleaned up and it looks like a lot of clean-ups too."

"Then we will leave you," Dominique says. "Good luck and I'd be inclined to check thoroughly."

"You can count on that," Zoe says and walks off down the corridor.

Dominique and Erika wait for Adrian to escort them back out.

"I'm not even going to ask," Adrian says, as he escorts them out to the attendant.

"I'm sure you'll hear," Dominique says conversationally.

With that, Dominique and Erika retrace their steps out of the palace and head home.

Chapter 31

A gentle knock on the door occurs before Dominique has had a chance to put her shoes on the rack. Erika having just taken her first steps into the lounge stops and looks towards the sound. Upon opening the door, Dominique sees the full team, Gavin, Laura, along with Jonathan and Matt. Erika heads into the lounge first.

"Come in, come in," Dominique says, ushering the whole group into her apartment. "Please find a seat when you're ready." Closing the door, she makes her way into the lounge.

She sits next to Erika on the sofa, as is their custom. When everyone has settled down into their seats, Matt, and Jonathan, as before, take the dining room chairs and set them down where they did the night before.

"I trust everything went well?" Dominique asks to the room in general.

"I had no problems," Gavin says simply.

"Everything went like clockwork," Laura confirms.

"I need to pass along the thanks of the King and Queen," Dominique says. "They explicitly asked me to make it clear that they were both very grateful for all you've done for them."

"That's hardly necessary," Gavin says.

"Perhaps," Dominique replies, "but they asked, and I have passed along the message, like a good messenger. Which is what we were this evening at the castle."

Jonathan laughs, "You should have seen the castle." He shakes his head, "There were plenty of problems there. I, or we, as predicted are fine. But the place is in turmoil. I don't know exactly who's implicated, but I don't imagine that those involved will be getting off any lighter than Andrew Haig."

"I'm fine," Matt says with a smile, clearly directed in Erika's direction.

"Thanks Matt," Jonathan says shooting him a look. "From what I can gather, they're incredibly grateful for what we've done. But it's going to take some time to find the underlying cause of what's happened, and I don't think they're all that happy about a soul warrior running around town. I trust that nobody saw either of you?"

"No, of course not," Gavin says, as if such a thing was possible. Laura confirms her intent by shaking her head.

"If I can ask," Erika enquires, "but what's a soul warrior? I've heard a lot about it tonight, but no idea what they're talking about."

Laura says, "We're soul warriors."

"Alright, but that tells me who is, not what is," Erika replies, her dislike of Laura currently forgotten.

"We kill things," Gavin says simply.

"What kind of things," Erika asks.

"All things. If for some reason, be it human, vampire, animal, etc., needs killing, then we do it," Gavin confirms with a glance at Laura.

"I told you he was good at what he did," Dominique says with a smile.

"You did, but you also neglected to mention that what he did was kill everything," Erika retorts.

"Only things that need killing," Dominique corrects. "Tonight was a busy night. It's not normally like this. It's normally running and pizza."

"Or Christmas pudding," Gavin says. "Have you all tried it?" Gavin looks at the blank expressions on all their faces. "I know you have, Dominique, you have the containers in the cupboard. Anyway, it's lovely. You buy a mature, maybe two- or three-year old pudding, cut off a slice and warm it in the microwave. Then," at this point he seems to get more enthusiastic, "warm some blood, and pour it all over. Eat a bit of pudding and lots of blood. Oh, it's lovely and before you ask, don't try making whipped blood, it doesn't work and is a waste."

"What are you going on about Gavin?" Laura asks.

"It's the spices they put in, with the spirits, brandy or whisky, stuff like that. Anyway, the tastes are fabulous together," Gavin looks at the blank looks and as his enthusiasm collapses, he sighs, "Fine, forget about it."

"Then what's a soul hunter?" Erika asks, glossing over the last bit of conversation.

"Soul warriors make soul hunters," Laura says simply. "So, to be a hunter, a warrior must make you. They're not quite as capable."

"How many are there?" Erika asks, "and how wary of them should I be?"

Laura looks for guidance from Dominique who says nothing, she then looks to Gavin who shrugs, leaving Laura to speak, "About fifty, as far as I know and quite a few more hunters. I don't think you have anything to be worried about when it comes to warriors or hunters. If in doubt, make sure you identify yourself. Do you remember how?"

Erika nods, "Yes, there's a phrase. Dominique made me memorise it."

"Good, because that's the thing that will stop a soul warrior if needs must. But I don't imagine that you're going to get yourself into a position where that'll be a problem. At least, I hope not," Laura says.

"You're an elder, just like they are," Dominique says, "so you should have a degree of professional curtesy. But, as Laura suggests, staying clear of anything that might require their services would be your best bet."

"Where do I fit into this?" Matt asks.

"Technically, your soul hunter level, so you fit in just the same. Be nice to them and identify yourself," Gavin says. "I don't see any reason to worry."

"Then to clarify a point that's been niggling at me," Matt asks, "does this mean that Erika has two soul warriors looking after her?"

Gavin nods, "Yes, it does. We are."

"How come nobody looked after me when I was new?" Matt asks.

"I think this is one for you Jonathan," Gavin says.

Jonathan sighs, "You had a soul hunter looking after you. I just didn't want you to know. He was there for five years. One before and the first four after. I accept that Erika's had the twins for two years before and will have them for another five years."

"Then why didn't you introduce me?" Matt asks.

"Because I didn't want you to get mixed up in all that...," Jonathan says waving his hand.

"You didn't want me to be a soul hunter?" Matt says.

"No, you couldn't really be a soul hunter, as you were made by me and I'm not a soul warrior," Jonathan says, "but, I didn't want you to get mixed up in violence, I wanted a more peaceful existence for you, at least for as long as possible."

Matt looks partly satisfied, but before he can ask additional questions, Erika asks, "How did you kill so many vampires so quickly?"

"You mean distant family?" Gavin questions.

"Yes, that," Erika responds.

"Trade secret," Gavin says with a knowing grin. "Soul warrior only information, we can't have all our secrets known to everyone. It would make us less effective. I would tell you, but then I'd have to kill you." He laughs at his own joke. "But, of course, I'm already too late for that."

"That was terrible," Dominique says.

"But you're one?" Erika asks Dominique.

Dominique shakes her head, "No, I just showed the appropriate aura."

Regaining a serious demeanour, Gavin says, "Be under no illusion, just because she's not a soul warrior, doesn't mean that she's not formidable. We all are, but she can kill us all before we know the battle has started. Does that answer your next question about what happened at the tube station?"

"No, not really," Erika replies.

"And I can tell you now, she'll never tell any of us what she did and how she did it that's Dominique's secret," Gavin says. "We all have our theories, but we don't know, and I doubt we ever will. I've asked many times and the answer is always the same."

"So how do you do it?" Erika asks Dominique.

"I think Gavin already answered your question," Dominique says.

"But...," Erika begins as she's cut off.

"But nothing. There's something that nobody can know. For me, this is one. Just as Gavin says, the warriors have their own secrets. It's best for those of us not privy to them, to just accept that we're not going to know. In time, you'll have your own, about which they won't know. It becomes your magic,"

Dominique says, making it clear that this is the end of this line of conversation.

"Honestly," Jonathan says, "there's no point."

"Alright, message understood," Erika says disappointed. "Then why did you lie to Richard and Zoe about what happened?"

"I'm hurt that you'd suggest I was lying," Dominique says, "and you a barrister too! I was nothing but cordial and polite. The quip about the Head of Security, I particularly liked."

"You said that you'd not be seeing the soul warrior again," Erika says prompting Dominique.

"I think you'll find I said that I probably, wouldn't be seeing him again," Dominique says. "The probably precludes me seeing him or not seeing him again. Besides, it doesn't pay for people to know that you are friends with a soul warrior or a soul hunter for that matter. That information would be more trouble than it's worth. You'd never hear the end of it, and they'd always be wanting to know where they were and what they were doing. They're feared for a reason and that has nothing to do with their prodigious killing reputation."

"Then what is it?" Erika asks. It's clear that Matt is extremely interested in the answer too.

"They're free agents," Dominique says, "and they show no allegiance to the local King and or Queen. They come and go as they please and there's nobody who can stay their power."

"So, they're a judge and jury killing machine?" Erika enquires, surprised at her own conclusion.

"To an extent, yes," Dominique confirms.

"But it's not random," Laura says, "we're not running our own agenda, just enforcing the law."

"There's a law?" Erika asks, her surprise deepening.

"You didn't tell her about the laws?" Laura asks Dominique.

"Of course, I told her about the rules," Dominique replies.

"Rules? Laws?" Erika says. "What's the difference and why the distinction? Or not?"

"Then let's be clear to both of you," Laura says, "there are only laws, no rules. Break one of the laws and you could find yourself on the wrong side of a soul hunter."

"Laura likes the laws, because she wrote them," Dominique says.

"I made them based off the ideas of the whole group at the time. I just got the short straw and had to write them down," Laura says in her defence.

"Nobody wants to be responsible for writing things down," Gavin says, "because they change the language too often."

"Originally, I thought it would be something that you and Laura had in common," Dominique says to Erika, "I thought it would give you a common bond."

"So, Laura's in charge of the laws and breaking one can get you killed without warning?" Erika confirms.

"No, of course not," Laura says, "you'd always be given a chance to justify your law- breaking and for the record, I wrote them down, I don't make them up and that was a long-time ago."

"But all of our society lives by them?" Erika queries.

"Without fail, under pain of unrecoverable death," Laura confirms.

"That's reassuring," Erika says, only to have Gavin's laughter ring out. Jonathan seems to be doing a better job of suppressing it.

"Don't feel bad," Gavin says, "you'll get used to it."

"Alright, then I have one more question," Erika says, "and that is did Richard and Zoe really mean what they said when we left?"

"Why do you ask?" Dominique asks. "Weren't you watching their aura as the meeting progressed?"

Erika nods, "Of course, you told me to always be watching aura."

"Then what did you see?" Dominique asks, back in training mode.

"I saw their aura's change. They seemed happy to see you, and me for that matter. Then, as the conversation progressed, they got less happy and more worried," Erika says. "But they could have been showing me what they wanted me to see."

Dominique shakes her head, "Outside of this room and excluding Matt, who should be doing better, very few of us can control their aura. The warriors and the hunters can. But very few others can and to be clear, Richard and Zoe cannot and will never be able to. They're not powerful enough. What you saw was their emotion, pure and direct."

Erika's face changes and it's almost possible to see the comprehension dawn on her face, "So that's why you've been pushing so hard with the aura. If nobody can control it, other than you, a few, then it shows what people are feeling and that gives away what they've done, what they will do and how they will react?"

"Yes, well done," Gavin says. "It's extremely important when interacting with strangers. It gives you an edge and I hope you see how being able to control it improves that edge. I have no doubt that the first guard you encountered at the tube station could see your auras. Which will have been different to what Dominique showed Tai Lin. One will have seen just a normal pale aura. The other when he checked, saw something completely different and I'm guessing terrifying. It's a powerful tool if you can back it up and in time, you'll be able to back it up."

"The more I learn about this, the more disconcerting it becomes," Erika says.

"Excellent," Gavin replies, "then we're finally making progress."

"Will every week be this intense, or is this a special one you did just for me?" Erika asks.

"This was just a special week for you," Gavin says grinning, "normally, it's sit around watching daytime TV."

"Now I'm traumatised," Dominique says returning the grin.

"There's one thing that I don't understand," Erika says to Dominique, ignoring her exchange with Gavin, "when you killed Tai Lin, why did you drink all his blood first?"

"Isn't that obvious?" Dominique replies.

"Maybe to everyone else, but not to me," Erika replies.

"Because it tastes so much better than the stuff in the fridge in the strawberry carton," Dominique says. "That's why we carefully share blood with each other. Nothing tastes better than the blood of another family member."

"So, it's just about taste?" Erika asks to Dominique's nod.

"Also," Matt chips in, "when you're drinking, always make sure the blood is clean. The last thing you want to do is give an associate blood that's contaminated. That leads them to become contaminated too. So, then the next time you feed on them, you'll become re-contaminated. Thus, spreading the infection throughout your network. It generally takes about twenty-four hours to clean up a tainted meal."

"Talking of dinner," Dominique says, "I've rearranged our dinner with Adam and Anita for Friday."

Erika leans over and whispers in Dominique's ear. Dominique smiles and says, "Alright everyone, time to go home."

"You know," Gavin says, "we all heard you. Vampires and villagers?"

"Good night, all," Dominique says grinning.

Biography

Kate Bean began her fascination with vampires at university, best not to dwell too much on that. Since then, her interest has only deepened. This set of stories are based on characters developed in the decades since.

Her interest in writing and developing her fictional world, encompasses vampires, magic, and all manner of supernatural creatures. Each one, developed lovingly over many years.

She has a keen interest in creating realism, even, if at times, her imagination takes her to places that don't yet exist. Kate enjoys writing, letting her imagination taking her to unexpected places and the telling of stories, so her having a range of business and fiction titles makes perfect sense. So, jump in and see what could be.

Thank you

I would like to thank you, the reader, personally for taking the time to read this tale. I hope you've enjoyed it. If so, please tell your friends. This encourages me to write more.

www.ingramcontent.com/pod-product-compliance
Lightning Source LLC
Chambersburg PA
CBHW070840260626
47170CB00007B/2452